"Writing in the cogent, swift-moving prose that good biography demands, Ciuraru personalizes the book by weaving her own reactions—modern, emotional, snarky—into each chapter. Our curator is always having fun in *Nom de Plume*, and, as a result, so are we."

—*Jewish Daily Forward*

"*Nom de Plume* is wildly entertaining, almost gossipy, but travels on the high end of the literary landscape. This book is beyond great."

—Bookazine

"Ciuraru's writing is bright, lively, and smart, making *Nom de Plume* both informative and extremely enjoyable to read. I strongly recommend this read for any fans of biography, especially writers, and perhaps even more especially, women writers."

—The Best Damn Creative Writing Blog

"Engaging without being breezy, informative without being pedantic, these essays offer insightful, fascinating literary portraits without the solemness and heft of so many literary biographies. Ciuraru gets to the essence of their lives efficiently and evocatively, which makes for pleasant and piquant summer literary nonfiction."

—The Reading Ape Blog

"A fascinating book on a fascinating subject. We all have other selves, but only some of us give them a name and let them loose in the world. Carmela Ciuraru steps behind a host of shadowy facades to interrogate the originals, and the result is both enlightening and wonderfully entertaining."

—JOHN BANVILLE, author of *The Sea*, winner of the Man Booker Prize

"What to make of the paradox that some of the boldest writers have hidden behind pen names? Carmela Ciuraru has performed a valuable service in examining the phenomenon through her charming, sprightly, and illuminating biographical essays."

—PHILLIP LOPATE

"*Nom de Plume* is a delicious investigation of what leads the likes of the Brontës, Samuel Clemens, and Karen Blixen to ditch their names for safer, more romantic identities when they write. Whether their reasons are practical or mysterious, their lives and choices are here charmingly limned by Carmela Ciuraru."

—HONOR MOORE, author of *The Bishop's Daughter*

Nom de PLUME

Nom de PLUME

A (Secret) History
of Pseudonyms

CARMELA CIURARU

HARPER PERENNIAL

NEW YORK • LONDON • TORONTO • SYDNEY • NEW DELHI • AUCKLAND

HARPER ● PERENNIAL

HarperCollins books may be purchased for educational, business, or sales promotional use. For information please write: Special Markets Department, HarperCollins Publishers, 10 East 53rd Street, New York, NY 10022.

FIRST HARPER PERENNIAL EDITION PUBLISHED 2012.

Designed by Cassandra J. Pappas

The Library of Congress has catalogued the hardcover edition as follows:
Ciuraru, Carmela.
  Nom de plume: a (secret) history of pseudonyms / Carmela Ciuraru.
     p. cm.
  Includes bibliographical references.
  ISBN: 978-0-06-173526-4
  1. Anonyms and pseudonyms—History. I. Title.
  Z1041.C55 2011
  929.4—dc22   2010053603

ISBN 978-0-06-173527-1 (pbk.)

12 13 14 15 16 ID/RRD 10 9 8 7 6 5 4 3 2 1

For Sarah, everything

(and for Oscar)

World is crazier and more of it than we think.
Incorrigibly plural. I peel and portion
A tangerine and spit the pips and feel
The drunkenness of things being various.

—LOUIS MACNEICE, "Snow"

On whom, then, my God, am I the onlooker? How many am
I? Who is me? What then is this gap between myself and me?

—FERNANDO PESSOA

"Must a name mean something?" Alice asked doubtfully.

"Of course it must," Humpty Dumpty said, with a
short laugh. "My name means the shape I am and a good
handsome shape it is, too. With a name like yours, you might
be any shape."

—LEWIS CARROLL, *Alice's Adventures in Wonderland*

The self is like a bug. Every time you smack it, it moves to
another place.

—PAT STEIR

Contents

Introduction   xvii

CHAPTER 1

ANNE, CHARLOTTE, AND EMILY BRONTË & ACTON, CURRER,   1
AND ELLIS BELL (1816–1855)

"Once there were five sisters. . . ."

CHAPTER 2

GEORGE SAND & AURORE DUPIN (1804–1876)   25

"It began with an ankle-length gray military coat,
matching trousers, a cravat, and a waistcoat. . . ."

CHAPTER 3

GEORGE ELIOT & MARIAN EVANS (1819–1880)   43

"Charles Dickens was suspicious. . . ."

CHAPTER 4

LEWIS CARROLL & CHARLES DODGSON (1832–1898)   63

"A show of hands if you've never heard of
Alice in Wonderland. . . ."

CHAPTER 5

MARK TWAIN & SAMUEL CLEMENS (1835–1910)   85

"How the protean Samuel Clemens became the world's
most famous literary alias will never be known for sure. . . ."

CHAPTER 6

O. HENRY & WILLIAM SYDNEY PORTER (1862–1910)   101

"If you are now reading or have recently read a short story by
O. Henry, you are most likely a middle-school student. . . ."

CHAPTER 7

FERNANDO PESSOA & HIS HETERONYMS (1888–1935)   119

"You will never get to the bottom of Fernando Pessoa. . . ."

CHAPTER 8

GEORGE ORWELL & ERIC BLAIR (1903–1950)   137

"Had Eric Arthur Blair been a working-class bloke from
Birmingham instead of an Old Etonian . . ."

CHAPTER 9

ISAK DINESEN & KAREN BLIXEN (1885–1962)   157

"Her childhood was filled with many of the traditional privileges
of a wealthy upbringing but she preferred the company of
servants. . . ."

CHAPTER 10

SYLVIA PLATH & VICTORIA LUCAS (1932–1963)   179

"She was a good girl who loved her mother. . . ."

CHAPTER 11

HENRY GREEN & HENRY YORKE (1905–1973)   195

"He's the best writer you've never heard of. . . ."

CHAPTER 12

ROMAIN GARY & ÉMILE AJAR (1914–1980) 215

*"He was a war hero, a Ping-Pong champion, a film director,
a diplomat, and an author who wrote the best-selling French
novel of the twentieth century. . . ."*

CHAPTER 13

JAMES TIPTREE, JR. & ALICE SHELDON (1915–1987) 237

*"On May 19, 1987, a seventy-one-year-old woman and her
eighty-four-year-old husband were found lying in bed together,
hand in hand, dead of gunshot wounds. . . ."*

CHAPTER 14

**GEORGES SIMENON & CHRISTIAN BRULLS ET AL.
(1903–1989)** 267

"He claimed to have had sex with ten thousand women. . . ."

CHAPTER 15

PATRICIA HIGHSMITH & CLAIRE MORGAN (1921–1995) 291

*"She was one of the most wretched people you could ever meet,
with mood shifts that swung as wildly as the stock market. . . ."*

CHAPTER 16

PAULINE RÉAGE & DOMINIQUE AURY (1907–1998) 307

*"Not many authors can boast of having written a best-selling
pornographic novel. . . ."*

Acknowledgments 333
Time Line 335
Bibliography 337

Introduction

At its most basic level, a pseudonym is a prank. Yet the motives that lead writers to assume an alias are infinitely complex, sometimes mysterious even to them. Names are loaded, full of pitfalls and possibilities, and can prove obstacles to writing. Virginia Woolf, who never adopted a nom de plume herself, once expressed the fundamental and maddening condition of authorship: "Never to be yourself and yet always—that is the problem." She was describing the predicament of the personal essayist, but identity can seem crippling to any writer. A change of name, much like a change of scenery, provides a chance to start again.

To a certain extent, all writing involves impersonation—the act of summoning an authorial "I" to create the speaker of a poem or the characters in a novel. For the audacious poet Walt Whitman, it was possible to explore other voices simply as himself. He embraced his multitudes. ("Do I contradict myself? / Very well then, I contradict myself.") But some writers are unable to engage in such alchemy, or don't want to, without relying on an alter ego. If the authorial persona is a construct, never wholly authentic (no matter how autobiographical the material), then the pseudonymous writer takes this notion to yet another level, inventing a construct of a construct. "[T]he cultivation of a pseudonym might be interpreted as not so very different from the cultivation *in vivo* of the narrative voice that sustains any work of words, making it unique and inimitable," wrote Joyce Carol Oates in a 1987 *New York Times* essay. "Choosing a pseudonym by which to identify the completed product simply takes the mysterious process a step or two further, officially erasing the author's (social) identity and supplanting it with the (pseudonymous) identity." Elide your own name, and imaginative beckoning can truly begin. As the French journalist and writer François Nourissier once noted (in a piece entitled "Faut-il écrire masqué?"), a nom de plume provides a space in which "obstacles fall away, and one's reserve dissipates."

The merging of an author and an alter ego is an unpredictable thing. It can become a marriage, like a faithful and sturdy partnership, or it can prove a swift, intoxicating affair. A clandestine literary self can be tried on temporarily, to produce a single work, then dropped like a robe; or the guise might exist as something to be guarded at all costs. The attraction is obvious and undeniable. Entering another body (figuratively, ecstatically) is almost an erotic impulse. Historically, many writers have been lonely outsiders, which is why inhabiting another self offers an intimacy that seems otherwise unobtainable. In the absence of real-life companionship, the pseudonymous entity can serve as confidant, keeper of secrets, and protective shield.

The term "alter ego" is taken from Latin, meaning "other I." This suggests the writer is not so much wearing a mask as becoming another person entirely. Have the two selves met? Maybe not, and it's probably better that way. Sometimes there's no reason to explore how or why the other half lives. Knowing that it does is enough.

In his influential 1974 book *The Inner Game of Tennis*, author Timothy Gallwey applied the notion of doubleness to the tennis player, describing how each self hinders or enhances performance. With almost no technical advice, he provides a prescriptive guide to mastery. He focuses on what he describes as two arenas of engagement: Self 1 and Self 2. When his book was first published, Gallwey's ideas were so radical that thousands of readers wrote to express their gratitude, saying that they'd successfully applied his principles to pursuits other than tennis, including writing.

Gallwey, who majored in English literature at Harvard University, portrays Self 1 as "the talker, critic, controlling voice," and notes its "persistence and inventiveness in finding opportunities to get in the way." Self 1 berates you, calls you an incorrigible failure. But the nonjudgmental Self 2 represents liberation in its purest form. As Gallwey writes, Self 2 is "much more than a doer. It is capable of a range of feelings that are the most uniquely human aspect of life. These feelings can be explored in sports, the arts . . . and countless other activities. Self 2 is like an acorn that, when first discovered, seems quite small yet turns out to have the uncanny ability not only to become a magnificent tree but, if it has the right conditions, can generate an entire forest." In the context of authorship, the freeing of an alternate identity (Self 2) can reveal not just a forest but new worlds, boundless and transgressive, thrilling beyond one's wildest dreams.

A pseudonym may give a writer the necessary distance to speak honestly, but it can just as easily provide a license to lie. Anything is possible. It allows a writer to produce a work of "serious" literature, or one that is simply a guilty pleasure. It can inspire unprecedented bursts of creativity and prove an antidote to boredom. For that rare bird known as the commercially successful author, there is typically less at stake in toying with a pen name. If the book produced by an ephemeral self fails, it will be viewed as a silly misstep. All is forgiven when an author retires a pen name and returns to giving critics and fans exactly what they want: the familiar. *Lesson learned, let's move on.* If you're writing the equivalent of high-fructose corn syrup, perhaps it's unwise to serve up organic spelt, even under a different brand name.

For best-selling authors like Nora Roberts (a truncated version of her actual name, Eleanor Robertson)—who has written more than two hundred novels, including under the pen name J. D. Robb—having a transparent or "open" pseudonym is a savvy marketing strategy, a way to keep up her busy production line and show off her versatility. Roberts had initially resisted writing as someone else, but her agent had talked her into it by explaining, "There's Diet Pepsi, there's regular Pepsi, and there's Caffeine-Free Pepsi." It's all about brand extension.

A new work by Stephen King, whose books have sold more than 500 million copies worldwide, is a reassuring promise of success to his publisher. It's also critic-proof. Yet in the late 1970s, feeling hemmed in by his phenomenally prolific output, King introduced the pen name Richard Bachman. As he later said, it was easy to add someone to his interior staff:

> The name Richard Bachman actually came from when they called me and said we're ready to go to press with this novel, what name shall we put on it? And I hadn't really thought about that. Well, I had, but the original name—Gus Pillsbury—had gotten out on the grapevine and I really didn't like it that much anyway, so they said they needed it right away and there was a novel by Richard Stark on my desk, so I used the name Richard, and that's kind of funny because Richard Stark is in itself a pen name for Donald Westlake, and what was playing on the record player was "You Ain't Seen Nothin' Yet" by Bachman Turner Overdrive, so I put the two of them together and came up with Richard Bachman.

King's practical measure to avoid saturating the market (and avoid openly competing with himself for sales) was a success. But in 1985, a bookstore clerk in Washington, D.C., did some detective work and exposed King's secret. The author subsequently issued a press release announcing Bachman's death from "cancer of the pseudonym." King dedicated his 1989 novel *The Dark Half* (about a pen name that assumes a sinister life of its own) to "the late Richard Bachman."

Prominent writers such as Robert Ludlum, Joyce Carol Oates, Anne Rice, Michael Crichton, John Banville, Ruth Rendell, and Julian Barnes are also known to have indulged in pseudonymous publication. The Nobel laureate Doris Lessing, who tested out a nom de plume in the early 1980s, learned that she was better off sticking with her own identity. One of her aims had been a respite from the public's perception of her work; she sought to upend preconceptions of what it meant to read a "Doris Lessing novel."

She also had something to prove. Lessing wanted to see how her books would be received if no one knew they were by the author of *The Golden Notebook* (a novel that had sold nearly a million copies), as well as more than twenty other books. "I wanted to highlight that whole dreadful process in book publishing that 'nothing succeeds like success,'" she said later in an interview. "If the books had come out in my name, they would have sold a lot of copies and reviewers would have said, 'Oh, Doris Lessing, how wonderful.'"

That's debatable, but on another level, Lessing had revenge in mind: the ruse was a way to strike back at critics who she felt had "hated" her then-recent Canopus novels, a five-volume science-fiction series of which she was extremely proud. (She considered the series her most important work.) So Lessing became "Jane Somers" and wrote the novel *The Diary of a Good Neighbour*, which her longtime UK publisher, Jonathan Cape, rejected, insisting that it was not commercially viable. The novel traced the friendship between two women: a middle-aged magazine editor and an octogenarian. After Lessing found a publisher, Michael Joseph, the book was released in the UK in 1983. (The coy jacket copy indicated, falsely, that Somers was the pen name of "a well-known English woman journalist.") It sold only a few thousand copies, and the American edition fared poorly, too.

Was its failure due to people's fixation on famous authors, or was it a bad book? Lessing blamed the former. Was her test nothing but an egotistical publicity stunt? A critic from the *Washington Post*, Jonathan Yardley, seemed to think so. He argued that it was not at all the "success syndrome" that had troubled Lessing, but rather that "reviewers refused to be seduced by her name on the 'Canopus' novels and picked them to pieces."

Regardless, Lessing followed up a year later with a Somers sequel, *If the Old Could*, and soon after its publication she confessed that she had written both books. "The reviews were more or less what I expected," she said of her experiment. "It was interesting to be a beginning writer again because I found how patronizing reviewers can be."

Of course, authorial charlatanism isn't always provoked by malice, fear, guilt, or any other dark motive. The best-selling author Tom Huff, who died in 1990, was a Texan who published gothic novels, but he rechristened himself Jennifer Wilde to venture convincingly into bodice-ripping historical romance. He did so with the 1976 novel *Love's Tender Fury*, and although he had used other female pseudonyms, none earned him the kind of success he experienced as Wilde.

Terry Harknett, the prolific author of nearly two hundred books, wrote westerns—as in gun slinging and tobacco chewing—using rancher-sounding names like George G. Gilman. Harknett once described himself as a frustrated suspense writer: "For fifteen long years, I wrote mystery novels that were published twice yearly—and sank without trace at the same rate." In a rather unlikely way, he had stumbled into the genre of westerns, and his Gilman novels went on to sell millions of copies. Not bad for a British man from Essex with a decidedly unmasculine name.

Sometimes, however, literary fakery crosses the line from being a harmless alias, employed for the author's private, benign purpose. It is perceived as mendacity, as an appalling betrayal of trust. The consequences of this exploitation can tarnish the poseur's reputation irrevocably. And when not only does the supposed background of an author prove fraudulent, but the material presented as autobiographical is itself a lie, the backlash is especially dreadful.

In early 2008, a writer named Margaret B. Jones published *Love and Consequences: A Memoir of Hope and Survival.* This was a harrowing story of the author's experiences as a foster child and a Bloods gang member in South Central Los Angeles. She recalled one of the crucial lessons she had learned in her former life: "Trust no one. Even your own momma will sell you out for the right price or if she gets scared enough."

Writing in the *New York Times,* in a review accompanied by the headline "However Mean the Streets, Have an Exit Strategy," the critic Michiko Kakutani called the book "humane and deeply affecting" and praised the author for writing "with a novelist's eye for the psychological detail and an anthropologist's eye for social rituals and routines."

The book was a fabrication, and "Margaret B. Jones" did not exist. (The author's duplicity was exposed by her own sister.) "Jones," it turned out, was the persona of Margaret Seltzer, a thirty-three-year-old white woman living with her daughter in a four-bedroom 1940s bungalow in Eugene, Oregon. Seltzer had grown up with her biological parents in affluent Sherman Oaks, California, and had attended a private Episcopal day school. She did not have a black foster mother whom she called "Big Mom," nor foster siblings named Terrell, Taye, Nishia, and NeeCee. She was neither a Blood nor a Crip. And she had not, at fourteen years old, received a gun as a birthday gift.

Riverhead Books, the publisher of *Love and Consequences*, promptly canceled the author's publicity tour, recalled copies of the book, and offered refunds to those who had purchased it. For her part, Seltzer claimed that her intentions had been honorable. "I thought it was my opportunity to put a voice to people who people don't listen to," she said in an interview. "I was in a position where at one point people said you should speak for us, because nobody else is going to let us in to talk. Maybe it's an ego thing—I don't know. I just felt that there was good that I could do and there was no other way that someone would listen to it." Seltzer had written much of the book at a Starbucks in Los Angeles.

The morbidly shy young writer JT LeRoy, a teenage drifter and re-covering drug addict from West Virginia, courted (mostly by phone, mail, and fax) the sympathetic attention of Hollywood celebrities such as Winona Ryder and Drew Barrymore, and prominent authors including Mary Karr and Dennis Cooper. Another fan of his work, Madonna, once sent LeRoy some books on kabbalah as a gift. No one actually met him.

He maintained an enigmatic allure, and it wasn't long before ru-mors circulated that there was no JT LeRoy. (Chloë Sevigny said that he was definitely real because "he's left several messages on my an-swering machine.") When the writer Mary Gaitskill wanted to meet him in person, the "real" LeRoy—Laura Albert, a former phone-sex operator from Brooklyn—paid a nineteen-year-old boy she'd met on the street ("You want to make fifty bucks, no sex?") to meet Gaitskill quickly at a San Francisco café, "get freaked out," and leave. Later, other "stunt doubles"—always wearing sunglasses and a blond wig—were hired to embody LeRoy for public appearances.

Following publication of the cult favorites *Sarah* and *The Heart Is Deceitful Above All Things*, LeRoy was praised as a wunderkind and his work described as a "revelation." Although both books were works of fiction, LeRoy's marketability (and his many celebrity friendships) depended on his image as a wounded kid with a hardscrabble back-ground. The director Gus Van Sant spoke to LeRoy by phone for hours every day, and gave him an associate-producer credit on the 2003 film *Elephant*. Dave Eggers edited (and wrote the foreword to) LeRoy's 2005 novella, *Harold's End*, which appeared first in *McSwee-ney's*. Eggers wrote that LeRoy's books would prove to be "among the most influential American books in the last ten years."

Several months later, a journalist revealed LeRoy's true identity, and the fallout was immediate and severe. A company that had op-tioned the film rights to *Sarah* successfully sued Albert for fraud. Still, in the wake of the ignominious scandal, the middle-aged author was unapologetic: "I went through a minefield," she said, "and I put on camouflage in order to tell the truth." Albert felt victimized by the media and insisted that she could not have written LeRoy's works under her own name. She denied that she had perpetrated a hoax. "It really felt like he was another human being," she told the *Paris Review* in a 2006 interview. "He'd tell the story and I was the secretary who would take it down and say, OK, thank you, now I'm going to try to turn it into craft. But while I wouldn't sit there and think of myself as JT, as long as I was writing I didn't have to be Laura either."

What's in a name? Everything. Nothing. Some writers find that crafting prose under the name they were born with is too restrictive. It can seem oddly false, or perhaps not grand enough to accompany their literary peregrinations. A name carries so much baggage; it can seem tired and dull. Too ethnic. Too stultifying. Too old. Too young. In such instances, an author may be unable to proceed if he is, say, Samuel Clemens, but feels capable of achieving impressive feats if he is Mark Twain. Imagination blooms. Assume an alias, and the depths of the mind can be plumbed at last, without fear of retribution, mockery, or—worst of all—irrelevance. The erasure of a primary name can reveal what appears to be a truer, better, more authentic self. Or it can attain the opposite, by allowing a writer to take flight from a self that is "true" yet shameful or despised.

A nom de plume can also provide a divine sense of control. No writer can determine the fate of a book—how the poems or novels are interpreted, whether they are loved or grossly misunderstood. By assuming a pen name, though, an author can claim territory, seize possession of a work before the reader or critic inevitably distorts it. In this way, the author gets the last laugh: *despise my book as much as you like; you don't even know who wrote it.* However petty, such trickery yields infinite pleasure. Obfuscation is fun!

"Every writer—after a certain point, when one's labors have resulted in a body of work—experiences himself or herself as both Dr.

Frankenstein and the monster," Susan Sontag once lamented. Authorial identity can become a trap that causes creative fatigue or even halts literary output altogether. As many writers know firsthand, the literary world is tough: one minute you're the toast of the town; the next minute you're just toast. The desire to emancipate oneself from the shackles of familiarity and start anew, under an altogether different name, makes perfect sense. In fact, why not *more* pseudonyms?

In the nineteenth century, the curious phenomenon of pseudonymity reached its height, and as early as the mid-sixteenth century, it was customary for a work to be published without any author's name. It is interesting that the decline of pseudonyms in the twentieth century coincided with the rise of television and film. As people gained more access to the lives of others, it became harder to maintain privacy—and perhaps less desirable. In today's culture, no information seems too personal to be shared (or appropriated). Reality television has increased our hunger to "know" celebrities, and even authors are not immune to the pressures of self-promotion and self-revelation; we are in an era in which, as the biographer Nigel Hamilton has written, "individual human identity has become the focus of so much discussion." This is not entirely new, but with the explosion of digital technology, things seem to have spiraled out of control. Fans clamor to interact, online and in person, with their favorite writers, who in turn are expected to blog, sign autographs, and happily pose for photographs at publicity events. Along with their books, authors themselves are sold as products. Even though the practice of pseudonymity is still going strong, it has lost the allure it once had, and for the most part it is applied perfunctorily in genres such as crime fiction or erotica. Today, using a pen name is less often a creative or playful endeavor than a commercial one. Reticence is not what it used to be.

For each of the authors in this book, hiding behind a nom de plume was essential. However varied their literary styles and their reasons for going undercover, all of them longed to escape the burdens of selfhood—whether permanently or for a brief period in their lives. To publish their work, many risked their reputations, their means of subsistence, and even the relationships they held most dear. Three of the authors committed suicide (Sylvia Plath, Romain Gary, and Alice Sheldon); others had contemplated killing themselves or attempted it; at least one author (Alice Sheldon) was bipolar; and several—including the Brontë sisters, George Eliot, Isak Dinesen, and George Orwell—suffered from chronic health issues. Many succumbed to strange compulsions, addictions, and self-destructive habits. Almost all were lonely, and few were adept at friendship, marriage, or parenthood. One was a convicted criminal. A number of them, including Henry Green, Georges Simenon, and Patricia Highsmith, were alcoholics. Some achieved literary success in their twenties, while others were late bloomers who found recognition in midlife. But the Portuguese writer Fernando Pessoa, who channeled more than seventy different identities, lived in obscurity and never achieved acclaim. At the time of his death, he left behind more than thirty thousand fragments of his unpublished writings in a trunk. For Romain Gary, the best-selling French author of the twentieth century, pseudonymity became a cage, much like fame.

Most of these authors had endured childhoods with domineering, neglectful, or cruel parents. They suffered profound trauma early on, such as the death of a parent (in the case of Dinesen's father, by hanging himself) or of one or more siblings. Mark Twain outlived his spouse and all but one of his children; Georges Simenon's daughter killed herself. For these troubled authors whose lives seemed to bring impediments without surcease, an alter ego served as a kind of buffer, protecting them (at least up to a point) from the painful aspects of their lives.

This book is a selective chronicle of pseudonymity over a hundred-year period, beginning in the mid-nineteenth century and ending in the mid-twentieth century. To explore this peculiar tradition is to tap into, among other themes, the complex psychological machinery of authorial identity; the perils of literary fame; the struggles of the artist within a society generally hostile to such a vocation; courage and faith; and the nature of creativity itself. In certain respects, delving into pseudonymity is a frustrating endeavor. No pithy or singular conclusions can be made. It's a puzzle. By definition, this is a history riddled with lacunae: there are thousands of recorded noms de plume, but many more that we will never know.

In reflecting on the tumultuous lives of the authors in this book, it's hard not to consider the literary deprivation we might have suffered had they not found the protective cover they needed to write. But that would mean contemplating a world without, say, *Jane Eyre*, *Middlemarch*, or *Alice in Wonderland*. Instead, let us celebrate the sense of liberation, however short-lived, that these writers found through pseudonymity. In carving out their secret identities, they went to astonishing lengths. Each of these authors possessed extraordinary determination and resilience.

Here are their stories.

Nom de PLUME

They were dead by the age
of forty

CHAPTER I

Anne, Charlotte, and Emily Brontë &
ACTON, CURRER, AND ELLIS BELL

Once there were five sisters. In 1825, Maria and Elizabeth Brontë, the two eldest, died of tuberculosis. That left Charlotte (born in 1816), Emily (born in 1818), and Anne (born in 1820), as well as a brother, Branwell, born in 1817. Their mother, Maria Branwell Brontë, died of cancer a year after Anne's birth. Their Irish minister father, Patrick, would outlive them all, dying in 1861 at the age of eighty-four.

The Brontë children grew up in a manufacturing village at the edge of the Pennine moors in West Yorkshire, England, and would spend, almost without exception, their entire lives at their father's parsonage at Haworth. The plain, two-story early Georgian building where they once lived is now a museum. Eventually, Haworth would be known as Brontë country. It might have been known as Brunty country, had their father not changed his family surname while studying at Oxford. ("Brontë" means "thunder" in Greek.)

Living with their father and an aunt, Elizabeth, who helped raise them (and whom they did not love), the children lacked playmates but had one another. Precocious and bookish, they retreated into their own private world. They roamed the moors, and, as Charlotte later wrote, Emily especially loved doing so. "They were far more to her than a mere spectacle; they were what she lived in and by, as much as the wild birds, their tenants, or the heather, their produce. . . . She found in the bleak solitude many and dear delights; and not the least and best loved was—liberty."

The children kept dogs, cats, and birds as pets, made drawings, and invented stories, creating elaborate fantasy worlds in which they could lose themselves. Lonely in the absence of their mother, the children developed rich sagas of imaginary cities and kingdoms. Their grand creation was "Great Glass Town Confederacy," presided over by the "Four Genii," named Tallii, Brannii, Emmii, and Annii. They conceived histories of Glass Town and even composed Glass Town songs. Later came the kingdoms of Angria, invented by Charlotte and Branwell, and Gondal, as dreamed up by Emily and Anne. There were kings, queens, pirates, heroes, romances, armies, schools, and struggles between good and evil. These apparently silly children's games gave rise to a flurry of literary activity, proving to be exercises in developing their craft. By their late teens, the Brontës had a command of plot, characterization, and pacing.

Another significant detail from their childhood was the rather unorthodox pedagogical method their father applied with them: the children would put on masks, and Patrick would question them intensively, one by one, about various subjects to test their knowledge. He believed that by wearing masks the children would feel unselfconscious and learn to speak with confidence and candor.

When Branwell created the *Young Men's Magazine* at the age of twelve, the siblings (most of all Charlotte) contributed essays, plays, and illustrations. Like Charlotte, Branwell was ambitious about his writing and desired a readership beyond the family. He believed he was destined for greatness. At twenty, he wrote a sycophantic letter about his literary efforts to William Wordsworth, enclosing samples of his own work, but the poet never replied. (Wordsworth reported to others that he was "disgusted" by Branwell's letter.)

At twenty-one, Charlotte also took the bold step of writing to a famous author, the poet laureate Robert Southey, asking for his opinion of her work. She shyly confessed to him that she longed "to be forever known" as a poet. Southey was a poor choice for a potential mentor; cranky, elderly, and in poor health, he had no interest in a young woman's literary aspirations. (She wrote to him using her own name.) Three months later, he replied by acknowledging her obvious talent and then putting her in her place. He issued a stern admonition that young poets hoping to get published "ought to be prepared for disappointment," and that, above all, "Literature cannot be the business of a woman's life, and it ought not to be." Surely he did not expect or even want a response to his missive, but he got one anyway: a letter from Charlotte that was almost comical in its expression of meek obedience. "In the evenings, I do confess, I do think," she wrote, "but I never trouble any one else with my thoughts. I carefully avoid any appearance of preoccupation and eccentricity, which might lead those I live amongst to suspect the nature of my pursuits. . . . Sometimes when I'm teaching or sewing I would rather be reading or writing; but I try to deny myself." She closed her letter by thanking him again "with sincere gratitude" for essentially crushing her dreams. If her misguided literary ambition should arise again, Charlotte told him, she would simply reread his letter "and suppress it."

The vast trove of Brontë juvenilia is larger than all their published works put together. Most of the material was recorded in nearly microscopic handwriting, on tiny folded sheets of paper—some only 2 inches by 1½ inches. These were stitched and bundled together, complete with title pages and back covers made from scraps of wrapping paper and bags of sugar. For her part, Charlotte was already documenting her own literary accomplishments—all twenty-two volumes—with a detailed record titled "Catalogue of My Books, With the Period of Their Completion Up to August 3, 1830," when she was just fourteen years old. Three years later she wrote a novella, *The Green Dwarf,* under the name "Wellesley."

The sisters wrote constantly, but had it not been for Charlotte, their efforts might have remained private. She dreamed of making writing her vocation and was unafraid to pursue it. Her foray into publishing was inspired not by her own work, however, but by Emily's.

Charlotte later described how she came across one of her sister's small notebooks and, although this was a violation of privacy, read what Emily had written: "One day, in the autumn of 1845, I accidentally lighted on a MS volume of verse in my sister Emily's handwriting. Of course, I was not surprised, knowing that she could and did write verse: I looked it over, and something more than surprise seized me—a deep conviction that these were not common effusions nor at all like the poetry women generally write. . . . To my ear, they had also a peculiar music—wild, melancholy and elevating." Emily was furious when she found out what Charlotte had done. It was only after breaking down her sister's resistance that Charlotte "at last wrung out a reluctant consent to have the 'rhymes' as they were contemptuously termed, published."

Left to her own devices, Emily probably would have kept her work private, much like another nineteenth-century Emily—Dickinson, the "belle of Amherst"—with whom she had a certain temperamental kinship. (Brontë's poem "Last Lines" would be read at Dickinson's funeral in 1886.)

Unlike Anne or Charlotte, Emily was by nature reclusive and always the least inclined to speak. She felt no need to reach the world beyond Haworth. As Charlotte later explained, her sister tended toward seclusion, and "except to go to church, or take a walk on the hills, she rarely crossed the threshold of home."

Anne, too, Charlotte noted, had "a constitutional reserve and taciturnity," but she was also ambitious. Finally, at Charlotte's urging, the sisters decided to publish, under assumed (and gender indeterminate) names, a volume of poems by all three of them: twenty-one poems by Emily, nineteen by Charlotte, and twenty-one by Anne. Branwell was excluded from this endeavor. His life—and his tremendous artistic potential—would be curtailed by alcoholism, opium addiction, and the often reckless behavior that embarrassed his family. He understood his predicament but felt helpless to fix it. "I have lain during nine long weeks utterly shattered in body and broken down in mind," he wrote during one of his typical bad stretches. Branwell was too much of a mess to be let in on his sisters' secret identities; they had to shut him out. He was a loudmouth drunk who would, they were sure, inevitably spill the news of their pseudonyms.

"My hopes ebb low indeed about Branwell," Charlotte wrote of the brother she had once idolized. "I sometimes fear he will never be fit for much." He was dead at thirty-one.

Charlotte took the initiative with regard to publication by sending query letters to publishers, but she had trouble even getting a response. Presenting herself as an "agent" writing on behalf of the authors, she sent a letter to the firm Aylott & Jones in January 1846:

> Gentlemen—May I request to be informed whether you would undertake the publication of a Collection of short poems in I vol. oct.
>
> If you object to publishing the work at your own risk, would you undertake it on the Author's account—I am gentlemen,
>
> Your obdt. Hmble. Servt.
>
> C. Brontë

They agreed to accept the book for publication, provided it was at the authors' own expense. Charlotte had very specific ideas about how the book should be presented: "I should like it to be printed in 1 octavo volume of the same quality of paper and size of type as Moxon's last edition of Wordsworth," she wrote. "The poems will occupy—I should think from 200 to 250 pages." She also expressed herself emphatically on the printing: "*clear* type—not too small—and good paper."

Having reached an agreement, Charlotte sent the manuscript (as "C. Brontë Esq") to Aylott & Jones. "You will perceive that the Poems are the work of three persons—relatives—their separate pieces are distinguished by their separate signatures," she explained.

When *Poems* by Currer, Ellis, and Acton Bell came out in the summer of 1846, the savvy Charlotte oversaw advertising and promotion. She had directed the design, and now she suggested how the book should be released to the public and which publications ought to review it. She was gratified by the positive critical reception that *Poems* received. "It is long since we have enjoyed a volume of such genuine poetry as this," one reviewer wrote, expressing curiosity regarding "the triumvirate" and wondering whether the Bells might be pseudonymous authors. Another contemplated the possibility that the trio might be "one master spirit . . . that has been pleased to project itself into three imaginary poets." Charlotte was more than happy to feed public curiosity: writing a letter to one magazine editor (under her pseudonym), she thanked him for his very kind review and referred to "my brothers, Ellis and Acton."

Four years later, in the posthumous editions of *Wuthering Heights* and *Agnes Grey*, Charlotte would explain fully the motive behind their pseudonyms:

> Averse to personal publicity, we veiled our own names under those of Currer, Ellis, and Acton Bell; the ambiguous choice being dictated by a sort of conscientious scruple at assuming Christian names positively masculine, while we did not like to declare ourselves women, because—without at that time suspecting that our mode of writing and thinking was not what is called "feminine"—we had a vague impression that authoresses are liable to be looked on with prejudice; we had noticed how critics sometimes use for their chastisement the weapon of personality, and for their reward, a flattery, which is not true praise.

Despite the positive reviews of the book, it was a failure financially. Only two copies were sold. (The initial print run was around a thousand.) Charlotte was not the least bit discouraged. "The mere effort to succeed had given a wonderful zest to existence," she wrote. "It must be pursued."

A year later, seeing that nothing had come of their poetic debut, Charlotte, tenacious as ever, sent copies of the slim green volume to various celebrated authors, including Tennyson, Wordsworth, and De Quincey, with an imploring letter to each:

> Sir,
>
> My relatives, Ellis and Acton Bell, and myself, heedless of the repeated warnings of various respectable publishers, have committed the rash act of printing a volume of poems.
>
> The consequences predicted have, of course, overtaken us; our book is found to be a drug; no man needs or heeds it. In the space of a year our publisher has disposed but of two copies, and by what painful efforts he succeeded in getting rid of these two, himself only knows.
>
> Before transferring the edition to the trunk-makers, we have decided on distributing as presents a few copies of what we cannot sell—We beg to offer you one in acknowledgement of the pleasure and profit we have often and long derived from your works.
>
> I am, sir, yours very respectfully,
>
> Currer Bell.

Undeterred by the Bells' lackluster debut, Charlotte wrote a follow-up letter to Aylott & Jones, advising them that "C. E. & A. Bell are now preparing for the Press a work of fiction—consisting of three distinct and unconnected tales which may be published together as a work of 3 vols. of ordinary novel-size, or separately as single vols—as shall be deemed most advisable." And she brashly advised them to respond soon, as other publishers might be interested as well. They declined the solicitation.

What they foolishly turned down, of course, were novels that would become part of the canon of English literature: Anne was writing *Agnes Grey*. Emily had begun *Wuthering Heights* (whose ferocity of emotion Charlotte found rather off-putting). And Charlotte had collected all the material she needed for her novel *Jane Eyre*, having worked, quite miserably, as a governess—but the novel she'd written first was *The Professor*, with its male narrator, Charles Grimsworth, who teaches at a girls' school in Brussels. The story, which she'd completed in June 1846, was based on her own formative time at a Brussels girls' school, where she fell in love (unrequited) with her headmaster before homesickness set in and she returned, deeply depressed, to the refuge of Haworth.

Though she tried submitting their works for consideration elsewhere, she had no luck. Finally, *Wuthering Heights* and *Agnes Grey* were accepted by a minor publisher, Thomas Cautley Newby, but he didn't want *The Professor*. Charlotte sent it to other publishers, and it was repeatedly rejected. In fact, she would not see the novel published in her lifetime. It came out in 1857, two years after her death.

Amazingly, the year 1847 would bring publication for all three sisters, almost at once. Charlotte completed *Jane Eyre*, which she'd written in small square books. As she wrote, she suffered from an almost unbearably painful toothache and gum disease that would linger for years. (By 1851, Charlotte had very few teeth left.) But she persevered, and *Jane Eyre* was accepted with enthusiasm by the obscure publishing house Smith, Elder and Company in London.

It wouldn't remain unknown for long; in the latter half of the century, Smith, Elder became known as the distinguished publisher of Elizabeth Gaskell, Matthew Arnold, George Eliot, Thackeray, Browning, and Ruskin. The firm's eventual success could be traced to having taken a chance on an unknown writer named Currer Bell.

Charlotte submitted the manuscript to her publisher in August 1847, with a note indicating casually that "[i]t is better in future to address Mr Currer Bell, under cover to Miss Brontë, Haworth, Bradford, Yorkshire, as there is a risk of letters otherwise directed not reaching me at present." Later, George Smith, the head of the firm, recalled his suspicions about Currer Bell: "For my own part I never had much doubt on the subject of the writer's sex; but then I had the advantage over the general public of having the handwriting of the author before me."

Published just six weeks later on October 16, *Jane Eyre*, with its declarative opening line—"There was no possibility of taking a walk that day"—proved shocking to many Victorians, and even an assault against decorum. Yet it was immediately recognized as a masterpiece, and could count among its admirers Queen Victoria, who read it aloud to her "dear Albert." Thackeray, who'd received an early review copy, wrote to Charlotte's publisher:

> I wish you had not sent me *Jane Eyre*. It interested me so much that I have lost (or won if you like) a whole day in reading it. . . . Who the author can be I can't guess, if a woman she knows her language better than most ladies do, or has had a "classical" education. . . . Some of the love passages made me cry. . . . I don't know why I tell you this but that I have been exceedingly moved and pleased by *Jane Eyre*. It is a woman's writing, but whose?

Elizabeth Barrett Browning thought it a fine novel (and superior to the subsequent *Shirley* and *Villette*) but wrote to a friend, "I certainly don't think that the qualities, half savage and half freethinking, expressed in *Jane Eyre* are likely to suit a model governess or schoolmistress." Although she found these "qualities" repugnant and expressed her disapproval, she was excited by the mystery of the authorship—particularly the scandalous gossip that "Currer Bell" was actually a young governess. Another critic declared that the novel was "[w]orth fifty Trollopes and Martineaus rolled into one counterpane, with fifty Dickenses and Bulwers to keep them company," but added that the author of *Jane Eyre* was "rather a brazen Miss."

Compared with her sisters' novels, Charlotte's debut achieved by far the greatest commercial and critical success. Sales exceeded all expectations, and within six months *Jane Eyre* went into a third printing. Charlotte—or, rather, her nom de plume—became the most celebrated author in England. Deepening the mystery was the book's curious title page: "*Jane Eyre: An Autobiography.* Edited by Currer Bell." It had been George Smith's idea to add the provocative subtitle. The novel was very autobiographical indeed—for Charlotte, that is. Some critics believed that Bell was a woman, but to others it seemed obvious that the novel was simply too good to have been written by a female author. "It is no woman's writing," wrote one reviewer confidently. "Although ladies have written histories, and travels, and warlike novels, to say nothing of books upon the different arts and sciences, no woman *could have* penned the 'Autobiography of Jane Eyre.' It is all that one of the other sex might invent, and much more." The critic George Henry Lewes wrote that the novel was perhaps not autobiographical "in the naked facts and circumstances," but it certainly appeared to be "in the actual suffering and experience."

Some speculated that perhaps Acton and Currer Bell were the same person. A baffled critic surmised that the author's identity was divided, "if we are not misinformed, with a brother and sister. The work bears the marks of more than one mind and more than one sex." One writer argued that the novel's "mistakes" about "preparing game and dessert dishes" proved beyond a doubt that the author was a man, because no female author would have been so clueless. But another claimed that "only a woman or an upholsterer" could have written the section about sewing on brass rings. Yet another reviewer was convinced that the name was a pseudonym, perhaps an anagram, and that the book was definitely by a woman from the north of England. "Who, indeed, but a woman could have ventured, with the smallest prospect of success, to fill three octavo volumes with the history of a woman's heart?"

As Elizabeth Gaskell wrote in her biography of Charlotte, following the publication of *Jane Eyre* Charlotte's life became "divided into two parallel currents," that of Bell and Brontë, and "there were separate duties belonging to each character—not opposing each other; not impossible, but difficult to be reconciled." Gaskell noted ruefully that when a man becomes an author, "it is probably merely a change of employment to him," but for a woman to take on the same role, especially in secret, the burdens seem too great to overcome. "[N]o other can take up the quiet, regular duties of the daughter, the wife, or the mother," Gaskell wrote. Sequestered at the parsonage, where the most exciting part of her day was the postman's call, Charlotte was somewhat protected from the pressures of her fame—but not entirely.

Literary London was buzzing about Currer Bell. Most agreed that whoever the author was, he or she had extraordinary talent. "This is not merely a work of great promise," one critic said, "it is one of absolute performance. It is one of the most powerful domestic romances which has been published for many years." There came an inevitable backlash—among other things, the novel was said to be coarse and immoral—but those reviews were drowned out by the praise. (Some critics wanted it both ways: *The Economist* declared the novel a triumph if written by a man, "odious" if written by a woman.)

Charlotte could not resist sharing a copy of the book (along with some laudatory reviews) with her gruff father, who had no idea that she'd been published. All of Patrick's support, interest, and hope for the future had been lost with his son. But he read the novel one afternoon, summoned his daughters to tea, declared the book "a better one than I expected," and did not mention it again for the next few years.

Although Charlotte found refuge in her anonymity, her happiness about the novel's triumphant reception was tempered by the drubbing that Emily took for *Wuthering Heights*. *Agnes Grey* (like poor Anne) did not stir a strong reaction in anyone. Their novels were published together in December 1847, just as Charlotte was preparing for the second edition of *Jane Eyre*. Unfortunately, Emily and Anne found their publisher to have done a shamefully shoddy job; their books were riddled with mortifying mistakes of spelling and punctuation that they'd corrected on proof sheets, and new errors had been introduced. Most of the reviews of *Wuthering Heights* were unkind. Although critics recognized the power of Ellis Bell's writing, one reviewer deemed the characters "grotesque, so entirely without art, that they strike us as proceeding from a mind of limited experience." And readers were warned that they would be "disgusted, almost sickened by details of cruelty, inhumanity and the most diabolical hate and vengeance" in *Wuthering Heights*. Emily, always reclusive, did not speak of her pain at reading the negative reviews; nor did she admit how hurtful it was to see Charlotte's work bask in adulation at the same time. But after her death it was discovered that tucked inside her desk, Emily had saved the clippings of the reviews comparing her novel unfavorably with *Jane Eyre*.

Meanwhile, Charlotte clutched the protective umbrella of Currer Bell as the storm of publicity raged around her. In a letter to her editor, she wondered "what author would be without the advantage of being able to walk invisible?"

For the third edition of *Jane Eyre*, she wrote a brief author's note "to explain that my claim to the title of novelist rests on this one work alone. If, therefore, the authorship of other works of fiction has been attributed to me, an honour is awarded where it is not merited; and consequently, denied where it is justly due. This explanation will serve to rectify mistakes which may already have been made, and to prevent future errors." Dated April 13, 1848, it was signed "Currer Bell." She'd written it as an irked response to Emily's and Anne's disreputable publisher, who had led readers to believe that one "Mr. Bell" was responsible for the works by all three sisters. The Bell brothers were thus accused of "trickery." This misrepresentation had brought trouble for Charlotte on a number of levels, including a need to assure her own publisher, George Smith, that his author was not working for a competitor behind his back.

That year, *Jane Eyre* was sold in the United States, also to great acclaim, and the New York publisher Harper & Brothers had eagerly submitted a high bid to acquire the rights to Currer Bell's next novel.

At home, people were clamoring to know who the elusive Bell was. Charlotte could not contain her secret much longer; nevertheless, she wrote to her publisher insisting that the author's identity remain protected at all costs. " 'Currer Bell' only I am and will be to the Public; if accident or design should deprive me of that name," she wrote, "I should deem it a misfortune—a very great one. Mental tranquility would then be gone; it would be a task to write, a task which I doubt whether I could continue."

In July 1848, Charlotte made a dramatic decision: without giving notice, she traveled to London to introduce herself—her real self— to Smith and to her editor, W. S. Williams. Deeply grateful for everything the firm had done for her, she felt obliged to be forthright and to prove that one author was not responsible for the novels of all three. Originally she'd planned to surprise Smith at his office accompanied by both Anne and Emily, but Emily refused to go. She was upset about the turn of events and viewed the confession as a betrayal. Charlotte felt terribly guilty. Following her visit to the office she wrote to Williams, asking him to pretend that their meeting had never happened, at least as far as Emily was concerned.

"Permit me to caution you not to speak of my sisters when you write to me," Charlotte advised. "I mean, do not use the word in the plural. Ellis Bell will not endure to be alluded to under any other appellation than the *nom de plume*. I committed a grand error in betraying his identity to you and Mr. Smith. It was inadvertent—the words 'we are three sisters' escaped me before I was aware. I regretted the avowal the moment I had made it; I regret it bitterly now, for I find it is against every feeling and intention of Ellis Bell." Even after her sisters died, she maintained "Currer Bell" as her authorial identity.

Apart from Emily's agitation about the trip, it had been wonderful in every way. Charlotte and Anne had stayed in Paternoster Row, in the shadow of St. Paul's Cathedral, at the Chapter Coffee House, which had once been a meeting place for luminaries such as Dr. Johnson—"the resort of all the booksellers and publishers; and where the literary hacks, the critics, and even the wits, used to go in search of ideas or employment," as Elizabeth Gaskell would describe it in her biography of Charlotte.

The sisters' arrival at the publisher's office was priceless: when Charlotte showed up, along with Anne, Smith was confused by the sudden appearance of two "rather quaintly dressed little ladies, pale-faced and anxious-looking." (He wasn't joking about the "little" part—at five feet three, Emily was the tallest of the sisters; Charlotte was a mere four feet nine.) He was also annoyed because the two strangers—women, at that—had shown up uninvited on a busy workday demanding to see him. They declined to give their names. "One of them came forward and presented me with a letter—addressed in my own handwriting to 'Currer Bell, Esq.,'" he recalled. "I noticed that the letter had been opened, and said with some sharpness: 'Where did you get this from?' 'From the post office,' was the reply. 'It was addressed to me. We have both come that you might have ocular proof that there are at least two of us.'"

However much Smith had suspected Currer Bell to be a woman, at first he could not put two and two together in the presence of Charlotte Brontë. Utterly stunned, he looked at the letter and at his author and back again at the letter. It took him a few moments to recover from his shock; Charlotte tried to suppress a laugh. As the truth dawned on Smith, he received them graciously—insisting that the sisters extend their London visit and entertaining them with trips to the opera, art museums, and more. Charlotte cautioned him that although they had disclosed the truth about their identities, the revelation should go no further: "To all the rest of the world we must remain 'gentlemen' as heretofore."

Because Smith could not tell anyone who his companions really were, his family and friends were perplexed as to why he had brought "a couple of odd-looking countrywomen," as Charlotte wryly recalled, to dine with them one evening. They were introduced as "the Misses Brown." What the urbane young Londoner was doing socializing with "these insignificant spinsters" was anyone's guess, but in typical British fashion, no one spoke of it. Charlotte and Anne were amused at the awkwardness and dazzled by the grandeur of Smith's family residence.

He later described Anne as "a gentle, quiet, rather subdued person, by no means pretty, yet of a pleasing appearance." Though he was fascinated by Charlotte and awestruck by her intellect, his appraisal of her appearance confirmed there was no danger of falling in love with his unmasked author (though her feelings for him were far more complex). For one thing, he took note of her missing teeth and her ruddy complexion. Also, "Her head seemed too large for her body. . . . There was but little feminine charm about her; and of this fact she was herself uneasily and perpetually conscious." Charlotte once lamented her "almost repulsive" plainness to her dear friend Elizabeth Gaskell, but understood that her power lay elsewhere. "Though I knew I looked a poor creature," she wrote, "and in many respects actually was so, nature had given me a voice that could make itself heard, if lifted in excitement or deepened by emotion."

She returned home from her London trip tired but giddy at having unburdened herself. The future seemed full of promise.

Instead, the next year of her life would bring extraordinary suffering. The dissolute lost soul, Branwell, died in September of tuberculosis. His sisters never told him about the novels they'd published. In a letter to W. S. Williams a month after Branwell's death, Charlotte admitted, "I do not weep from a sense of bereavement—there is no prop withdrawn, no consolation torn away, no dear companion lost—but for the wreck of talent, the ruin of promise, the untimely, dreary extinction of what might have been a burning and a shining light."

The worst was still to come. Emily caught a severe cold at Branwell's funeral and had difficulty breathing. Her health deteriorated steadily from then on, and she did not leave the house again. She developed consumption but refused medical treatment, and her behavior became increasingly erratic; she would not rest or eat and bristled at familial displays of sympathy. (Charlotte described witnessing her sister's abrupt decline as causing "pain no words can render.") Just thirty years old, Emily died on December 19, 1848, at two o'clock in the afternoon. Three days later a memorial service was held, and her beloved bulldog, Keeper, accompanied the family to the church. (After her death, he had howled outside her door.) Emily was buried in the vault of the same church where her mother and brother now lay. Her coffin was only seventeen inches wide.

"For my part I am free to walk on the moors," Charlotte wrote later, "but when I go out there alone—everything reminds me of the times when others were with me and then the moors seem a wilderness, featureless, solitary, saddening—My sister Emily had a particular love for them, and there is not a knoll of heather, not a branch of fern, not a young bilberry leaf, not a fluttering lark or linnet but reminds me of her." Charlotte did not think she could go on as a writer: "Worse than useless did it seem to attempt to write what there no longer lived an 'Ellis Bell' to read," she informed her publisher.

Because Anne had shared a bedroom with Emily, it was not entirely shocking that in January 1849 Anne was diagnosed with tuberculosis. She had managed to publish another novel, *The Tenant of Wildfell Hall*, the year before, but it would be her last. As if she'd had a presentiment of her death, in the sharply worded preface to the novel's second edition she boldly defended the need for authorial privacy. The essay reads almost as a manifesto:

Respecting the author's identity, I would have it to be distinctly understood that Acton Bell is neither Currer nor Ellis Bell, and therefore let not his faults be attributed to them. As to whether the name be real or fictitious, it cannot greatly signify to those who know him only by his works. As little, I should think, can it matter whether the writer so designated is a man, or a woman, as one or two of my critics profess to have discovered. I take the imputation in good part, as a compliment to the just delineation of my female characters; and though I am bound to attribute much of the severity of my censors to this suspicion, I make no effort to refute it, because, in my own mind, I am satisfied that if a book is a good one, it is so whatever the sex of the author may be. All novels are, or should be, written for both men and women to read, and I am at a loss to conceive how a man should permit himself to write anything that would be really disgraceful to a woman, or why a woman should be censured for writing anything that would be proper and becoming for a man.

July 22nd, 1848.

Anne died on the afternoon of May 28, 1849, at the age of twenty-nine. A lifelong friend of Charlotte later recalled the last words Anne had uttered to her sister: "Take courage, Charlotte."

"When my thoughts turn to Anne," Charlotte said of her sister, "they always see her as a patient, persecuted stranger,—more lonely, less gifted with the power of making friends even than I am." She wrote a poem in Anne's memory that began, "There's little joy in life for me, / And little terror in the grave; / I've lived the parting hour to see / Of one I would have died to save."

In life, Anne had been overshadowed by her sisters (and her legacy remains so), yet her preface is a deeply captivating personal document, remarkable for its forcefulness of expression and eloquence. Her argument is also impossible to refute.

As the only survivor of her siblings, Charlotte was inconsolable. "Why life is so blank, brief and bitter I do not know," she wrote. Her faith sustained her: "God has upheld me. From my heart I thank Him." She proceeded with her next novel, *Shirley*, which she completed in August 1849. "[T]hough I earnestly wish to preserve my incognito," she wrote to her editor, "I live under no slavish fear of discovery—I am ashamed of nothing I have written—not a line." Still, she thanked him for preserving her secret.

That *Shirley* is considered her weakest novel can be forgiven, considering the circumstances under which it was written. Regardless, it had been a balm for the author, who admitted to her editor that in the aftermath of enormous losses, work was her favorite companion: "[H]ereafter I look for no great earthly comfort except what congenial occupation can give."

It was published in October to mostly respectable reviews, and Charlotte said that she would have to be a "conceited ape" to be dissatisfied with them. But the best thing to come of the book's publication was a warm letter from Elizabeth Gaskell. In response, Charlotte explained, "Currer Bell will avow to Mrs. Gaskell that her chief reason for maintaining an incognito is the fear that if she relinquished it, strength and courage would leave her, and she should ever after shrink from writing the plain truth." Aside from keeping up the nom de plume, the sentiments expressed in Charlotte's letter were completely honest.

Gaskell was delighted at having extracted some small bit of biographical information from the mysterious author. She excitedly wrote to a friend: "Currer Bell (aha! What will you give me for a secret?) She's a she—that I will tell you."

In 1850, Charlotte's social circle began to widen, and she met Mrs. Gaskell in person during a visit to the Lake District. "She is a woman of the most genuine talent," Charlotte said, "of cheerful, pleasing and cordial manners and—I believe—of a kind and good heart." They became close, and Gaskell's loving and sympathetic (if flawed) biography, *The Life of Charlotte Brontë* (published in 1857), is still considered one of the great works of Victorian literature. Gaskell's book was significant for being the first full-length biography of a woman novelist written by another woman. The legend, long upheld by scholars and readers alike, of Charlotte as the saintly sister—dutiful, modest, almost mouselike, and above reproach—can be traced to Gaskell, who created it.

After the deaths of her sisters, Charlotte made regular visits to London, where she had the privilege of meeting writers she admired, including Thackeray. She attended lectures, saw plays, and visited museums. She even sat for a portrait by the popular artist George

Richmond—a gift from George Smith to Charlotte's father that now resides in London's National Portrait Gallery, along with Branwell's iconic painting of Emily, Anne, and Charlotte, circa 1835, with his own image inexplicably blurred out of the portrait.

Even as she extended herself beyond Haworth, Charlotte remained discreet about her alter ego. She railed against "vulgar notoriety," yet speculation was rampant. She was even openly confronted, though she tried to brush such incidents aside. One evening, at a dinner party at Thackeray's home, the author called Charlotte "Currer Bell" in front of the other guests. She was not amused. "I believe there are books being published by a person named Currer Bell," she said curtly, "but the person you address is Miss Brontë—and I see no connection between the two." (Thackeray had himself used various noms de plume in his early works, including Michael Angelo Titmarsh, George Savage Fitz-Boodle, and Charles James Yellowplush.)

Charlotte was also on the defensive with George Lewes, who had initially praised her work, offering advice and encouragement, but who began lecturing "Bell" sternly in his letters and then maligning the author in reviews. She entered reluctantly into what became a rather contentious correspondence. It seems bizarre that the man who would become George Eliot's most passionate supporter just a few years later would engage in reductive criticism on grounds of gender, but he did. "I wish you did not think me a woman," she wrote to him in 1849. "I wish all reviewers believed 'Currer Bell' to be a man; they would be more just to him. You will, I know, keep measuring me by some standard of what you deem becoming to my sex; where I am not what you consider graceful, you will condemn me." She went on: "I cannot when I write think always of myself— and of what is elegant and charming in femininity—it is not on those terms or with such ideas I ever took pen in hand; and if it is only on such terms my writing will be tolerated—I shall pass away from the public and trouble it no more. Out of obscurity I came—to obscurity I can easily return."

Lewes ignored her response, reviewing *Shirley* in the *Edinburgh Review* and finding fault with the work based on the author's gender. (The headlines of the article's first two pages read, "Mental Equality of the Sexes?" and "Female Literature.") Charlotte was outraged and hurt by what she viewed as his cruelty toward her, and at having her fiction judged by a double standard. The note she subsequently addressed to "G. H. Lewes, Esq." was damning and brief: "I can be on guard against my enemies, but God deliver me from my friends." It was signed "Currer Bell." (About a year later, after Charlotte met him in person, she said, "I cannot hate him.")

At home as well, her secret had begun to unravel. Her father had started telling neighbors who his daughter was. Excited fans made pilgrimages to the village, hoping to come upon the genius in person. And on February 28, 1850, a local newspaper announced, in a burst of pride, that Charlotte Brontë, the reverend's daughter, was "the authoress of *Jane Eyre* and *Shirley*, two of the most popular novels of the day, which have appeared under the name of 'Currer Bell.'" The charade was officially over.

In 1851, thirty-five-year-old Charlotte received the third marriage proposal of her life and the third she would decline. (When the latest suitor approached her to propose, Charlotte admitted, "my veins ran ice.") Caring for her aging father, and suffering from health problems of her own, including a liver infection, she was lonely—but she didn't want a husband.

Discouraging her further was the news that despite all her success, Smith, Elder still declined to publish *The Professor*. The firm suggested that she instead begin work on a new novel, and she did—often in a state of despair. Two years later, *Villette* was published. The title page read, "VILLETTE. BY CURRER BELL, AUTHOR OF 'JANE EYRE,' 'SHIRLEY,' ETC." Feeling burned after having her pseudonymous cover unmasked, Charlotte longed to become invisible again. She had asked George Smith if he might consider publishing *Villette* under yet another pen name: "I should be much thankful for the sheltering shadow of an incognito," she implored. But "Currer Bell" was now an enviable brand in Victorian society; "he" was a towering figure whose name on a book almost guaranteed sales. The publisher reluctantly denied her request.

Villette, which Virginia Woolf would later deem to be Brontë's "finest novel," drew on Charlotte's own breakdowns and was her most overt exploration to date of the struggle between a woman's will and the constraints of society. Even though it made demands on the reader and lacked a happy ending, it proved a great success. George Eliot, then still known as Mary Ann Evans, read it three times. "I am only just returned to a sense of real wonder about me, for I have been reading *Villette*, a still more wonderful book than *Jane Eyre*," she wrote to a friend. "There is something almost preternatural about its power." She would later praise Charlotte to George Lewes, who had met Charlotte and saw her as a plain "old maid." Eliot, however, recognized the beauty of Charlotte's inner life: "What passion, what fire in her!" she said. "Quite as much as in George Sand, only the clothing is less voluptuous." Charlotte happened to have great respect for Sand, whom she considered "sagacious and profound"; this favorable view was in contrast to her opinion of Jane Austen's work, which she found uninteresting, with its "ladies and gentlemen, in their elegant but confined houses."

In 1853, Charlotte was just two years from her death. She'd begun writing yet another novel, but abandoned it after reluctantly marrying her father's curate, Arthur Bell Nicholls, who had pursued her for years. (The sisters' pseudonymous surname was taken from his middle name.) She consented to marry Nicholls in June 1854, only a short time after George Smith had married. (That event was quite painful for Charlotte to digest.) She married Nicholls accepting that there was only companionship, not passion, between them. At least she would no longer be alone. "Doubtless then it is the best for me," she wrote to a friend. Soon after marrying, she offered a sober assessment of her new role: "It is a solemn and strange and perilous thing for a woman to become a wife. . . . My time is not my own now."

In the early hours of March 31, 1855, Charlotte died at the age of thirty-eight. She is believed to have been pregnant at the time.

The defiant opening stanza of Emily Brontë's most famous poem conveys the inspiring resilience and fierce spirit of Emily, Anne, and Charlotte:

> *No coward soul is mine,*
> *No trembler in the world's storm-troubled sphere:*
> *I see Heaven's glories shine,*
> *And faith shines equal, arming me from Fear.*

The Brontë sisters had aggressively offended, challenged, and violated Victorian morals with their revolutionary works, which were profoundly disturbing for their era. In concealing their true identities, the Brontës could speak the truth without facing judgment. By overturning rigid societal notions of a distinctly "male" or "female" imagination, they raised provocative questions about the nature of creativity.

"If men could see us as we really are," Charlotte once wrote, "they would be amazed."

She was a bisexual, cigar-smoking cross-dresser

CHAPTER 2

George Sand & AURORE DUPIN

It began with an ankle-length gray military coat, matching trousers, a cravat, and a waistcoat. Clothes may make the man, as Mark Twain famously noted, but in this instance, they made the woman the man.

She was born Amandine-Aurore-Lucile Dupin in Paris in the summer of 1804, shortly before Napoleon became emperor of France. She was known as Aurore. "My father was playing the violin and my mother wore a pretty pink dress," she would report of her birth in her epic, two-volume memoir, *Histoire de ma vie.* "It took but a minute." Her parents had married secretly weeks before, making their daughter legitimate. In later years Aurore claimed to have walked at ten months, and to have been an adept reader by age four. "My looks gave promise of great beauty, a promise unkept," she recalled, with no trace of regret. "This was perhaps my own fault, because at the age when beauty blossoms, I was already spending my nights reading and writing."

Even in childhood Aurore was unconventional, finding delight and power in her own precociousness. She was an explorer, constantly testing boundaries in her behavior and pushing back at authority figures.

Though her mother valued beauty above all, Aurore deplored the notion of "living under a bell jar so as to avoid being weather-beaten, chapped, or faded before your time." She shunned hats and gloves and lessons in becoming a proper young lady. Gestures of reticence and grace were of no interest. She didn't rebel for the sake of rebellion, but "I could not be coerced." She daydreamed endlessly, befriended boys and girls alike, and cultivated a certain wildness of intellect and character. Already she displayed hints of the adult she would become, magnanimous and brave.

Aurore's identity evolved largely in opposition to her mother's character. Yet in one regard, her mother unwittingly exerted a profound influence. A former stage actress and prostitute, Antoinette Sophie-Victoire Delaborde Dupin had a lifelong tendency toward melodrama and instability—thus teaching Aurore that selves could be cycled through and discarded at will. Aurore's mother was raised in poverty, the daughter of a bird seller; her husband was descended from a family of aristocrats. (Both had illegitimate children from previous relationships—he had a son, Hippolyte; she had a daughter, Caroline.) The class schism was a source of tension in their relationship, and would become a recurring theme in Aurore's fiction. Antoinette's mother-in-law came to accept, and even adore, Aurore but could not endorse her son's marriage, which she deemed "disproportionate," and she considered his wife contemptible. The best state the two women would ever settle into was a kind of benign antipathy.

Over the years Antoinette preferred to be called Victoire, and then, after her marriage, Sophie. At times she had only a tenuous grip on reality, and this condition worsened as she aged. She was impulsive and manipulative. Roles and selves were interchanged to suit her circumstances. "When she was in good spirits," Aurore recalled of her mother, "she was truly charming, and it was impossible not to be swept up in her buoyant gaiety and vivid witticisms. Unfortunately, it would never last an entire day; lightning would strike from some remote corner of heaven."

At least one thing kept the mother-daughter relationship close: the art of storytelling. As a girl, Aurore delighted in hearing her mother read stories and sing lullabies to her. She loved the sounds of words, developed a rich imagination, and became a compulsive storyteller herself. "I used to compose out loud interminably long tales which my mother used to call my novels," she later recalled.

She had a knack for embellishment, or perhaps a dubious memory (though she once dismissed forgetfulness as unintelligence or inattention). In her autobiography, Aurore shared what she claimed was the first memory of her life, an incident that occurred when she was two years old and that she recalled in remarkable detail:

> A servant let me fall out of her arms onto the corner of the fireplace;
> I was frightened, and I hurt my forehead. All the commotion, the
> shock to the nervous system opened me to self-awareness, and I saw
> clearly—I still see—the reddish marble of the mantelpiece, my blood
> running, the distraught face of my nursemaid. I distinctly remember
> the doctor who came, the leeches which were put behind my ears,
> my mother's anxiety, and the servant dismissed for drunkenness.

Was this recollection accurate in every, or even any, aspect? Did the incident happen at all? No matter. Aurore cast her younger self at the center of a drama vividly told. She was both subject and object. She also claimed to remember perfectly the apartment her family lived in a year later, on Rue Grange-Batalière, and she said that from then on, "my memories are precise and nearly without interruption." It's an astonishing claim, regardless of how attentive young Aurore must have been to the world around her.

Since her mother was often unavailable physically and emotionally, Aurore spent countless hours in solitude. She craved touch. When she wasn't telling stories to her rapt listener, a pet rabbit, she was beginning to discover the thrills of playing with different personae. The first time she called out into the empty flat and heard her own voice call back the same words, she recalled thinking, "I was double and somewhere nearby was another 'me' whom I could not see but who always saw me since it always answered me." She didn't realize that it was only the echo of her own voice calling back until her mother later told her this, but the idea of "doubleness" had been planted, and it delighted her. She gave the voice a name and would call out, *"Echo, are you there? Do you hear me? Hello, echo!"*

Although Sophie's husband, Maurice Dupin, a military officer, was rarely present, his letters home showed how much he loved his family: "How dear is our Aurore!" he wrote in September 1805, two days before the Battle of Austerlitz. "How impatient you make me to come back and take both of you into my arms! . . . Tell me about your love, our child. Know that you'd destroy my life if you should cease to love me. Know that you're my wife, that I adore you, that I love life only because of you, and that I've dedicated my life to you." Elsewhere he implored, "May you always feel gloomy in my absence. Yes, beloved wife, that is how I love you. Let no one see you, think only of taking care of our daughter, and I'll be happy as I can be far from you."

Sophie seemed to take his words to heart. In her husband's absence, the Dupin house, with only mother and daughter, was lonely and listless. (The illegitimate children mostly lived elsewhere, though Hippolyte would become quite close to his half sister Aurore.) Maurice's periodic returns invigorated their lives, at least temporarily. "[My parents] found themselves happy only in their little household," Aurore would later recall. "Everywhere else they suffocated from melancholy yawning, and they left me with this legacy of secret savagery, which has always made society intolerable for me and 'the home' a necessity."

In the autumn of 1808, Maurice was thrown from his horse, Leopardo, and instantly killed. He was thirty. Just eight days earlier, he and Sophie had suffered the devastating loss of their infant son, Louis. After Maurice died, Aurore saw her mother crying one day and shyly approached her. "But when my daddy is through being dead," she said, "he'll come back to see you, won't he?"

She recalled that the house was "plunged into melancholy." Sophie's fragile, shifting self may have been a means of resilience against the hardships she suffered. But whatever the cause, her condition worsened after the deaths of Maurice and Louis, and her perpetual instability provided a template for Aurore's own ideas about identity: "It seems to me that we change from day to day and that after some years we are a new being," she reflected late in life. This notion was liberating—Aurore was a fearless risk-taker, rushing headlong into new experiences—but it also had a grievous effect, leaving her with a lifelong pining for love and intimacy that, occasional salves aside, would never be filled.

Following the losses of her brother and father, Aurore's love of daydreaming and storytelling became obsessive; imagination was no longer merely a retreat from boredom and solitude but a life raft, a need. "She's not trying to be difficult; it's her nature," her mother would explain. "You may be sure that she's always meditating on something. She used to chatter when she daydreamed." Aurore never relinquished her belief in the virtues of clinging to the imagination: "To cut short the fantasy life of a child is to go against the very laws of nature," she wrote.

Her grandmother was increasingly troubled by her peculiar behavior, and in 1817 Madame Dupin decided to rectify it by sending the thirteen-year-old to a convent, Couvent des Anglaises, in Paris. Aurore later recounted her grandmother's harsh assessment of her at the time: "You have inherited an excellent intelligence from your father and grandparents, but you do all in your power to appear an idiot. You could be attractive, but you take pride in looking unkempt. . . . You have no bearing, no grace, no tact. Your mind is becoming as deformed as your body. Sometimes you hardly reply when spoken to, and you assume the air of a bold animal that scorns human contact. . . . It is time to change all this."

At the convent, Aurore alternated between subversive behavior ("Let me say in passing that the great fault of monastic education is the attempt to exaggerate chastity," she later wrote), and austere withdrawal. Despite the excessive instruction, she admitted, "I still slouched, moved too abruptly, walked too naturally, and could not bear the thought of gloves or deep curtsies." Aurore said that when her grandmother would scold her for these "vices," "it took great self-control for me to hide the annoyance and irritation these eternal little critiques caused me. I would so like to have pleased her! I was never able to." Aurore could not (and had no wish to) shake off her propensity for daydreaming—"my mind, sluggish and wrapped up in itself, was still that of a child." She wrote poems at the convent, and even completed two novels; the second was "a pastoral one, which I judged worse than my first and with which I lit the stove one winter's day."

During this period, her grandmother exerted tremendous control over Aurore's education and development. (She accomplished this by threatening to disinherit Aurore.) Dying, Madame Dupin was concerned, as ever, about what she saw as the toxic effects of Sophie's influence on her granddaughter. She was determined to instill in Aurore moral and intellectual development; a socially acceptable degree of independence; a permanent distrust of Sophie and her family; and to remove Aurore from a "lower-class environment" into established society—which also meant finding a proper husband.

As a result, Sophie gave up custody of Aurore for a time. "It seemed as though she was ready to accept for herself a future in which I was no longer an essential party," Aurore wrote of her mother. Resigned to Madame Dupin's authority and dominance, Sophie would not engage in a contest of wills with her mother-in-law. The distance between mother and daughter was painful. "My mother seemed to have abandoned me to my silent and miserable struggle," Aurore recalled. "I was desolate over her apparent abandonment of me after the passion she had showered on me in my childhood." Maternal nurturing was provided instead by a nun, Sister Alicia, the first woman for whom Aurore had powerful feelings of love. In later years, with other women, Aurore would find physical intimacy, great passion, and much torment.

She left the convent in 1820, at age sixteen; within two years, she was married. It was the result of an extensive contractual agreement, following lengthy negotiations and financial haggling between the families. Her husband, Casimir Dudevant, the son of a baron, was a handsome twenty-seven-year-old sublieutenant in the French army. Sophie never warmed to him, explaining her dislike by saying that his nose didn't please her. But Aurore found him an agreeable and reasonable companion, if not an ideal romantic suitor: "He never spoke to me of love, he admitted to being little disposed to sudden passion, or enthusiasm, and in any case, was incapable of expressing these sentiments in a seductive manner," she recalled.

Nonetheless, by the spring of 1823 her first child was on the way: a son, Maurice, named for her father. And she already had stirrings of doubt about her marriage. Self-abnegation did not suit Aurore, who recognized it as an essential but unpleasant aspect of her union. "In marrying, one of the two must renounce himself or herself completely," she noted. "All that remains to be asked, then, is whether it should be for the husband or the wife to recast his or her being according to the mould of the other." On a family trip to the Pyrenees on her twenty-first birthday, she wrote in her diary: "I have to get used to smiling though my soul feels dead."

Despite periods of depression, she delighted in motherhood and gave birth to a daughter, Solange, in the fall of 1828. Aurore was dissatisfied with her marriage intellectually, emotionally, and sexually. It was a functioning partnership, nothing more. She was slowly recasting herself, but hardly as the dutiful wife—though she had genuinely tried: "I made enormous efforts to see things through my husband's eyes and think and do as he wished," she later wrote. "But the minute I had come to agree with him, I would fall into dreadful sadness, because I no longer felt in agreement with my own instincts."

The headstrong young woman was keenly interested in exploring other, more flamboyant and expansive roles. Just a year before she married, Aurore had made her first public appearance in a male disguise. She'd been riding her horse, Colette, one day, dressed in equestrian clothes, and was mistaken for a man. In a nearby village, she'd been addressed as "monsieur" by a woman, who had blushed and narrowed her eyes in "his" presence. Aurore was thrilled about her cross-dressing experiment and delighted by her own power. The illicit erotic charge wasn't bad, either.

Although she was certainly adjusting to the mold of another, her new form did not belong to the dull Casimir but to George Sand, her literary persona, who would become France's best-selling writer and would be among its most prolific authors. In considering what Sand accomplished, and the inspiring way she went about it, a dictum from the inimitable artist Louise Bourgeois comes to mind: "A woman has no place in the art world unless she proves over and over again she won't be eliminated."

Both Aurore and Casimir had casual affairs during their marriage, but at twenty-six, Aurore met a young Parisian who would play an important role in her life. When they fell in love, Jules Sandeau was nineteen and, like her, a writer. The first syllable of his surname (Sand) would become the surname of her pseudonym. Though their love affair didn't last long, Sandeau proved enormously influential and helped her find her path toward a wholly independent life. "Inspiration can pass through the soul just as easily in the midst of an orgy as in the silence of the woods," she wrote in her autobiography, "but when it is a question of giving form to your thoughts, whether you are secluded in your study or performing on the planks of a stage, you must be in total possession of yourself." By 1830, she was well on her way.

The following year, she decided to assert her will rather forcefully. She told Casimir that she would live in Paris for half the year with Solange, returning in the other months to care for Maurice. Yet she went through many periods of replicating her own mother's treatment of her—abandoning both children for long (and damaging) stretches to caretakers and tutors, in the single-minded pursuit of her own desires and ambitions. She wrestled with this but did not always remedy the situation to her children's liking.

Aurore's loneliness in Paris, at first, was "profound and complete." She felt useless. There was no doubt in her mind that literature alone "offered me the most chance of success as a profession." The few people she confided in about it were skeptical that writing and monetary concerns could successfully coexist—at least for a woman.

She dabbled in other, more pragmatic attempts at work. Feeling despair over not being able to help the poor in any meaningful way, she became "a bit of a pharmacist," preparing ointments and syrups for her clients gratis. She tried translation work, but because she was meticulous and conscientious with the words of others, it took too long. In attempting pencil and watercolor portraits done at sittings, she said, "I caught the likenesses very well, my little heads were not drawn badly, but the métier lacked distinction." She tried sewing, and was quick at it, but it didn't bring in much money and she couldn't see well enough close up. In another profitless venture, she sold tea chests and cigar boxes she'd varnished and painted with ornamental birds and flowers. "For four years, I went along groping, or slaving at nothing worthwhile, in order to discover within me any capability whatsoever," she recalled. "In spite of myself, I felt that I was an artist, without ever having dreamed I could be one."

Jules Sandeau would play an integral role in her becoming a "public" writer, as she had already written prolifically in private. He was part of a bohemian circle that Aurore eagerly joined, one that provided stimulating political, artistic, and intellectual discourse. These were people she felt an affinity with (as she most certainly did not with her husband), and they would become her close friends. It was an exciting time, and she took full advantage, throwing herself passionately into the affair with Sandeau.

The tricky issue of financial independence lingered. In the winter of 1831, Aurore reluctantly arranged an interview, through an acquaintance, with the publisher of *Le Figaro*, Henri de Latouche. She cringed at the thought of newspaper work, but recognized it as a useful entry point to literary endeavors. Also, she appreciated Latouche's intensity and fervent antibourgeois sensibility. He offered Aurore a job as columnist—making her the only woman on the staff and paying her seven francs per column. She was more than willing to prove herself. "I don't believe in all the sorrows that people predict for me in the literary career on which I'm trying to embark," she wrote in a letter to a friend. But when she called on an author to seek advice about the Parisian publishing world, the meeting was a disaster: "I shall be very brief, and I shall tell you frankly—a woman shouldn't write," he said before showing her the door. She recalled in her autobiography that because she left quietly, "prone more to laughter than anger," he ended his harangue on the inferiority of women with "a Napoleonic stroke that was intended to crush me: 'Take my word for it,' he said gravely, as I was opening the outer door to his sanctum, 'don't make books, make babies!'"

Never mind: Aurore was more determined than ever. As she once wrote, in another context, "I was not a coward, and I could not have been if I tried."

She continued to immerse herself in her social circle, and she and Sandeau collaborated on their writing. They received enthusiastic support from Balzac, who would drop by Aurore's flat from time to time. She later described him fondly as "childlike and great; always envious of trifles and never jealous of true glory; sincere to the point of modesty, proud to the point of braggadocio; trusting himself and others; very generous, very kind, and very crazy." Other notable men she called her friends included Baudelaire, Turgenev, Dostoevsky, Zola, Henry James, and Dumas. (John Ruskin, William Thackeray, and Thomas Carlyle, however, disliked her work intensely.) Later, Flaubert became a lifelong friend and confidant. Their letters were beautiful and mutually consoling. "There you are feeling sad and lonely, you say, and here I am feeling the same way," Flaubert wrote to her in 1866. "Where do they come from, do you think, these black moods that engulf us like this? They rise like a tide, you feel as if you are drowning and you have to escape somehow. What I do is lie, floating, letting it all wash over me." In 1876, a few months before she died, Flaubert wrote: "[Y]ou've never done me anything but good and I love you most tenderly."

At the end of the summer of 1831, Aurore and Jules began work on the bawdy *Rose et Blanche*, a planned five-volume novel for which they'd secured a publishing contract, and which they'd signed with the joint pseudonym "J. Sand." (Latouche, who had become a devoted mentor to Aurore, invented the name.) But Aurore ended up doing the bulk of the writing.

The novel was released to mixed reviews, yet it had moderate success and gave Aurore the confidence to publish entirely on her own. The following year, she published *Indiana*—a semi-autobiographical novel, and an unapologetic denunciation of marriage that she expected "to please very few people." Instead, it won international acclaim and became a best seller. An envious Victor Hugo (her rival for the status of France's best-selling author) called it "the finest novel of manners that has been published in French for twenty years." The author of this lauded novel was "George Sand," a name that would not only endure as her nom de plume but serve as her identity for the rest of her life. After completing *Indiana*, "I was baptized," she explained. "The [name] I was given, I earned myself, after the event, by my own toil. . . . I do not think anyone has anything to reproach me for."

She was amused by the number of reviewers who spoke enthusiastically of "Mr. G. Sand," but insisted that a woman must have had a hand in refining some of the novel's more emotional aspects. They were stumped because "the style and discrimination were too virile to be anything but a man's."

In 1832, her romantic relationship with Sandeau collapsed, and just as she was beginning to achieve professional success, she felt increasingly isolated. But in January 1833, she met Marie Dorval, a famous stage actress in her mid-thirties whose presence toppled and intoxicated Sand, and who would become—as she later described it—the one true love of her life. Both women were married (and had other lovers) at the time, but Sand legally separated from her husband in 1835. She pursued Dorval—initially, in the name of "friendship": "For my part I feel I love you with a heart brought back to life and rejuvenated by you," Sand wrote to her early on. "If it is a dream, like everything else I have wished for in life, do not steal it from me too quickly. It does me so much good." Meanwhile, Dorval's lover at the time, Alfred de Vigny, gave a detailed assessment of his rival: "Her hair is dark and curly and falls freely over her collar, rather like one of Raphael's angels," he wrote of Sand. "She has large black eyes, shaped like those of mystics whom one sees in paintings, or in those magnificent Italian portraits. Her face is severe and gives little away, the lower half is unattractive, the mouth ill-shaped. She has no grace of bearing, and her speech is coarse. In her manner of dress, her language, her tone of voice and the audacity of her conversation, she is like a man." Vigny had good cause to be concerned.

Sand played a male role in public because doing so offered her a much broader range of experience, and she loved freedom. Elizabeth Barrett Browning affectionately called her "thou large-brained woman and large-hearted man." She wrote a sonnet, "To George Sand: A Recognition," in 1844:

> *True genius, but true woman! dost deny*
> *Thy woman's nature with a manly scorn,*
> *And break away the gauds and armlets worn*
> *By weaker women in captivity?*
> *Ah, vain denial! that revolted cry*
> *Is sobbed in by a woman's voice forlorn!—*
> *Thy woman's hair, my sister, all unshorn*

Floats back disheveled strength in agony,
Disproving thy man's name: and while before
The world thou burnest in a poet-fire,
We see thy woman-heart beat evermore
Through the large flame. Beat purer, heart, and higher,
Till God unsex thee on the heavenly shore
Where unincarnate spirits purely aspire!

Sand was a cigar-chomping rebel who had brazen affairs as she wished, and with whomever she desired. She could practically roll a cigarette with her eyes closed, and she loved to smoke a hookah. She reveled in her own mischief. In one of her novels, Sand boldly suggested that monogamous marriage was an abnormal, unnatural state that deprived men and women of experiencing true sexual pleasure. Her significant lovers included Alfred de Musset, Franz Liszt, and Frédéric Chopin, who reported to his family, "Something about her repels me." Her decade-long relationship with Chopin ended badly in 1847, when Sand suspected that he had fallen in love with her daughter.

Even after it became an open secret in literary circles (and a source of malicious gossip) that Aurore Dupin was the notorious George Sand, she continued her transgressive style of dress and behavior, simply because she enjoyed it. She loved the idea of being in disguise. With her trousers, vest, military coat, hat, and tie, "I was the perfect little first-year student," she recalled in her autobiography. "My clothing made me fearless." And walking in her solid, sturdy boots was far preferable to the fussy discomfort of women's shoes: "With those little iron heels, I felt secure on the sidewalks. I flew from one end of Paris to the other." In her male attire, she was a voyeur, seeing without being seen. "No one knew me, no one looked at me, no one gave me a second thought; I was an atom lost in the immense crowd."

At theaters, she sat in the pit, where only men were permitted, and she always pulled off the ruse with ease—"the absence of coquettishness in costume and facial expression warded off any suspicion," she explained. "I was too poorly dressed and looked too simple—my usual vacant, verging on dumb, look—to attract or compel attention. . . . There is a way of stealing about, everywhere, without turning a head, and of speaking in a low and muted pitch which does not resound like a flute in the ears of those who may hear you. Furthermore, to avoid being noticed as a man, you must already have not been noticed as a woman."

In her autobiography, Sand recalled that one of her friends, who was privy to her sartorial secret, began calling her "monsieur" in public. But just as he would get used to addressing her this way, she would appear the following day dressed as a woman, and he couldn't keep up with the relentless change of costume. Confused by her various corrections, he took to addressing her only as "monsieur" from then on.

There was a less amusing aspect to dabbling in androgyny: having to deal with the fallout from her marriage. Casimir meticulously kept a log of his (soon to be former) wife's crimes and misdemeanors—among them, "She writes novels." Even worse, "Mme D. affecting the manners of a young man, smoking, swearing, dressed as a man and having lost all the feminine graces, has no understanding of money." Once tolerant and blithe about their marital arrangement, which allowed her to veer off on an independent path, Casimir came to detest the liberty she'd achieved and was disgusted by her "bohemian" lifestyle. She had to enter a nasty and protracted legal battle to end the marriage, and in the end had to divide her fortune with him.

No matter how messy her personal life became at any given time, she held steady with her writing, producing a staggering number of novels, plays, essays, and other works. She also painted, and she was an astonishingly prolific letter writer; her published correspondence includes more than fifteen thousand letters. Yet she also happily engaged in so-called women's work—making jam, doing needlework, and immersing herself in her beloved garden. Although she would periodically take stock of "the irregularity of my essentially feminine constitution," she was never shaken by what she viewed as the mutability of the self. Given the choice between conforming to prevailing customs and doing as she wished, she simply alternated between the two. It was not always easy, yet she was constitutionally incapable of remaining in a fixed state:

> I was not a woman completely like those whom some moralists censure and mock; I had in my soul an enthusiasm for the beautiful, a thirst for the true; and yet I was a woman like others—dependent, nervous, prey to my imagination, childishly susceptible to the emotionalism and anxieties of motherhood. But did these traits have to relegate me to secondary standing in artistic and family life? That being society's rule, it was still within my power to submit patiently or cheerfully.

As Sand's biographer Belinda Jack noted, "[H]er modernity lies less in her feminism or her socialism, and more in her acceptance of loose, even freewheeling ideas about the self. . . . She had strong intuitions about the subconscious and the need to be aware of our inner unthinking, but acutely responsive, selves."

To Sand, this was a natural, normal idea. It was far ahead of her time; she worked tirelessly so that others might embrace it. In her autobiography, Sand expressed a desire to achieve societal acceptance not for herself only, but for other women. "I was going along nourishing a dream of male virtue to which women could aspire," she wrote, "and was constantly examining my soul with a naïve curiosity to find out whether it had the power of such aspirations, and whether uprightness, unselfishness, discretion, perseverance in work—all the strengths, in short, that man attributes exclusively to himself—were actually unavailable to a heart which accepted the concept of them so ardently. . . . I wondered why Montaigne would not have liked and respected me as much as a brother."

No less than George Eliot's future partner, the critic George Henry

Lewes, declared in 1842 that Sand was the most remarkable writer of the century. Dostoevsky considered her "one of the most brilliant, the most indomitable, and the most perfect champions."

The last years of her life were often filled with sadness, as by then many of her friends and former lovers were dead. But she was one of the most influential and famous women in France, and possessed remarkable serenity after all that she'd endured. Unfortunately, her reputation did not hold up well after her death. Her prodigious output was eclipsed by the shocking, scandalous details of her life. Compared with her contemporaries, she is hardly read today. "The world will know and understand me someday," Sand once wrote. "But if that day does not arrive, it does not greatly matter. I shall have opened the way for other women." In that regard, she succeeded beyond measure.

"What a brave man she was," Turgenev recalled of Sand, "and what a good woman."

Her old friend Flaubert, a notorious misanthrope and recluse, outlived her by four years. Of her funeral in 1876, he said: "I cried like an ass."

She had a big nose and the face
of a withered cabbage

CHAPTER 3

George Eliot & MARIAN EVANS

Charles Dickens was suspicious. "I have observed what seem to me to be such womanly touches, in those moving fictions, that the assurance on the title-page is insufficient to satisfy me, even now," he wrote to George Eliot in January 1858. The candid letter was written a year after the publication of *Scenes of Clerical Life*, a collection of three stories first serialized, anonymously, in *Blackwood's Edinburgh Magazine*. Dickens praised their "exquisite truth and delicacy" but was convinced that the writer was a woman. Elizabeth Gaskell, however, insisted that the author was a man named Joseph Liggins of Nuneaton. The *Saturday Review*, meanwhile, harbored its own suspicions, noting that George Eliot was rumored to be "an assumed name, screening that of some studious clergyman . . . who is the father of a family, of High Church tendencies, and exceedingly fond of children, Greek dramatists and dogs."

Not quite: George Eliot was a thirty-eight-year-old woman named Mary Anne (Marian) Evans, a politically progressive atheist raised in a stern, religious household, unmarried, childless, and living openly with a married man. She was a formidable intellectual who had begun educating herself after her mother's death in 1836 and would publish seven astonishing novels in her lifetime, including *The Mill on the Floss*, *Middlemarch*, and *Daniel Deronda*. How Evans became one of the great Victorian novelists is the story of an eccentric young woman from the Midlands region of England who broke just about every taboo of her time. "She was never content with what was safely known and could be taken for granted," one critic wrote of her extraordinarily restless life.

Born on November 22, 1819, in Warwickshire, she was her parents' third child, following the birth of a daughter and a son. (Her father, Robert, also had two children from a previous marriage; his first wife died.) The birth of a second daughter was terribly disappointing. Sons were valued and valuable; girls, until married off, were a financial drain and nothing but a burden on the family. Mary Anne was no great prize. Twin boys arrived fourteen months later, but they died soon after birth, and Mary Anne's mother, Christiana, never recovered from the loss. She made no effort to hide that fact from her daughter.

Mary Anne eventually dropped the "e" from "Anne" and later changed her name to Marian, but at the end of her life, she reverted to "Mary Ann." (That's why, in biographies, you'll find her first name spelled with confusing variation: what to call her?) Since she lived with a mother who never doted on her, her childhood was marked by isolation and sadness. Luckily, her father was kinder, and gave her a copy of her very first book: *The Linnet's Life*. But whatever bond she shared with him, it was never enough to replace the maternal affection she was denied.

Unkempt, frequently melancholy, and extremely sensitive, she was an unsightly irritant to Christiana, who may have blamed her own poor health and depression on having given birth to Mary Anne. The Evanses' youngest child was obstinate, fearful, and given to emotional outbursts. At the age of five, in 1824, she was sent to a boarding school. A few years later, her parents would move her to another boarding school, where Mary Anne became close to a teacher named Maria Lewis. Even for the Victorian era, five was quite young to be shipped away for one's education, though she did come home on weekends. A timid and socially awkward student, Mary Anne would eventually find academic success and earn the admiration of her peers, but her insecurity lingered and she was always harshly critical of her own achievements.

At seven, Mary Anne began reading Sir Walter Scott's *Waverley*. This event marked the first hint of her future vocation: when the book was returned to a neighbor before she'd had a chance to finish reading it, she was terribly upset. She did the next best thing by writing out an ending herself.

When she was twelve, Mary Anne attended a girls' school in the Midlands run by evangelical sisters. She excelled there, impressing her teachers with her mastery of every subject, especially literature. She received a novel in the mail from her beloved former teacher Maria Lewis, and sent a thank-you letter back, describing the sustaining role that books had played in her life. "When I was quite a little child I could not be satisfied with the things around me," she wrote. "I was constantly living in a world of my own creation, and was quite contented to have no companions that I might be left to my own musings and imagine scenes in which I was chief actress." It was Lewis, in 1839, who encouraged Mary Anne to submit her work for publication. The poem, her print debut, was signed "M.A.E." and appeared in the *Christian Observer*. It began:

> As o'er the fields by evening's light I stray,
> I hear a still small whisper—come away;
> Thou must to this bright, lovely world soon say
> Farewell!

The effects of her feeling of estrangement from those around her— and dealing with her mother's death, when she was seventeen years old—would lead her to be perpetually in search of mother figures and to form fierce attachments to the people she loved—including her brother Isaac. (Their close yet complex bond informed the sibling relationship of Maggie and Tom Tulliver in *The Mill on the Floss*.) She was desperate for intimacy, a longing that never left her. "Before I had your kind letter," she wrote to a friend in 1842, "one of the ravens that hovered over me in my Saul-like visitations was the idea that you did not love me well enough to bestow any time on me more than what I had already robbed you of, but that same letter was a David's harp that quite charmed away this naughty imagination." (By this time, too, she had begun spelling her name Mary Ann.)

After her mother died, she became more withdrawn. While caring for her widowed sixty-three-year-old father, she dutifully—though not happily—took over running the household, and felt like little more than a maid. But she used the seclusion to further her education. In what spare time she had, she read (and reread) widely: history, literature, poetry, philosophy, science, and music (she became an accomplished pianist), and studied Latin, Greek, German, French, and Italian. With her capacity for deeply felt emotion, she could not ignore the fact that daily life was constricting and pallid. Still, her emotional deprivation was offset by the riches of learning, of cultivating a powerful and capacious intellect. The hunger of the heart was sublimated into the hunger of the mind.

Always a thoughtful, contemplative girl, Mary Ann grew increasingly analytical and developed a keen interest in ideas concerning morality, modesty, and character. She was also intrigued by the conflict between individual will and the stifling demands of convention. "Certainly those determining acts of her life were not ideally beautiful," Evans, as Eliot, would write in *Middlemarch*, widely regarded as her greatest work. "They were the mixed result of young and noble impulse struggling amidst the conditions of an imperfect social state, in which great feelings will often take the aspect of error, and great faith the aspect of illusion. For there is no creature whose inward being is so strong that it is not greatly determined by what lies outside it." As a novelist, Eliot would prove to be an astute social observer, a historian, and a philosopher. Yet she also captured the despair of insatiable yearning, a condition she understood all too well.

The fervent desire to love and be loved, which had driven her back upon herself throughout her childhood, stayed constant even after it had been fulfilled. Despite her reputation as an author whose novels reflected her vast intellect, she was very much invested in matters of the heart.

The English poet William Ernest Henley, best known for his 1875 poem "Invictus," once dismissed Eliot as "George Sand plus Science minus Sex." Yet the heart, if not sex, was more present in Eliot's work than is generally recognized. In *Middlemarch* she wrote (in the voice of her heroine, Dorothea Brooke) that "surely the only true knowledge of our fellow-man is that which enables us to feel with him—which gives us a fine ear for the heart-pulses that are beating under the mere clothes of circumstance and opinion. Our subtlest analysis of schools and sects must miss the essential truth, unless it be lit up by the love that sees in all forms of human thought and work, the life and death struggles of separate human beings."

Even in her personal correspondence, such matters weighed on her mind, as in a letter to Lady Mary Elizabeth Ponsonby, the wife of Queen Victoria's Private Secretary, with whom Mary Ann corresponded until Ponsonby's death: "Consider what the human mind *en masse* would have been if there had been no such combination of elements in it as has produced poets. All the philosophers and *savants* would not have sufficed to supply that deficiency. And how can the life of nations be understood without the inward life of poetry—that is, of emotion blending with thought?"

That Mary Ann had such a propensity stemmed from the extreme loneliness of her growing-up years. "I have of late felt a depression that has disordered my mind's eye and made me *alive* to what is certainly a fact (though my imagination when I am in health is an adept at concealing it), that I am *alone* in the world," she wrote to a friend at the age of twenty-one. "I do not mean to be so sinful as to say that I have not friends *most* unreservedly kind and tender, and disposed to form a far too favourable estimate of me, but I mean that I have no one who enters into my pleasures or my griefs, no one with whom I can pour out my soul, no one with the same yearnings, the same temptations, the same delights as myself." Four years later, in another letter, she reflected on her years of suffering: "Childhood is only the beautiful and happy time in contemplation and retrospect: to the child it is full of deep sorrows, the meaning of which is unknown." She was absolutely convinced that "the bliss of reciprocated affection" was something she would never know.

Mary Ann had been marked early on as an ugly duckling, a characterization that would take on an even crueler edge for her as an adult. Someone once told her that she was, in fact, too ugly to love. Henry James called her the "great horse-faced bluestocking." And her publisher, upon learning her identity, described her to his wife as "a most intelligent pleasant woman, with a face like a man." Many went so far as to regard her as Medusa-like—not merely plain but hideous. She had a large head, a big nose, and unflattering physical proportions. She dressed badly. And she was rather humorless, a trait that added severity and heaviness to her face. She was the first to acknowledge her ungainly appearance, once describing herself as "a withered cabbage in a flower garden." Still, she had kind eyes, and Henry James wrote of this "magnificently ugly, deliciously hideous" woman that "in this vast ugliness resides a most powerful beauty which, in a very few minutes, steals forth and charms the mind, so that you end, as I ended, in falling in love with her." Even her obituary in the *Times*, though praising her as "a great and noble woman," could not refrain from mentioning her "irradiated features that were too strongly marked for feminine beauty."

She had been raised in an intolerant family, which rejected those who didn't readily fit in. Aside from her "ugly" appearance, she held, from an early age, provocative views that distanced her from her family, particularly her father. Although she'd read theology texts passionately and had gone through a lengthy period of religious fervor, she became disenchanted. Eventually, her love of science and her passion for rational thought took over; a love of Wordsworth began to steer her into Romanticism and away from God. Moreover, when she and her father moved to Coventry, in 1841, she happily came into contact with agnostics, atheists, and freethinking intellectuals. She became especially close to her neighbors Cara and Charles Bray, both of whom openly enjoyed affairs outside their marriage.

Soon afterward, Mary Ann renounced her faith and stopped going to church. Rather than give up her newfound principles, she told her outraged father that she would leave home and make her own way in the world. He made no effort to stop her. She eventually returned to care for him, and even attended church again, but their last years together, until his death in 1849, were difficult. "My life is a perpetual nightmare," she confided to a friend, "and always haunted by something to be done, which I have never the time, or rather the energy, to do." While serving as her father's nurse, she did read aloud to him a recently published novel, *Jane Eyre*, by a writer called Currer Bell. And in his final months, she managed the frivolous task of translating Spinoza's *Tractatus Theologico-Politicus*.

This period was yet another that led her to ruminate on notions of obligation versus independence, fulfilling duty versus chasing desires. In *Romola*, her historical novel set in fifteenth-century Florence, she would explore the question of where "the duty of obedience ends and the duty of resistance begins."

How Mary Anne, Mary Ann, or Marian Evans—full of secret ambition but lonely, prim, and lacking confidence—transformed herself into George Eliot is a remarkable story. She often felt that she'd been given the mind of a man but not his opportunities. At thirty-one, she was numb, still grieving after her father's death, revealing in a letter that "the only ardent hope I have for my future life is to have given to me some woman's duty—some possibility of devoting myself where I may see a daily result of pure calm blessedness in the life of another." Around this time, she became Marian, another in a line of appellation shifts. And somewhere, "George Eliot" was patiently waiting to meet her.

Charles and Cara Bray had introduced Marian to Ralph Waldo Emerson, who commented on her "calm and serious soul." Her provincial world had expanded considerably. And with the support of Charles, she began writing book reviews (anonymously) for the newspaper he owned. She was still about a decade away from publishing her first novel. But one friend was wise enough to observe of Marian at thirty-two that "[l]arge angels take a long time unfolding their wings; but when they do, soar out of sight. Miss Evans either has no wings or, which I think is the case, they are coming, budding." She was right.

Charles also took a great interest in Marian's head—or, to be more specific, her skull. As a keen believer in phrenology, Bray introduced Marian to one of its leading proponents in London. "Miss Evans' head is a very large one," the expert astutely concluded. He added in his assessment that "the Intellect greatly predominates" (true), and that "in the Feelings, the Animal and Moral regions are about equal; the moral being quite sufficient to keep the animal in order." That sounded about right, too. Most promising of all, he said, "She was not fitted to stand alone."

Companionship would come later. For now, Marian was writing and editing for London's *Westminster Review.* However, there was one small snag in her newfound work. As Eliot's biographer Brenda Maddox has noted in her lively account, "A female editor was as unheard of as a female surgeon; to be known to have one would have done no service to the review." While, in her own way, Marian was becoming entrenched in London's intellectual circles (the rare woman to have done so), she had to keep quiet about it. She was there, she was known socially, but her name could not be attached to the work she produced. Still, for the first time in her life, she experienced a real sense of popularity and demand for her presence. Young women she encountered, dazzled by her supple mind, developed crushes on her.

Considering her privileged position, Marian was more than happy to comply with the discretion demanded of her, and was even helpful in suggesting how to manage the situation. She told her boss that it might be best if "you are regarded as the responsible person, but that you employ an Editor in whose literary and general ability you confide."

This rush of good fortune was cold comfort, however. She still lacked a husband, and she wanted one. But meeting a man named George Lewes would prove transformative. She could never legally marry him, but their relationship would become the most significant of her life. He was a prolific author, two years older than she, and they'd gotten to know each other better through a friend. She didn't know much about Lewes's personal life, but her first impression of him was that he talked too much. Soon she admitted, "He has quite won my liking, in spite of myself." She found out that he was unhappily married, the father of four sons, and that he had a well-earned reputation for promiscuity. It was public knowledge that his wife, Agnes, had been having an affair with a friend of his, too. Lewes was even "uglier" than Marian, with a pockmarked face, an unkempt mustache, and unfashionable clothing, all of which she found off-putting. Even his friends called him "Ape" and declared him the ugliest man in London. (Charlotte Brontë, however, once remarked that she saw something of her sister Emily in him.) Henry James found him "personally repulsive."

Lewes was cosmopolitan and Evans was provincial; his family, with its background in theater, was as flamboyant as hers was listless and austere. But by March 1853, she was already telling a friend that she found Lewes "genial and amusing," and that he had "won my liking, in spite of myself."

Within a year, they were living together—and she started calling herself Marian Evans Lewes. Though he was still married to Agnes, Evans was able to confide to a friend, "I begin this year more happily than I have done most years of my life." Divorce was out of the question for Lewes, but both he and Marian, despite their trepidation about whisperings of their supposed immorality, charged forward in their relationship—living together "in sin" and hoping that her reputation in particular would not suffer irrevocably. They were prepared to lose friends to preserve their love, and did. "I have counted the cost of the step I have taken and am prepared to bear, without irritation or bitterness, renunciation of all my friends," she wrote. "I am not mistaken in the person to whom I have attached myself."

Both she and Lewes had already experienced their own forms of social persecution and were familiar with its toll. Yet they lost family, too: Marian had waited a few years to reveal her relationship to her siblings, and when she did, her brother Isaac (whom she adored) cut her off and encouraged his sisters to ostracize her. Defiant, she referred to Lewes as "my husband."

"We are leading no life of self-indulgence," she wrote, "except indeed that, being happy in each other, we find everything easy." Further, she insisted that she wasn't prepared to settle into someone else's notion of a virtuous life. She could be only herself. "Women who are satisfied with light and easily broken ties do *not* act as I have done," she wrote. "They obtain what they desire and are still invited to dinner." She paid the penalty without complaint or regret.

It is fair to say that without this passionate, supportive partnership, which would last until Lewes's death in 1878, George Eliot would not have been born. Lewes offered Evans a kind of love she had never known, unquestioning and absolute. (Despite rumors of his infidelity, there is no known evidence.) He wasn't an entirely enlightened man—after all, he had once claimed condescendingly that even the best women writers were "second only to the first-rate men of their day"—but he did heartily encourage her to write a novel. Journalistic work provided money but little satisfaction. "It is worth while for you to try the experiment," he urged her—and finally, in 1856, she confided in her journal: "I am anxious to begin my fiction writing."

She embarked on this phase of her writing career by sending stories to John Blackwood, editor of *Blackwood's Edinburgh Magazine*; the first was published in January 1857 under the name "George Eliot." She didn't send the pieces directly to Blackwood—she submitted them via Lewes, who was already a regular contributor to the journal, as an added buffer. A month later, she wrote to Blackwood's brother and colleague, William: "Whatever may be the success of my stories, I shall be resolute in preserving my incognito, having observed that a *nom de plume* secures all the advantages without the disagreeables of reputation."

Eliot was, of course, not the first woman to adopt a male pseudonym: the Brontës had done it, and so had the French writer George Sand, who was much admired by Eliot. But she felt that her controversial subject matter—depicting the lives of clergymen in her own native county of Warwickshire, and invoking autobiographical ideas about religion, faith, and unrequited love—demanded secrecy. Not only that, but her social position was shaky enough because of her unconventional living situation. She was already infamous.

It turned out to be a good thing that she'd kept her identity hidden, as Blackwood wrote to Lewes (in a letter whose subtext was none too subtle): "I am glad to hear that your friend is, as I supposed, a clergyman. Such a subject is best in clerical hands."

In 1858, *Scenes of Clerical Life*, which contained the stories serialized in *Blackwood's* magazine, was published in two volumes, under the name George Eliot. She was now a real author, and asked her publisher to send review copies to contemporaries she admired, including Dickens, Ruskin, and Tennyson.

The first part of her new pen name was inspired by her devoted partner (and was also the name of her uncle); the surname "Eliot" was chosen simply because she thought it was a "good mouth-filling, easily pronounced word." "Under what name could she have published her fiction?" wrote a critic in 1999, referring to her various names. "It is clear that neither 'Evans' nor 'Lewes' would have done. Her invented title became the only fixed point in a shifting world of reference."

When John Blackwood showed up at Lewes's flat one day, hoping to meet the esteemed Mr. Eliot in person, the couple broke the news to him in a rather playful way. "Do you wish to see him?" Lewes asked. He and Marian left the room, then walked right back in—and Blackwood was introduced to the man (woman) himself.

He was more than gracious about it, and happy to keep their secret safe. In 1859, with the publication of *Adam Bede* (a masterful depiction of rural domestic life, whose title character was based on her father), Marian kept her gender and name private—though not for long. For one thing, too much of the story was recognizable, with identifiable characters; her brother Isaac read it and said that no one but his sister could possibly be the author. But the greater issue, as had been true for Charlotte Brontë with *Jane Eyre*, was the book's success: Queen Victoria was a fan. Dickens raved, "I cannot praise it enough," even though *Adam Bede* had outsold *A Tale of Two Cities*. Alexandre Dumas called it "the masterpiece of the century." And the *Times* declared that the mysterious author ranked "at once among masters of the art." Critics loved *Adam Bede*, and so did the public—a rare feat. The novel was a huge best seller. People wanted to know who George Eliot was, and false "authors" came forward to claim the glory. One man from Warwickshire insisted that he had written *Adam Bede* and *Scenes of Clerical Life*, and that he'd been cheated out of royalty payments.

Marian's efforts to hide her identity were increasingly in vain. It did not escape the notice of the Leweses' friends that their purchase of a large house, filled with new furniture and staffed by servants, happened to coincide with the launch of George Eliot. One friend wrote to Marian saying that she would "go to the stake" if Marian was not George Eliot. She received a warm, open, but stern reply from the author: "Keep the secret solemnly till I give you leave to tell it, and give way to no impulses of triumphant affection." Lewes added to the letter that "you mustn't call her Marian Evans again; that individual is extinct, rolled up, quashed, absorbed in the Lewesian magnificence!" From those who did realize the truth, the author pleaded for discretion. "Talking about my books," she explained, "has the same malign effect on me as talking of my feelings or my religion."

When *The Mill on the Floss* came out in 1860, she was by then one of the most acclaimed authors of her day, and it became well known that George Eliot was a woman living with a married man. (Why she clung to her pseudonym even after her true identity was revealed is unclear.) People loved her books but judged her as immoral for her unorthodox relationship. Lewes's wife was cast as the victim in this drama, and Marian Evans as the predator. Never mind that Agnes had given birth to not one but another four sons outside her marriage. Although Lewes had forgiven her, he had ceased to think of her as his wife. He went on with his life in a discreet and dignified manner—and did not embarrass Agnes as she had embarrassed him. He continued to support his family financially, yet his loyalty to Marian was unwavering. And she did not live with him until she knew that he would never again live under the same roof with Agnes.

In response to the flurry of scandal, "George Eliot" took full ownership of her new self, replying to letters addressed to "Miss Evans" with a chilly correction, informing one friend, "I request that any one who has a regard for me will cease to speak of me by my maiden name." Marian Evans represented a lonely, ugly country girl whom the author no longer knew and now deemed "extinct." George Eliot, her "real" self, was famous and influential (however immoral). She produced *Silas Marner* in 1861, and *Romola* two years later. Set in Renaissance Florence, *Romola* was a poorly received departure from her earlier works. She was not dissuaded by disappointment, and kept writing: *Felix Holt the Radical* came out in 1866—and four years later came her masterpiece, *Middlemarch*. (Emily Dickinson wrote to a cousin: "What do I think of *Middlemarch*? What do I think of glory?")

By 1876, when Eliot published *Daniel Deronda*, another breathtaking accomplishment (notable for its sympathetic portrait of Jews), she was forgiven. She was the pride of her country and was proclaimed the greatest living English novelist. Her work, finally, spoke for itself, and a judgmental public had listened and fallen silent. She was adored and admired, a literary giant—and a very wealthy woman. Whereas she and Lewes had once been exiles in London society, now they were celebrated, visited by Emerson, Turgenev, and other eminent intellectuals. A handsome American banker, John Cross, whom they affectionately called "dear nephew," managed their business affairs. All was well.

But on November 30, 1878, Lewes was dead by evening. Eliot had reported months earlier to a friend that Lewes was "racked with cramps from suppressed gout and feeling his inward economy all wrong." The sixty-one-year-old had succumbed to cancer, though he had never received the diagnosis.

They'd been together for more than two decades, and although Eliot was melancholic by nature, these had been the best years of her life. In a sense, Lewes had made everything possible. And when Eliot had received a manuscript of *Adam Bede*, bound in red leather, from her publisher, she had inscribed it to Lewes: "To my dear husband, George Henry Lewes, I give this M.S. of a work which would never have been written but for the happiness which his love has conferred on my life. Marian Lewes, March 23, 1859."

In her grief-stricken stupor, she felt unable to attend his funeral. Each new day without him represented "a new acquaintance with grief." Her old friend Turgenev sent a letter of condolence assuring her that the whole of "learned Europe" mourned with her. When she responded to such letters, she signed herself "Your loving but half dead Marian." She was severely depressed and weighed just over a hundred pounds. She found a sense of purpose by establishing a £5,000 grant in Lewes's name at Cambridge University, and by devoting her waking hours to editing his final work. Eliot never wrote another novel. She would be dead within two years.

Her fans demanded her attention more than ever; it seemed that her fame had grown after her loss, which she found deeply unsettling. Requests for photographs of the famous George Eliot were politely declined, as the author explained that she treasured her privacy and did not wish to be stared at in public. One particularly aggressive autograph hunter was finally silenced with a form letter, a reply that the author had dictated: "Mrs. Lewes (George Eliot), whom he has mistakenly addressed as Miss Marian Evans, has no photograph of herself and systematically abstains from giving her autograph."

One might expect that at this late stage of life—she was sixty— her knack for courting scandal would have been a distant memory. But she provoked rebuke once again, in May 1880, by marrying John Cross, who was twenty years her junior. He'd proposed to her three times before she accepted. Now she would have the legal marriage she'd always longed for; in this regard, she was rather old-fashioned, and had suffered from being unable to legitimize an otherwise blissful longtime union. At last, she could marry, if not the love of her life, a man she loved.

For their honeymoon, John and Marian traveled to Venice, where a strange mishap occurred. One morning, suffering from a depressive episode, Cross jumped from the balcony of their suite at the Hotel Europa (where luminaries such as Proust and Verdi had stayed) and landed in the Grand Canal. He was perhaps embarrassed, but physically unharmed. Venetian newspapers reported the incident, and the local police recorded it as a suicide attempt. Eliot alerted John's brother by telegram, and he joined them for the rest of their honeymoon. They blamed the heat for John's bizarre leap, and the trio traveled on to Munich.

Upon their return home, the couple attended a dinner party in their honor, after which a guest wrote a petty and unkind missive to her sister: "George Eliot, old as she is, and ugly, really looked very sweet and winning in spite of both. She was dressed in a short soft satin walking dress with a lace wrap half shading the body, a costume most artistically designed to show her slenderness, yet hiding the squareness of age." She added that there was not a single person in the room (including Eliot's husband) "whose mother she might not have been. . . . She adores her husband, and it seemed to me it hurt her a little to have him talk so much to me. It made her, in her pain, slightly irritated and snappish. . . . He may forget the twenty years difference between them, but she never can."

Evans changed her name yet again, to Mary Anne Cross, but the marriage lasted less than a year. She died unexpectedly on December 22, 1880, at sixty-one—the same age at which Lewes died. Only a few days earlier, she and John had attended a concert and seen a performance of *Agamemnon*. In what is believed to be her final utterance, she complained of "great pain in the left side." Then she was gone.

Left to tend to the legacy of this towering figure, Cross had his own minor identity crisis; he was referred to as "George Eliot's widow." He only bolstered his image as "Mr. Eliot" when he published a biography of his late wife in 1885. It would be a stretch to assume that his marriage to Eliot had been consummated, but he is said to have truly loved and revered her. "I am left alone in this new House we meant to be so happy in," he wrote to a friend. He never remarried.

Even in death, Eliot paid a steep price for her unconventional life: in her will, she asked to be buried at Westminster Abbey, but the request was denied. She was dismissed as "a person whose life and opinions were in notorious antagonism to Christian practice in regard to marriage, and Christian theory in regard to dogma." (This was certainly true.) Further, the church noted that despite the author's wish for a funeral in the Abbey, "[o]ne cannot eat one's cake and have it too. Those who elect to be free in thought and deed must not hanker after the rewards, if they are to be so called, which the world offers to those who put up with its fetters."

It was not until the centenary of her death that she would receive a memorial stone in Poet's Corner. (She was in good company in that regard: Lord Byron, whose life was shockingly scandalous, died in

1824 and wasn't given a stone until 1969.) The eminent scholar Gordon Haight had the honor of delivering the speech for the unveiling of her stone at Westminster Abbey on June 21, 1980, five years before his own death. "The novels of George Eliot provide the most varied and truthful picture we have of English religious life in the nineteenth century," he said. Whereas the novel had often previously served as a trivial pastime, he noted, Eliot elevated it into "a compelling moral force."

After Eliot died, Henry James paid her a glorious tribute: "What is remarkable, extraordinary—and the process remains inscrutable and mysterious—is that this quiet, anxious, sedentary, serious, invalidical English lady, without animal spirits, without adventures, without extravagance, assumption, or bravado, should have made us believe that nothing in the world was alien to her; should have produced such rich, deep, masterly pictures of the multifold life of man."

Today we take for granted how much Eliot sacrificed to become one of the greatest authors in the history of Western literature. She is simply *George Eliot*, literary master, staid historical figure, required college reading, admired by generations of authors. Her iconic Victorian visage now adorns posters, calendars, coffee mugs, stationery. But this pioneer could never forget the toll of her fame.

Reflecting on her story, it is tempting to interpret one of the concluding passages of *The Mill on the Floss* as the author's weary assessment of her own life:

Nature repairs her ravages, but not all. The uptorn trees are not rooted again; the parted hills are left scarred; if there is a new growth, the trees are not the same as the old, and the hills underneath their green vesture bear the marks of the past rending. To the eyes that have dwelt on the past, there is no thorough repair.

He was obsessive-compulsive and collected books about fairies

CHAPTER 4

Lewis Carroll & CHARLES DODGSON

A show of hands if you've never heard of *Alice in Wonderland*. That's what I thought. You'd have to have fallen down a rabbit hole to be unfamiliar with Lewis Carroll's 1865 masterpiece, which in the past hundred years has been adapted for television and film numerous times, including three silent films, a British musical, a pornographic movie, an animated Disney version, a Japanese anime TV series (*Fushigi no Kuni no Alice*), and in 2010, a 3-D blockbuster directed by Tim Burton. It has been turned into graphic novels, plays, and operas, and it was even appropriated as the title of an execrable album by Jewel (*Goodbye Alice in Wonderland*). It has been translated into 125 languages, including Yiddish, Swahili, and Pitjantjatjara, an Aboriginal language of Australia. It has influenced James Joyce and Jefferson Airplane. There have been *Alice* theme parks, mugs, teapots, soap dishes, chess sets, T-shirts, and tea towels. Aside from Shakespeare, and the Bible, it's the most widely translated and quoted book of all time. Following the first edition illustrated by John Tenniel, subsequent versions have been accompanied by drawings from artists such as Arthur Rackham, Mervyn Peake, Ralph Steadman, and Salvador

Dalí. Many woefully misguided authors have attempted sequels to *Alice*. Parodies have been published—some brilliant, some without merit. Vladimir Nabokov translated a Russian edition when he was just twenty-four years old. And through all its iterations, *Alice* has never been out of print.

This classic story, perhaps the most-read children's book in the world, has also been banned on at least a few occasions. In the early twentieth century, a high school in New Hampshire censored *Alice in Wonderland* owing to its "expletives, references to masturbation and sexual fantasies, and derogatory characterizations of teachers and of religious ceremonies." (Fair enough.) And in 1931, China deemed it forbidden material because "animals should not use human language."

The author of *Alice's Adventures in Wonderland* (its original title) was Lewis Carroll, but that name was a hiding place. The eccentric Reverend Charles Lutwidge Dodgson, a shy, eminent Oxford mathematician and lecturer, had created the nom de plume as a means of shelter from which he could let his imagination run wild. He wanted his "day job" to remain undisturbed and private. Reflecting his obsession with wordplay since childhood, the pseudonym was a clever transposition of his real name: "Lewis" was the anglicized form of *Ludovicus* (Latin for "Lutwidge"), and "Carroll" was an Irish surname similar to the Latin *Carolus*, from which the name "Charles" is derived.

He was so mortified by publicity that he refused to acknowledge his alter ego. Whenever he was a guest in someone's home, if the name "Lewis Carroll" arose in conversation, he would leave. Autograph hunters were turned away without exception.

Her Majesty Queen Victoria loved *Alice* and its sequel, *Through the Looking-Glass*, so much that she wrote a letter to Lewis Carroll, asking if he would send her the rest of his books. Unable to decline a request from the Queen, the humble author obliged as best he could, sending her numerous volumes—all by Charles Dodgson, and all mathematical texts, including the popular beach read *Condensation of Determinants, Being a New and Brief Method for Computing Their Arithmetical Values.*

Until the end of his life, this reticent polymath maintained a strict divide between himself and the fanciful Lewis Carroll. "For 30 years I have managed to keep the 2 personalities distinct," he boasted in a letter written three years before his death, "and to avoid all communication, *in propria persona*, with the outer world, about my books."

Fastidious in everything he did—today, we might apply the clinical term "obsessive-compulsive," a mental disorder—Dodgson went so far as to conceal his own handwriting. When he had to handle official correspondence for Lewis Carroll, he'd ask someone to copy out his response so that no one would have a sample of his writing. In 1883, he wrote to the divinity school at Oxford, begging the staff never to release anything he had handwritten. "It is a thing I often have to do—people seeming to assume that *everybody* likes notoriety," he explained, "and scarcely believing me when I say I dislike it particularly. My constant aim is to remain, *personally*, unknown to the world."

More than a hundred years after his death, it is still hard to believe that the same man who wrote whimsical, exuberant classics of Victorian literature also produced arcane texts such as *Notes on the First Two Books of Euclid, Designed for Candidates for Responsions*; and *An Elementary Treatise on Determinants with Their Application to Simultaneous Linear Equations and Algebraical Geometry.* No wonder he needed a pen name.

To recount, even broadly, the achievements of Dodgson's life is the equivalent of tracing the lives of ten extraordinary men. The sheer vastness and absurd variety of his accomplishments, beyond his literary success, is exhausting to contemplate. He defies comprehension; only speculation is possible.

His beginnings were unremarkable. Charles Lutwidge Dodgson was born in Daresbury, Cheshire, on January 27, 1832, the third child (and first son) of eleven children—there would be five more sisters and three brothers. His father, Charles Dodgson, and mother, Frances Jean Lutwidge, were first cousins. This genetic intermix might be to blame for the severe stammer that afflicted their son throughout his life, as well as most of his siblings. In childhood, he suffered a high fever making him permanently deaf in his right ear.

The young Dodgson had a fantastic imagination. He devised elaborate games with lists of rules, performed magic tricks to entertain his family, and created a puppet theater, writing plays and handling the troupe of marionettes himself. He wrote stories and poems (including acrostics), drew sketches, and wrote, edited, and illustrated magazines for his family. This was a common activity for many Victorians; what was unusual was for a young boy to lead the creative efforts and make all the booklets almost entirely alone. He was educated at home in his early years and proved a precocious reader, supposedly tackling *The Pilgrim's Progress* at age seven. Frances, who doted on her son, kept a record of his endeavors—"Religious Reading: Private," "Religious Reading with Mama," and "Daily Reading: Useful—Private." In an 1898 biography of Dodgson, his nephew Stuart Dodgson Collingwood wrote that "the boy invented the strangest diversions for himself . . . [and] numbered certain snails and toads among his intimate friends. . . . [He] lived in that charming 'Wonderland' which he afterwards described so vividly; but for all that he was a thorough boy, and loved to climb the trees and to scramble about in the marl-pits." It was an idyllic childhood.

He may have been a "thorough boy," but he was wary of other boys. "I am fond of children (except boys)," he famously wrote, and admitted once that "little girls I can now and then get along with . . . but with little *boys* I'm out of my element altogether." His negative sentiment might be traced to his time at Richmond Grammar School, where he was sent at the age of twelve. In a letter home, he recounted his unhappy initiation: "The boys have played two tricks upon me which were these—they first proposed to play at 'King of the cobblers' and asked me if I would be king, to which I agreed, then they made me sit down . . . and immediately began kicking me and knocking on all sides." He was bitten by another student, too. Although this was a rude awakening from his early years at the parsonage at Daresbury, where his father was a vicar (eventually rising to archdeacon), the boy quickly adapted to his new life. The headmaster sent an enthusiastic report to Dodgson's father, saying that "he possesses, along with other and excellent natural endowments, a very uncommon share of genius."

He switched schools after a year and a half, but left feeling confident, intellectually superior to his peers, and, toughened by experience, unafraid to challenge would-be bullies. For the next four years he attended the public school Rugby; founded in 1567, it was one of Britain's most prestigious boarding schools (and the source of the sport). At the time Dodgson enrolled, Rugby was considered the best public school in England. Here, however, the hazing and cruelty proved far more brutal than had been the case at Richmond.

In 1849, he returned home, where he would stay before heading off to Christ Church, Oxford, two years later, following in his father's footsteps. His university education got off to a bittersweet start, as his mother died at forty-seven, just two days after he'd arrived at Oxford. He had been especially close to her, and this loss marked the definitive end of his childhood.

At twenty-one, he wrote a poem called "Solitude" that revealed, despite his love of jokes, puzzles, and riddles, a pensive side, glum and highly sensitive. It also revealed what would become a lifelong craving for a return to innocence, manifested in his preference for close friendships with children rather than adults. The final stanzas of the poem read:

For what to man the gift of breath,
If sorrow be his lot below;
If all the day that ends in death
Be dark with clouds of woe?

Shall the poor transport of an hour
Repay long years of sore distress—
The fragrance of a lonely flower

Make glad the wilderness?

Ye golden hours of Life's young spring,
Of innocence, of love and truth!
Bright, beyond all imagining,
Thou fairy-dream of youth!

I'd give all wealth that years have piled,
The slow result of Life's decay,
To be once more a little child
For one bright summer-day.

Even as he earned a degree in mathematics at Christ Church, Dodgson wrote poems and stories on the side. In 1855, he submitted "Solitude" for publication in a literary journal called *The Train*. This is the earliest recorded appearance of "Lewis Carroll." Two years earlier, he'd placed a poem and a short story in another literary journal, signing both with the alias "B. B."

He was tall (six feet), slim, and handsome, yet he often showed considerable discomfort in social situations. Then there was the matter of his being ordained, which further isolated him from a wider community. However, as the bishop of Oxford recalled years after Dodgson's death, he did not pursue his religious studies as far as he might have done. "He was ordained," the bishop wrote, "but he never proceeded to priest's orders. Why he stopped at the Diaconate I do not know, but I think his stammer in speech may have had something to do with it. He was rather sensitive about this and it made him shy of taking clerical duty in church." Although Dodgson was not prepared to devote himself wholly to parochial life, as his father had, the bishop wrote, "No one who knew him could doubt that he took his position as an ordained man seriously, or that his religion was a great reality to him, controlling his thoughts and actions in a variety of ways." It may have not only controlled but crippled him. Dodgson never married or had children;

many scholars have asserted that the relationship with his young muse, Alice Liddell, was the single great romance of his life.

Dodgson found a home at Christ Church, partly by winning a distinguished "studentship" honor, given to only the best undergraduates. This appointment offered him lodgings and a small stipend for the rest of his life, along with permanent affiliation with Christ Church—and access to its astounding resources with no obligation to teach or publish academic papers. There was a catch, of course; he could keep the fellowship as long as he never violated its restrictions. As a fellow, he was required to remain celibate and unmarried, and to progress to holy orders as an ordained priest. It's unclear why he never got further than deacon; instead, he appealed to the dean, Reverend Henry George Liddell, for permission not to advance. For reasons also unknown, Liddell allowed him to retain his position as Christ Church fellow, even though this was a violation of the rules and unprecedented. Despite deciding against entering the priesthood, Dodgson was by all accounts devout and pious, obsessed throughout his life by notions of sin and guilt. He was extremely conservative in his political and personal beliefs. This is yet another reason why he seems inscrutable, and so unlikely as the creator of Lewis Carroll.

The transition from stellar undergraduate to undergraduate tutor was not enough for him. As one writer commented of Dodgson's living quarters at the college, "the very intensity of his tidiness indicates what forces were pent up within this environment." To the extent that he could, he satisfied his creative yearnings by slyly infusing his mathematical lessons with puzzles and riddles. One former student recalled, "I always hated mathematics at school, but when I went up to Oxford I learnt from Mr. Dodgson to look upon my mathematics as the most delightful of all my studies." But something larger and more urgent stirred in his blood, and could not stay pent up for long.

At the age of twenty-three, Dodgson now had a secure position as a scholar and lecturer, and a regular income. His life changed profoundly when he was introduced to Dean Liddell's children.

Among his many skills and hobbies, Dodgson took an early interest in photography when it was still a wondrous new invention. Like Mark Twain, Dodgson was a gadget freak—whatever the nineteenth-century equivalents of iPhones and iPods, he couldn't wait to try the next big thing. The camera was no exception, and with his eye for composition, his artistic sensibility, and his desire to tinker with new toys, Dodgson loved taking pictures. It was a cumbersome process, the very opposite of today's point-and-shoot, but he enjoyed it all, including the preparation of the plates. He constantly sought out subjects for his photographs, especially children.

As Liddell, a photography enthusiast himself, became better acquainted with Dodgson, he invited the young man to take pictures of his family. Dodgson began spending time with Liddell's little girls, Lorina (known as Ina), Alice, and Edith, and their brother, Harry, taking them on picnics and boating trips.

The "golden afternoon" of July 4, 1862, would prove transformative for them all. Years later, Alice Liddell recalled the day: "The sun was so hot we landed in meadows down the river, deserting the boat to take refuge in the only bit of shade to be found, which was under a newly made hayrick. Here from all three of us, my sisters and myself, came the old petition, 'Tell us a story,' and Mr. Dodgson (that is Lewis Carroll) began it." He made it up as he went along.

In the presence of children, particularly the Liddells, there was no awkwardness: Dodgson was at his most charming. That July afternoon, as he later remembered it, "in a desperate attempt to strike out some new line of fairy-lore, I had sent my heroine straight down a rabbit-hole, to begin with, without the least idea what was to happen afterwards." Ten-year-old Alice begged him to write down for her the story that he'd told. He sat up the entire night, working on a draft, and eventually made it into a green leather booklet called *Alice's Adventures Under Ground*, which he illustrated himself and gave to her as a Christmas gift.

Dodgson shared his story with a select few, including his friend Henry Kingsley, a novelist, who urged him to consider publishing it. He expanded and revised the manuscript, commissioned John Tenniel (already celebrated for his political cartoons for *Punch*) to do the illustrations, and submitted it to Macmillan, which agreed to publish *Alice's Adventures in Wonderland* by Lewis Carroll. The first chapter, "Down the Rabbit Hole," began:

> Alice was beginning to get very tired of sitting by her sister on the bank, and of having nothing to do; once or twice she had peeped into the book her sister was reading, but it had no pictures or conversations in it, 'and what is the use of a book,' thought Alice, 'without pictures or conversations?'
>
> So she was considering in her own mind (as well as she could, for the hot day made her feel very sleepy and stupid) whether the pleasure of making a daisy chain would be worth the trouble of getting up and picking the daisies, when suddenly a white rabbit with pink eyes ran close by her.

The book was initially released in 1865, but only fifty copies of a planned edition of two thousand were issued. Publication ceased when an unhappy Tenniel insisted on suppressing it because of imperfections in the printing process, which had affected his illustrations. Those who had purchased early copies were asked to return them to the publisher, and Macmillan donated the rejected books to children's hospitals.

After the necessary corrections were made and a new printer was found, *Alice* was published, in 1866, in an edition of four thousand that Dodgson proudly declared to be a "perfect piece of artistic printing." (Only twenty-three copies of the withdrawn 1865 version are known to survive, and in 1998 an anonymous buyer paid $1.54 million at auction for one of those precious books.)

Alice was an instant success and sold out right away. Dodgson was thrilled at the reviews proclaiming his book "a glorious artistic treasure." Like Charlotte Brontë, Dodgson requested that his publisher send him clippings of every review that came out, and he kept records of them in his diary.

The sequel, *Through the Looking-Glass, and What Alice Found There*, which made no reference to its predecessor, was published in time for Christmas 1871, with a first printing of nine thousand copies bound in gilt-stamped red cloth. Today, the original manuscript is in the British Museum.

A section called "The Wasp in a Wig" had been omitted from the second book at Tenniel's suggestion, partly because he didn't think it could be drawn. He dismissed it with no small amount of condescension, informing the author that "the '*wasp*' chapter doesn't interest me in the least . . . a *wasp* in a *wig* is altogether beyond the appliances of art." Tenniel was apparently something of a diva—he'd initially refused to sign on as the illustrator for *Looking-Glass*, and only after more than two years of nudging was Dodgson able to persuade him to say yes. Tenniel agreed, but noted that he would draw the pictures only if he could find the time.

Although *Looking-Glass* was not as universally praised as *Alice* had been, it was a best seller. Immediately after the first printing sold out, Macmillan went back to press for six thousand more. It's no wonder that the critical reaction to the book, while favorable, was not entirely rapturous. The sequel, though brilliant, was more of an acquired taste than its predecessor (those coded chess moves!), if no less enchanting.

As the novelist Zadie Smith commented in her introduction to the 2001 Bloomsbury edition, *Looking-Glass* is "a more tenebrous animal than its sister, both in style and quality of its fame. When I came to pick it up once more after an absence of years, I found I couldn't quite remember it other than as the repository where missing stories you *thought* were in *Wonderland* turn out to be—like a second, darker, larder."

Looking-Glass introduced what many consider to be the greatest piece of nonsense verse ever written, "Jabberwocky." It ranked in the top ten in a poll of Britain's favorite children's poems, along with Edward Lear's "The Owl and the Pussycat" and T. S. Eliot's "Macavity the Mystery Cat." "Jabberwocky" begins:

> 'Twas brillig, and the slithy toves
> Did gyre and gimble in the wabe;
> All mimsy were the borogoves,
> And the mome raths outgrabe.
> "Beware the Jabberwock, my son!
> The jaws that bite, the claws that catch!
> Beware the Jubjub bird, and shun
> The frumious Bandersnatch!"

Carroll went on to write other books, including, in 1876, the mock-heroic nonsense poem *The Hunting of the Snark* (141 rhymed four-line stanzas) and important texts on mathematics and logic, but the *Alice* books remained his crowning achievements. His writing career had reached its apogee. As Robert McCrum wrote in the *Guardian* on the occasion of Tim Burton's "charmless mash-up" of a movie adaptation, the *Alice* books "continue to exert an indestructible spell: teasing, phantasmagorical, narcotic, existential and profoundly English."

That he knew fame (not to mention great wealth) in his lifetime was a decidedly mixed blessing for C. L. Dodgson, as he was often known. Managing it filled him with terrible anxiety. On the rare occasions when he admitted that Dodgson and Carroll were the same man, he was either speaking openly with friends or corresponding with children and encouraging their letters. Otherwise, he said once, "I use the name of 'Lewis Carroll' in order to avoid all *personal* publicity." Over and over, he lamented the unrelenting pressure to become a "public figure," since he'd chosen a pseudonym precisely to protect himself from the burdens of celebrity. Dodgson hated the idea of strangers knowing anything about his personal life or what he looked like. Even those close to him could not resist feeding the myth of his enigmatic nature. He was "not exactly an ordinary human being of flesh and blood," one friend reported, but rather "some delicate, ethereal spirit, enveloped for the moment in a semblance of common humanity."

To that end, when he received letters for "Lewis Carroll," he marked most of them "Return to sender." Requests for photographs, even from relatives, were routinely denied. (He gave out photographs of himself only to children, usually young girls.) He begged friends to keep his real name private. When a bookshop catalog cited him as the author of *Through the Looking-Glass*, he wrote a letter demanding that Charles Dodgson's name no longer be printed "in connection with any books except what he has put his name to."

Desperate to keep his pseudonym private, he implored the Bodleian Library at Oxford to delete all cross-references between his names. The request was refused. Even though his identity as Carroll was an open secret, he was distressed by his inability to control its distribution.

He achieved a minor triumph when an editor contacted him for the *Dictionary of the Anonymous and Pseudonymous Literature of Great Britain*. "I use a name, not my own, for writing under, for the one sole object, of avoiding *personal* publicity," he wrote, "that I may be able to come and go, unnoticed, to all public places." He added that "it would be a real unhappiness to me to feel myself liable to be noticed, or pointed out, by strangers." And he begged for respect in not "breaking through a disguise which it is my most earnest wish to maintain."

The *Dictionary* editor, surprisingly, agreed to omit his name—and so the book was published in 1882 with a glaring omission: this very famous pseudonym was nowhere to be found.

Dodgson remained a vigilant sentry of his privacy. In 1890, exasperated by the barrage of mail he received, he printed a circular to be enclosed with all replies to letters addressed to "Lewis Carroll." The statement declared that Mr. Dodgson "neither claims nor acknowledges any connection with any pseudonym, or with any book that is not published under his own name." (He might as well have added,

"So please bugger off.")

There's a passage from *Alice in Wonderland* that invites interpretation as a commentary on the double-edged sword of fame, with its demands, expectations, and vicissitudes—and as an expression of Dodgson's ambivalence toward his legacy:

> "It was much pleasanter at home," thought poor Alice, "when one wasn't always growing larger and smaller, and being ordered about by mice and rabbits. I almost wish I hadn't gone down that rabbit-hole—and yet—and yet—it's rather curious, you know, this sort of life! I do wonder what can have happened to me! When I used to read fairy-tales, I fancied that kind of thing never happened, and now here I am in the middle of one! There ought to be a book written about me, that there ought!"

(The meaning is heightened, too, if you buy into the notion that the heroine is a stand-in for the author.) By all accounts, what Dodgson desired most was the power of invisibility. Though he was a fanatic about photography and loved taking pictures of people, he treasured his own privacy, and struggled to reconcile this requisite to his well-being with the fame he'd achieved. "I don't want to be known by sight!" he once said in despair.

He may have been paranoid about fame, but he was pragmatic. In 1879, he wrote to his publisher: "I cannot of course help there being many people who know the connection between my real name and my 'alias,' but the fewer there are who are able to connect my face with the name 'Lewis Carroll' the happier for me." After all, he'd never intended to make *Alice in Wonderland* public; it had been created as a gift for Alice Liddell, and only at the urging of friends had he considered publishing it. He had hardly conceived it as a commercial product. Another reason for his strict separation of church (Dodgson) and state (Carroll) was purely professional: he wanted his mathematical books to be regarded seriously, and feared that if scholars connected him with Carroll, those works would be dismissed.

Although Dodgson could accept that at a certain point his real name was not exactly a secret, there was the matter of preserving his privacy. He bristled at what he considered even the slightest invasion of his personal life—such as being accosted in public to receive compliments about his work. It was exhausting. ("But it's no use now," says Alice after falling down the rabbit hole, "to pretend to be two people! Why, there's hardly enough of me left to make *one* respectable person!")

His encounters with eager fans left him uncomfortable, and he confessed that among the things he hated most were "having a tooth drawn" and listening to a stranger talk about his books. The notion of being gracious to admiring fans was lost on him. In 1891, he reported to a friend an anecdote he'd read about a pompous author who greeted someone with the line, "Have you read my book?" It left him mortified. "If ever *I* ask such a question of a stranger," he wrote, "it will be due to 'temporary insanity!'"

Even though some biographical accounts of Dodgson portray him as a cloistered academic, he wasn't that, exactly. Between the age of twenty-nine and his death at sixty-five, he wrote a staggering number of letters—nearly a hundred thousand in all—proving that although he was shy with his public, he was not a recluse. That most of his letters were addressed to children shows his frequent unease in the world of adults; for the children he adored, he kept records of their birthdays and sent them letters with jokes, puns, puzzles, acrostics, and drawings. He toyed with inventive forms for his correspondence, including looking-glass letters that the recipient had to hold up to a mirror to read; rebus letters to be decoded; pinwheel-shaped letters; and delightful letters composed in such tiny script, on paper the size of a postage stamp, that a magnifying glass was needed to read them.

Because Carroll was a writer of the highest achievement who was also widely popular, it's understandable that his interactions with adults were sometimes marked by wariness and formality, rather than the broad affection he showed children. For them, he was whatever they wanted him to be. There is no evidence, in his diaries or elsewhere, of any long-term romantic relationships with women, which surely contributed to suggestions (however indirectly, even in his lifetime) of pedophilia. There was his affinity for taking photos of nude girls, of course. However, in the Victorian era, child nudes were not an uncommon artistic subject; it was perhaps Dodgson's excessive ardor for little girls, and his compulsive pursuit of their friendship, that called his behavior into question. (One might regard him as a Victorian-era Michael Jackson, but that is a topic for another time.)

Considering Dodgson's conscientious temperament, his open-heartedness, and his religious fervor, it seems likely that his sexual urges, however inappropriate, remained repressed and were never acted on. Still, adding to the intrigue are four volumes missing from Dodgson's diaries of various periods dating from 1853 to 1863. (Nine volumes in all have survived.) What happened? Did he have something to hide? Was he chaste or deviant? Did a relative remove the diary pages after his death, to protect the family's reputation or the author's own? A record by the Lewis Carroll Society on Dodgson's "Journal 8" (from the period of his burgeoning acquaintance with Alice Liddell and her siblings) comments:

> A noticeable feature of this journal is the use Dodgson makes of these pages for recording prayers and supplications to help him lead a better life. Although prayers occurred in earlier volumes, the frequency and earnestness began to take on greater proportions in this journal. There has been much speculation about the reasons and purposes of the prayers. Reading them in the context of his unfolding life, there is no clear and obvious reason which can account for them. They do show that he experienced moments of great self-doubt and guilt. Some prayers indicate that feelings of slothfulness and lack of attention to his duties as mathematical lecturer gave rise to regret. However, there are some prayers which are more personal and poignant. One gets a deep sense of Dodgson's inability to come to terms

with the troubles in his mind, and a feeling that he was unable to control these feelings which caused him such anguish and concern, whatever the cause may have been.

In 1863, a falling-out occurred with the Liddell family, and even though the mysterious rift was mended, the relationship was sporadic from then on. Was Dodgson a man with ignominious secrets? Did this partly explain his extreme need to protect himself from the scrutiny surrounding "Lewis Carroll"? Was the shame he carried regarding his fixation on prepubescent girls the reason he never progressed from deacon to priest? Why were his diaries filled with angst-ridden contemplations of guilt, temptation, and self-rebuke?

Taken together, these questions are no more answerable today than they have been over the past century, but Alice's refrain throughout her journey in Wonderland—"Who in the world am I?"—resonates further when one considers the author's complex history. For unknown reasons, Dodgson often felt tormented by his own thoughts: he once wrote of having been "haunted by some worrying subject of thought, which no effort of will is able to banish."

The man who loved puzzles was himself a deep mystery. Photography, which had once captivated him, was abandoned in the summer of 1880. Over more than two decades, he'd become an excellent photographer and had even considered earning a living with his hobby. He'd taken thousands of pictures, yet that year stopped the activity that had given him so much pleasure. As far as anyone knows, Dodgson never took another photograph for the rest of his life. One reason may be the unpleasant rumors that circulated about his penchant for photographing nude children. He was quite aware of how it might be perceived, telling one mother that her children's "innocent unconsciousness is very beautiful, and gives one a feeling of reverence," and expressing remorse if he had overstepped any bounds with them. Though he discussed plans for future portraits, they were dropped. Another, more mundane, explanation for this may have been his extreme disdain for the latest, more advanced photographic processes, which he regarded as inferior.

In no way did this curious mathematician add up. He was a distinguished member of society, though he wore his hair longer than was considered proper for a Victorian gentleman. His letters alone were often works of genius, as exhilarating and imaginative as his *Alice* books, yet many who knew Dodgson found him stodgy and dull. "He held himself stiffly," a relative recalled, "one shoulder slightly higher than the other; in his almost overemphasized erectness there was an old-fashioned seriousness, an air of punctiliousness." Even Alice Liddell remembered him as having "carried himself upright, as if he had swallowed a poker." In the company of adults, if he knew someone well and felt at ease, he appeared handsome, charming, funny, and confident; yet one colleague called him "peculiar and paradoxical, and the topics on which he loved to dwell were such as would bore many persons."

Dodgson was quite odd. He wrote most of his books, including *Alice*, while standing up. (He calculated that he could work standing at his desk for up to ten hours.) His contradictions, eccentricities, and obsessive routines were truly astonishing—apart from standing to write, he would map out entire journey routes well in advance, determining the precise time required to complete each leg of the trip. He also tallied the amount of money he would need at each stop, for each potential activity, and planned accordingly. Even his tea-brewing was a fanatical ritual: it must be steeped for exactly ten minutes, not a second more or less, or he would consider it undrinkable. And as it brewed, he would walk up and down his sitting room, swinging the teapot gently back and forth—always for precisely *ten* minutes. When he entertained dinner guests, he prepared a seating chart and kept records of their dining preferences for future events. ("By keeping the cards," he wrote, "one gets materials for making up other dinner-parties, by observing what people harmonise well together.") As a mathematician, he was fascinated by theories of randomness, but in life he was indefatigably controlling.

He loved taking long walks—sometimes for twenty miles—as an

aid to problem solving, composing verse, and reflection. During his treks, he liked to time himself, record his average speed, then compare the numbers with those from previous walks. It makes sense that his mathematician's mind would have found satisfaction in this self-tracking; it's harder to understand why he took extensive notes on the condition of his feet after each walk.

Steeped as he was in logic and science, Dodgson believed that Tuesday was his lucky day and forty-two his lucky number. He was a charter member of the Society for Psychical Research and the Ghost Society. He collected books about fairies and the occult.

Charles Dodgson would have been a fascinating subject of study had he done nothing but produce the *Alice* books. One could spend years dissecting them and attempting to "know" the man whose phenomenal imagination made them possible. For those accomplishments alone, his name—or, rather, Lewis Carroll's—would have been embedded in the popular psyche for generations to come. But he spent his lifetime bursting with acts of invention, none of which adds up to a cohesive whole.

Where to begin? Dodgson can be credited with the idea of printing the title of a book on the spine of its dust jacket, which he conceived for *The Hunting of the Snark*. (That innovation proved fairly influential, to say the least.) He also developed, in his late forties, a system to correct flawed voting procedures that resulted in unjust outcomes; elements of his "Parliamentary and Proportional Representation" theory are still used in elections today. He also applied it to lawn tennis tournaments in which superior players were unfairly eliminated in early rounds, and in 1883 he published the treatise *Lawn Tennis Tournaments: The True Method of Assigning Prizes*. (This from the guy who wrote "Jabberwocky"?) Then there was his role as Common Room Curator at Christ Church, which was not curatorial in any artistic sense; Dodgson spent an inordinate amount of time organizing the wine cellars, creating accounting systems, conducting audits, and doing other tedious but important administrative tasks.

But wait, there's more: Dodgson lobbied for government support to relocate to Australia or the Cape the residents of Tristan da Cunha, an archipelago off the coast of South Africa considered the most remote inhabited locale in the world. (He'd adopted this as a political cause after his youngest brother, Edwin, had served as an Anglican missionary there in the 1880s.) He wrote both "serious" poems and comic verse. He spoke out on the benefits of vaccinations. He invented a portable chessboard. He was a passionate theatergoer and had corresponded with W. S. Gilbert and Arthur Sullivan—as in Gilbert and Sullivan—about a collaboration to set his poems to music and produce a musical *Alice*. (It never happened.) He created sketches to improve a kind of three-wheeled cycle known as the velociman, making it easier to steer. Shunning celebrity himself, he enjoyed meeting famous people of his time such as Trollope, Tennyson, and Ruskin. Portmanteau words such as "chortle" and "galumph" originated with Dodgson. He invented a new kind of postal money order, double-sided adhesive strips, a method for right-margin justification on a typewriter, an *Alice in Wonderland* postage-stamp case, a variation on conventional backgammon, a mnemonic system known as *Memoria Technica* for recalling dates and events, a writing tablet called a Nyctograph that could be used for taking notes in darkness (take that, iPad!), brainteasers, and word games, including an early version of what endures today as Scrabble.

Despite all that he accomplished in his life, he was always modest. Dodgson wanted his work, regardless of context, to stand alone. When a friend once inquired about what *The Hunting of the Snark* "means," he replied in a letter, "I'm very much afraid I didn't mean anything but nonsense. Still, you know, words mean more than we mean to express when we use them; so a whole book ought to mean a great deal more than the writer means. So, whatever good meanings are in the book, I'm glad to accept as the meaning of the book." (Humpty Dumpty was just as cagey in explaining the meaning of his utterances. As he told Alice, "When I use a word . . . it means just what I choose it to mean—neither more nor less.")

In his final years, Dodgson continued lecturing, sketching, writing letters, juggling work projects, and making time for the friends he cherished. He suffered increasingly from bronchial trouble, and he died on January 14, 1898, two weeks before his sixty-sixth birthday. He left instructions that his funeral be "simple and inexpensive, avoiding all things which are merely done for show," and that there be "no expensive monument. I should prefer a small plain head-stone."

As someone who had always drawn gossip with what might gently be called an unconventional lifestyle, Dodgson did little to dispel the rumors that swirled around him. Despite ugly whispers about his relations with children, he gave widely to charities that advocated on their behalf—and kept all his donations private. He supported more than two dozen child-welfare organizations, and was so generous in giving away money that he incurred debt; a bank manager had to set limits on his overdrafts. As Morton N. Cohen noted in his excellent 1995 biography, *Lewis Carroll*, Dodgson never judged himself based on the opinions of others:

> Charles recognized earlier than one might suppose that his inner springs differed from most men's, that his heart beat to a different drum, that in order to be true to himself he would be compelled to lead a life that was not only outside the norm but would come under particular scrutiny and raise suspicions, one not generally condoned and subject to severe reprimand, sneers, lampoons, and ridicule. Be that as it may, he determined to follow his own star in spite of raised eyebrows and possible social censure. "Let them talk" was his answer; his own conscience would be his only judge.

"People want Carroll to be some sort of mad hatter," the chairman of the UK Lewis Carroll Society said in a 2010 interview. "They find it difficult that somebody who could write something as crazy as *Alice in Wonderland* could still be a jolly decent chap."

He was a profligate spender who smoked forty cigars a day

CHAPTER 5

Mark Twain & SAMUEL CLEMENS

How the protean Samuel Clemens became the world's most famous literary alias will never be known for sure. Sly and droll, never one to shy away from the making of his own myth, Clemens claimed that his pen name derived from the years he spent working on riverboats, where water at a depth of two fathoms, or twelve feet, was considered safe for the boat to pass over. This distance was measured on a sounding line, a length of rope with lead on the end. The crew would call out, "*Mark twain!*" (meaning the mark on the line was at two fathoms) to indicate clear passage.

Look up the archaic word "twain" in the *Oxford English Dictionary* and you will find an interesting entry. The adjective is defined as "[o]ne more than one, two; forming a pair, twin." "Consisting of two parts or elements; double, twofold." "Separate, apart; estranged, at variance." As in the eighteenth-century hymnal by the priest and Oxford tutor John Keble: "Five loaves had he, / And fishes twain." Or, from the Shakespearean sonnet, "We two must be twain, / Although our undivided loves are one." The noun is defined as "[t]wo persons or things identified contextually." In a nautical context, "[t]wo fathoms. Esp. in mark twain, the two fathom mark on a sounding-line."

Clemens liked to explain that his appellation had been swiped from a man named Captain Isaiah Sellers—a well-known steamboat man and sometime river correspondent for New Orleans newspapers. In *Life on the Mississippi*, Twain wrote that the captain "was not of literary turn or capacity, but he used to jot down brief paragraphs of plain practical information about the river, and sign them 'MARK TWAIN,' and give them to the *New Orleans Picayune*. They related to the stage and condition of the river, and were accurate and valuable. . . . At the time that the telegraph brought the news of his death, I was on the Pacific coast. I was a fresh new journalist, and needed a nom de guerre; so I confiscated the ancient mariner's discarded one, and have done my best to make it remain what it was in his hands—a sign and symbol and warrant that whatever is found in its company may be gambled on as being the petrified truth; how I have succeeded, it would not be modest in me to say."

There are other stories and legends as to how "Twain" came to be. Perhaps to varying degrees all versions are true, perhaps none. Some have ascribed to Clemens a Jekyll-and-Hyde nature; some have remarked on pseudonymity as a conventional choice for Victorian humorists, especially those tilted sharply toward satire. Perhaps both are true. One thing is beyond dispute: Twain is the best-known author in America's history, and his work is taught in every high school and college. With his pitch-perfect ear for the American vernacular, he is unrivaled (or, at least, secure among the all-time greats). "I am not an American," he wrote in his notebook in 1897. "I am the American."

Adopting a pseudonym was for Clemens an exercise in playfulness, in fooling the public simply because he could. "Some people lie when they tell the truth," Clemens once said in an interview. "I tell the truth lying." (The poet, philosopher, and critic George Santayana once described truth as "a jewel which should not be painted over; but it may be set to advantage and shown in a good light"—an aphorism that Twain would surely have endorsed.) And because he was some-one who occasionally made enemies with his writing, having the pseu-donymous cloak gave him a small measure of protective cover.

The jocular master of obfuscation was savvy about his own brand, eventually registering his alias as a trademark. He was his own best publicist and marketing director. He even incorporated himself under his nom de plume, so he officially became Mark Twain, Inc. He also trademarked the slogan on a box of "Mark Twain"–branded cigars that read "MARK TWAIN: KNOWN BY EVERYONE—LIKED BY ALL." Al-though this pen name was the one that stuck, it was not his first: he'd previously experimented with other names, including "W. Epami-nondas Adrastrus Blab," "Rambler," "Josh," "Sergeant Fathom," and "Thomas Jefferson Snodgrass."

Among his contemporaries, the use of pseudonyms was not only common practice but considered a fashionable accessory. Humorists in particular adopted pen names: Charles Farrar Browne was a famous writer and lecturer who signed his writing as "Artemus Ward"; he was greatly admired by Abraham Lincoln and known for his delightfully awful puns. Other popular humorists included David Ross Locke, who wrote as "Petroleum V. Nasby"; and Robert Newell, whose pen name "Orpheus C. Kerr" was a pun on "office seeker."

"Mark Twain" was born in 1863, but Samuel Langhorne Clemens was born on November 30, 1835, in Florida, Missouri, in a two-room rented cabin. The red-haired infant's arrival was two months prema-ture and he narrowly survived his birth. He spent his first four years frail and bedridden. Even his mother later admitted, "I could see no promise in him."

He was one of seven children, three of whom would die young, and was raised in the nearby riverside town of Hannibal. "If you are born in my state, you pronounce it *Missourah*," he once said. "If you are not born in my state, you pronounce it *Missouree*. But if you are born in my state, and you have to live your entire life in my state, you pronounce it misery."

He adored his mother, Jane, and avoided his stern, aloof father, John, whom he could not remember ever having laughed. (John died of pneumonia when Clemens was eleven years old.) He was a high-strung child, a sleepwalker, and he suffered from nightmares. Yet he was as exuberant, magnetic, and funny as his father was austere. It's no wonder that Clemens struggled to escape the provincial, restrictive milieu of his boyhood and went in search of a more expansive world. Despite being a poor student, he displayed an early knack for language and mimicry and a great love of storytelling. If he found little enchantment in his own house, he cultivated it endlessly through his fertile imagination. At sixteen, he was already working for a small newspaper, the *Hannibal Western Union*, and writing humorous sketches. And the first in a lifelong series of get-rich-quick schemes hooked him at the age of eighteen—he had a quixotic plan to sail the Amazon, where he would make a vast fortune in "a vegetable product of miraculous powers" that he'd read about. It was said to be "so nour-ishing and so strengthening that the natives of the mountains of the Madeira region would tramp up hill and down all day on a pinch of the powdered coca and require no other substance." This claim about being able to tramp up and down hills all day was undoubtedly true. "Coca" is better known today as cocaine.

Clemens was detoured from his grand plan, however, and went to work as an apprentice steamboat pilot, eventually getting his license. It was a job he loved. The stint ended with the advent of the Civil War, and it had been marked by tragedy. Clemens had convinced his younger brother Henry to join him in steamboat work, and Henry died in 1858 when the steamboat he was working on exploded. Clem-ens never forgave himself for his brother's death. Adding to his horror and guilt, he'd had a dream, not long before Henry died, in which he saw his brother lying in a metal casket.

In the summer of 1861, at his brother Orion's insistence, Clemens had headed west by stagecoach, hoping to strike it rich in Nevada's silver rush. He failed as a prospector. A job as a mill laborer didn't work out, either. One day Clemens asked his boss for a raise, naming the figure of $400,000 a month in his request. He was promptly fired.

His next move brought better luck, if modest pay: he was hired as a reporter, at a salary of twenty-five dollars a week, by the *Territorial Enterprise*, a newspaper in Virginia City, Nevada. Well liked and clearly talented, Clemens soon upped his wages to six dollars a day. "Everybody knows me," he boasted in a letter to his mother, "& I fare like a prince wherever I go, be it on this side of the mountains or the other. And I am proud to say I am the most conceited ass in the Territory."

"Mark Twain" made his debut on February 3, 1863, launched in an *Enterprise* column with the line, "I feel very much as if I had just awakened out of a long sleep." It was signed, "Yours, dreamily, Mark Twain." Two years later, while living in San Francisco, Twain became an official success: his short story "Jim Smiley and His Jumping Frog" was published in the *Saturday Press* in New York. It was reprinted all over the country (later retitled as "The Celebrated Jumping Frog of Calaveras County") and won him nationwide acclaim. "The foremost among the merry gentlemen of the California press, as far as we have been able to judge," wrote one New York critic, "is one who signs himself 'Mark Twain.' He is, we believe, quite a young man, and has not written a great deal. Perhaps, if he will husband his resources and not kill with overwork the mental goose that has given us these golden eggs, he may one day rank among the brightest of our wits."

It was obvious from the start, even in his slightest pieces, that down to his marrow Twain was a writer: "The difference between the almost right word and the right word is really a large matter—it's the difference between the lightning bug and the lightning," he once noted.

As Clemens's career as a newspaper reporter took off, he used his Twain pseudonym irregularly, but eventually it supplanted his real name. He slipped into Twain as if into an elegant new pair of shoes. Some of his friends began calling him "Mark," and his letters home were signed that way, too. As Twain's biographer Ron Powers has noted, even early correspondence displayed the young man's knack for embellishment: "His indifference to the boundary between fact and fantasy became a hallmark of his literature, and later, of his consciousness." At the age of twenty-eight, the transformation was complete: Clemens was a buried man. The sobriquet stuck, and everything published subsequently would appear under this alter ego. "Mark Twain" gave Clemens a kind of solid self-confidence he had never known as a boy. At one point he even joked that an "independent Double" was going around causing the kind of mischief that Sam Clemens wouldn't dream of attempting: "It gets intoxicated—I do not. It steals horses—I do not. It imposes on theatre managers—I never do. It lies—I never do." He was a restless lover of reinvention, and his new name allowed him to step into a role that he had conjured, and that he alone controlled.

When his book *The Innocents Abroad* was published in 1869, it was an instant hit. But his 1867 story collection, *The Celebrated Jumping Frog of Calaveras County, and Other Sketches*, had been a huge flop, and Twain said he hoped that every remaining copy would be burned. Even so, his public lectures had already made him a much-adored entertainer, with packed houses, and audiences hanging on his every word and rewarding his droll performances with roaring applause and standing ovations. (Powers has described Twain as "the nation's first rock star.") He charmed everyone he met. For the most part, he was able to repress his darker side and the grudges he held against those perceived to be his enemies. Yet he was gripped by bouts of depression and suicidal impulses, and often craved public validation as a means of steadying himself again. Periods of idleness threatened his equilibrium. Even in good times, though, he could be unpredictable, acting like a petulant prima donna: yelling at hotel employees in cities he visited; canceling lectures at the last minute; smashing a window shutter with his fists over a scheduling glitch; angrily throwing his shirts out a window.

He became a husband at thirty-five, marrying Olivia Langdon, the daughter of a wealthy merchant from Elmira, New York. Her skeptical father asked his future son-in-law for references, one of whom reported, "I would rather bury a daughter of mine than have her marry such a fellow." However difficult Clemens could be (which was very), and however frequent his absences from home, he and his wife were utterly devoted to each other until her death left him a widower.

The couple met on New Year's Eve 1867, through her family, and spent the evening in Manhattan attending a reading by Charles Dickens. Their courtship lasted seventeen months. Marrying into money left Clemens conflicted—after all, he had humble beginnings and claimed to hate the rich. (He would mock the nation's culture of materialism and greed in 1874's *The Gilded Age*.) Yet Mark Twain had boundless ambition and extravagant tastes. It seems fair to assume that even as he commissioned the ostentatious Gothic Revival mansion in Hartford, Connecticut, where he would settle with Olivia (known as Livy), some part of him must have burned with self-loathing. Louis Comfort Tiffany and Company designed part of the interior, which included custom stained-glass windows, polished marble floors, ornate brasswork, a carved oak Venetian bed, a mantelpiece from a Scottish castle, a billiards room, and modern conveniences such as central heating and flush toilets. In all, there were nineteen rooms and seven bathrooms. Although Twain would experience his greatest literary success while in that residence, it was also where he would experience ravaging losses. (Eventually, beset by financial ruin, he would be forced to sell the house.) In Buffalo, New York, he and Livy had already suffered the death of their first child, who died of diphtheria at eighteen months old. In Hartford, where the couple would spend the next twenty years, they raised three girls—Susy, Clara, and Jean—who venerated and feared their father. Harriet Beecher Stowe was the family's next-door neighbor, though she lived in a much more modest brick house.

Twain's admirers included Charles Darwin, Joseph Conrad, William Faulkner, T. S. Eliot, Eugene O'Neill, Oliver Wendell Holmes, and George Bernard Shaw. Twain would rarely admit to reading other writers, but he liked Shaw, whom he praised as "quite destitute of affectation." Shaw wrote a letter to Twain in 1907, mentioning that he'd met William Morris, an "incurable Huckfinomaniac." He addressed the letter to "My dear Mark Twain—not to say Dr Clemens (though I have always regarded Clemens as mere raw material—might have been your brother or your uncle)." A year later, Thomas Edison remarked, "An American loves his family. If he has any love left over for some other person, he generally selects Mark Twain." Nietzsche recommended *The Adventures of Tom Sawyer* to friends.

At the height of his fame, Twain was bombarded by fan mail, including manuscripts from aspiring writers who wanted his opinion of their work and assistance with publication. Letters poured in from around the world, some addressed simply to "Mark Twain, Hartford, Connecticut." Some asked for money. He filed away many letters under the heading, "*From an ass.*" He wrote to his mother, "I have a badgered, harassed feeling, a good part of the time." Yet he was paradoxical as ever: even though he often checked into hotels incognito, using a variety of aliases including "S. L. Samuel" and "C. L. Samuel," he was always thrilled to be recognized. Sometimes he would actually strut up and down busy streets in Manhattan, just as church services were ending and crowds were pouring out, so that he could bask in the sight of heads excitedly turning toward the great celebrity in their midst.

Once Twain was asked why the fame of many other humorists had been so ephemeral. "Because they were merely humorists," he replied. "Humorists of the 'mere' sort cannot survive. Humor is only a fragrance, a decoration. Often it is merely an odd trick of speech or of spelling . . . and presently the fashion passes and the fame along with it." Restless and ambitious all his life, Twain knew that to secure his legacy, his output had to transcend "mere" comic sketches and journalism. His reputation would ultimately rest on two masterpieces: *The Adventures of Tom Sawyer*, published in 1876 when the author was forty-one; and *The*

Adventures of Huckleberry Finn, published nearly a decade later. Ernest Hemingway claimed that all of American literature was derived from from the latter novel, calling it "the best book we've ever had. There was nothing before. There's been nothing as good since." The playwright Arthur Miller once said of Twain in an interview, "He wrote as though there had been no literature before him."

Twain, a popular writer, was also one hell of a trickster. As the scholar John Seelye notes of Tom Sawyer in his introduction to the Penguin edition of *Huckleberry Finn*, Tom is "a prankster from the start," not unlike the author himself, who adored practical jokes. "Where Huck Finn seems to be a projection of something mysterious deeply hidden in Mark Twain's psyche, Tom Sawyer is clearly an active agent of the author," Seelye writes.

Swindler, con man, histrionic showman: Tom represents, at least on the surface, the essential Twain. Huck goes deeper; he evinces both halves of the author's troubled psyche (Clemens/Twain), with all its contradictions, anxieties, and follies. But as Twain grew older, his private, Clemensesque qualities floated disruptively to the surface, threatening the impish, rambunctious public man he had become. The blithe, witty charmer was far more mercurial than his admiring public ever knew, and struggled (often painfully) to manage the two worlds and selves he inhabited. When he was drunk, however, his carefully constructed mask came undone. As one friend observed, "He was always afraid of dying in the poorhouse. The burden of his woe was that he would grow old and lose the power of interesting an audience, and become unable to write, and then what would become of him?" The more Clemens drank, the worse it got; there was no Twainian joviality or playful wit to accompany his alcohol consumption. Instead, his friend said, he would "grow more and more gloomy and blue until he fairly wept at the misery of his own future."

In April 1894, the world's most famous author declared bankruptcy. The wealth he'd amassed could not match his debts, and he'd had to embark upon a grueling round-the-world tour to repay creditors and become solvent again. Like his late father, Clemens had an almost manic relationship to money and had invested his considerable earnings dreadfully. He'd backed failed gadgets and fraudulent schemes, founded a money-losing publishing company, and patented a few unsuccessful inventions of his own, at great expense. Among them was an adjustable elastic waist strap for men that could be buttoned onto the back of a pair of trousers to keep them from falling down.

Foolishly, even though he was among the first Americans to have a telephone at home, he had declined to invest in Alexander Graham Bell's invention. He wasn't convinced that the telephone had much of a future. Twain himself acknowledged his gift for squandering his fortune. "Now here is a queer fact," he wrote, "I am one of the wealthiest grandees in America—one of the Vanderbilt gang, in fact—and yet if you asked me to lend you a couple of dollars I should have to ask you to take my note instead." Even he must have appreciated the perverse irony of having succumbed to the Gilded Age—a lifestyle that he so despised.

Having brought his family to the brink of ruin, Clemens would endure greater tragedies in subsequent years. He lost several friends and relatives. His daughter Susy died in 1896; Livy died of heart failure in 1904, at the age of fifty-eight; and his daughter Jean died in 1909.

These catastrophic events left him lonely, bitter, brokenhearted, vindictive, and paranoid. Sam Clemens depended on Mark Twain to keep going, but the gentle, irreverent humor in his work gave way to a more cynical, dyspeptic edge. (He took to calling his famous white uniform his "don'tcareadam suits," and boasted that they made him the most conspicuous man alive.) Although he'd always abhorred critics, he had previously displayed tolerance toward what he regarded as a necessary evil. "I believe that the trade of critic, in literature, music, and the drama, is the most degraded of all trades, and that it has no real value," he wrote. "However, let it go. It is the will of God that we must have critics, and missionaries, and Congressmen, and humor-ists, and we must bear the burden." Now, however, he was inclined to be far more bilious. If it's true that Clemens and Twain were polar opposites within the same deeply divided man, then it seems there was little actual Twain left in him at the end.

His insecurity often overwhelmed him, and his corrosive obses-sions—success, wealth, fame—revealed a volatility that baffled even him. The "periodical and sudden changes of mood in me," he once wrote, "from deep melancholy to half-insane tempests and cyclones of humor, are among the curiosities of my life." He loved playing billiards, which provided yet another excuse for his explosive temper to manifest itself. "When his game was going badly," Albert Bigelow Paine wrote in his 1912 Twain biography, "his language sometimes became violent and he was likely to become critical of his opponent. Then reaction would set in, and remorse."

Today, Mark Twain is still viewed as the mythic "Colonel Sand-ers without the chicken, the avuncular man who told stories," as Ron Powers has described him. "He's been scrubbed and sanitized." Yet a more comprehensive version of Twain emerged in 2010 with the publication of the first installment of his rambling three-volume auto-biography. It presents Twain raw and uncensored; he instructed that his unedited recollections be withheld from the public for one hun-dred years after his death. (As ever, what a brilliant marketing ploy.) He dictated most of the 500,000-word manuscript to a stenographer during the four years before he died, then postponed its publication for a century to preserve his genial reputation and legacy. The strategy worked. Among towering American literary figures, Twain remains essentially unknowable. As one contemporary journalist aptly put it, he's "still a mystery, a riddle wrapped in an enigma shrouded in a white suit."

The biographer Justin Kaplan—whose 1966 account of Twain won the Pulitzer Prize and the National Book Award—has spoken of the author's dark moods, which are more fully revealed in the new

Autobiography. The private Twain evinced a side filled with "rage and resentment . . . where he wants to get even, to settle scores with people whom he really despises. He loved invective," Kaplan noted in an interview. For instance, after having stayed in 1904 with his family in Florence, Italy (where Livy would die), Twain unleashed his fury against the rather unaccommodating countess who owned the villa they'd rented. He characterized her as "excitable, malicious, malignant, vengeful, unforgiving, selfish, stingy, avaricious, coarse, vulgar, profane, obscene, a furious blusterer on the outside and at heart a coward." A lawyer and fellow investor who betrayed him was attacked as having "the pride of a tramp, the courage of a rabbit, the moral sense of a wax figure, the sex of a tapeworm." And Twain's secretary and household manager, Isabel Van Kleek Lyon, with whom he had a close, tempestuous relationship for the last several years of his life, was in the end an object of obsessive condemnation. In a letter to his daughter Clara, Twain fumed that Isabel was "a liar, a forger, a thief, a hypocrite, a drunkard, a sneak, a humbug, a traitor, a conspirator, a filthy-minded & salacious slut pining for seduction & always getting disappointed, poor child."

In the years before his death in Redding, Connecticut, on April 21, 1910, Twain was at his most miserable, full of malice and sadness and vitriol. His health was terrible, too, no doubt owing to his having smoked forty cigars a day for most of his life. Toward the end, he spent much of his time in bed.

Facing his own mortality, he hoped for reconciliation. "I think we never become really and genuinely our entire and honest selves until we are dead," he once wrote, "and not then until we have been dead years and years. People ought to start dead and then they would be honest so much earlier." Not long before drifting off to sleep for the last time, he mumbled something about "dual personalities." He died in his carved oak bed, with his daughter Clara at his side. Two days later, a letter appeared in the *New York Times*.

To the Editor:

I wish to draw your attention to a peculiar coincidence.

Mark Twain, born Nov. 30, 1835.

Last perihelion of Halley's comet, Nov. 10, 1835.

Mark Twain died, April 21, 1910.

Perihelion of Halley's comet, April 20, 1910.

It so appears that the lifetime of the great humorist was nearly identical (the difference being exactly fifteen days) with the last long "year" of the great comet.

R. FRIDERICI.

Westchester, N. Y., April 22, 1910

Mark Twain would have loved that coincidence. In fact, he had once predicted it himself: "The Almighty has said, no doubt: 'Now here are these two unaccountable freaks; they came in together, they must go out together.'" The comet was visible from Earth when he died, the final triumph of an inimitable showman.

He was Federal Prisoner 30664

CHAPTER 6

O. Henry & WILLIAM SYDNEY PORTER

If you are now reading or have recently read a short story by O. Henry, you are most likely a middle-school student. He was the greatest short story writer of his generation, but O. Henry—who died at forty-seven with twenty-three cents in his pocket—isn't read much these days, except as homework.

His stories are known for their irony, aphorisms, plot twists, and moral lessons, and the surprise endings he called "snappers." They were formulaic, but the formula worked. "[H]e never told his story in the first paragraph but invariably began with patter and palaver; like a conjurer at a fair, it was the art of the anecdote that hooked the public," wrote the critic Francis Hackett. "He planned, first of all, to make his theme straight and clear, as a preacher does who gives the text. Then he established his people with bold, brilliant strokes, like a great cartoonist. But the barb was always a surprise, adroitly prepared, craftily planted, and to catch him at it is an exercise for a detective."

William Sydney Porter was born in Greensboro, North Carolina, on September 11, 1862. His middle name was originally spelled

"Sidney," but he changed it; later in life he would drop "William" and be known as Sydney Porter.

By the time he was three years old, his mother was dead of tuberculosis. Along with his father, Dr. Algernon Sidney Porter, William moved into a boardinghouse run by his grandmother. Algernon—a heavy drinker, just as William would become—was also an aspiring inventor with plans for a flying machine and a horseless carriage driven by steam.

The year 1865 brought the end of the Civil War and the assassination of President Lincoln. William began attending a one-room schoolhouse run by his aunt, who served as a surrogate mother and whom he later credited with inspiring his love of art and literature. As a boy he had a talent for drawing, thanks to his aunt's attentive instruction; and he devoured Dumas, Hugo, Thackeray, Dickens, Wilkie Collins, and others. "I did more reading between my thirteenth and my nineteenth years than I have done in all the years since, and my taste was much better then," he once told a reporter.

Although he loved learning, college was for the rich, which meant that for him it was out of the question. At fifteen, William was sent to work in his uncle's pharmacy, and at nineteen he became a licensed pharmacist. "The grind in the drugstore was an agony to me," he later admitted. Had he not received an invitation in 1882 to join a family friend in Texas, doing ranch work, William Porter might have lived and died a pharmacist rather than become the prolific writer O. Henry.

La Salle County, Texas, was not destined to be his last stop, but it was at least an escape from his tedious life at home. He was always reading poetry, especially Tennyson, and while herding sheep, he carried around a copy of *Webster's Unabridged Dictionary*. He wrote stories, too, but after reading them aloud to a family friend, he'd rip them up and throw them away.

Next he made his way to Austin, where, supposedly, he first used his future pen name: he had a habit of calling "Oh, Henry!" to a girlfriend's cat, said to respond only to that greeting. (True or not, the phrase has no connection to the candy bar of that name, launched in 1924.) He signed his girlfriend's autograph album as "O. Henry," and composed a poem, "A Soliloquy by the Cat," using this name. When he proposed marriage to his girlfriend, she rejected him; she came from a wealthy family, and he was a nobody with a dead-end job. Although he lost the girl, he'd found his pen name. Or so one version of the story goes; there are many. Porter was a good liar who enjoyed spinning fabrications about himself.

He had a series of drab jobs, finally working as a draftsman at the Texas Land Office, where he earned a hundred dollars a month. He wasn't thrilled by the work, but had no trouble finding friends. He played cards, charmed rapt listeners with his storytelling, and joined local singing and theater groups. He became a popular local figure and was known for always being impeccably dressed.

In 1888, following a speedy courtship, Porter eloped with seventeen-year-old Athol Estes. They had a son who died the day he was born. A year later, the couple had a daughter, Margaret. Porter, feeling settled and happy, was ready to pursue his true ambition: writing. After sending a journalism piece to the *Detroit Free Press*, he received an encouraging reply: "Am sorry it is not longer," the editor wrote. "Check will be sent in a few days. Can you not send more matter— a good big installment every week?" Porter began selling freelance articles, mostly humor pieces, to newspapers and journals around the country.

In 1891, he took a job as a teller at the First National Bank of Austin, a position that seemed ideal at first—it was mindless, and would allow him to write in the evenings—but would later turn out to have damaging and long-lasting consequences. After working at the bank for three years, he resigned when an audit revealed shortages in his till. Though he was charged with embezzlement, the case was dismissed for lack of evidence. Porter decided to focus on his writing, and he turned entrepreneurial, buying a used printing press and publishing an eight-page weekly satirical magazine called *The Rolling Stone*, for which he served as writer, illustrator, typesetter, and printer. "It rolled on for about a year," he said later, "and then showed unmistakable signs of getting mossy." He shut it down but had no regrets; the experience had boosted his confidence. His family moved to Houston, where he worked as a reporter, cartoonist, and columnist for the *Houston Post*, a job he loved.

Unfortunately, his falling-out with the Austin bank came back to haunt him just six months later. The embezzlement case had been reopened by federal auditors, and he was arrested. Although he insisted that bank executives regularly "borrowed" money without keeping records of their transactions (and that they rarely repaid what they'd withdrawn), he had no proof. Whether Porter was a fall guy or a criminal, no one will ever know, but he couldn't face the thought of imprisonment. After being released on a $2,000 bond posted by his wealthy father-in-law, Porter hopped on a night train to New Orleans, and, a few weeks later, boarded a freighter bound for Honduras. It was a frightening experience at the time, but would prove excellent fodder for fiction. (Life as a South American fugitive was chronicled in his 1904 debut story collection, *Cabbages and Kings*.) When asked once why he did not read more fiction written by others, he replied, "It is all tame, as compared with the romance of my own life."

Porter regretted his evasion of justice, but he argued until the end of his life that he was an innocent man who had no choice other than to flee. "I am like [Conrad's] Lord Jim," he told a friend, "because we both made one fateful mistake at the supreme crisis of our lives, a mistake from which we could not recover." Honduras was a smart choice—it had no extradition treaty with the United States—and he had some vague plan for his wife and daughter to join him in exile. It never happened. When Porter found out that Athol was dying of tuberculosis, he rushed back home.

A year later, after a three-day trial in Austin, Porter—now a grieving widower with a ten-year-old daughter—pleaded not guilty. He was convicted of embezzlement and sentenced to five years in a Columbus, Ohio, penitentiary. "I care not so much for the opinion of the general public," he wrote in a letter to his mother-in-law, "but I would have a few of my friends still believe that there is some good in me."

Becoming Federal Prisoner 30664 would launch his writing career and complete his transformation into O. Henry. Despite a painful separation from Margaret, with whom he was close, prison was the ultimate writing colony. The three years he spent there proved to be his MFA program, his refuge from the demands of the outside world.

He wrote stories during his night shifts in the prison infirmary, a plum job he had obtained because of his background as a licensed pharmacist. After saving the life of a warden who'd overdosed on arsenic, Porter gained additional privileges with minimal supervision, including sleeping at the infirmary and being able to roam the grounds more freely than other prisoners. Still, the inhumane conditions were difficult to witness, and the experience of being in prison left him shattered. Even after his early release for "good behavior," he was never quite the same. Imprisonment left him ashamed, ended relationships, exacerbated his volatile temper, and turned a gregarious, easygoing man into a solitary hard drinker (often consuming two quarts of whiskey a day)—a habit that would kill him in the end.

But in prison, Porter was disciplined and productive in his writing, making the best of grim circumstances. A guard recalled his routine: "After most of his work was finished and we had eaten our midnight supper, he would begin to write. . . . He seemed oblivious to the world of sleeping convicts about him, hearing not even the occasional sigh or groan from the beds which were stretched before him in the hospital ward, or the tramp of the passing guards. After he had written for perhaps two hours he would rise, make a round of the hospital, and then come back to his work again."

He was already a published author; his first short story, "Miracle of Lava Canyon," appeared the year his wife died. He didn't use a pseudonym, exactly, but he did sign the story as the eminent-sounding

"W. S. Porter." For other stories, he'd toyed with various pen names: Sydney Porter, James L. Bliss, T. B. Dowd, Howard Clark, S. H. Peters, and Olivier Henry. Even in his personal correspondence, he sampled all sorts of names, signing letters as Panhandle Pete, S. P., Hiram Q. Smith, and so on. Later, working with the young editor Witter Bynner (who would become a poet and scholar), Porter almost never called him by his actual name. Instead, he addressed Bynner affectionately as Honored Sir, Doubleyou B, Mr. Man, Pal, My Dear Person, Willie, Witt, B. Binny, and Mr. Bitterwinter, among other appellations.

From prison, Porter published more than a dozen stories, signing them "O. Henry," the name with which he became the most widely read author of his time. He kept a small notebook in which he recorded the names of his stories and where they had been submitted. The first story he published as O. Henry was "Whistling Dick's Christmas Stocking," which appeared in *McClure's Magazine* in 1899. Because he used an intermediary in New Orleans to submit his stories to editors, no one knew they were written by a convicted felon. His friend would place each story in a different envelope and then mail them from his own address.

In 1901, Porter was a free man. He'd made sure that Margaret had no idea where her father had been during his absence; she knew only that he was away on "business." He'd written letters to her regularly from prison:

July 8, 1898. MY DEAR MARGARET: You don't know how glad I was to get your nice little letter to-day. I am so sorry I couldn't come to tell you good-bye when I left Austin. You know I would have done so if I could have. Well, I think it's a shame some men folks have to go away from home to work and stay away so long don't you? But I tell you what's a fact. When I come home next time I'm going to stay there. . . . Now, Margaret, don't you worry any about me, for I'm well and fat as a pig and I'll have to be away from home a while yet and while I'm away you can just run up to Nashville and see the folks there. And not long after you come back home I'll be ready to come. And I won't ever have to leave again. . . . Look out pretty soon for another letter from me. I think about you every day and wonder what you are doing. Well, I will see you again before very long. Your loving PAPA.

Porter was a changed man. He'd cut off several friendships rather than reveal the fact of his imprisonment. He had no wish to explain himself, and he hoped that no one would ever learn how he'd spent the past thirty-nine months of his life. He was determined to keep his secret and start anew.

The first step toward reinvention was no surprise: he shut down the name William Sydney Porter. Having adopted O. Henry in prison (and with no one able to trace it to an actual person), he made the transition easily. As William Porter, he was merely a journalist; as O. Henry, he was an author.

In 1902 he moved to New York City. The geographic change brought him closer to the center of the publishing industry and provided distance from his former self. In New York, where he had no friends or acquaintances, he was more prolific than ever, writing and publishing hundreds of stories. His popularity soared.

From 1903 to 1907, Porter lived in Manhattan's Gramercy Park neighborhood, which had been created in 1831 by the developer Samuel Ruggles. The area was just as Ruggles had envisioned it: "a bastion of civility and serenity." Over the years, Gramercy Park became known for its literary figures—among them, Henry James, William Dean Howells, Herman Melville, Mark Twain, and the impoverished Stephen Crane, who lived with three aspiring artists in a tiny studio apartment. Melville, a customs inspector by day, was a resident for nearly thirty years, suffering there through the tepid reception of each of his novels, including *Moby-Dick*. Yet Porter—or O. Henry—is perhaps the author most closely identified with the neighborhood. He lived at 55 Irving Place in a first-floor brownstone apartment, and for the first time in his life, he was financially comfortable, having been given a contract by the *New York World* to write a weekly story, at the rate of a hundred dollars each.

Despite the financial incentive, he often missed deadlines—perhaps owing to his drunkenness. His editor refused to pay him until they arranged a compromise. For the first half of the story he delivered, he'd receive an advance; after submitting the other half, he'd be paid the remainder of his fee. Critics have noted that some of the beginnings and endings of O. Henry's stories seem disconnected, almost like Mad Libs. His quirky payment system might have had something to do with that.

Later, as his fame grew, various stories were released about the origins of his pen name. Porter told the *New York Times* that he came across the surname "Henry" in the society pages of a New Orleans newspaper, and that he wanted something short for a first name. A friend suggested using a plain initial. "O is about the easiest letter written," Porter decided, "and O it is."

There was yet another version. After having dabbled in a number of pseudonyms, Porter took his name from Orrin Henry, a guard at the Columbus prison. Some said that the pseudonym came from the French pharmacist Etienne-Ossian Henry. Others said that the author had used "O. Henry" as an expletive so often that someone suggested it as his pen name.

The scholar Guy Davenport had his own rather dubious theory about the name, arguing that it was an assemblage from the first two letters of "Ohio" and the second and last two of "penitentiary."

So, take your pick.

In 1904, Porter got a shock when he was asked to meet with an editor at the *Critic*, a monthly literary magazine. The editor said, "You are O. Henry, are you not?" Caught off-guard, Porter didn't deny it, but he did claim that there was no real mystery about writing under a different name. He hoped that a mundane story would defuse any desire by the editor to publish an exposé, and to dig into his past. He spoke as if confiding in the editor, saying that he was simply shy and averse to publicity, and that his lack of confidence had led him to use pen name. He then changed the subject, and hoped that the matter would go no further.

But a few weeks later, he picked up the new issue of the *Critic* and saw that the editor had proceeded with his scoop anyway. The article noted that the public was delighted by "certain fantastic and ingenious tales" bearing "the strange device O. Henry as a signature." It went on: "No one seemed to know the author's real name, and immediately vague and weird rumors began to be afloat and the nom de guerre was soon invested with as much curiosity as surrounds an author after his decease." Fortunately for Porter, the editor had simply published what he'd been told—so now it would be known, at least to some, that Porter was O. Henry, but no one had connected him back to the bank teller who'd been arrested and convicted. "[L]ike most mysteries, when it was probed there was no mystery," the article said of the unmasking. "O. Henry's real name is Mr. Sydney Porter, a gentleman from Texas, who, having seen a great deal of the world with the naked eye, happened to find himself in New York." Porter's real secrets remained safe. Still, he fretted over how the *Critic* had found the story in the first place, who had tipped off the editor, and how the magazine had gotten hold of an old photograph of him to accompany the story. Luckily, the fact of Porter's pseudonym did not spread to the rest of the country right away. He could relax for a while, though he lived in fear that at any time he'd be found out and ruined. He decided that even if some people knew that he was O. Henry, he would at least minimize how much information was known about William Porter.

After the publication of O. Henry's well-received *Cabbages and Kings* came *The Four Million*, in 1906, spreading his fame even further. The book included what would become his most celebrated story, "The Gift of the Magi," with its famous opening:

One dollar and eighty-seven cents. That was all. And sixty cents of it was in pennies. Pennies saved one and two at a time by bulldozing the grocer and the vegetable man and the butcher until one's cheeks burned with the silent imputation of parsimony that such close dealing implied. Three times Della counted it. One dollar and eighty-seven cents. And the next day would be Christmas.

There was clearly nothing to do but flop down on the shabby little couch and howl. So Della did it. Which instigates the moral reflection that life is made up of sobs, sniffles, and smiles, with sniffles predominating.

The much-anthologized story is required reading for most students, but the story behind it is not well known. The night that the piece was due, his editor, in desperation, sent an illustrator out to track down O. Henry and extract it in person. When the illustrator arrived at the writer's apartment, he found that O. Henry had not even started. Supposedly, O. Henry then handed him a roughly drawn sketch and said, "Just draw a picture of a poorly furnished room. . . . On the bed, a man and a girl are sitting side by side. They are talking about Christmas. The man has a watch fob in his hand. . . . The girl's principal feature is the long beautiful hair that is hanging down her back. That's all I can think of now, but the story is coming." Then he finished a few hours later.

As usual, the details of anything to do with William Porter are sketchy at best. According to another story about "The Gift of the Magi," O. Henry wrote the entire story in a booth at Pete's Tavern, near Gramercy Park—a bar established in 1864 whose tagline is "The Tavern That O. Henry Made Famous." He is said to have gone to Pete's every morning. When he was in the midst of writing, though, he would order a bottle of Scotch to be delivered to him.

Gilman Hall was the magazine editor who'd given Porter his first writing contract, and they became friends. "I was sure that he had a past," he once recalled, "though he did not tell me of it and I did not inquire into it. It was not till after his death that I learned of the years spent in Columbus. I used to notice, however, that whenever we entered a restaurant or other public place together he would glance quickly around him as if expecting an attack."

Porter did a fine job of keeping the most painful parts of his past a secret. In a wide-ranging interview he gave to the *New York Times* in the spring of 1909, the reporter George MacAdam commented that "so far as the public is concerned, all he will do is to materialize between the covers of magazine and book . . . while he himself remains invisible behind the pen name."

Noting that "for the past six or seven years O. Henry has been one of the most popular short-story writers in America," MacAdam mentioned that even though "he has kept himself under a bushel," his real name was now well known, having "leaked from a hundred and one different sources."

The *Times* was clearly proud of having obtained unprecedented access to its elusive subject. MacAdam showed a dash of smugness in pointing out, "Many are the interviewers who have sought him, but he has turned a deaf ear to their siren song."

Now Porter was talking, but he wasn't necessarily telling the truth. "Let me see: I was born in 1867," he told the reporter. (He wasn't.) Taking out a pencil and a scrap of paper to calculate his age, he added, "That makes me 42, almost 43 years old, but put down 42."

He was asked what he had done after *The Rolling Stone* had ceased publication.

"A friend of mine who had a little money . . . suggested that I join him on a trip to Central America," he said, "whither he was going with the intention of going into the fruit business." (Or, more accurately, whither Porter was going to avoid being sent to prison.) After that, instead of mentioning where he'd actually spent the next three years, he said that he moved to New Orleans and "took up literary work in earnest." If by "New Orleans," he meant "Columbus,

Ohio," then yes, he was telling the truth. There was no mention of his years in Austin, his years in prison, or even his marriage and daughter.

His few straightforward responses in the interview came when he was asked to talk about his writing. On his advice to young writers: "I'll give you the whole secret to short story writing," he said. "Rule 1: Write stories that please yourself. There is no Rule 2." And on the virtues of his work, he said, "People say I know New York well. Just change Twenty-Third Street in one of my New York stories to Main Street, rub out the Flatiron Building, and put in the Town Hall and the story will fit just as truly in any upstate town. At least, I hope this can be said of my stories. So long as a story is true to human nature all you need do is change the local color to make it fit in any town."

A woman who knew Porter socially in New York once spoke of how difficult it was to engage him in conversation, except superficially, because "he protected himself from the crude and rude touch of the world in a triple-plated armor of mirth and formality." He bristled at personal questions (though he didn't mind reminiscing about his early years in North Carolina), and felt most at ease in the role of raconteur. "His wit was urbane, sophisticated, individual; entirely free from tricks and the desire to secure effects," the woman recalled. "It was never mordant nor corrosive; it did not eat or fester; it struck clean and swift and sure as a stroke of lightning."

It must have flattered him when, in his early days in New York, as his fame was growing and people began to speculate about his true identity, at least one impostor emerged. Gilman Hall recalled that only a few editors knew who O. Henry was and where he lived. An editor from a competing magazine boasted to Hall one day that he'd just learned that "the real O. Henry" was a college undergraduate who'd "admitted" that he was the author. Hearing this, Hall laughed and informed the editor that the *real* "real O. Henry" had in fact just left his office. When Hall related the amusing anecdote to Porter, he replied that so long as the paychecks were sent to the right man, he didn't care how many other aspiring O. Henrys there were.

Having established himself as an important writer was all the more reason to guard his privacy—particularly any unsavory aspects of his past that didn't conform to his image as a man of letters. His rise to prominence was remarkable: one critic argued that O. Henry "took the place of Kipling as a literary master," and said that on "the shelf of my prized American classics" were Poe, Thoreau, Whitman, Crane, Sarah Orne Jewett, W. D. Howells—and O. Henry.

Another critic insisted that O. Henry should be considered a source of national pride: "More than any author who ever wrote in the United States, O. Henry is an American writer. And the time is coming, let us hope, when the whole English-speaking world will recognize in him one of the great masters of modern literature."

Porter's personal life, too, had finally brought a measure of happiness—if short-lived, yet again. In 1905, after reading one of O. Henry's short stories, a childhood friend from Greensboro, Sara Lindsey Coleman, wrote a letter to the author inviting him to visit her. She'd gained her own impressive reputation as a short story writer, albeit locally, in North Carolina. Her family was prominent, as her father had served as a colonel in the Confederate army. She was witty and gracious, and Porter corresponded with her for a while before inviting her to come visit him in New York. (A diehard southerner, she admitted to him that she loathed the city.) Upon seeing her again, on his forty-fifth birthday, Porter fell in love and proposed. He confessed the entire (true) story of what he said was his wrongful imprisonment, and his journey to becoming a writer. They were married on November 27, 1907, in Asheville, and Gilman Hall served as best man. But within two years, owing mostly to Porter's alcoholism, the marriage deteriorated. They never divorced, however. His wife lived until the age of ninety-one; she died in North Carolina in 1959. She outlived even her husband's daughter: Margaret died in California at the age of thirty-seven.

But 1907 was a good year for the author: he was married and at the height of his fame. The third O. Henry story collection, *The Heart of the West*, was published, as well as a fourth, *The Trimmed Lamp*. He repeated the same feat for the next few years, issuing two story collections annually—but these were his final years. (He would die at the age of forty-seven.) Porter had begun to resent his success and admitted that he felt constrained by it. Everyone by now knew what an "O. Henry story" was, and even he had tired of his predictable story structure. He boasted that he would write a novel, but he never did.

Although his fame was accompanied by a very comfortable income, Porter was perpetually in debt. He used his earnings to buy Scotch, wine, and beer; tipped waiters at restaurants in amounts that matched the check for his meal; gave money freely to panhandlers; and generously treated his friends. He was compulsive in his giving, always ending up flat broke himself. Some of his debt, apparently, could be traced to silencing blackmailers. One woman from Austin was prepared to reveal to the press that he was a convicted embezzler. For her silence she requested a thousand dollars, an astronomical sum at the time, and he caved in to her demands. Perhaps fearing that she could be arrested for blackmail, she left Porter alone and never approached the media with her story.

Despite the agony he had suffered over his past and the memories that haunted him, he received adulation from the public. Fans wrote to him asking for autographs, inscribed books, and photographs (which he usually declined to provide).

By 1909, his wife was living in North Carolina with her mother while Porter remained in New York. When he saw a doctor that summer, he was told that he had an enlarged heart, bad kidneys, and a severely compromised liver. During periods of relative recovery, he smoked and drank heavily, in denial that he was killing himself, and was more deeply in debt than ever.

On June 3, 1910, his kidneys failed. He called for help, then passed out. When he arrived by taxi (at his insistence) at New York Polyclinic Hospital on East Thirty-fourth Street, he wanted to protect his privacy. He requested permission to register under an assumed name, and as if casually checking into a hotel, he signed in as "Will S. Parker." Following an emergency operation, his condition stabilized, and his wife began to make her way up to New York by train from North Carolina. She arrived too late to see him alive again.

At around midnight on June 5, Porter told a hospital nurse: "Turn up the lights. I don't want to go home in the dark." He was dead before seven o'clock in the morning.

His career had been brief—just under a decade—but in that time he'd won international acclaim and his work was translated into a dozen languages. Two years after he died, Doubleday published a deluxe, limited edition of his collected stories, which included an original manuscript page with each copy. Only twelve were printed. Priced at $125, they sold out right away.

In the obituary that ran in the *New York Times*, Porter was called "one of the best short story writers in America." The article also noted that a year before his death, "O. Henry did something he was not in the habit of doing. He gave to the *New York Times* a story of his life, and it was the real story and not the invented narrative that went the rounds." (He died having fooled the *Times*.)

The "real" story came out only in 1916, in the first biography of O. Henry, which fully exposed the imprisonment of William Porter and the launching of O. Henry's writing career. Additional volumes of O. Henry's short stories were released posthumously, and continued to sell millions of copies. In 1918, the O. Henry Memorial Award Prizes were established, given each year to the best short stories published in the United States and Canada, and intended to "strengthen the art of the short story and to stimulate younger authors." Doubleday published the first collection of prizewinning stories in 1919. Today, Porter is best known for this award, rather than his own work, but at the time it proved that his name, above all others, was synonymous with the short story.

O. Henry was buried in Riverside Cemetery in Asheville, North Carolina. In honor of those famous first six words of "The Gift of the Magi," visitors have made a tradition of leaving $1.87 at his grave—money he would no doubt have spent if he could.

He died a virgin

CHAPTER 7

Fernando Pessoa & HIS HETERONYMS

You will never get to the bottom of Fernando Pessoa. There are too many of him.

"After looking for him in the poems, we look for him in the prose," wrote the scholar and translator Edwin Honig. Yet we find him nowhere. This was, after all, a poet whose maxim was, "To pretend is to know oneself." Cyril Connolly noted that Pessoa "hived off separate personalities like swarms of bees." He pretended relentlessly, employing more than seventy personae in his self-searching circus. They were not so much disguises as extensions and iterations of himself. "How idyllic life would be," he once wrote, "if it were lived by another person." When he looked in the mirror, he saw a crowd.

For some authors, the task of writing is a descent into the self. Pessoa ventured in the opposite direction, using his heteronyms as a means of departure and claiming that within his mini-populace, he was the least "real" and compelling of the bunch. The others were constellations swirling around him. In the context of psychoanalysis, a split identity is seen as a wound that needs healing. But in Pessoa's mind(s), there was nothing disorienting about it. "I've divided all my humanness among the various authors whom I've served as literary executor," he explained. "I subsist as a kind of medium of myself, but I'm less real than the others, less substantial, less personal, and easily influenced by them all."

Although the basic facts of his life are now known, attempting to create a "biography" of Pessoa is a slippery task indeed. "There never was a good biography of a good novelist," F. Scott Fitzgerald wrote in his journals. "There couldn't be. He is too many people, if he's any good."

Fernando António Nogueira Pessoa was very, very good.

Some things about him can be said for sure. He was born on June 13, 1888, in Lisbon, Portugal, and spent his first seven years there. His surname, ironically, means "person" in Portuguese. He was five when his father, the music critic Joaquim de Seabra Pessoa, died of tuberculosis. Six months later, Fernando's infant brother, Jorge, died. His paternal grandmother suffered from episodes of insanity and was in and out of mental hospitals for the last twelve years of her life. After his father died, his mother, Maria Madalena Nogueria Pessoa, remarried, and the family moved to South Africa, where the boy's stepfather, João Miguel Rosa, served as the Portuguese consul of Durban, a British-governed town. By that time, the precocious Pessoa could read and write, thanks partly to his cultured, nurturing mother. He produced what is believed to be his first poem in the summer of 1895, when he was seven years old, in response to learning that the family would be moving to South Africa. The poem was called "To My Dear Mother":

Here I am in Portugal,
In the lands where I was born.
However much I love them,
I love you even more.

He attended a primary school run by French and Irish nuns and became fluent in French and English. Later, at Durban High School, he was a brilliant student. He won awards and shunned sports. A former classmate, Clifford Geerdts, recalled a boy who was morbid, as well as "meek and inoffensive and inclined to avoid association with his schoolfellows."

Pessoa gained three younger half siblings from his mother's second marriage: Henriqueta (with whom he was closest), Luís, and João. He read and loved Keats, Shelley, Shakespeare, Dickens, Poe, and Byron. He began using false names to write: Charles Robert Anon, also known as C. R. Anon, and Alexander Search, for whom he printed calling cards. (Search once wrote a short story called "A Very Original Dinner," in which the guests feast on human flesh.) Then there was Jean Seul, who wrote only in French. The shy boy created poems and stories, and even "edited" fake newspapers—not unlike an early-twentieth-century version of *The Onion*—with news, spoofs, editorials, riddles, and poems, all written by a staff of "journalists" who'd sprung from his imagination and whose biographies he'd made up. Later, in recalling his childhood, Pessoa wrote that "[a]ny nostalgia I feel is literary. I remember my childhood with tears, but they're rhythmic tears, in which prose is already being formed." Nothing really mattered to him apart from his writing. Real life was beside the point. "I've always belonged to what isn't where I am and to what I could never be," he once wrote, conceding his fixation on dreaming and escape. "All I asked of life is that it go on by without my feeling it."

In 1905, at the age of seventeen, Pessoa returned to Lisbon to attend university. (He would never again leave the city.) Though he dropped out after two years, he got a fine education on his own by sequestering himself in the National Library to read literature, history, religion, and philosophy. He began writing short stories, some of them under the name "David Merrick," as well as poems and essays, occasionally in Portuguese but more often in French and English.

Pessoa, who had very poor vision and wore glasses, lived with relatives or in rented rooms, chain-smoking, reading, writing, and earning a modest salary as a translator for companies that conducted business abroad. Later he worked as a bookkeeper. He had few friends. "Since childhood I had the tendency to create around me a fictitious world, surrounding myself with friends and acquaintances that never existed," he wrote later. (As a boy, he'd invented the Chevalier de Pas, a faithful "playmate" who sent letters to him.) In 1910, the twenty-two-year-old admitted that "[t]he whole constitution of my spirit is one of hesitancy and doubt. Nothing is or can be positive to me; all things oscillate round me, and I with them, an uncertainty unto myself." That his identity seemed so unstable was both distressing and consoling: "Am I happy or sad?" he asked in one poem. "My sadness consists in not knowing much about myself. But then my happiness consists in that too."

His heteronyms, too, were filled with contradictions. "In each of us there is a differingness and a manyness and a profusion of ourselves," wrote one of his mental offspring. This notion of endless expansiveness offered tremendous freedom. "I suffer the delicacy of my feelings with disdainful attention," Pessoa explained, "but the essential thing about my life, as about my soul, is never to be a protagonist. I've no idea of myself, not even one that consists of a nonidea of myself. I am a nomadic wanderer through my consciousness." Put it like that, and you can't help but envy him.

It is crucial to make the distinction that Pessoa's "others" were heteronyms rather than pseudonyms. He insisted that they were separate from him. "I'm the empty stage where various actors act out various plays," he once wrote. In Pessoa country, unification was not possible or even desired. He was a breeder of beings, and always in pursuit of another. "I break my soul into pieces," he wrote, "and into different persons." He explained:

A pseudonymic work is, except for the name with which it is signed, the work of an author writing as himself; a heteronymic work is by an author writing outside his own personality: it is the work of a complete individuality made up by him, just as the utterances of some character in a drama of his would be.

Although Pessoa was timid and introspective and lived accordingly, he was no hermit. Nor did he attempt to hide his heteronyms—he was quite transparent about the fact of their existence. Unlike many pseudonymous authors, Pessoa was not secretive but the opposite: utterly guileless, psychologically honest, earnest rather than serving up ironic posturing. His heteronymic conceit didn't spring from a desire to fool anyone or attract attention. This was a private matter.

In his writings, Pessoa went so far as to explain the genesis of his heteronyms; he understood that readers would be curious. Suggesting that the identities derived from "an aspect of hysteria that exists within me," he diagnosed himself as either "simply a hysteric" or a "neurasthenic hysteric," but leaned toward the latter. Also, he noted, "The self-division of the I is a common phenomenon in cases of masturbation."

He claimed that the various people he had "procreated" often sent him greetings, and that he could hear and see them, even if no one else could. ("Imaginary figures have more depth and truth than real ones," he once wrote.) Was this the result of talent or sickness? He stopped short of calling himself crazy. Throughout his life Pessoa grappled with the possibility of his insanity—an anxiety undoubtedly fueled by his grandmother's illness—but he was never able to draw conclusions about himself one way or the other. Perhaps he recognized that what mattered was being sound enough to produce his work. That he was so obsessively drawn to Shakespeare's Hamlet was more telling than he may have realized.

He argued that just as a novelist becomes annoyed when readers assume that a character's feelings and experiences are mere stand-ins for the author's own, so too should people accept that Pessoa's heteronyms were utterly separate from him. If the heteronyms occasionally happened to express his ideas, so be it; but this was not by calculation on his part, only chance. Although he acknowledged the strangeness of all this, he felt it was not for him to judge whether the heteronyms actually did or did not exist. Besides, he noted, he wasn't even sure which one, Hamlet or Shakespeare, was more real—or "real in truth."

(He added that he had no proof that Lisbon existed, either.) Further, he said that he agreed with some of the theories expressed by his heteronyms but disagreed with others. All their work was dictated to him, yet they weren't seeking his advice or consent. He was not artist but amanuensis, nothing more.

Pessoa kept tight control over his social interactions, meeting acquaintances in coffeehouses and restaurants. One scholar noted that people who knew Pessoa described him as cordial, if inscrutable: "He could be a delightful man, full of charm and good humor, a humor that was very British, though with none of the traditional grossness in it. But this role was also that of a heteronym, which saved him from intimacy with anyone while allowing him to take a modest part in the normal feast of daily life." A man who knew Pessoa in later years recalled, "Never, when I bade him goodbye, did I dare to turn back and look at him; I was afraid I would see him vanish, dissolved in air."

There is no evidence that Pessoa yearned for more than his "modest part" in daily life, or that, in any case, he was willing to exert much effort. He once wrote that he wanted to be loved, but never to love: "Passivity pleased me. I was only content with activity just enough to stimulate me, not to let myself be forgotten."

He was a lifelong outsider, but in 1910 he founded the magazine *A Águia*, and eventually he became part of the nascent Portuguese avant-garde, a group of intellectuals in Lisbon who founded a journal, *Orpheu*, introducing modernist literature to the country. Initially, it was ridiculed, but soon the publication won respect, and the criticism that appeared in *Orpheu* became highly influential. Only a few issues were released before it folded—but within this group of intellectuals, Pessoa found a strong sense of kinship. He went on to work with other literary journals (both as editor and writer), publish chapbooks, issue a political manifesto called *O Interregno*, and start a press called Olisipo, which failed. For a London editor, he translated into English three hundred Portuguese proverbs. The years leading up to 1920 were most productive for this young bohemian.

Literary activity constituted his "real" life, but Pessoa paid the bills with his dreary day job, working as a clerk. (He had this dull occupation in common with fellow toiling authors Herman Melville, Franz Kafka, and Constantine Cavafy.)

He wrote and wrote—in the daytime when he could, or else at night, and usually while standing up. On March 18, 1914, he had a kind of breakthrough: "I wrote some thirty-odd poems, one after another, in a sort of ecstasy, the nature of which I am unable to define," he recalled. "It was the triumphant day of my life. . . . What followed was the appearance of someone in me to whom I immediately gave the name Alberto Caeiro. Forgive the absurdity of the sentence: In me there appeared my master."

Caeiro, the first of Pessoa's major heteronyms, had been "born" in 1889, lived with an elderly aunt in the country, and would die in 1915. He had "no profession or any sort of education," was of medium height, pale, with blue eyes, and died consumptive. Once, Caeiro spoke in an "interview" of his humble accomplishments: "I don't pretend to be anything more than the greatest poet in the world," he said. "I noticed the Universe. The Greeks, with all their visual acuity, didn't do as much." He was joined by another heteronym, Álvaro de Campos, born in Tavira on October 15, 1890 ("at 1:30 pm"). Campos was a bisexual, unemployed naval engineer who'd studied in Glasgow and was now living in Lisbon. He was tall, Pessoa noted—"1.75 meters tall, two centimeters taller than I"—and "slender with a slight tendency to stoop." He was "fair and swarthy, a vaguely Jewish-Portuguese type, hair therefore smooth and normally parted on the side, monocled." And he was a dandy who smoked opium and drank absinthe. In him, Pessoa invested "all the emotion that I allow neither in myself nor in my living." Ricardo Reis was a classicist and physician born in 1887 ("not that I remember the day and the month, though I have them somewhere," Pessoa wrote) and living in Brazil. Pessoa explained that Reis "is a Latinist by virtue of school training and a semi-Hellenist by virtue of his own efforts."

Then there was the "semi-heteronym" Bernardo Soares, an assistant bookkeeper living in downtown Lisbon who "seems always to be tired or sleepy." He was the closest to Pessoa's own voice, experience, and sensibility, and therefore the closest identity to a pseudonym. These men formed Pessoa's "dramatic ensemble," and Campos even claimed that Pessoa did not exist.

Because he never had children of his own, Pessoa was father to his heteronyms, and they were quite a handful. There was the suicidal Baron of Teive, who produced just one manuscript, *The Education of the Stoic*, having allegedly destroyed everything else he had written. Raphael Baldaya was an astrologer. Maria José was a nineteen-year-old hunchback consumptive suffering madly from unrequited love. And Thomas Crosse was an ardent advocate of Alberto Caeiro's work. Yes, Pessoa's heteronyms actually critiqued—sometimes savagely, sometimes kindly—one another's writings. They also collaborated on projects (Crosse worked with his brother, I. I. Crosse) and translated one another's work. These diverse personae—or, Pessoae, you might say—wrote thousands and thousands of pages, and most of those texts were left behind as fragments to be transcribed and translated after Pessoa's death. It's a vast archive, much of it untouched even to this day.

Aside from Pessoa's almost spiritual devotion to his work, his life in Lisbon was uneventful and his routine predictable. He was a strange and lonely man. He smoked eighty cigarettes daily and drank a lot. He hated having his photograph taken. He never arrived on time for an appointment, always showing up too early or too late. He had terrible posture. He was very interested in the occult. He dressed formally, with a bow tie and homburg hat. Obsessed with horoscopes, he considered making his living as an astrologer. He produced horoscopes for himself, his acquaintances, and even his heteronyms. He lost some of the few friends he had to suicide.

He is known to have had only one significant love affair—with a young woman named Ofélia de Queirós. (She eventually married, and died in 1991.) When they met, the aptly named Ofélia was nineteen and working as a secretary at the same firm where the thirty-one-year-old Pessoa worked. He declared his love for her one day with lines taken from *Hamlet*, and then kissed her, she recalled, "like a madman."

After the failure of the relationship, Pessoa decided that love was a false notion, anyway. "It's our own concept—our own selves—that we love," he wrote, arguing that "the repression of love sheds much more light on its nature than does the actual experience of it." Yet Ofélia claimed that Pessoa was entirely to blame for their breakup. "Little by little, he withdrew until we stopped seeing each other altogether," she recalled. "And this was done without any concrete reason whatsoever. He did not appear or write for several days because, as he said, there was something wrong with his head and he wanted to go to the insane asylum." He had written her more than fifty letters—some affectionate, drunk with love, others bitter and accusatory: "Why can't you be frank with me?" he demanded in March 1920. "Why must you torment a man who never did any harm to you (or to anybody else) and whose sad and solitary life is already a heavy enough burden to bear, without someone adding to it by giving him false hopes and declaring feigned affections? What do you get out of it besides the dubious pleasure of making fun of me?"

Elsewhere, he expressed moments of insecurity and alienation: "I'm all alone—I really am. . . . I'm going crazy from this sense of isolation and have no one to soothe me, just by being near, as I try to go to sleep." Yet he was just as quick to assume control and withdraw. "By the way," he wrote a few weeks later, "although I'm writing you, *I'm not thinking about you.* I'm thinking about how much I miss the days *when I used to hunt pigeons.*" Pessoa also had Alvaro de Campos ("Naval Engineer") write to Ofélia on his behalf, explaining that his friend's "mental state prevents him from communicating anything, even to a split pea."

Some scholars contend that Pessoa was a latent homosexual who sublimated his sexual impulses.

Ultimately, the author remains, like his work, "vastly unfinished, hopelessly unstructured, and practically unknown," as the Pessoa scholar and translator Richard Zenith has written. It is no accident that one volume of verse Zenith translated is titled *Pessoa & Co.* The Portuguese writer formed a Corporation of One, of which he was CEO and every employee from the top of the ladder to the bottom rung. Pessoa's dozens of constructed alternate selves, Zenith noted, "were instruments of exorcism and redemption. They were born to save him from this life that he felt ill-equipped to live, or that offended his aesthetic and moral sensibilities, or that simply bored him." Although alter egos had become fashionable accessories for European writers in the early twentieth century, no one took the device as far as Pessoa did—and certainly no one has done so since. As the scholar Jorge de Sena said in 1977, at the first international symposium on Pessoa's work (held at Brown University), Pessoa was hardly the first to eradicate any trace of autobiography from his writing. Yet de Sena noted that even though the alter egos of modernists such as Gide, Joyce, and Eliot produced masterpieces, they never went to the extremes that Pessoa did. He annihilated himself in the name of artistic creation. "Unceasingly I feel that I was an other, that I felt other, that I thought other," Pessoa wrote. "I am a spectator of myself. . . . I created myself, crevasse and echo, by thinking. I multiplied myself, by introspection. . . . I am other even in my way of being."

"Poets don't have biographies," Octavio Paz wrote in his introduction to *A Centenary Pessoa.* "Their work is their biography." Who could make a stronger claim to this than Pessoa? "I am, in large measure, the selfsame prose I write," he confessed. "I unroll myself in periods and paragraphs, I make myself punctuation marks. . . . I've made myself into the character of a book, a life one reads."

George Steiner called Pessoa "one of the evident giants in modern literature." John Hollander declared that if Pessoa had never existed,

Jorge Luis Borges would have had to invent him. C. K. Williams praised Pessoa's "amazing audacities, his brilliance and his shyness." Harold Bloom included Pessoa on a list of twenty-six writers he considered essential to the Western canon, including Dante, Shakespeare, and Proust, and argued that Pessoa was not a madman but a reborn Walt Whitman, "who gives separate names to 'my self,' 'the real me,' or 'me myself,' and 'my soul,' and writes wonderful books of poetry for all of them."

Pessoa was the loving ringmaster, director, and traffic cop of his literary crew. He tended to each of their biographies with meticulous specificity, and attentively varied their styles, idioms, techniques, genres, ideologies, and interests. He killed some off and let others live. Whereas the work of poets is typically fed by outside stimuli, Pessoa's creativity seems to have fed off itself—like one of the contemporary artist Dana Schutz's famous "Self-Eater" paintings. One persona stirred another and another, and perhaps that apparently arbitrary transmission of energy explains why so much of the work by Pessoa & Co. took shape in unfinished fragments. The ideas born of this collective were too much for one man to set down on paper. "My character of mind is such that I hate the beginnings and the ends of things, for they are definite points," he explained.

What was Pessoa aiming for with his menagerie? What drove him to it? Because "true" biographical information about him is so limited, it is difficult to say. All we have are his written accounts of his motives and the speculations of others. It seems that Pessoa was in pursuit of self-abdication. He wanted to escape both body and mind. "Pessoa sought to expel not only his sexual desires," Zenith wrote, "but his friendly affections, his religious tendencies, his aggressive feelings, his humanitarian urges, his longing for adventure, his dreams, and his regrets." Anyone attempting to define Pessoa reductively as a cluster of pathologies should think again. As Zenith noted, "Psychoanalysis is too poor a science to explain the case of Pessoa, who seems to have been simply, mysteriously, possessed by a demon—that of detachment."

In a 1977 interview, Edwin Honig echoed the notion of Pessoa's essential unknowability: "Being both complex and simple, he is always hovering over some piece of mysterious ground, like moonscapes with mile-deep craters—terribly attractive but also very forbidding." It's understandable that Pessoa has been compared to T. S. Eliot and Wallace Stevens, both masters of the elusive. "Reading [Pessoa's] best poems," Honig said, "you never know if you're plumbing the depths or if you're dangling there above without even touching ground. There's always that paradox in his secret, something unanswerable. Though he invites you to share it, he resists your advance the moment you accept the invitation." (This was not unlike his personal life. In work and in his social dealings, he always preferred a bit of distance.)

By taking leave of himself, becoming invisible to the extent that he could, he was free to roam in contradiction, paradox, and complexity without being labeled as this or that kind of writer. He could hold up mirrors, play with them, and then smash them to bits. As Borges wrote in his "Ultra Manifesto," the true artist does not reflect himself, but razes himself and creates from there. "Two aesthetics exist: the passive aesthetic of mirrors and the active aesthetic of prisms," he wrote. "Guided by the former, art turns into a copy of the environment's objectivity or the individual's psychic history. Guided by the latter, art is redeemed, makes the world into its instrument, and forges—beyond spatial and temporal prisons—a personal vision."

In private life, Pessoa was a demure and awkward man. But his "personal vision" as a writer was startling and brave, anything but ordinary.

Much more than mere pseudonyms, Pessoa's heteronyms were so wildly different from one another that they allowed him to explore his imagination endlessly, without paying any price. Well, up to a point: that very messiness, the refusal to be defined as just one man, explains why he is not more widely known today. (Pessoa once described his oeuvre as "a drama divided into people instead of into acts.")

Certainly to literary types he is a significant figure (the blessing of Harold Bloom is no small thing), but his books are not easily found. It's true that more of his work has been translated into English over the past decade, but Pessoa hardly helped the matter of his legacy: he left behind a trunk full of journalism, cultural criticism, philosophy, plays, poems, political essays, and horoscopes, much of the work illegible and unfinished. The trunk was discovered, after his death, in his rented room in Lisbon.

The material—nearly thirty thousand manuscript pages—is daunting for even the most intrepid scholar to sift through. Some have begun, then abandoned, their Pessoa projects. The task of deciphering, organizing, and translating his work is still in progress, and perhaps will never be finished. Pessoa wrote haphazardly in different languages, on loose scraps of paper, in journals and notebooks, on the backs of envelopes, and on the official stationery of the firms for which he worked. As Richard Zenith has written, the work stands "like variously sized building blocks—some rough, others exquisitely fashioned—of an impossible but marvelous monument." Pessoa didn't care for cohesiveness in any area of his life. Yet the quality of much of these thousands of texts, however fragmented or arbitrary, is generally exceptional; these are much more than the ramblings of a crazy person.

In his lifetime, he wasn't quite the Emily Dickinson of Lisbon— except for having apparently died a virgin. Mostly he kept to himself, to be sure, but he also published hundreds of poems, journalistic pieces, and essays. He became a respected intellectual figure, if not quite a celebrity, yet his literary genius was not widely recognized until after he died. In his home country he is now considered the greatest Portuguese poet since Luís de Camões, the sixteenth-century author of the epic *Os Lusíadas* (which Pessoa is said not to have cared much about). He is also regarded as one of the greatest modernists in any language and is one of the most fascinating figures in the history of literature.

On November 29, 1935, the forty-seven-year-old Pessoa suffered from abdominal pain and developed a high fever. He was taken to the Hospital de São Luís in Lisbon, where he wrote, in English, his last words: "I know not what tomorrow will bring." The next day he died from cirrhosis of the liver.

A statue of Pessoa now stands near one of the coffeehouses he used to frequent. At the time of his death, those who knew his work understood that the country had lost an important man. "Fernando Pessoa is dead," a young doctor (later to become a distinguished literary figure) named Miguel Torga wrote in his journal. "As soon as I heard the news in the paper, I closed my surgery and plunged into the mountains. There, with the pines and the rocks, I wept for the death of the greatest poet of our times, whom Portugal watched pass by in his coffin, on his way to immortality, without even asking who he was."

In the opening lines of what is perhaps his best-known poem, "The Tobacco Shop," Pessoa declares:

I'm nothing.
I'll always be nothing.
I can't want to be something.
But I have in me all the dreams of the world.

He was someone who felt like "nothing" to such an extent that he strove for self-expulsion, yet like Whitman, he contained everything that he needed, desiring nothing from the universe beyond his imagination. His statement presents the speaker as both meek and grandiose: *I have nothing, I am nothing, but don't you wish you had what I have? Don't you wish to be what I am?* Pessoa's self-abnegation is the source of his power and vitality. In his free-floating way, he implicates us, his readers, in the telling and interpretation of his story.

As he wrote in his posthumously published masterpiece, *The Book of Disquiet:*

> I am the suburb of a non-existent town, the prolix commentary on a book never written. I am nobody, nobody. I am a character in a novel which remains to be written, and I float, aerial, scattered without ever having been, among the dreams of a creature who did not know how to finish me off.

Pessoa has been dead for decades. We haven't even begun to finish him off.

He slept with prostitutes, hated bad smells, and dressed like a tramp

CHAPTER 8

George Orwell & ERIC BLAIR

Had Eric Arthur Blair been a working-class bloke from Birmingham instead of an Old Etonian, George Orwell might never have existed. By the age of six, Blair aspired to become a writer, and as a young man he knew that he wanted to explore the lowest stratum of society in his work. Given his genteel family background, this kind of subject matter might have been problematic. If he wanted to write, he would have to conceal himself.

Blair was born on June 25, 1903, in Motihari, a village in colonial India near the Nepalese border. His parents were stationed there while his father, Richard, held a minor post with the Indian Civil Service. They were not wealthy—Eric would later describe his family as "lower-upper-middle-class"—but both his parents came from prominent families in decline. Richard was descended from West Indian slave owners (his great-grandfather was rich and had married the daughter of an earl), and was instilled with a strong sense of public service; Blair's mother, Ida, grew up in Burma, the daughter of a French timber merchant who himself came from a distinguished family of artisans.

Ida was working at a boys' school in India when she met Richard, who was thirty-nine, unmarried, and in a dead-end job that paid poorly. He was eighteen years older than Ida. They married in 1897, and she gave birth to a daughter, Marjorie, the following year. (Another daughter, Avril, was born five years after Eric, in 1908.) Without being affluent, they enjoyed the usual perks of colonial life, including servants and access to a whites-only club. Soon after Eric was born, Ida took the children back to England; she wanted them to enjoy a comfortable middle-class existence (and education) in Oxfordshire. In the town where they settled, which dated to the fourteenth century, Ida found an active social life, something she'd missed terribly.

Growing up, Blair was keenly aware of his family history and of the divisions of caste and class systems. He would later reject organized religion and declare himself an atheist, but he had a strong sense of moral duty (even when he didn't live up to his own code, which was often). He was a stubborn, sensitive, and studious boy who loved reading Dickens, Swift, Defoe, and especially Kipling, whom he called a "household god" and whose work would greatly influence his own. His mother recorded his first word, uttered when he was eighteen months old: "beastly."

In temperament, Blair was more like his soft-spoken, introverted father than his outgoing, chatty mother, and he found unbearable the frivolous tea parties he was forced to attend. "As a child I was taught to say 'Thank you for having me' after a party, and it seemed to me such an awful phrase," he recalled later. Ida loved being part of a well-to-do social set, playing croquet, shopping, going to theater and music events in London, attending a local regatta, and watching tennis at Wimbledon. Yet she was an attentive, loving mother, and Blair is said to have inherited his vicious wit from her. "I barely saw my father before I was eight," he recalled in the opening of his 1946 essay, "Why I Write." "For this and other reasons I was somewhat lonely, and I soon developed disagreeable mannerisms which made me unpopular throughout my schooldays."

Coming of age in Edwardian England, when "the sheer vulgar fatness of wealth" was everywhere, and "without any kind of aristocratic elegance to redeem it," Blair assumed the stance of a critical outsider. "[T]he social status of nearly everyone in England could be determined from his appearance, even at two hundred yards' distance." Social order was not an abstract notion; it was present in his everyday life, and he was made to understand its significance both at home and at school. "I was forbidden to play with the plumber's children; they were 'common' and I was told to keep away from them," he wrote in his 1937 book *The Road to Wigan Pier*. "This was snobbish, if you like, but it was also necessary, for middle-class people cannot afford to let their children grow up with vulgar accents. So, very early, the working class ceased to be a race of friendly and wonderful beings and became a race of enemies."

It was partly because of his chronic ill health that Blair was highly attuned to disparities in social conditions. (He had defective bronchial tubes and a lesion in one lung, which was not diagnosed until later in his life.) He knew what it was to feel helpless, to feel apart from one's own community, to be judged as weak and inferior. He was not yet two years old when he endured a bout of bronchitis, the first of many (along with influenza) to recur throughout his life. A decade after failing an army medical exam in 1940, Blair would be dead of tuberculosis at the age of forty-six. His entire life was spent with a sense of urgency regarding his work, with the constant knowledge that he was running out of time. "Until I was about thirty I always planned my life not only on the assumption that any major undertaking was bound to fail, but that I could only expect to live a few years longer," he once wrote.

Perhaps because he was confined to bed so often as a child, in enforced solitude, he developed a rich imagination. He believed in ghosts and was enchanted by ghost stories. He also believed that his dreams had symbolic meaning and were sometimes prescient. And he was highly superstitious, a believer in black magic. When his father died in 1939, he placed pennies on Richard's eyes and threw the pennies into the sea.

In fact, years later, Blair is said to have thought that assuming a pseudonym meant no one could use his real name against him for evil purposes. The notion of peeling off identities appealed to him, anyway. "I had the lonely child's habit of making up stories and holding conversations with imaginary persons," he later recalled, "and I think from the very start my literary ambitions were mixed up with the feeling of being isolated and undervalued."

Blair produced his first poem at the age of four, dictated to his mother. Seven years later, in 1914, he published an exuberantly patriotic poem in a local newspaper, with the opening stanza:

Oh! Give me the strength of the lion,
The wisdom of Reynard the fox,
And then I'll hurl troops at the Germans,
And give them the hardest knocks.

He also produced what he later described as "bad and unfinished 'nature poems' in the Georgian style," a rhyming play, and short fiction—most of which he regarded as embarrassing. But he recognized his facility with language and his love for it. "From a very early age, perhaps the age of five or six, I knew that when I grew up I should be a writer," he later recalled. "Between the ages of about seventeen and twenty-four I tried to abandon this idea, but I did so with the consciousness that I was outraging my true nature and that sooner or later I should have to settle down and write books."

Even in childhood he was cultivating "the making up of a continuous 'story' about myself, a sort of diary existing only in the mind. . . . As a very small child I used to imagine that I was, say, Robin Hood, and picture myself as the hero of thrilling adventures, but quite soon my 'story' ceased to be narcissistic in a crude way and became more and more a mere description of what I was doing and the things I saw." (That storytelling self would later be manifested as George Orwell.) He always felt a need to describe things, events, and people, and his early stories were, if nothing else, impressive in their descriptive quality.

In 1911, a fateful event occurred: Ida decided to send her son away to St. Cyprian's, a fashionable preparatory school in Sussex for boys aged eight to thirteen. The five years he spent there traumatized him and filled him with contempt, yet the school's "values" did shape his socialist views—and proved formative in the making of George Orwell, whom V. S. Pritchett called "the conscience of his generation."

He set down an account of his sufferings at the "expensive and snobbish school" in the ironically titled, fifteen-thousand-word essay, "Such, Such Were the Joys," which took him years to write. (It was not published in the UK until 1968, after the widow of the cruel headmaster died.) Soon after his arrival at St. Cyprian's, he recalled, "I began wetting my bed. I was now aged eight, so that this was a reversion to a habit which I must have grown out of at least four years earlier." The guilt and self-mortification he'd acquired from a Catholic school education was exacerbated by his time at St. Cyprian's. "[I]t was looked on as a disgusting crime which the child committed on purpose and for which the proper cure was a beating," he wrote. "Night after night I prayed, with a fervour never previously attained in my prayers, 'Please God, do not let me wet my bed! Oh, please God, do not let me wet my bed!' but it made remarkably little difference."

For such an elite institution, "the standard of comfort was in every way far lower than in my own home," Blair recalled bitterly, "or, indeed, than it would have been in a prosperous working-class home." He found that there was never enough food, and what was available tasted awful—including porridge containing unidentifiable black lumps. (He resorted to stealing stale bread from the pantry in the middle of the night.) The boys were allowed a hot bath only once a week, and the towels were damp, with a foul smell. "Whoever writes of his childhood must beware exaggeration and self-pity," Blair admitted. "But I should be falsifying my own memories if I did not record that they are largely memories of disgust."

He was surrounded by boys boasting about "my father's yacht," "my pony," "my pater's touring car," and the like. "How much a year has your pater got?" "What part of London do you live in?" "Is that Knightsbridge or Kensington?" "Have you got a butler?" and "How many bathrooms has your house got?" were the kinds of interrogations intrinsic to the school's culture. The boys were constantly keeping score and ranking themselves socially above or below their peers; Blair was always below. He was well aware that aside from money or a title, he lacked every other virtue that might bolster his standing—athleticism, good looks, confidence, and charm.

One of his few friends at St. Cyprian's was the future literary critic Cyril Connolly, who later recalled Blair's appearance as grotesque: "Tall, pale, with his flaccid cheeks, large spatulate fingers, and supercilious voice, he was one of those boys who seem born old."

Blair was bullied as well as beaten at school, and he found no comfort in his holidays at home. His father, now fifty-five, had retired with a modest pension and returned to the family. Ida, having been left alone to raise three children, was chilly and remote to Richard. He was a stranger to Eric and did nothing to cultivate closeness between them. Eric felt no love for his father, and was mortified by Richard's habit of removing his false teeth and setting them on the table at mealtime. "Most of the good memories of my childhood, and up to the age of about twenty, are in some way connected with animals," he wrote in "Such, Such Were the Joys."

Even then, as a morose and timid boy, haunted by "a sense of desolate loneliness and helplessness," as he once recalled of his younger self, Blair aspired to greatness. He knew he would become an author someday—and not just any, but a famous one. He announced that his writing name would be the distinguished-sounding "E. A. Blair," rather than "Eric Blair," which he deemed too plain.

His education at St. Cyprian's prepared him for a spot at the Mount Olympus of English public schools, Eton, where he was awarded a scholarship in 1916. (His parents could never have afforded the full boarding and tuition fees.) But Blair had already been worn down by his unhappy experience at St. Cyprian's, and he hated Eton. He felt more miserable than ever, and even more alone. One of his classmates once described him in even more unflattering terms than did Cyril Connolly (who also attended Eton with Blair), as having had "a large, rather fat face, with big jowls, a bit like a hamster." Another said that Blair was "pretty awful" and "a bit of a bastard." One boy Blair particularly disliked was Philip Yorke— the oldest brother of Henry Yorke, who would assume the authorial name Henry Green.

At Eton, Blair cranked out stories and plays in his notebooks, all of which he signed "Eric the FAMOUS AUTHOR." He savored a few aspects of his time there, including having been taught French by Aldous Huxley. And his reading experiences were extraordinary: Zola, Maupassant, Flaubert, Twain, and Milton were among his favorites. He also took up smoking and cultivated a rebellious streak, which won him the admiration of his peers.

At St. Cyprian's, Blair had at least soared academically, but at Eton his grades were poor. His tutor found him lazy and impudent. Upon graduation, for reasons he never explained, Blair took a commission with the Indian Imperial Police in Burma, where he spent five monotonous years feeling exiled. (Among his few pleasures were frequent visits to Burmese brothels, which, as a sexual late bloomer, he found addictive.) Perhaps his decision to enter government service was an easy way to deal with his confusion about what to do next, and to figure out what kind of man he should become. The experience would buy him time. Cambridge and Oxford—the two universities of destiny for Eton's finest—held no interest for him, and in any case he was considered by Eton to be "unsuitable" for either. That was upper-class code for "an embarrassment."

In 1927, Blair returned to England a heavy smoker, gaunt (having suffered his usual bronchial problems, along with dengue fever), and, as one of his parents' neighbors noted, someone who "looks as though he never washes." His classmates from Eton had already started to publish and even achieve renown. Although Blair would eventually exorcise the bad memories from his time in Burma, which represented wasted years (and lost innocence), in his 1934 novel *Burmese Days*, for the time being he was still six years away from his publishing debut, *Down and Out in Paris and London.*

He rented a cheap room in Notting Hill for a while to fashion himself into a "FAMOUS AUTHOR," but it wasn't until he set off for Paris that things seemed to click into place. Like so many other literary expatriates, Blair felt that in Paris life would truly begin. He arrived in 1928 in search of culture, education, writing material, and undoubtedly romance. (Brothels were legal at the time, so sex could be obtained one way or another.) The city had a buzz that dour London seemed to lack. Henry Miller was there, as were Joyce, Hemingway, and Fitzgerald, among other famous writers.

Blair soon managed to complete his first novel, but when it was rejected for publication he burned it. At that time his heart was still set on fiction—he had no intention of becoming a celebrated essayist, even though he was deeply political (while refusing to join any one party) and interested in provocative reportage. He wasn't sure how he intended to use the sketches he wrote about the beggars and tramps he encountered on the city's streets, but "common people"—the kind he'd been raised to ignore, like a good and proper snob—interested him most. The self-declared socialist was drawn to down-and-out types much more than to writers or artists, and least of all to anyone with the odor of affluence.

With political unrest brewing in Europe, Blair eased up on his single-minded focus on fiction; he needed money. Even though he also wrote poetry, he realized that no earnings would come of it. He started writing for a left-wing weekly publication and other newspapers, with an eye toward stories with sociological and political issues—in particular the implications of censorship (exploring ideas that would incubate and later shape his dystopian masterpiece *Nineteen Eighty-four*), and the homeless. He started signing these pieces "E. A. Blair."

Unfortunately, he was hardly getting by in Paris; he would learn firsthand what it felt like to be impoverished. His experiences there felt desultory. He was reduced to fishing (without success) in the Seine, rationing his food supply, and even pawning some of his possessions. "I underwent poverty and the sense of failure," he recalled of his time in Paris. "This increased my natural hatred of authority and made me for the first time fully aware of the existence of the working classes."

After doing menial work and finding it wretched, he was pleased that a publication in London had accepted one of the essays he'd submitted. He decided that moving back to London would not signify failure but offer greater potential for becoming a professional writer. In December 1929 he left Paris and returned to his parents' house. "England is a very good country when you are not poor," he wrote a few years later. Still, it was better to struggle in his own country than in France.

In no way embarrassed by having to work as a babysitter and take occasional odd jobs, Blair (who looked like a bum) started writing a nonfiction book about beggars and outcasts, based on his own experiences, which would evolve into *Down and Out in Paris and London*. He also began publishing criticism. It didn't earn him much money, but he established himself as a respected reviewer, or at least the beginnings of one.

Though slowly finding his way toward his vocation, Blair didn't fit neatly into any single category: he came from a snobbish family that was not wealthy; he'd been given the most prestigious public school education a student could hope for—yet unlike many of his contemporaries, who had already achieved fame and wealth, he had little to show for it. He disowned Eton but wore it as a badge of honor. He spoke in a posh accent but dressed in ill-fitting, rumpled clothing.

And having immersed himself in Shakespeare, Chaucer, Twain, Poe, Ibsen, Dickens, and Thackeray, among others, he was well read and intellectual, but he had rejected a university education. Although he was bitter about not having gone to Oxford or Cambridge, it was also a point of pride that he had not. He was austere, but he enjoyed comfort. He was stridently political and deplored politics. He was unlucky in love and perpetually unable to sustain relationships with women. (Prostitutes, however, he did fine with.) He appeared to love women and despise them; even some of his friends described him as a misogynist. He sought out tramps and beggars, yet he was an intellectual snob and ill at ease in the presence of those who did not share his interests. He relished immersing himself in vagrant life, but had a pathological aversion to bad smells and dirt, and was oblivious to the foul stench of his own smoking habit. He was happy only when writing, but no matter how hard he worked, he couldn't earn a living doing it. He was frustrated by his frequent illnesses, which kept him from writing, yet he did not take responsibility for his health—he smoked heavily even while coughing up blood. All the intriguing contradictions of Eric Blair would find their way into the work of George Orwell. Blair might be judged by others as mentally unstable, paranoid, troubled, sadistic, and aberrant—but George Orwell? He was a noble and brilliant author.

Regardless of his quirks, and there were many, it was almost unnerving to see how little Blair cared about others' opinions of him. Still, he kept his writing ambition largely private. Slowly, Blair was developing a pioneering, novelistic style that blended reportage and memoir. His work was investigative yet highly personal, driven by a sense of moral outrage at social injustices. (The genre might be called Proletarian Lit—not exactly sexy stuff.) He had also taken to hanging out with vagrants in London and sometimes dressing like a tramp, sleeping in Trafalgar Square covered in newspapers. "He didn't look in the least like a poor man," a friend recalled of Blair decades later. "God knows he was poor, but the formidable look didn't go with the rags."

Nor did the rags go with the name Eric Arthur Blair. It was time to invent George Orwell. Blair had always been secretive in every respect; adopting a pseudonym would allow him to release the various facets of his personality. Doing so was not without some degree of shame: he wrote in *A Clergyman's Daughter* (in which a character uses a pseudonym) that "[i]t seemed a queer thing to have to do, to use a false name; dishonest—criminal, almost."

As Eric Blair, he accepted a teaching job at a boys' school—hardly a posh one—which would make the twenty-nine-year-old seem somewhat respectable in the eyes of his parents. (Even though he had no university degree, his Eton schooling was impressive enough to win him the job.) He was bored by the work, and described the school as "foul."

That summer, he received the best news he'd heard in a long time: he'd found a publisher for *Down and Out in Paris and London*. Under a different title, the manuscript had been rejected by Jonathan Cape, and also by T. S. Eliot at Faber and Faber—Eliot's elitist sensibility did not exactly savor tales of the malodorous downtrodden. In refusing the book, he wrote to Blair that it was "too loosely constructed."

The final version of the manuscript was a semiautobiographical story narrated by an anonymous, penniless English writer—or, rather, it was a collection of essays about Blair's own experiences, recounted in fictionalized form. Most of the events in the book had occurred, but some fabrications were thrown in. It was startling for its up-close exploration of street people and others left behind by society. It was also a shocking exposé of harsh, filthy, inhumane conditions in the restaurant kitchens of Paris, where Blair had toiled as a lowly dishwasher.

"I can point to one or two things I have definitely learned by being hard up," the narrator reflects in the book's final paragraph. "I shall never again think that all tramps are drunken scoundrels, nor expect a beggar to be grateful when I give him a penny, nor be surprised if men out of work lack energy, nor subscribe to the Salvation Army, nor pawn my clothes, nor refuse a handbill, nor enjoy a meal at a smart restaurant. That is a beginning."

The publisher Victor Gollancz had accepted the work and paid Blair an advance of forty pounds. After some discussion about the title and potential libel issues, there was one significant matter to settle: the name of the author. Blair had informed his agent that he wished to use a pseudonym. "If by any chance you *do* get it accepted," he wrote, "will you please see that it is published pseudonymously, as I am not proud of it." (Perhaps he was ashamed by the rejections he'd received, and certain that his execrable book was doomed to failure.) Then there was the matter of his family: he did not want to embarrass them with sordid (if thinly disguised) tales of his adventures. He also wrote to Gollancz that "if the book has any kind of success I can always use the same pseudonym again." The editor suggested simply signing the book with the letter "X," but Blair wished to find a suitable name, perhaps thinking about his future career. He had trouble settling on a nom de plume, so he sent Gollancz four suggestions: H. Lewis Allways, P. S. Burton, Kenneth Miles—and George Orwell, which was his favorite.

His anxiety about concealing his authorship from his parents may have been genuine, but he didn't try very hard. Portions of the book had already appeared in literary periodicals under his own name; he confessed to his sister Avril that he was publishing his first book using a pseudonym; and he allowed his mother to read the book. Still, the pen name at least shielded the family from public scrutiny. It seems that another compelling reason for using an alter ego was the fact of his background. How credible was it for an Eton graduate to go undercover by living on the margins of society, rejecting respectability, and plunging himself into the lives of outcasts? It could also be perceived as highly offensive that such a genteel young man would "slum it" for the sake of creating a literary masterpiece. For him, vagrancy was a choice: if his situation became too dire, he could always borrow money from his mother;

and he could find a place to sleep whenever he wished. He was certainly in a bad way, yet he could afford to be a part-time tramp; it was a role to play more than anything else.

Writing about poverty demanded authorial authenticity, and that meant erasing all traces of Eric Arthur Blair. He had to "pass" as a man living on the margins, and Eric Blair was not that man. Changing his name was also appealing because he claimed to detest his birth name. Perhaps it had to do with the strained relationship he'd had with his father.

Down and Out in Paris and London by George Orwell was published in January 1933, with an initial print run of 1,500 copies. The author was relieved to have some validation of his efforts. "Isn't it a grand feeling when you see your thoughts taking shape at last in a solid lump?" he wrote to a friend.

There are a few reasons why Blair had settled on "George Orwell" as his literary persona. Some have speculated that the first name came from his admiration for the late-nineteenth-century writer George Gissing, who influenced his work. The surname seemed to have derived from the River Orwell in Suffolk, which Blair is said to have loved—Defoe had written of it—or from the village of Orwell in Bedfordshire, which Blair had once passed through.

In any case, it seemed perfect, and "George Orwell" became the most famous English pseudonym of the twentieth century. As well, thanks to his novel *Nineteen Eighty-four*, the adjective "Orwellian" became part of the lexicon. (It has a much better ring than, say, Milesian or Allwaysian, had he settled on his other choices.)

Anthony Powell once asked his friend if he'd ever considered adopting "George Orwell" as his legal name. "Well, I have," he told Powell, "but then, of course, I'd have to write under another name if I did." Why he felt such a profound need to separate himself in private life from his "writing self" is a mystery. But duality is present throughout his work: in *A Clergyman's Daughter*, for instance, and elsewhere Orwell's characters lead double lives and harbor hidden selves. "He was as secretive about his private life as any man I ever knew," a friend recalled of him.

The book was well received in England and, upon its international publication, by critics abroad. "George Orwell is but trembling on the age of 30 this year, but he appears to have had about as much experience so far as the seamy side of life is concerned as a man of 50," wrote a reviewer in the *New York Times* in 1933, adding that Orwell's chilling account "is apt to put an American with a ticklish stomach off filets mignon in the higher-priced hotel restaurants for ever. It is Mr. Orwell's argument bolstered by numerous horrible examples, that the more you pay for food in Paris, the less clean it is."

With the modest success of *Down and Out*, Blair's metamorphosis into George Orwell was complete. He'd received fan letters addressed to Orwell, and had, for the first time, even signed a book review as Orwell. The persona endured. His family, friends, publisher, and agent knew him as Eric Blair, but to the public he was firmly established as George Orwell. He'd accepted that neither Eric Arthur Blair nor even "E. A. Blair" had ever found success as a writer, and that only Orwell would be taken seriously. Eric Blair was a loser.

His books came in rapid succession: *Burmese Days* (1934), *A Clergyman's Daughter* (1935), *Keep the Aspidistra Flying* (1936), *The Road to Wigan Pier* (1937), *Homage to Catalonia* (1938), and in the last few years of his life, *Animal Farm* (1945) and *Nineteen Eighty-four*, published a year before his death. Even when he was highly productive, his usual reaction was to be dismissive of his output. "I have never been able to get away from this neurotic feeling that I was wasting time," he wrote in his diary. "As soon as a book is finished, I begin, actually from the next day, worrying because the next one is not begun, & am haunted with the fear that there never will be a next one." Nevertheless, despite having exasperated so many people with his polemics, he had by then endeared himself, more or less, to the literary establishment. "He writes in a lucid conversational style which wakens one up suddenly like cold water dashed in the face," V. S. Pritchett wrote of Orwell's work.

Although he instructed later that *A Clergyman's Daughter* and *Keep the Aspidistra Flying* not be republished once they had fallen out of print—he dismissed them as "silly potboilers"—they were crucial building blocks in what would prove a highly successful and even lucrative career.

A friend once commented on Orwell's obsessive writing process. He walked in one day to find Orwell sitting at a table with books by W. Somerset Maugham and Jonathan Swift, reading passages from both, closing them, then copying out sections from memory. "I'm trying to find a style which eliminates the adjective," Orwell explained. It was not unusual for Orwell to write for ten hours a day, to rewrite entire book drafts three times, or to revise individual passages five or ten times, until he was satisfied.

His fussiness also extended to his personal life. In an entry written in 1940 for an American directory of authors, he revealed, "I dislike big towns, noise, motor cars, the radio, tinned food, central heating and 'modern' furniture." His list of approved things included English beer, French red wine, Indian tea, strong tobacco, vegetable gardening, and comfortable chairs. He added: "My health is wretched, but it has never prevented me from doing anything that I wanted to. . . . I ought perhaps to mention that though this account that I have given of myself is true, George Orwell is not my real name."

In 1941, a critic (and former Eton classmate) named Christopher Hollis wrote a withering review of Orwell's book *The Lion and the Unicorn*, attacking the author as a coward: "Many things interest me about Mr. Orwell," he wrote, "and not the least among them the question why he prefers to confront the world with that peculiar name rather than with the very respectable one under which I have had the honour of knowing him for the last quarter of a century." This must have come as a shock to those acquaintances who knew Orwell only as Orwell. By that time, he was signing his work correspondence "George Orwell," and sometimes signing personal letters "E. A. B. (George Orwell)." Most of his old friends still called him Eric. Despite the confusion, he refused to have his name legally changed. He may have taken some pleasure in being able to flit at will between one self and the other, as suited the occasion.

The 1930s had been a kind of golden age for the author, apart from his occasional hospitalizations and periods of convalescence. He established himself as a famous writer and he found love, or at any rate an acceptable version of it. After meeting an Oxford graduate named Eileen O'Shaughnessy at a party, he decided that she was "the type of girl I'd like to marry." In 1936, they did, but like so many other things in his life, the marriage would prove ephemeral. In 1944, they adopted an infant son, whom they named Richard Horatio, but Eileen died a year later during an emergency operation. Because Orwell had been unfaithful to her, his grief was mingled with guilt. "It wasn't an ideal marriage," he admitted to his housekeeper. "I don't think I treated her very well." Her absence left him lonely and depressed, and with his recurrent bouts of flu and bronchitis, reminded him that he was probably running out of time himself.

He was eager to find another wife, and at the age of forty-six his wish was fulfilled. On October 14, 1949, the Associated Press issued a brief announcement: "George Orwell, novelist, married yesterday Miss Sonia Brownell, an editor, in University College Hospital, where the author, who is suffering from tuberculosis, is confined." Orwell remarked on their travel plans. "I don't know when I shall be allowed to get up," he said, "but if I am able to move, we shall go abroad for the worst part of the winter, probably for January and February."

He was dead by the end of January.

V. S. Pritchett paid tribute to Orwell, calling him "sharp as a sniper" and praising him as "a writer of extraordinary honesty, if reckless in attack; to the day he died, nearly three weeks ago, he had never committed an act of political hypocrisy or casuistry." Six decades after his death, Orwell was named by fifty Penguin authors as the publisher's most popular author ever. *Animal Farm* and *Nineteen Eighty-four* are still required reading in schools. He influenced scores of writers, including Kingsley Amis, Norman Mailer, and Anthony Burgess. And he is considered one of the twentieth century's finest essayists. "If you want to learn how to write non-fiction, Orwell is your man," wrote Jeremy Paxman in the *Daily Telegraph* in 2009. "The impeccable style is one thing. But if I had to sum up what makes Orwell's essays so remarkable is that they always surprise you."

After Orwell's death, his friends remembered him fondly while acknowledging that he was often difficult. One spoke of him, aptly, as having been "easier to love than to like." Stephen Spender offered a more generous assessment: although he found Orwell disingenuous in earnestly aligning himself with the working class, Spender recognized his essential decency and the purity of his motives. "Even his phoniness was perfectly acceptable," he recalled. "Orwell had something about him like a character in a Charlie Chaplin movie, if not like Charlie Chaplin himself. He was a person who was always playing a role, but with great pathos and great sincerity."

She weighed seventy pounds
when she died

CHAPTER 9

Isak Dinesen & KAREN BLIXEN

Her childhood was filled with the traditional privileges of a wealthy up-bringing, but she preferred the company of servants. Karen Cristenze Dinesen was born on April 17, 1885, and over the course of her life would be known alternately as Tanne, Tanya, and Tania by her family and close friends. "Tanne" was a nickname that originated from her youthful mispronunciation of her own name (and was one she was said to dislike), but it stuck nonetheless. She grew up on her family's estate in Rungstedlund, on the Danish coast midway between Copenhagen and Elsinore. Her father bought the house, a former inn, in 1879, and Dinesen would spend her final years there in relative seclusion.

Karen's great-grandfather on the side of her mother, Ingeborg, was a ship baron and one of the wealthiest men in Copenhagen. Her father, Wilhelm, came from a family of major landowners. After the Franco-Prussian War, he traveled to America, where he spent time among Indians who gave him the name "Boganis," meaning hazel-nut. He later published a book, *Letters from the Hunt,* using Boganis as a pseudonym, which was Karen's first encounter with a nom de plume. She was the second of five children, raised in a puritanical household, and easily her father's favorite; they had a close, confiding relationship that seemed to exist in its own private, obsessive realm, outside the rest of the family. But in 1895, a month before Karen's tenth birthday, Wilhelm hanged himself at the age of fifty. She never forgave him for abandoning her. She was left, as she would later say, with an abiding terror "of putting one's life into, and abandoning one's soul to something that one might come to lose again."

Even at a young age, Karen knew the depths of sadness. She struggled to find a secure place within her competitive family and used her rich fantasy life as a frequent means of escape. She wrote thoughtful, world-weary plays, essays, stories, and poems and kept a diary. Her mother was strict, forbidding the children to enter certain rooms of the house without permission and refusing to intervene in sibling squabbles. "Whoever is angry must absent himself from the public spaces, and from the stairs and corridors, so long as the anger lasts," she decreed. (Crying aroused neither Ingeborg's sympathy nor any gestures of maternal comfort.)

At fourteen, Karen fell in love with Shakespeare, marveling at the epic scale of his romances and tragedies. She read widely: Stendahl, Chekhov, Voltaire, Conrad, Turgenev, Hans Christian Andersen, and poets such as Percy Bysshe Shelley. She was passionate about art and at eighteen was accepted at the Royal Academy in Copenhagen. The following year, in 1904, Karen began to write what she called "Likely Stories," which revealed even then her predilection for the gothic and fantastical. Her favorite poet was Heinrich Heine, and she often recited these lines from his *Buch der Lieder*: "You haughty heart, you wanted it like this! / You wanted to be happy, infinitely, / Or infinitely wretched, haughty heart, / And now you are wretched."

At the Royal Academy, she met someone who would become her first reader (apart from her family) and literary mentor: Mario Krohn, a young intellectual whose father was a museum curator. She spent a lot of time with Krohn, though her affection for him seems to have been largely platonic. (He died of tuberculosis in 1922.) With his encouragement, she sent her stories to the editor of Denmark's most prestigious literary journal, who responded to one piece by calling it "too broad and a little too artistically contrived, and the whole tone too hearty and simpleminded. It is also too long." Yet he recognized her talent and decided to accept one of the stories, "The Hermits." She would publish two more stories in the journal, all under the pseudonym "Osceola." This she'd borrowed from an unlikely source: her father's German shepherd. It was a name that Wilhelm had borrowed from a leader of the Seminole Indians in Florida. Osceola had led his tribe's resistance when the American government tried to remove the Seminoles from their land, and he died in prison a few months after being captured.

Before giving birth to Isak Dinesen, Karen Dinesen would have to meet the man who would become her husband: her Swedish second cousin, Baron Bror von Blixen-Finecke, a distant cousin of King Christian of Denmark. (Bror had a twin brother, Hans, whom Karen was in love with, but he was not interested in her.) Bror, who pursued her assiduously until she relented, was handsome and gregarious. Karen did not find him compelling or even intelligent. Her family was not impressed, either. Bror was inept with money, a fact that would have disastrous consequences for the couple later on. Still, their early years together were fairly happy, and when Bror's uncle suggested, "Go to Kenya, you two," they did.

In 1913, the Blixens set off for what was then British East Africa, setting up a 4,500-acre coffee plantation called the Swedo-African Coffee Company, twelve miles from Nairobi. (Eventually they would own 6,000 acres.) Bror was giddy at the financial potential of the business. Never mind that he knew nothing about growing coffee. Nor did he consider fluctuating coffee prices or realize that locusts, droughts, acidic soil, and the elevation of the land made it inhospitable for his ambitious endeavor, and destined it to fail. "The land was in itself a little too high for coffee," Karen recalled with typical understatement in *Out of Africa*, "and it was hard work to keep it going; we were never rich on the farm. But a coffee-plantation is a thing that gets hold of you and does not let go, and there is always something to do on it: you are generally just a little behind with your work. . . . Coffee-growing is a long job." But in Africa she had found a spiritual home, and she described the thought of ever leaving as "Armageddon. After that—nothing."

In addition to her own elegiac memoir—with its famous opening line ("I had a farm in Africa, at the foot of the Ngong Hills") and notable omissions (not much mention of her husband, and only a platonic rendering of her lover, the hunter Denys Finch Hatton)—many accounts of her years in Africa have been written elsewhere: the decline of the plantation; the pileup of financial debt; her contracting of syphilis (from which she never recovered) from her philandering husband in the first year they were married; the breakdown of her marriage; her relationship with Finch Hatton; and so on. Those years, by turns enchanting and filled with frightening adversity, had a profound impact. "When I was a young girl," she recalled later, "it was very far from my thoughts to go to Africa, nor did I dream then that an African farm should be the place in which I should be perfectly happy. That goes to prove that God has a greater and finer power of imagination than we have."

Even after her marriage ended, she continued to manage the farm on her own. At the time, this was certainly an odd way for a woman of her class to live, but it was a testament to her attachment to the land and its people. "Here at long last one was in a position not to give a damn for all conventions, here was a new kind of freedom which until then one had only found in dreams," she said.

Partly because of the collapse of the coffee market, she was eventually forced to sell the plantation and return to Denmark. The decision broke her heart. "I was driven out of my house by the fear of losing it," she wrote. "When in the end, the day came on which I was going away, I learned the strange learning that things can happen which we ourselves cannot possibly imagine, either beforehand, or at the time when they are taking place, or afterwards when we look back on them."

The painful losses she endured—of her farm, of her beloved horses and dogs, of Finch Hatton (who died in a plane crash in May 1931)—drove her back to Denmark and to writing.

"I really began writing before I went to Africa," she told the *Paris Review* in an interview six years before her death. "But I never once wanted to be a writer." (That single-minded devotion to process—the ardor for writing *itself*, rather than the vanity of *having written*—is, of course, the mark of a true writer.) She had done some writing in Africa as well; two of the stories in *Gothic Tales*, believed to be "The Dreamers" and "The Old Chevalier," were written there. She wrote them while trying to distract herself from the distressing problems of the farm. "One of my friends said about me that I think all sorrows can be borne if you put them into a story or tell a story about them, and perhaps this is not entirely untrue," she said years later. In Africa she refined her skills as a storyteller: "I had the perfect audience," she told the *Paris Review*. "White people can no longer listen to a tale recited. They fidget or become drowsy. But the natives have an ear still. I told stories constantly to them, all kinds. And all kinds of nonsense. I'd say, 'Once there was a man who had an elephant with two heads' . . . and at once they were eager to hear more. 'Oh? Yes, but Memsahib, how did he find it, and how did he manage to feed it?' or whatever. They loved such invention." In a 1957 interview with the *New York Times*, she insisted, "I am not a novelist, really not even a writer; I am a storyteller." Some would dispute that assessment. When Hemingway was awarded the Nobel Prize in 1954, he said that he would have been "happy—happier—today" if it had gone instead to "that beautiful writer, Isak Dinesen."

When she returned to Denmark from Africa, in 1931, she was a lost soul. Even her identity was in tatters; she'd lost her title as baroness after Bror remarried in 1929 and found a new Baroness Blixen.

Though Karen was often accused, perhaps unfairly, of being a vain snob, she did cherish her title and was angry and indignant when she was stripped of it. People continued to call her the Baroness in later years, which surely pleased her. But at that point, she didn't know what to call herself. And at forty-six years old, she was destitute, forced to move back to her mother's home. (In a 1986 essay, John Updike, an admirer of Dinesen's work, described her return at that time as "ignominious," noting that she was received into the household as "a prodigal daughter, a middle-aged adolescent.") In a letter that year, Karen told her brother Thomas, "I have wondered whether I could learn to cook in Paris for a year or two, and then perhaps get a post in a restaurant or a hotel." She also suggested that she could take care of "mad people." Fortunately, she set her ambitions elsewhere, confiding to Thomas, "I have begun to do what we brothers and sisters do when we don't know what else to resort to—I have started to write a book." She decided to write in English because it had been her primary language in British East Africa, and she was comfortable with it; and because she believed that potentially, an English-language book would reach a larger audience and be more profitable. (She was right.)

The book she was writing became *Seven Gothic Tales*. She said later that she used the word *tale* after Shakespeare, or "in the naïve view of a child or primitive who sees a story as neither tragic nor comic but marvelous."

Of course, Karen needed to support herself as she wrote, so she asked Thomas to finance her for two years, promising that by the end of this time she would become independent. Writing from her family's estate, Karen felt the presence of her father once again. After all, he had gone to America and lived with the Plains Indians, then returned to Denmark to write his books. "So you see, it was natural for me, his daughter, to go off to Africa and live with the natives and after return home to write about it," she explained to the *Paris Review*.

Biographical events intersected in other ways. Not long after the farm was sold to a Nairobi real estate developer, Karen had attempted suicide by slashing her wrists. And shortly before her father's suicide, Wilhelm was told by a doctor that he had a disease "which could only conclude in a dark, helpless future." (It was most likely syphilis.) "My father's destiny has, curiously enough, to a great extent, been repeated in my own," she said.

Three years after the scaffolding of her life collapsed beneath her, Karen would become a published author in England and the United States. She would evolve into Isak Dinesen. The transformation was a struggle, however. ("No one came into literature more bloody than I," she once said.) In those days—as is true in today's publishing climate—a short story collection, especially by an unknown author, was not a desirable commodity. Publishing is a profit-driven business, like any other, and story collections aren't known for being lucrative. Karen's manuscript was rejected by at least two publishers, including the London house of Faber and Faber, which was then a relatively new (founded in 1929) but prestigious firm.

Karen had been preparing the material that would form *Seven Gothic Tales*, on and off, for a decade. She later described her process as beginning with a "tingle, a kind of feeling of the story I will write. Then come the characters, and they take over, they make the story." She said that she began only with the "flavor" of a tale, and that her characters led her toward their fates—"I simply permit them their liberty," she explained. (In his 1976 *Paris Review* interview, John Cheever—speaking not of Dinesen specifically, but of the notion that fictional characters take on identities of their own—dismissed the romantic idea of the author as a passive creative vessel. "The legend that characters run away from their authors—taking up drugs, having sex operations, and becoming president—implies that the writer is a fool with no knowledge or mastery of his craft," he said.)

In any case, Karen would devote herself fully to writing, well aware of the radical nature of her task. Two decades later, she admitted in a speech that if she had been a man, "it would be out of the question for me to fall in love with a woman writer." Working away in her father's old office—which was also the same room where, in the late eighteenth century, Denmark's greatest lyrical poet of the era, Johannes Ewald, was said to have written—she sat at the Corona typewriter she'd brought home from Kenya, allowing few intrusions into her time and space. She was openly resentful of social interruptions, whether from family or friends; as a result, some visitors who came to the house were put off by her foul mood and deemed her behavior selfish (not an adjective one might have ascribed to a male writer). Her seclusion provided a kind of freedom, psychological if not physical: the permission for her imagination to roam at will, exploring and reaching beyond the bounds of self, mining the material of both her dreaming and her waking life.

She later explained that her decision to publish under a pseudonym was not unlike how her father "hid behind the pseudonym Boganis. . . . [It was to] express himself freely, give his imagination a free rein. He didn't want people to ask, 'Do you really mean that?' Or, 'Have you, yourself, experienced that?'" She decided to use her maiden name, Dinesen, and chose the first name Isak, meaning "laughter" in Hebrew. (In the Old Testament, Isaac was born to Sarah when she was quite old; his birth seemed almost like a miraculous prank by God.) The name reflected Karen's comic spirit and her love of humor, particularly irony. It was an element in her work, even in the "tragic" stories, that was never given its proper due by most critics. Also, as an author who "gave birth" to her first book at the age of forty-nine, she was a late bloomer herself; the name was apt.

When she completed her manuscript in 1933, she took it first to London, where a family friend arranged a luncheon for her. Karen was introduced to an American-born publisher, Constant Huntington of the British firm Putnam's. She charmed him and asked if he would be willing to read her work. When she mentioned that it was a collection of short stories, he threw up his hands and refused even to look at it. "A book of short stories by an unknown writer? No hope!" he said. She returned home angry and despondent, almost ready to give up.

But one of her mottoes in life was: "Often in difficulties, never afraid."

She made use of a contact from her brother Thomas—an American author, Dorothy Canfield Fisher, who lived in Vermont. She mailed her the manuscript, hoping something might come of it. Fisher immediately recognized its value and passed it along to her neighbor, the publisher Robert Haas, who accepted it, taking a big chance on an unknown European writer. (When Random House bought the firm owned by Haas and his partner, Harrison Smith, the company acquired not only Isak Dinesen but other prominent authors, including Jean de Brunhoff and William Faulkner.) Haas considered the deal a labor of love, and imposed two conditions before publication: that the book include a foreword by Fisher, a distinguished figure whose name might generate some good publicity; and that he not pay an advance until at least a few thousand copies had been sold. Dinesen agreed to his terms, but wrote to Fisher to express concern regarding authorship. "I don't want the book to come out under my own name," she wrote, "and at the same time I don't want people to know that it is myself who has written it, even though that is not a serious problem in America!—I'm going to have to find a name to publish it under."

When *Seven Gothic Tales* was published in January 1934, it was a critical and commercial success. (Dinesen's first check from Haas, for $8,000, arrived that Christmas.) Upon seeing that the book had met with such great acclaim, Constant Huntington wrote a letter to Haas, praising the book, pleading for the author's address, and—oh, the audacity—insisting that he (and Putnam's) publish the British edition. Dinesen was amused. "He had met me as Baroness Blixen," she recalled later, "while Mr. Haas and I had never seen one another. Huntington never connected me with Isak Dinesen." Putnam's released the work in England in September 1934.

The persona "Isak Dinesen" made the author a figure of mystery in the literary world. Rumors swirled about the true identity of this "slender, pale, large-eyed, middle-aged Danish woman," as a critic would later describe her. They said she was really a man, or "Isak" was a woman, or argued that the author was a collaboration between a brother and sister. He or she was a recluse. A nun. Actually French, not Danish. And so on.

In "The Dreamers" (the penultimate story in *Seven Gothic Tales*), the character Pellegrina Leoni, an alter ego of sorts for Dinesen, implores another character to lose himself: "Be many people," she says. "Give up this game of being one. . . . You must, from now, be more than one, many people, as many as you can think of. I feel, Marcus— I am sure—that all people in the world ought to be, each of them, more than one, and they would all, yes, all of them, be more easy at heart." This reflected the author's desire to escape her own self. For her, the willful expanse of identity was a path that led away from suffering, from the daily sorrows that trapped her.

A passage in the story "The Old Chevalier" seemed to express Dinesen's need, after so much loss, to overturn the circumstances of her life and start anew: "Reality had met me, such a short time ago, in such an ugly shape, that I had no wish to come into contact with it again," she wrote. "Somewhere in me a dark fear was still crouching, and I took refuge within the fantastic like a distressed child in his book of fairy tales. I did not want to look ahead, and not at all to look back."

Themes of truth and deceit are everywhere in Dinesen's fiction. In "The Deluge at Norderney," the opening story of *Gothic Tales*, a cardinal explains the virtues (and power) of masquerade: "The witty woman, Madame, chooses for her carnival costume one which ingeniously reveals something in her spirit or heart which the conventions of her everyday life conceal; and when she puts on the hideous long-nosed Venetian mask, she tells us, not only that she has a classic nose behind it, but that she has much more, and may well be adored for things other than her mere beauty. So speaketh the Arbiter of the masquerade: 'By thy mask I shall know thee.'"

Isak Dinesen's lauded debut was a Book-of-the-Month Club selection, with a print run of fifty thousand copies—an astonishing number at the time. The BOMC newsletter ran an announcement, along with a simple notice: "No clue is available as to the pseudonymic author." On March 3, 1934, the *New York Times* posted the selection in its "Book Notes" column: "*Seven Gothic Tales*, by a European writer who uses the pen name of Isak Dinesen, is to be the Book-of-the-Month Club choice for April. Smith & Haas will publish it, with an enthusiastic introduction by Dorothy Canfield." Five weeks later, John Chamberlain, a columnist for the newspaper's "Books of the Times," wrote that he was unimpressed by the selection: "[W]e found it impossible to get interested in Isak Dinesen's *Seven Gothic Tales. . . .* We are willing to grant the eerie light in the book, and the slanting beauty of phrase, but the predicaments of the characters leave us cold. If you prick Mr. Dinesen's people, they do not bleed."

Regardless, it was a hit, and Dorothy Canfield Fisher's introduction to *Seven Gothic Tales* encouraged a sense of intrigue about the author's identity. She proved a great advocate for the book, writing, "I am so much under its spell (it feels exactly like a spell)," and also letting the reader know that the material did not fit easily into any familiar genre or literary movement. "The person who has set his teeth into a kind of fruit new to him," Fisher wrote, "is usually as eager as he is unable to tell you how it tastes. It is not enough for him to be munching away on it with relish. No, he must twist his tongue trying to get its strange new flavor into words, which never yet had any power to capture colors or tastes."

Devour the book, she urged, but claimed she could offer no insight into who had written it: "I can't even tell you the first fact about it which everybody wants to know about a book—who is the author." Fisher continued, cryptically: "In this case, all that we are told is that the author is a Continental European, writing in English although that is not native to his pen, who wishes his-or-her identity not to be known, although between us be it said, it is safe from the setting of the tales to guess that he is not a Sicilian."

But Isak Dinesen was perhaps the shortest-lived pseudonym in literary history. The book had created such a stir that the Danish press immediately set out to learn the author's real identity, and, following a tip that "he" was in fact a "Danish lady," reporters from the newspaper *Politiken* found her. At the end of April, Smith and Haas announced formally that Isak Dinesen was Baroness Blixen of Rungstedlund. A week later, the competition began among Danish publishers to acquire translation rights to her book. She decided to undertake the job of translation herself, a practice she would follow from then on—writing most of her stories first in English, then in Danish. But these were never direct translations; she would rewrite as well, even changing the endings to create original stories for a different audience.

Seven Gothic Tales (or *Syv Fantastiske Fortaellinger*) was published in Denmark in September 1935, when Dinesen was fifty (the same age at which her father committed suicide). The critical reception was decidedly harsh. Her work was dismissed as too artificial, too perverse, too shallow, too elitist, and too foreign. One young reviewer criticized the book on many counts, noting that "[t]he erotic life which unfolds in the tales is of the most peculiar kind." In the end, he wrote, "There is nothing . . . behind [the author's] veil, once it is lifted."

Some critics were annoyed by Dinesen's decision to write first in English—an apparent breach of etiquette—and by the fact that her breakthrough had occurred in the United States rather than her homeland. To avoid offending them again, subsequent books were issued simultaneously in Danish and English—or first in Danish. Also, she reserved her pseudonym only for books that came out in North America; in Denmark she reverted to Karen Blixen—perhaps in an attempt to prove her "authenticity" and appeal to national pride. Still, she never felt that she achieved enough popularity in Denmark, certainly not compared with the adulation she received abroad. In the United States, she had an impressive roster of admirers. Truman Capote yearned for a movie adaptation of "The Dreamers," with Greta Garbo in the lead role. Ralph Ellison, Pearl Buck, and Marianne Moore loved her work. Orson Welles said that he considered

Dinesen superior to Shakespeare. William Maxwell praised Dinesen as "the most original, the most perceptive, and perhaps the best living prose writer." Eudora Welty called her "a great lady, an inspired teller of her own tales, a traveler, possessed of a learned and seraphic mind." Carson McCullers was also a fan. "When I was ill or out of sorts with the world," she said, "I would turn to *Out of Africa*, which never failed to comfort and support me." In 1957, Dinesen was made an honorary member of the American Academy of Arts and Letters; other member inductees that year included John Dos Passos, Flannery O'Connor, Mary McCarthy, and W. S. Merwin. Meanwhile, at home, Dinesen confided to a friend, "Lately, I have had the feeling in Denmark of being under suspicion, almost as if I were on parole."

When *Out of Africa* was published in 1937, it, too, was a Book-of-the-Month Club selection. With its lovely, straightforward prose, not the least bit baroque or decadent, and with no questionable subject matter, the memoir elicited a positive critical response in her homeland. Grounded in the story of a land and its people, it was "realistic" rather than fantastical. In Denmark she called the book *Den afrikanske Farm* (*The African Farm*); for the American edition, she'd chosen the title *Ex Africa*, but Robert Haas persuaded her to use *Out of Africa* instead. Dinesen insisted that it be published on the same day in the United States, Scandinavia, and England, rather than releasing first to Danish readers and then elsewhere—a request her publisher resisted because of the logistics. "America took me in when I could not even make the publishers in Europe have a look at my book," she explained, "and the American reading public received me with such generosity and open-mindedness as I shall never forget. I was delighted with the reviews of the American critics. I feel the deepest gratitude toward you all." She worried (however irrationally) that delaying American publication might convey the impression that she had lost interest in her fans there or no longer valued them. Despite the case she'd made, her request was denied, thus preserving a schism in her literary identity that could not be made whole: living as one persona abroad and another at home.

Out of Africa was praised by *Time* magazine as "a restrained, formalized book, which has little in common with her first book." She captured the African landscape, its people and animals "with the eye of a painter and a novelist." The *New York Times* called the book "rare and lovely," and praised its "penetration, restraint, simplicity and precision which, together, mark the highly civilized mind, and that compassion, courage and dignity which mark civilization, in the best sense, in the human heart."

It must have annoyed Dinesen that a book by her former husband came out at the same time—also a memoir of Africa, published by Knopf. *Time* magazine was scathing in its review: "By comparison with his former wife's volume, 50-year-old Baron von Blixen-Finecke's *African Hunter* is little more than a handbook for big-game hunters. . . . Baron Blixen-Finecke does not care much for natives. Now married to an adventurous, pretty, 29-year-old Englishwoman, he remembers his first wife (Isak Dinesen) for one incident, when she flew unarmed at two lions that had attacked an ox, lashed them into the jungle with a stock whip." (Bror would marry a third time and die in a car crash in Sweden in 1946.)

On May 10, 1943, Dinesen's third book, *Winter's Tales*, was published in the United States. (It had come out in Denmark a year earlier.) This, too, was sold to the Book-of-the-Month Club and was a huge success. Despite having been unmasked seven years earlier, Dinesen still had a seductive aura of intrigue, one that cast her as imperious and remote. William Maxwell noted that although "Isak Dinesen" was "now generally known to be the pen-name of a Danish woman . . . the Baroness herself is still something of a mystery. The facts concerning Baroness Blixen supplied by her publishers are definite enough; there just aren't many of them." And when the *New York Times* columnist Orville Prescott reported the publication of *Winter's Tales*, his piece, with its dramatic opening, read more as if he were writing about a witch than an author: "In Denmark lives a baroness, a strange and grandly gifted woman who by some odd chance has strayed into the twentieth century from distant regions beyond time and space. . . . A serene and frosty genius, she is an artist of précieux and impeccable talent who scorns the conventional, the direct and the clearly understandable. A writer, she forsook her native Danish tongue and has written her books in an English of such coldly glittering beauty she has hardly a living rival as a literary stylist. Her books are signed Isak Dinesen." Prescott proclaimed the arrival of another book from this enchantress as "rather like a nightingale singing in a boiler factory, like a phoenix materializing in Union Square on May Day." He may as well have been referring to the author herself when he said that *Winter's Tales* was "aloof and separate from every world that ever was."

Winter's Tales—which was Dinesen's own favorite of her books—had a rather unlikely path to publication. This collection came out of Denmark in the midst of World War II, by secret diplomatic mails, to America. First Dinesen had traveled with the manuscript to Stockholm, where she visited the American embassy with an odd request: would someone there be willing to carry the manuscript on one of the planes headed for the United States? She was told that only political or other official papers could be transported. Then she went to the British embassy to make the same request. After she provided a few references in high places (including Winston Churchill), the favor was granted and the manuscript was sent to America on her behalf. Along with her stories, Dinesen had enclosed a note to her publisher, indicating that she was unable to communicate further: "I can sign no contract and read no proofs," she wrote. "I leave the fate of my book in your hands."

She would have no idea how things turned out until the war ended. "I suddenly received dozens of charming letters from American soldiers and sailors all over the world," she said later. "The book had been put into *Armed Forces Editions*—little paper books to fit a soldier's pocket. I was very touched. They gave me two copies of it;

I gave one to the King of Denmark and he was pleased to see that, after all, some voice had spoken from his silent country during that dark time."

The book was critically well received, though without making the same splash as *Seven Gothic Tales*. "Many people, I feel sure, will read all eleven *Winter's Tales* as I did—as fast as possible in order to have as soon as possible the pleasure of reading them for the second, the third, and, inevitably, the fourth time," William Maxwell wrote. Still, Dinesen was feeling bored, restless, and frustrated—partly because of the monotony of daily life brought on by the war—and suffered through periods of poor health, due to the syphilis she'd contracted years earlier. She was convinced that she would never produce a novel, but held out hope that she might.

A Frenchman named Pierre Andrézel would do it for her.

Here was yet another persona for Dinesen, at the age of fifty-nine, during the German occupation of Denmark. She had created Andrézel out of boredom, because she felt caged in as herself and wished to toy with a new disguise. The novel, *The Angelic Avengers*, was (as its title suggests) a thriller. Years later, Dinesen would laugh it off as "my illegitimate child." She had done it, she insisted, simply to amuse herself. She asked her Danish publisher in Copenhagen for an advance, and for a stenographer to whom she could dictate the novel. Unsure of the story before she began, she wrote by improvising, dictating a little each day. "It was very baffling to the poor stenographer," she said. It was also problematic: she would begin a session by announcing that a certain character would enter a room, only to be reminded by the stenographer, "Oh dear, he can't! He died yesterday in Chapter Seventeen."

When the book came out, Dinesen denied that she had anything to do with it (or with Andrézel), despite a surge of rumors fueled by her own publisher. She said that even if she were the author, she would never admit it. When a friend wrote to say that he'd read the novel and found it "a profound joke," she replied that she knew who the author was, but refused to reveal his identity until others discovered it for themselves (just as she knew, inevitably, they would).

The novel, which some readers interpreted as an allegory of the fall of Nazism, was published as *Ways of Retribution* in Copenhagen, in 1944. Although Dinesen refused to claim authorship, it wasn't long before she was unmasked, again by the pesky press. Dinesen was upset that journalists would not respect her desire to go incognito, a privilege lost to her long ago. The book became a best seller in Denmark (it was reviled by critics) and was published in the United States a few years later. The Book-of-the-Month Club chose it as half of the dual selection for January 1946 (along with *Mr. Blandings Builds His Dream House*, by Eric Hodgins). In its announcement, the BOMC remarked that *The Angelic Avengers*—"a fascinating story of mystery, adventure, and pure young love"—was written in wartime, and that "Pierre Andrézel" was surely a pseudonym, but: "Of whom? There were shrewd guesses, but nobody ever really knew. The author, whoever it is, continues to guard this anonymity. All that has been divulged by him (or her) is a plainly fictitious autobiographical note sent to the American publisher."

Despite the author's contention that her latest novel was a bit of an embarrassment, something she had written to have "a little fun," *The Angelic Avengers* marked another grand success, selling ninety thousand copies in America. One reviewer wrote that Dinesen was dealing with "somewhat coarser material than in the best of her tales, but dealing with it in such a way that this novel will certainly widen the circle of her readers."

After the publication of *Winter's Tales* and *The Angelic Avengers*, Dinesen didn't publish again for more than a decade. In the final years of her life came *Last Tales* (1958), which she dictated to her assistant and said was written "with a leg and a half in the grave"; two years later came *Shadows on the Grass* and *Anecdotes of Destiny*. Her health had steadily worsened, owing to the syphilis. There were periods in which she would rally, but once her decline had begun she was never quite the same. A frail, gaunt figure, weighing less than eighty pounds, Karen was in and out of the hospital. In the morning she took amphetamines, stimulants that caused her to talk compulsively, in an odd, almost trancelike state. At night she swallowed barbiturates to fall asleep. Because of the wasting away of her spine, she was sometimes unable to stand or walk. In those last years she led a fairly isolated life, and in periods of illness she was especially ill tempered, sarcastic, depressed, and paranoid. Her moods, she admitted, were "coal black."

Dinesen was well aware that she could be as difficult as she was charming. "As long as I live it will be bothersome for you to have to deal with me," she once told a dear friend. She was a leading contender for the Nobel Prize until her death but never won, a fact that proved an ongoing disappointment. Yet by the time she died, in 1962, she was an international celebrity and her books had been published in twelve languages. When Sydney Pollack's Academy Award–winning film adaptation of *Out of Africa* was released in 1985, a new audience was drawn to Dinesen's work, and there was a resurgence of interest in the author as well. To the end, whether inhabiting Tanne, Karen, Isak, or any of her other selves, she believed absolutely that it was her right to assume a pseudonym, and that readers were obliged to respect it. Although her aliases had been promptly uncovered, a friend once wrote of his unknowable, inscrutable friend that "Karen Blixen as a person was always pseudonymous in varying degrees, [and] that she always wanted to be suspected behind her texts but under no circumstances caught."

In her final months, she grew weaker still, her weight down to seventy pounds. She subsisted on glasses of vegetable and fruit juice, oysters, and biscuits—the few things she could keep down. She could no longer stand without losing her balance, and admitted in a letter to a friend that a doctor had said "that I have all the symptoms of a concentration camp prisoner, one of them being that my legs swell so that they look like thick poles and feel like cannon balls. This last thing is terribly unbecoming and for some reason very vulgar. Altogether I look like the most horrid old witch, a real Memento Mori." On September 7, 1962, she spent the evening listening to Brahms. That night she fell into a coma and died in her narrow wooden bed. She was buried on the family property under a beech tree.

Five years before her death, an interviewer asked Dinesen whether she had led a happy life. "Yes, and with all my heart," she replied. "At times I have been so happy that it has struck me as overwhelming, almost as supernatural." She was asked what, exactly, had made her so happy. "In a way I believe that the only true, sure happiness one can talk about here is the pure joy of living, a sort of triumph simply because one exists."

She found sexual satisfaction
in picking her nose

Sylvia Plath & VICTORIA LUCAS

She was a good girl who loved her mother. That, at least, was the benign impression Sylvia Plath gave the outside world—a smiling façade of conformity; feminine, pure of heart; accommodating, polite, bright-eyed, and pretty. She admired her mother, Aurelia, and was desperate for her approval. There were no secrets between them. Aurelia was nurturing and boundlessly devoted; Sylvia was her dutiful, adoring daughter. Such was the seamless porcelain exterior of their relationship, and both players were invested in protecting it. Meanwhile, writing in her journals, Plath recorded the brutal truth. "I lay in my bed when I thought my mind was going blank forever and thought what a luxury it would be to kill her, to strangle her skinny veined throat which could never be big enough to protect me from the world," she wrote on December 12, 1958, following a session with her therapist. "But I was too nice for murder. I tried to murder myself: to keep from being an embarrassment to the ones I loved and from living myself in a mindless hell." She resigned herself to the ineluctable role she'd been cast in: "I could pass her on the street and not say a word, she depresses me so. But she is my mother." Sylvia was adept at dealing with Aurelia. Before speaking to her, it was as if Sylvia had trained herself to neatly tuck in her fury and put it to bed, permitting it to stir again only in her mother's absence.

Plath's biography is familiar to just about every English literature major, reader of contemporary poetry, and suicidal teenager. She was toxic because she was so seductive, and seductive because she was so toxic. Her fame is immeasurable. Even many nonliterary types know that Sylvia Plath was the mercurial poet who gassed herself in an oven.

She was born at 2:10 p.m. on October 27, 1932, in a suburb of Boston, Massachusetts. Her father, Otto Plath, was a biology professor at Boston University, a well-regarded etymologist, and twenty-one years older than his wife. "At the end of my first year of marriage," Aurelia later wrote, "I realized that if I wanted a peaceful home—and I did—I would simply have to become more submissive, although it was not my nature to be so."

By the time she was three years old, Sylvia proved quite brilliant. Once, while her mother was baking in the kitchen, she played alone on the living room floor. She was unusually quiet. Otto went to check on her, and, as Aurelia recalled, both parents were stunned to see what their daughter had done. Using a set of mosaic tiles she'd received as a gift, she reproduced "unmistakably the simplified outline of the Taj Mahal, the picture of which was woven into a mat in our bathroom."

When Sylvia was eight years old, her father died of an embolism brought on by complications of diabetes. We know how well she came to terms with that loss; those who don't should read her notorious poem "Daddy," which says it all.

She had a younger brother, Warren, born in 1935, with whom she felt competitive for her parents' affection, especially her mother's. Sylvia was always driven to be the best, and often was. The siblings' relationship did not become markedly closer until she attended Smith College (on a scholarship) and Warren was at Phillips Exeter Academy and then Harvard. Years later, their mother described the family with her typical fondness for nostalgia (steeped in denial). This false portrait presented a family close and uncomplicated in its affections: "We three loved walking by the sea, in the woods, huddling close by the fire and talking, talking, talking—or sharing a companionable silence," she said.

Plath always knew that she stood apart from others. Because she was viewed as "dangerously brainy," she felt it was in her interest to mask her sharp intellect and turbulent emotions. Not only did she embody the role of a perfect, straight-A student, but she was determined to become popular. She also pursued the approval of adults, both at school and at home. Other students might merely work hard, but she burned with determination. Before her first short story appeared in *Seventeen* (in the August 1950 issue), Plath had submitted forty-five pieces to the magazine. At eighteen, she berated herself in her journal: "What is my life for and what am I going to do with it? I don't know and I'm afraid. I can never read all the books I want; I can never be all the people I want and live all the lives I want."

One of her early poems, written when she was in tenth grade, was called "I Thought That I Could Not Be Hurt." A teacher who read it expressed amazement that "one so young could have experienced anything so devastating." In this instance, the source of suffering was her unwitting grandmother, who had accidentally smudged one of Plath's pastel drawings. The final stanza read,

(How frail the human heart must be—
a mirrored pool of thought. So deep
and tremulous an instrument
of glass that it can either sing,
or weep.)

Such intensity of feeling would never leave her, despite her efforts to conceal and tame it. Aurelia added to this unbearable pressure by making Sylvia feel responsible for the well-being of both mother and daughter. Yet Aurelia might also be credited for Sylvia's supreme sense of confidence, her innate belief that she was "special" and destined for greatness. "The worst enemy to creativity is self-doubt," Plath once wrote, but when it did creep in, she pounded it like a Whac-A-Mole until her achieving self could surface once again. Then all was right with the world. And she was at least able to find consolation in what she once described as the "minute joys" in life: she admitted in her journals that she loved the "illicit sensuous delight" she felt when picking her nose. "God what a sexual satisfaction!" she wrote.

Early on, Plath was a baffling mix: highly empathetic but also self-obsessed. She absorbed everything and everyone around her. By the age of seventeen, she was investigating the bounds of the self and how to manage her troubled psyche. "Sometimes I try to put myself in another's place, and I am frightened when I find I am succeeding," she wrote in her diary in 1949. "How awful to be anyone but I. I have a terrible egotism. I love my flesh, my face, my limbs with an over-whelming devotion. . . . I want, I think, to be omniscient. . . . I think I would like to call myself 'The girl who wanted to be God.' Yet if I were not in this body, where *would* I be? . . . But, oh, I cry out against it. I am I—I am powerful, but to what extent? I am I."

The struggle between selves would torment her for her entire life—in poems such as "An Appearance," "Tulips," and "In Plaster," among others—and it served as a frequent subject of her journals. At Smith, she wrote a long paper on the theme of double personal-ity in Dostoevsky's novels. Even when she was relatively happy, or at least emotionally stable, her inner turmoil never abated. It must have been exhausting. Often her fixation on duality and falseness reached a crisis pitch. "Look at that ugly dead mask here and do not forget it," she wrote in a lacerating note to herself in a 1953 diary, referring to a recent photograph. "It is a chalk mask with dead dry poison behind it, like the death angel. It is what I was this fall, and what I never want to be again." That year, she attempted to kill herself by overdosing on sleeping pills.

Despite her recurring depressions, treatments with electroshock therapy, and flirtations with suicide, she was not entirely obsessed with death. As much as she was preoccupied with it, she was also seeking to end her ego self, with its oppressive, needy demands that were impossible to fulfill. Perhaps it wasn't her whole life she wanted to stop, but a "shameful" part of herself. Over and over she expressed frustration at not measuring up to other poets and for feeling stalled in her work. "I, sitting here as if brainless wanting both a baby and a career," she wrote in her journal in 1959. "What inner decision, what inner murder or prison-break must I commit if I want to speak from my true deep voice in writing . . . and not feel this jam up of feeling behind a glass-dam fancy-façade of numb dumb wordage."

What she seems to have craved most, in fact, was a chance at rebirth, at resurrection. Even though she was sometimes able to produce (or recover) what she deemed an "authentic" self, the success did not prove sustainable. Plath's obsession with split selves—the pretty, superficial good girl who does everything easily and well, versus the raging, violent demon lurking within—left her perpetually confused: Which one was real? Which one should be shed? Which one should she kill off? In the end, the demon won.

In 1961 Plath won the Eugene F. Saxton Memorial Fellowship, a writing grant of $8,000. She had by then graduated summa cum laude from Smith, published poems and stories, and won a Fulbright scholarship to Cambridge University. There she met the dashing British poet Ted Hughes, whom she married on June 16, 1956. (That date is Bloomsday.) After winning the Saxton, she was especially excited because she had applied previously, for poetry, but had been rejected. This time, she'd gone for it with a different project in mind. Although she had in fact completed her first novel, *The Bell Jar*, and even signed a contract for the manuscript with the British publisher Heinemann, this award would give her time to make revisions before the book's publication and provide monthly living expenses as well. Money was extremely tight. That fall, Plath wrote one of her usual cheery letters home to her mother, assuring her that all was well. (Many of Plath's missives to Aurelia opened with the effusive "Dearest-Mother-whom-I-love-better-than-anybody.")

She mentioned that the *New Yorker* had just accepted her poem "Blackberrying" and shared the news about the Saxton. "Well, I applied for a grant for prose this time and got the amount I asked for," she wrote. "They pay in quarterly installments as parts of a project are completed, so I should get my first lot in a week or two!" She continued: "Life in town has been more and more fun." The letter began and ended with her standard loving greeting ("Dear Mother") and sign-off ("x x x Sivvy").

Less than two weeks later, she sent Aurelia another chatty letter, referring again to the grant but neglecting to explain what, exactly, her writing project was about. "I finished a batch of stuff this last year, tied it up in four parcels and have it ready to report on bit by bit as required," she reported vaguely. "Thus I don't need to write a word if I don't feel like it. Of course, the grant is supposed to help you do writing and is not for writing you've done, but I will do what I can and feel like doing, while my conscience is perfectly free in knowing my assignments are done."

What "Sivvy" failed to mention was that the "batch of stuff" was an autobiographical novel that would have killed her mother, or at least broken her heart. The narrator's voice, as in Plath's poetry, was icy and lucid. It was about the "crackup" of a well-behaved young woman named Esther Greenwood, described in the flap copy of the 1971 Harper & Row hardcover edition as "brilliant, beautiful, enormously talented, successful—but slowly going under, and maybe for the last time." The story was also, to put it mildly, an exploration of Esther's strained relationship with her mother, and how her repressed anguish leads to madness. There was only one way this devastating novel could be published by a "good girl" such as Plath, and that was to hide behind a pseudonym. She chose "Victoria Lucas": "Victoria" was a favorite cousin of Ted Hughes; "Lucas" was the name of

Hughes's good friend Lucas Myers. Heinemann published *The Bell Jar* in London on January 14, 1963. Twenty-eight days later she killed herself.

Plath lived long enough to read the reviews of her novel, and they didn't please her. The reception in Britain was tepid and condescending. "There are criticisms of America that the neurotic can make as well as anyone, perhaps better, and Miss Lucas makes them brilliantly," Laurence Lerner wrote in the *Listener*. A critic in the *Times Literary Supplement* wrote that "if [Lucas] can learn to shape as well as she imagines, she may write an extremely good book." Worse, Plath had hoped for publication in the United States, too, but that didn't seem forthcoming. Just after Christmas, she'd received a jarring letter of rejection from Alfred A. Knopf in New York, which had published her poetry book *The Colossus* the year before. A second rejection came from Harper & Row ("The experience remains a private one," the editor wrote of the narrative, which seemed more a "case history" than a novel.) In the letter from Knopf, the editor expressed her regret: "We didn't feel that you had managed to use your materials successfully in a novelistic way. . . . Up to the point of her breakdown the attitude of your young girl had seemed a perfectly normal combination of brashness and disgust with the world, but I was not at all prepared as a reader to accept the extent of her illness." The same could be said of Plath. No one—not even those closest to her, who were well acquainted with her despair—could fully comprehend its sheer velocity, its manic and unstoppable force.

The 1989 Plath biography *Bitter Fame*, by the poet and critic Anne Stevenson, opens with an apt epigraph from Dostoevsky's *The Devils*:

There was a tremendous power in the burning look of her dark eyes; she came "conquering and to conquer." She seemed proud and occasionally even arrogant; I don't know if she ever succeeded in being kind, but I do know that she badly wanted to and that she went through agonies to force herself to be a little kind. There were, of course, many fine impulses and a most commendable initiative in her nature; but everything in her seemed to be perpetually seeking its equilibrium and not finding it; everything was in chaos, in a state of agitation and restlessness. Perhaps the demands she made upon herself were too severe and she was unable to find in herself the necessary strength to satisfy them.

Plath, volatile to say the least, was once described by the poet W. S. Merwin as "a cat suspended over water." Like many others who knew her, he found her a "determined, insistent, obsessive person who snapped if things did not go her way, and flew into sudden rages."

The manuscript of *The Bell Jar* is another interesting manifestation of Plath's fragmented selves. Here she had produced the most shocking work of her young life, filled with harrowing insights into her own psyche—yet she typed these words on dainty pink Smith College memo paper. "Got a queer and most overpowering urge today to write, or typewrite, my whole novel on the pink, stiff, lovely-textured Smith memorandum pads of 100 sheets each," Plath wrote in her journal on March 3, 1958, while she was back at Smith, working as an instructor in the English department. She proudly noted that she'd helped herself to plenty of school stationery: "Bought a rose bulb for the bedroom light today & have already robbed enough notebooks from the supply closet for one & 1/2 drafts of a 350 page novel."

Well before the novel came out, the phrase "bell jar" had popped up in Plath's writings. At Smith, she described feeling overwhelmed by her own mind, by the demands made on her, socially and otherwise—and admitted that she found things especially hard without a prescribed routine to follow. She could never give herself a break:

Working, living, dancing, dreaming, talking, kissing—singing, laughing, learning. The responsibility, the awful responsibility . . .

is rather overwhelming when there is nothing, no one, to insert an exact routine into the large unfenced acres of time—which is so easy to let drift by in soporific idling and luxurious relaxing. It is like lifting a bell jar off a securely clockworklike functioning community, and seeing all the little busy people stop, gasp, blow up, and float in the inrush (or rather outrush) of the rarefied scheduled atmosphere—poor little frightened people, flailing impotent arms in the aimless air. . . . What to do? Where to turn?

Elsewhere, she wrote that "it's quite amazing how I've gone around for most of my life as in the rarefied atmosphere under a bell jar." And a 1959 journal entry recorded feelings of frustration and gloom: "The day is an accusation. Pure and clear and ready to be the day of creation, snow white on all the roof tops and the sun on it and the sky a high clear blue bell jar."

The few years leading up to the publication of *The Bell Jar* had brimmed with creativity. That period provided an argosy of material, but it may have ultimately contributed to her death. In the spring of 1959, she was writing the searing poems of *The Colossus*. Those took a toll, and the book's themes would inform her novel as well. She also had an appendectomy, and in 1960 she gave birth to a daughter, Frieda. After suffering a miscarriage, she became pregnant again, and in January 1962 gave birth to her son, Nicholas. (He would have his own lifelong battle with depression; he died in 2009 by hanging himself.) By the fall, her marriage had fallen apart: Hughes left her for another woman. This time, recovery was not possible.

The following January, as an overwhelmed, exhausted, and isolated young mother, Plath numbly witnessed her novel's debut. She was living in a dreary London flat (where W. B. Yeats had once lived) at 23 Fitzroy Road in St. Pancras. There was no telephone and electricity was intermittent. That winter in England, following a "bone cold" autumn, was bleak, snowy, and icy, one of the worst on record. Plath and her children had the flu, and she was terribly anxious about money.

At night, she could not fall asleep without medication. She was waking at four o'clock each morning to crank out the poems of *Ariel*. (Several drafts had already been handwritten on the reverse of the "lovely-textured" pink Smith College stationery on which she had typed her *Bell Jar* manuscript.) On February 11, 1963, as her children lay sleeping, she sealed off the door to their bedroom with wet towels and opened their window wide. She left them milk and bread. Then she put her head inside that infamous gas oven and ended it all.

As she'd immersed herself in the early stages of her novel, Plath had been understandably secretive with her mother about writing *The Bell Jar*, but she had openly shared her fiction-writing ambition with a friend: "I have been wanting to do this for ten years but had a terrible block about Writing a Novel. Then suddenly . . . the dykes broke and I stayed awake all night seized by fearsome excitement, saw how it should be done, started the next day & go every morning to my borrowed study as to an office & belt out more of it." This was a real breakthrough, considering Plath constantly berated herself for not having accomplished enough. "Prose writing has become a phobia to me: my mind shuts & I clench," she wrote in her diary in 1957. "I can't, or won't, come clear with a plot." Her self-flagellation is present throughout her journals. "Why can't I throw myself into writing?" she wrote. "Because I am afraid of failure before I begin."

In an entry dated December 12, 1958, Plath wondered, "Why don't I write a novel?" Following that question, she'd gone back a mere three years later and giddily amended the entry: "I have! August 22, 1961: THE BELL JAR."

To describe the writing of it as cathartic is an understatement. Plath called *The Bell Jar* "an autobiographical apprentice work which I had to write in order to free myself from the past." She had found a safe alter ego in Esther Greenwood—rendered even more secure by the mask of Victoria Lucas—through which the author could exorcise, among other things, her electroshock therapy, mental breakdowns, repressed sexual desires, and hatred of her mother. In one scene, Esther expresses revulsion at watching her mother awaken: "My mother turned from a foggy log into a slumbering, middle-aged woman, her mouth slightly open and a snore raveling from her throat. The piggish noise irritated me, and for a while it seemed to me that the only way to stop it would be to take the column of skin and sinew from which it rose and twist it to silence between my hands." With such cruelly drawn characters, Plath could malign anyone who'd ever caused her pain or failed to give her what she craved—and her mother above all would be punished.

Years after Plath's death, Aurelia refused to accept her daughter's dark feelings toward her, attributing the lapse to mental anguish. "My mother was always my best friend and I'd hoped that my daughter would be too," she said. "She became ashamed of our friendship during her breakdown. I don't want to accuse anybody. I don't want to blame anybody, but . . . somebody had to be the scapegoat."

The American edition of *The Bell Jar* wasn't published until April 1971, and it would remain on the *New York Times* best-seller list for six months (fueled no doubt by the author's posthumous fame). Finally, the novel also achieved critical acclaim. When the paperback was issued a year later, three editions sold out within a month.

Aurelia had done her best to stop publication. The year before, she implored Plath's editor at Harper & Row to reconsider. "I realize that no explanation of the *why* of personal suffering that this publication here will create in the lives of several people nor any appeal on any other grounds is going to stop this, so I shall waste neither my time nor yours in pointing out the inevitable repercussions," she wrote. Nearly every character in *The Bell Jar*, she claimed, "represents someone—often in caricature—whom Sylvia loved; each person had given freely of time, thought, affection, and, in one case, financial help during those agonizing six months of breakdown in 1953 [the year in which the novel is set] . . . as this book stands by itself, it represents the basest ingratitude."

To Aurelia, the novel also gave the world a gross distortion of her daughter's supposedly true self, undone by mental illness. "Sylvia never wanted it to be published here," she told a *New York Times* reporter in a 1979 interview, which took place in the white frame suburban house where Sylvia and Warren grew up. "She'd had two babies and an appendectomy and needed money. 'I have to write a best-seller,' she told me. 'I want to write a potboiler. What would you suggest for a subject that wouldn't fail?' I suggested a child-parent conflict. I little knew what shape it would take." As usual, Aurelia made everything all about her, and she came across as self-absorbed and self-pitying. She spoke repeatedly of her vulnerability and painted herself as a victim. "When *The Bell Jar* came out in 1971, it became a very hard time for me," she said. "It was accepted as an autobiography, which it wasn't. Sylvia manipulated it very skillfully. She invented, fused, imagined. She made an artistic whole that read as truth itself."

Just a few days before Plath died, she had written optimistic letters about her future—including horseback riding again, an activity she loved. When she committed suicide, the first rumor in the United States was that she had died of pneumonia, a rather sunnier cause of death that Aurelia Plath, always in willful denial of monstrous truths, wanted to believe. (The official cause was deliberate carbon monoxide poisoning.) Ted Hughes handled the grim task of identifying his wife's body and confirming her name, age, occupation, and address. Their children did not attend the funeral. Plath's tombstone inscription read, EVEN AMIDST FIERCE FLAMES THE GOLDEN LOTUS CAN BE PLANTED.

Sixteen years after her daughter's death, Aurelia continued to reckon with the grotesque portrait of herself that was presented in *The Bell Jar*. "Can you imagine what it is like to relive it over and over and over again?" she said of her daughter's crippling legacy. "It is only because I've been compelled to. It is because I have the name Plath. Anytime I meet anyone, the same thing happens. It happens to my daughter-in-law, their two girls, my son, of course. I was on

Nantucket recently having a joyous time with a dear friend. She introduced me at a party and the other woman said: 'Oh . . . you are, aren't you?' I just can't escape it. The warm greeting until the name strikes them and they think of *The Bell Jar*, and of Mrs. Greenwood, the uncaring mother. 'Oh so you are Mrs. Greenwood,' they say."

Aurelia once wrote to the scholar and poet Judith Kroll, who had published the first full-scale critical study of Plath's poetry, *Chapters in a Mythology*. It was evident in her letter that Aurelia's trauma would never heal. (She died at the age of eighty-seven in 1994.) "[Sylvia] made use of everything and often transmuted gold into lead," she explained. "These emotions in another person would dissipate with time, but with Sylvia they were written at the moment of intensity to become ineradicable as an epitaph engraved on a tombstone. . . . She has posthumous fame—at what price to her children, to those of us who loved her so dearly and whom she has trapped into her past. The love remains—and the hurt. There is no escape for us."

He was a stinky drunkard with
brown teeth and dirty hair

CHAPTER II

Henry Green & HENRY YORKE

He's the best writer you've never heard of. If you have read any or all of Henry Green's nine novels, you know that you're in on a too-well-kept secret. You probably wish that everyone with fine literary taste (such as yours) could experience the intense pleasure of reading him for the first time. That's no easy feat, since most of his books are out of print and the few that aren't are nearly impossible to find. Quiz a bunch of people who consider themselves well read, and a surprising number will admit that they have never read Green's books and are not even familiar with his name. Depending on your temperament, this response will leave you feeling disappointed or smug.

Henry Green was the nom de plume of Henry Vincent Yorke, an Englishman born on October 29, 1905, in Gloucestershire. He grew up in a fourteenth-century manor, called Forthampton Court, on a 2,500-acre estate. Henry came from fancy stock: his handsome, athletic father, Vincent, had attended Eton and Cambridge and was a former archaeologist and explorer turned businessman; his mother, Maud, was the daughter of a baron who owned one of the grandest houses in England, a man who was among the richest British aristocrats of his era. One of her uncles was prime minister. Her great-grandfather was an earl and a well-known patron of the arts, one of the first supporters of J. M. W. Turner. Although Maud was an affectionate mother to her three sons—Henry and his older brothers Philip, who would die at sixteen of lymphatic leukemia, and Gerald—she preferred spending time with her beloved dogs and horses and indulging in her great love, reading. She was born with a curvature of the spine, yet had been quite athletic in her youth—shooting pheasants, hunting avidly, and breeding racehorses. (She'd continued riding horses well into the sixth month of her pregnancy with Henry; he later insisted this had undermined his health and been the source of his neurotic temperament.) Maud, who spoke in a clipped military diction, was a witty, intelligent woman who loved to gossip. She was an eccentric character, said to have instructed her gardener to bowl turnips down a grass slope so that she could shoot at them. Maud almost always wore black or navy blue, and because she was a chain-smoker (of Turkish cigarettes), she was left in old age with only one brown-stained tooth. She refused to wear dentures.

In childhood, the Yorke boys were left largely in the care of nannies and servants who taught them proper manners and reined them in when necessary. Their father was an aloof presence in their lives. "We were well brought up and saw our parents twice a day," Henry later wrote, "that is to say my father worked in London and we only saw him at weekends." When he was there, Vincent was taciturn to the point of hostility. Unlike Maud, he lacked a sense of humor, and he envied her social ease. Most often, Vincent behaved toward his family like an irascible bully. Affection played no part in his emotional repertoire.

Philip and Gerald appeared somewhat more in the mold of their father—brash, confident, excellent athletes and hunters—but their younger brother was timid, awkward, lonely, and plump. He had no knack for academics or sports. (Henry described gym class as "harrowing.") He took his family's wealth for granted, yet he also felt estranged from it, identifying with servants, butlers, and working-class men far more than with his fellow aristocrats, whose company he found boring. Opulence was lost on him, which partly explained why Vincent found Henry such an awful disappointment.

Nicknamed "Goosy" at home, Henry was educated at Eton and Oxford but was not able to match the impressive academic records of his brothers. His time at Eton was unremarkable. Philip in particular had been a star there, and after his death in 1917, Henry felt even more inadequate. "I needed praise badly," he wrote later, "and if I had had it might be even less of a person now, but from the lack of it at that time found everything pointless, so blind that no effort at work or play ever seemed worth while."

But he and some friends did form a Society of Arts, a creative outlet that gave him a sense of belonging, and he began writing short stories. "This point is a watershed, after this there was no turning back," he later wrote. "I determined to be a writer . . . and a nom de plume was chosen, of all names Henry Michaels." He published a few pieces in *College Days*, the school literary magazine, an accomplishment his parents regarded with suspicion and disdain. One of his stories, "Bees," which appeared in 1923, follows a clergyman from "a slum parish in Liverpool" who suffers from malaise in a "sleepy, unenthusiastic" village. Though brief and spare, it is well written and reveals a certain psychological acuity; one wouldn't necessarily guess that the story had sprung from the mind of an eighteen-year-old:

All day long he thought of how he was to stand the blow of his daughter's death, and, although it was eighteen months since she had died, he was still composing answers in his mind to the letters of condolence that never came. In the busy buzz of his bees he detected the sympathy he could not discover in the world outside. His wife, whom he always regarded as a drone, could do nothing with him. He was sure that every man's hand was against him. He detected an insult in the butcher boy's whistling as he delivered the meat. So he turned to his bees, who always sympathized, and were so practical, and who were not useless like his family.

Without telling Henry, his mother sent his stories to a friend, the Scottish writer John Buchan (most famous for *The Thirty-nine Steps*, adapted into a film directed by Alfred Hitchcock). Buchan offered encouraging words about Henry's work. "Whatever your boy's stories are, they are not a waste of time," he wrote. "They are curious stories, rather like the kind of thing that Hans Christian Andersen wrote in his youth. They show great powers of observation, great sensitivity to scenery, and the nuances of temperament, and a strangely mature sense of the irony of life." He added, however, that one ought to use writing as a hobby rather than a profession, and that Henry "seems to have literary gifts of a high order, but he wants the discipline of more normal subjects. It would be exceedingly good for him to try his hand at concrete objective narrative for a change." Concreteness, as readers would later discover, was perhaps the quality most absent in Henry's writing—and perhaps most abhorred by him.

Henry became close to one of his Eton classmates, Anthony Powell, who would become an author as well. The boys shared their enjoyment of storytelling and even began (but abandoned) collaborating on a novel. Years later, Powell recalled his friend as "always interested in words, repeating unfamiliar ones (e.g., hirsute) over to himself, laughing at them, discussing them." Another close friend, Robert Byron, admired Henry's peculiarity and shared his irreverent humor. Byron later said of him, "He can talk like no other person I've ever met."

In 1924, Henry began writing a draft of what would become his impressionistic first novel, *Blindness*, published when he was just twenty-one. The original typescript was signed "Henry Browne." Eventually he would settle on the bland pseudonym "Henry Green"— never publishing a book under his real name. That choice may have had to do with his aristocratic upbringing, which frowned upon such a self-centered vocation. His friend and classmate Harold Acton did not approve of his pseudonym. "There are Greens of so many shades writing novels that one wishes he had selected another colour," he said. (Henry "Green" later befriended the novelist Graham Greene, whose full name was Henry Graham Greene.) Henry was forever caught between the desire for revelation, for confession, and the reticence expected of someone of his class. He wanted to remain enigmatic and private while at the same time fully exploring human emotion and experience. Anonymity seemed to offer a comfortable compromise. "Names distract, nicknames are too easy, and if leaving both out . . . makes a book look blind then that to my mind is no disadvantage." Perhaps he meant that in making a book "blind," cloaking it cleverly enough, more distance would be placed between reader and writer; keeping the reader slightly "in the dark" was not a bad idea. The author himself could not be examined too closely—only his work. *Res ipsa loquitur*: the thing speaks for itself.

At Oxford, Henry's tutor was C. S. Lewis, who had no respect for Henry's literary interests, especially for his appreciation of "experimental" writers. Henry regarded Lewis as "rude and incompetent." Studying was not Henry's priority, anyway. He estimated that he put in no more than six hours of academic work a week. Most nights he was drunk. He played billiards, stayed up late, and slept until around noon. His first meal of the day, accompanied by a brandy and soda, was always fried sole and sausages because "I thought that by not varying my food I was giving my stomach less to do." He had another routine: going to the cinema every afternoon, sometimes twice a day, and returning to his room to write; he admitted that "it became the last foothold to write just one more page a day, the last line of defence because I was miserable in fits and starts and felt insane."

Henry's debut novel, which he characterized three decades later as "mostly autobiographical," follows the callow sixteen-year-old John Haye ("It sounds an awful thing to write, but I seldom meet anyone who interests me more than myself," he admits). Like the author, John enjoys reading Carlyle, Turgenev, and Dostoevsky. On his way home from a repressive boarding school called Noat (a thinly disguised Eton, which was "Note" in earlier drafts), John is blinded. The account of his accident is clinical: a boy throws a rock at a train; the window smashes; John, sitting behind it, loses his sight. His stepmother (who is obviously Maud) spends her time hunting and horseback riding. She tries to marry him off to any girl of the "right" social class, so she won't have to spend the rest of her life caring for him. The story is told from multiple points of view, including those of a young girl and a drunken clergyman. Henry dedicated the novel to his mother.

A review appeared in the *New York Times* on November 14, 1926, shortly after the book was released in the United States: "It is reported to be the first novel of a very young man. In spite of certain defects of workmanship, of prolonged episodes, meandering dialogue and confusion of method, it does convey a sense of character under stress. It is a creditable performance."

Blindness doesn't have much of a plot—Green, like modernists such as Woolf and Joyce, was far more interested in the interior life, memory, emotion, language, and metaphor than in creating tidy, linear, plot-driven stories. "I write for about six people (including myself) whom I respect and for no one else," he once said. In Green's work, there was no authorial guidance as to how a reader should "feel" about any character. Ambivalence reigned. Henry was already an eccentric and sophisticated thinker. He understood that less is more, and that sometimes, nothing is even more.

The gaps and flaws in *Blindness*, including its too-abrupt ending, could be attributed to the immaturity of the author (of which he was well aware), yet even in later novels he favored an oblique approach that did not fill in many narrative blanks. Of his nine novels, not one is like another. Motifs change from book to book. Likable characters are not considered crucial. There are no feel-good endings. And no character learns a moral lesson or is transformed by experience. Life simply goes on. In a sense, you might say that Green was the

Jerry Seinfeld of his day. Calling to mind the comedian's approach to humor, with his "show about nothing," Green believed that "the novel should be concerned with the everyday mishaps of ordinary life," as he told an interviewer in 1950. (John Updike once proclaimed Green "a saint of the mundane.")

With its knotty diction and odd syntax, his fiction, he knew, was not for everyone. Fortunately, Henry found a sympathetic ear in Nevill Coghill, an Irish don at Oxford who became a close friend; Coghill believed absolutely in the young writer's talent and proved a steady source of support and advice. In a 1925 letter, written while on holiday, Coghill was filled with regret as he reported that his brother and a cousin had picked up Henry's manuscript and were not so taken with it: "Alas they think it difficult, depressing, ungrammatical (!!!) carelessly written!!! This so infuriates me that I shout at them, telling them it is a work of undying genius and that they are too crapulous to understand it. To which they reply 'Ah, but I like a good story.' Poor Henry. I am so sorry. But I am sure that your way of writing is a very good way and is right for you."

At the time, Henry may not have been aware of Emily Dickinson's "Tell all the truth but tell it slant— / Success in Circuit lies," but he certainly practiced it in his writing. He was keenly interested in playing with different stylistic techniques, and in applying Chekhov's notion of significant irrelevance, in which details were teased out through indirect means. "Irrelevancy means so much," he wrote to Coghill, "it shows you what a person is & how he thinks, & conveys atmosphere in a way that is inconceivable if you have not seen Tchekov's Cherry Orchard." He finished his novel on May 30, 1925, a few months before his twentieth birthday, noting the precise time and date of completion on the last page of the manuscript. He promptly (and rather boldly) sent it to Chatto & Windus, the distinguished London publishing house of authors such as Wilkie Collins and Samuel Beckett, and the first English translation of Marcel Proust's novel *À la recherche du temps perdu*. (Henry was a great admirer of Proust.)

The editor who received Henry's novel was not impressed. "I do not make much of this MS., which depressed me at the start (by the boringness of the schoolboy mind) and went on depressing me (by the boringness of everything) to the end," he wrote in a memo. "Nevertheless," he added, "the author should not be lightly condemned, because he evidently is very fluent, and his talent may develop."

He mailed the manuscript back to the author with a standard letter of rejection. Henry was furious and told Coghill that Chatto was a "despicable firm." His friend suggested that he send his work to the publisher J. M. Dent, who accepted it after requesting some revisions. An editor there asked Henry, "How did you ever come to write anything so good?"

Dent was known for creating the Everyman's Library—handsome limited editions of classic literature, offered at an affordable price (one shilling). Because Henry was still legally a minor when his book was accepted, his father had to sign his publishing contract. Gerald Yorke later described their parents' response to the novel as "not quite horror but complete misunderstanding and great doubt." They did nothing to assuage Henry's anxiety about disappointing or upsetting them. One of Henry's aunts interpreted *Blindness* as a cry "for sympathy which he doesn't find at home."

At Oxford in the fall of 1926, Henry was very lonely. Many of his friends had graduated and moved on, and he fell into a depression. He wanted out. "Everyone is rich and vapid or poor and vapid & one & all talk about Oxford day & night," he complained in a letter to his mother. He wanted to go to work "in a factory with my wet podgy hands" for the Birmingham branch of H. Pontifex and Sons, his family's coppersmithing company. Vincent Yorke had several enterprises, including positions in banking, insurance, and railways—all secured for him by his father, John Reginald Yorke, who had purchased Pontifex for him as well. The company, which was then failing, had once made plate engravings for William Blake. Vincent proved a savvy businessman, making Pontifex profitable again by moving the factory to a cheaper site

(Birmingham instead of London) and by expanding the manufacturing business into bathroom plumbing and brewery equipment.

Henry decided that he was finished with Oxford's academic pressures. He resented being forced to spend his time studying, he said, "when I have my own work always running in my mind." In December, shortly after the publication of *Blindness*, he dropped out of Oxford without earning a degree. His friend Evelyn Waugh, at work on his own first novel at the time, was enthusiastic about Henry's literary debut: "It is extraordinary to me that anyone of our generation could have written so fine a book."

Henry was eager to trade his stuffy university environment for the factory floor, partly because he sensed that the rhythms and sounds of proletarian idioms could provide material for his next novel, and partly because he longed to experience what he called "the deep, the real satisfaction" of manual labor. (His interest in the working class was not unlike that of his contemporary, and fellow pseudonymous writer, George Orwell.)

In January 1927, Henry reported at the Midlands iron foundry, where he would quickly build up his muscles moving heavy machinery for eight hours a day, earning twenty shillings a week. Although coworkers assumed that he'd been assigned the job as some kind of shameful punishment, it was at Henry's insistence that he started as an apprentice, working his way up from the bottom and living in a Victorian boardinghouse.

The setting was as unrefined as he'd hoped for, and he toiled away at Pontifex quite happily for the next two years. "I had been an idler who had at last found something to occupy his mind and hands," he later wrote. A hundred and fifty people worked at the factory that he would one day control. There was no lack of colorful characters to keep him entertained. Henry proudly reported to his mother that he had met a man who "bites the heads off mice to kill them when the trap hasn't." Despite working harder physically than he ever had, he still found time to indulge in one of his favorite hobbies—his addiction to the cinema—and to write a few hours each day. "Going home it would be dark again and I would be tired," he later recalled. "But after no more than thirty minutes in a chair I was ready for hard work again." His moviegoing and his writing were not unrelated; Henry aptly described the draft of what would become his second novel, *Living*, as "a kind of very disconnected film." The novel, tentatively titled "Works," was set in a Birmingham iron foundry and captured the monotony of the workers' lives. Written with extraordinary sensitivity and empathy, without a trace of condescension or sentimentality, it was a reflection of the author's lifelong affection for the working class, and of his ambivalence about his own pedigree. He once told his mother bluntly that she should accept the fact that "by nature I am not the sort of person who dresses for dinner every night, in fact I am not what is generally known as a gentleman."

He led two lives. By day, he was Henry Yorke, laborer and aspiring businessman; in his private writing time, he was Henry Green. He preferred that the two personae would never meet. For one thing, as he later explained, "I write books but I am not proud of this any more than anyone is of their nails growing." And for another, as he explained in a 1958 *Paris Review* interview with a close friend, the American novelist Terry Southern, "I didn't want my business associates to know I wrote novels." The role of artist seemed pretentious and ill fitting. While contemporaries such as George Orwell (Eric Blair) were engaged in polemical writings and political activism, Green was quietly crafting his strange fiction. He shied away from publicity, avoided being photographed in public, and had deliberately chosen a pseudonym that was unremarkable and did not call attention to itself. He explained that "if you are trying to write something which has a life of its own, which is alive, of course the author must keep completely out of the picture." As Sebastian Yorke (Henry's son) later noted, Henry's own father regarded his son's books "with silent contempt because they did not make money," which only reinforced the notion that Henry Yorke ought to remain as invisible as he could.

In 1949, upon the U.S. publication of Green's fifth novel, an American critic asked:

> Who is Henry Green? Well, there's an elaborately built-up mystery about that, though you could probably soon find out in England. Particularly if you could inspect British income-tax records. He is [according to his publisher] a fellow with a passion for anonymity, a Birmingham manufacturer, an Etonian, an Oxonian, possibly a Bolognian, too, no less. . . . It may be that he is really Graham Greene. It may be that he is Ivy Compton-Burnett's great-grandfather.

By 1958, most of his colleagues at Pontifex, at least, were well aware that Henry Yorke had an alter ego called Henry Green, and he admitted in his interview with Southern that the revelation had affected his relationships with them. "Yes, yes, oh yes—why, some years ago a group at our Birmingham works put in a penny each and bought a copy of a book of mine, *Living*," he said. "And as I was going round the iron foundry one day, a loam molder said to me, 'I read your book, Henry.' 'And did you like it?' I asked, rightly apprehensive. He replied, 'I didn't think much of it, Henry.'"

It was no wonder: aside from the brilliant music of common speech, which Green captured beautifully ("I got you fixed in me mind's eye tucking away lamb with mint sauce"), his prose style was scrambled and demanding. There were sentences with loose grammar, absent nouns, cryptic references, and articles dropped at will: "Hundreds went along road outside, men and girls." "Range made kitchen hotter." "Baby howled till mother lifted him from bed to breast and sighed most parts asleep in darkness."

Although Green's admirers placed him alongside authors such as Woolf, Joyce, Lawrence, Kafka, and Sterne, he claimed no influences himself. "As far as I'm consciously aware," he said, "I forget everything I read at once, including my own stuff." He explained, too, that "Joyce and Kafka have said the last word on each of the two forms they developed. There's no one to follow them. They're like cats which have licked the plate clean. You've got to dream up another dish if you're to be a writer."

By the time Green was twenty-four, he'd already written two boldly experimental novels. Yet in the memoir—if you can call it that—that he published in 1940, *Pack My Bag*, he hardly mentions the publication of either book, or his third novel, *Party Going*, which came out the year before; or any sense of pride in his accomplishments. He names almost none of the people in his life, not even his wife and young son; he does not reveal that the main schools he attended were Eton and Oxford; and in no way does he describe the effect that Philip's death had on him. He entirely skips the decade of his life prior to 1938 (his story stops when he is twenty-four). And he does not even bother to explain why Henry Yorke had become Henry Green. The book's subtitle, "A Self-Portrait," seems a kind of joke. It is a work of great originality, but one in which the author, as usual, omits the most basic details and presents the rest mostly through a blurry viewfinder. (Kingsley Amis said of the book that it seemed "the author was drunk whilst writing it.") There is a willful perversity in the way Green hoards and obfuscates information. Evelyn Waugh wrote to him at the time that "it was a book no-one else could have written and it makes me feel I know [you] far less well than I did before which, in a way, I take to be its purpose."

Despite its baffling omissions, *Pack My Bag* was deeply important to the author. Written when Green was thirty-three, his "interim autobiography" was the result of his terror that he would die in the impending war. He published his book hastily because "we who may not have time to write anything else must do what we now can."

The memoir finished as enigmatically as it began, and abruptly, too—though on a somewhat tender note, alluding at the very end to his epistolary courtship of the woman he would marry: "It was not hunting when it was no fun, not having to go shooting, it was not having to be polite to masters who were fools, it was to lose convictions, at a blow it was life itself at last in loneliness certainly at first, but, in that long exchange of letters then beginning and for the ten years now we have not had to write because we are man and wife, there was love."

Green delivered his tersely titled novels in efficient succession: *Party Going* (1939), *Caught* (1943), *Loving* (1945), *Back* (1946), *Concluding* (1948), *Nothing* (1950), and *Doting* (1952). Then came silence, a literary purgatory that lasted until Green's death in 1973.

In 1929, the year that Henry Green published *Living*, Henry Yorke married an upper-class Englishwoman, Mary Adelaide Biddulph, known as Dig. Waugh affectionately called the couple "Mr H. Yorke the lavatory king and his pretty wife." Henry, along with his parents, had decided that once he'd completed his latest novel, he would move to London and assume a new role at the family firm: managing director. He knew that the structure of an office job would keep him stable, yet he was also "violently depressed" at the time. "My fucking novel is so absolutely mediocre," he told Anthony Powell. His editor, too, had commented that Green's elliptical prose style was "difficult, & a trifle affected." When it was released, the book was neglected critically, perhaps owing to the crowded, exceedingly impressive publishing field that year: Ernest Hemingway, Italo Svevo, Rebecca West, V. S. Pritchett, and Robert Graves all brought out new works. But Green's prominent literary friends helped boost his spirits, providing a welcome antidote to reviews such as one from the *Times Literary Supplement*, which asserted that the author "does not seem to care in the least whether the reader is thrilled, bored, delighted, or irritated." Waugh considered *Living* a masterpiece and compared Green's dazzling technical feats to those of T. S. Eliot. He also emphasized that the author's radically ambitious aims made it "necessary to take language one step further than its grammatical limitations allow. The more I read it the more I appreciate the structural necessity of all the features which at first disconcerted me." Regardless of its originality, the novel failed to sell many copies.

The decade-long interval between the publication of Green's second and third novels was the result of frustrations and distractions, bouts of depression and paranoia; the demands of business, of upper-class society, of fatherhood (his son was born in 1934); and the onset of the war. As one critic later wrote of Green, the neglect of his literary legacy came about partly because he "lived several lives not sequentially but in parallel." He never fully inhabited one identity or the other. The ambivalence evident in his work was also reflected in his personal attitudes. As Anthony Powell noted of his friend, "[I]f one side of Yorke found the silver spoon a handicap to respiration, another accepted it as understandably welcome; and coming to terms with opposed inner feelings about his family circumstances, his writing, his business, his social life, was something he never quite managed to achieve to his own satisfaction."

During the London Blitz, Green volunteered for the Auxiliary Fire Service, an experience that would provide material for *Caught*. His preceding novel, *Party Going*, comically followed a group of aimless young rich people stranded in London's Victoria Station during a heavy fog. Not much happens, and the characters aren't particularly likable. (Seinfeld again comes to mind.) The novel's startling, bizarre opening line set the tone for the disorientation that lay ahead: "Fog was so dense, bird that had been disturbed went flat into a balustrade and slowly fell, dead, at her feet."

After the war, Henry assumed his position as managing director at Pontifex, and the novels he continued to write were greatly admired by W. H. Auden, Christopher Isherwood, Elizabeth Bowen, Roald Dahl, and other prominent literary figures. He also kept busy as a serial philanderer who was as cruel as he was charming. "Hurting—that should be the title of your next novel," one of his girlfriends suggested bitterly.

That Henry Green published nothing after 1952 is explained by the sad decline of Henry Yorke. His lifelong despair started to overtake him and never loosened its grip, eventually leaving him adrift even from himself. Although he was mostly deaf (a condition that worsened during the war), he refused to wear a hearing aid, which isolated him still further from others. He drank and drank. Half his days were spent in pubs, and sometimes he'd return to a pub after dinner and stay until closing time. "To the regulars he was simply Henry who always sat at the same table wearing his raincoat and hat with a glass of gin and water beside him," Sebastian recalled of his father.

Henry had not lost sight of the mission of writing fiction, but he could no longer fulfill it. "Prose is not to be read aloud but to oneself alone at night," he believed, "and it is not quick as poetry but rather a gathering web of insinuations which go further than names however shared can ever go. Prose should be a long intimacy between strangers with no direct appeal to what both may have known. It should slowly appeal to feelings unexpressed, it should in the end draw tears out of stone."

He once claimed that he could "only get myself right by writing." He insisted that writing alone had given him happiness, and that he relied upon it to stay sane. Yet, for some reason, he could no longer gain access to the part of himself that yielded such pleasure.

Henry continued to oversee Pontifex, which had experienced a brief postwar boom, but the company too began to decline. With his stubborn inattention to detail, his pessimism and pathological indecisiveness, and his increasingly erratic behavior, he proved a poor chairman, and the company suffered. In 1958, it was discovered during a board meeting that Henry's water glass contained neat gin. He was forced to retire a year later.

After 1960, the man whom Terry Southern had called a "writer's writer's writer" rarely left his house. He dictated the beginning of an intended sequel of sorts to his memoir, called "Pack My Bag Repacked," a project that, like many others, he soon abandoned. In one draft, he refers to himself in the third person: "Green lives with his wife in Belgravia. He has now become a hermit. . . . Green can write novels, but his present difficulty is to know quite how to do it." He spent much of his time watching TV, especially sports. He often wandered around the house in a shabby state, littered with cigarette ash and wearing mittens because he said that his hands were always cold. Sebastian recalled that his father's hearing grew steadily worse. He once phoned home and asked to speak to "Mummy," to which Henry replied, "So sorry, I have absolutely no money."

In 1962, a BBC interviewer asked Green, "Are you going to write any more books?" He replied wearily: "No—never—never. . . . It's too exhausting, I can't do it." He'd lost his drive and was convinced that no one wanted him to find it again. "I'm absolutely finished as far as the public's concerned," he said. "I mean, I'm out, I don't sell books any more, and the critics despair of me. No, I don't exist any more."

In spite of his black moods, he wasn't entirely gone. He loved reading books (but hated talking about them), and consumed about eight a week—always novels, no poetry or nonfiction. Contemporary British and American fiction appealed to him; he had catholic tastes and read widely, but he refused to read Georges Simenon or C. P. Snow. Like Simenon, Henry idolized Faulkner, and meeting him in 1950 was one of the highlights of Henry's life. He told an interviewer that he wanted Faulkner, more than anyone else, to read his books. (It isn't known whether Faulkner did.)

Over the years, Henry alienated many of his friends with his drunken, maudlin, self-destructive behavior, and they stopped calling on him. He'd become a charmless embarrassment. One friend recalled observing his rare presence at a dinner party, "talking away as if driven by a demon, looking very much the worse for wear." Another compared him to F. Scott Fitzgerald: "He drank because he couldn't write and he couldn't write because he drank." This was perhaps the most succinct diagnosis of Henry's predicament. And in a letter to Nancy Mitford, Evelyn Waugh, who could be quite vicious about Henry's diminished state, described him with sheer disgust: "He looked GHASTLY. Very long black dirty hair, one brown tooth, pallid puffy face, trembling hands, stone deaf, smoking continuously throughout meals, picking up books in the middle of conversation & falling into maniac giggles, drinking a lot of raw spirits, hating the country & everything good. . . . I really think Henry will be locked up soon." In 1968, after much coaxing, Sebastian convinced his father to accompany him to an event at London's Albert Hall, to which Henry came unshaven and wearing bedroom slippers.

What had become of the promise of Henry Green, a writer who, as the author and translator Tim Parks put it, "must be the most highly praised, certainly the most accomplished, of twentieth-century novelists not to have made it into the canon, not to be regularly taught in universities, not to be considered 'required reading'"? One critic astutely described Green as having shown "more subtlety and virtuosity than any other novelist of his generation in England. And yet Green's very mastery of his medium has kept him from the recognition he deserves." Eudora Welty, who'd met Green once and adored him, lavished praise on his underappreciated work in a 1961 essay: "The intelligence, the blazing gifts of imagery, dialogue, construction, and form, the power to feel both what can and what never can be said, give Henry Green's work an intensity greater, this reader believes, than that of any other writer of imaginative fiction today." And the critic James Wood has written that after D. H. Lawrence and Virginia Woolf, Green was the greatest English modern novelist.

The fact remained that despite occasional success (*Loving* had appeared briefly on best-seller lists in the United States), no single book of his had sold more than ten thousand copies in England. His novels had slipped in and out of print even in his lifetime. Of course, Green had sabotaged himself through bizarre financial and marketing decisions: declining offers for paperback sales because of paranoia about income tax debt, and refusing to provide photographs or biographical information to his publishers. Though he reluctantly agreed to come to New York to help launch *Loving*, he registered at his hotel under another pseudonym, H. V. Yonge, whose initials at least matched those of his real name. But he didn't mask his hatred of publicity and made it as difficult as possible for admirers to meet him. Considering how disinclined he seemed to achieve a wider readership, it is no surprise that his publishers were unable to earn a profit from his work. They promoted him as best they could under rather challenging circumstances, undoubtedly out of absolute belief in his prodigious talent. As with everything else to do with him, nothing was straightforward or even rational.

After he'd stopped publishing, Green succumbed to sporadic bouts of inconsolable weeping, telling anyone who would listen that he suffered from a lack of recognition and believed he was a failure. Once, while visiting his brother and sister-in-law, he cried as he complained, "I've never won any of the good prizes." If Green was misunderstood or neglected, he seemed oblivious that any of this was his own doing.

Of the relatively few people who were aware of Green's novels, perhaps too many shared the view of the *New York Times* critic who found his work baffling to the point of irritation, and who dismissed Green as another case of Emperor's New Clothes. Green was blasted by the critic for writing "peculiar, artificially mannered novels of limited appeal which are extravagantly overpraised by a few critics whose pride it is to admire books which lesser mortals don't appreciate." This naysayer, however, later revised his opinion, admitting, "I didn't like green olives the first few times, either. Maybe Mr. Green is an acquired taste."

Henry Yorke died at the age of sixty-eight on December 13, 1973, from bronchial pneumonia, after being bedridden for quite some time. Henry Green had been dead for years. "He was a very very complicated and tricky person," Anthony Powell recalled of his old friend. "And although we knew each other so well, of all the people I've ever known I really never got to the bottom of him."

He could fool some of the people
all of the time

CHAPTER 12

Romain Gary & ÉMILE AJAR

He was a war hero, a Ping-Pong champion, a film director, a diplomat, and an author who wrote the best-selling French novel of the twentieth century. Being famous made him tired. He wanted to be someone else, but one invented persona was not enough.

Roman Kacew was born on May 8, 1914, in Vilna, Russia, and raised by a Jewish single mother, Nina Owczinski, a former stage actress. By the age of thirteen, he believed that he was destined to become a great writer. At this age, too, he took up smoking, a habit encouraged by his mother. (She would smoke three or four cigarettes when she woke each morning, and happily shared her Gauloises with her son.) Nina was a devout Francophile, and emigrated with her son in 1928 to Nice, where she instructed Roman to change his name so he could become famous. "You must choose a pseudonym," she said. "A great French writer who is going to astonish the world can't possibly have a Russian name."

He began experimenting with pen names—spending hours each day hunched over his exercise book and testing out "noble-sounding" noms de plume in red ink. He toyed with "Hubert de la Vallée" and

"Romain de Roncevaux," among many others. "The obvious trouble with pen names," he discovered, "even with the most inspired and impressive ones, was that they somehow failed to convey truly the full extent of one's literary genius."

Such healthy self-regard was inspired in no small part by his mother, who considered her son the center of the universe. Anyone who failed to recognize that fact was an idiot. Neighbors who were annoyed by Nina's constant proclamations of his glory were denounced as "dirty little bourgeois bedbugs." If her son scored poor marks at school, it was everyone else's fault. In his fictionalized 1960 memoir *Promise at Dawn*, he recalled an exchange that occurred one day when his mother asked how things were going at school:

> "I got another zero in math."
> My mother thought this over for a moment.
> "Your teachers don't understand you," she said firmly.
>
> I was inclined to agree. The persistence with which my teachers kept giving me zeros in science subjects seemed to indicate some truly crass ignorance on their part.
>
> "They'll be sorry one day," my mother assured me. "The time will come when your name will be inscribed in letters of gold on the wall of their wretched school. I'll go and tell them so tomorrow."

Roman found his mother's relentless adoration both awe-inspiring and paralyzing. She encouraged him to become a "giant of French literature" only after suffering disappointment that he was not a violin prodigy, a budding Jascha Heifetz. She'd pointed out that if he *were* to become a famous violinist, "our real name, Kacew, or even better, my stage name, Borisovski, would be excellent." But it was not to be. After Nina bought Roman a secondhand violin when he was seven years old, she'd signed him up for private lessons, but the instructor dismissed him after three weeks. "A great dream had left us," Roman recalled.

He and his mother led an itinerant life, dependent mostly on the latest way she'd devised to reinvent herself. He would grow up in Russia and Poland and on the French Riviera. "My mother was always waiting for the intrusion of the magical and marvelous into her life," he wrote, "for some *deus ex machina* that would suddenly come to her rescue, confound the doubters and the mockers, take the side of the dreamer and see to it that justice was done." She earned a living making hats, running a hotel, selling furs and antiques, and other occupations, but perhaps her most memorable venture was in "second-hand teeth"—buying teeth containing gold or platinum, then reselling them at a highly marked-up price.

Though Nina eventually achieved financial security, her dream of being a famous actress never left her. This larger-than-life woman was the consummate stage mother, pushing her son to succeed as the artist she would never become. Roman was instilled with ambition, fear, frustration, and dread, but he was always determined to please her, to lay the world at her feet. In search of the vocation that would bring them acclaim and fortune, they exhausted various possibilities—such as painting, acting, and singing—before settling on literature, which he later noted "has always been the last refuge, in this world, for those who do not know where to lay their dreaming heads." Not only did Nina expect her son to become an artist of renown, but she dreamed that someday he would become an ambassador of France and wear bespoke suits made in London. (Both came to be true.)

As mother and son plotted his future, Roman applied himself to crafting the pseudonym that would inspire literary masterpieces to flow like water. It was, he later recalled, no easy task to discover a name "grand enough to compensate for my own feeling of insecurity and helplessness at the idea of everything my mother expected from me." Despite Roman's intensive brainstorming, nothing seemed right—and both he and Nina were chagrined that names such as "Shakespeare" and "Goethe" were already spoken for. "We were both getting terribly impatient to know, at last, under what name we were to become famous," he recalled. Fifteen years later, when he heard the name "Charles de Gaulle" for the first time, he felt it would have been the perfect pseudonym. None of the names he came up with satisfied him or his mother: "Alexandre Natal," "Armand de la Torre," "Romain de Mysore"—these just weren't good enough.

Nina suffocated her son in a more significant way: she believed that no other woman should ever have him. He belonged to her alone. Worse, she refused to give herself to another man, and took great offense at the suggestion that she ought to try. Any attempts by the teenage Roman to explore his sexual appetite with beautiful young women were invariably crushed by his mother. "I am not saying that mothers should be prevented from loving their young," he wrote later. "I am only saying that they should have someone else to love as well. If my mother had had a husband or a lover I would not have spent my days dying of thirst beside so many fountains."

The grievous effect of such vast and forceful love was that for the rest of his life, Roman would seek, in vain, to recapture it. His craving for companionship was best fulfilled by a succession of devoted friends—notably, Mortimer, Nicholas, Humphrey, and Gaucho, all of them cats—and a dog named Gaston.

As he and his mother steeped themselves in French culture, Roman became "Romain." Whenever Nina was harassed in France as an outsider, mocked as a "dirty foreigner," she would retort by coolly informing the moronic offender that her son "is an officer of the French Air Force and he tells you *merde*!" Romain noted his mother's inability to distinguish between "is" and "will be." (Her ardent idealism and willful denial were part of her charm.)

Meanwhile, Romain felt desperate to somehow make his mark. He discovered that despite his failure at sports such as swimming, running, and tennis, he had a real knack for Ping-Pong. One of the engraved medals he later won at a tournament sat on Nina's bedside table until the day she died.

In his late teens, he also grew more serious about writing. "Attacked by reality on every front, forced back on every side and constantly coming up against my own limitations, I developed the habit of seeking refuge in an imaginary world where, by proxy, through the medium of invented characters, I could find a life in which there was meaning, justice and compassion," he recalled. But because Romain had inherited that marvelous flair for self-mythologizing, he could not simply sit down and write. Under the watchful eye of his mother, as ever, he took a Method-acting approach to his craft. That was the only way he could become, as he hoped, "the youngest Tolstoy of all time," and thus reward his mother for all the sacrifices she had made on his behalf.

Romain flung himself headlong into his task. His dramatic first step was to assemble a pile of three thousand sheets of paper, which he estimated to be equivalent to the manuscript of *War and Peace*. Then, he recalled,

> My mother gave me a dressing gown of ample proportions, modeled on the one which had already made a great literary reputation for Balzac. Five times a day she opened the door, set a plate of food on the table and tiptoed out again. I was, just then, using François Mermonts as a pen name. Since, however, my works were regularly returned to me by the publishers, we decided that it was a bad choice, and substituted for it, on my next effort, that of Lucien Bulard.

Still no luck. But in 1933, at the age of nineteen, Romain finally won a respite from his mother's overwhelming expectations. He enrolled, as a practical consideration, in law school at the University of Aix-en-Provence. He described the experience of bidding goodbye to Nina as "heartrending." It was a healthy and much-needed separation. He spent his free time lingering at cafés, and managed to write a novel. He promptly sent the manuscript to various publishers, and one responded by including a report from an acquaintance—a well-known psychoanalyst to whom he had shown the novel. She indicated in her report that the author of this demented book suffered from a castration complex, a fecal complex, necrophilic tendencies, and other pathologies. In any case, the manuscript was politely declined. Undaunted, Romain took pride in being told that he had a fecal complex, which he felt marked him indisputably as a tormented soul—and a genuine artist. He completed law school in Paris, neglecting his studies to spend several hours a day on his writing. Eventually, he published a few of his stories, and was thrilled to learn that one had even been translated and published in the United States. His early work, signed as "Romain Kacew," was marked by a maturity and economy of prose that was impressive in someone not yet twenty-two years old. In 1935, he became a naturalized French citizen.

During the Nazi occupation, Romain was admitted to what was regarded as the oldest and "most glorious" bomber squadron, the Lorraine, serving under de Gaulle in the Free French forces. Around this time he had begun using the surname "Gari," anglicized as "Gary." For some reason he never explained this rather crucial fact in *Promise at Dawn*. The name was not a random choice; it was yet another tribute to his mother, who had used "Gari" as one of her stage names.

During World War II he had various postings throughout Europe and North Africa. Despite the physical and emotional battering he suffered, he was nonetheless chastised from afar by his ever-looming mother, who insisted that he ought to keep up with his writing. He knew that it would be futile to defend his inactivity by reminding her that there was a war on. So the obedient son set himself to work.

Noting that it was hard to unleash his creative genius "on a ship's deck or in a tiny cabin shared by two others," he persisted, attempting to cobble together stories that might turn into a coherent whole. Part of what would become his first novel, *Éducation européenne* (*A European Education*), was written on a steamer ship that carried him into battle. The latter half was composed at night, in a shared corrugated-iron hut. Every night, Romain—wearing his flying jacket and fur-lined boots—would write until three or four in the morning, "with numbed fingers, my breath rising in visible vapor in the freezing air." He completed the novel in 1943, in Surrey, England.

Later, Romain recalled his harrowing wartime experiences, the aftermath of which left him in a state of alienation unlike any he had ever known—and one he would never quite shake. "After four years of fighting with a squadron of which only five members are still alive, emptiness has become for me a densely populated place," he recalled. "All the new friendships I have attempted since the war have made me only more conscious of that absence which dwells beside me." He also shared an insight about himself that would acquire an eerie and profoundly tragic meaning after he died. "A fool I shall always be, when it is a matter of . . . smiling in the face of nothingness," he admitted. "There is no despair in me and my idiocy is of the kind that death itself cannot defeat."

His combat service transformed him in many ways. He had survived dangerous missions, typhoid fever, and a plane crash that killed everyone aboard but himself. He was decorated with some of France's highest honors, including the Cross of the Liberation, the Legion of Honor, and the Croix de Guerre. Upon his return to Paris, he married Lesley Blanch, a British writer and former features editor at *Vogue*. He also entered the diplomatic corps, serving first with the French embassy in Bulgaria, then Moscow, then Switzerland. Later, he became first secretary of the French delegation to the United Nations, as well as the French Consul General in Los Angeles. The postwar years were an exciting time and would launch the amazing Romain Gary in earnest. (In 1951, it became his legal name.) He would satisfy his mother's great expectations after all.

Only one essential source of happiness was missing: his mother. Romain had returned home from the war to learn that she had been dead for more than three years. How was that possible? He had received a steady flow of letters from her all along. That's because just a few days before she died, Nina had written more than two hundred short, undated letters to her son and sent them to a friend in Switzerland, with instructions to forward them to Romain at regular intervals. And so, as far as he'd known during combat, his mother had been there for him, sending constant words of love and support. The last letter he'd received ended, "Be tough, be strong. Mama."

In 1945, the year after he was married, *A European Education* appeared in print to great acclaim and won the Prix des Critiques. The author and journalist Joseph Kessel raved, "In the last ten years, ever since we heard the names of Malraux and Saint-Exupéry, there has not been a novel in French fed by a talent as deep, new, and brilliant as this one." Raymond Queneau declared Gary's debut a triumph, with "such a particular and original tone." Jean-Paul Sartre considered it possibly the finest novel about the Resistance. Gary received an admiring letter from Albert Camus. And in reviewing the American edition, published in 1960, the *New York Times* noted, "He can forge a great conception with all the incandescence of a romance novelist—then give it final definition by tempering it in sad irony."

This new toast of the literary world, thirty-one years old in 1945, was on his way to becoming what he'd always wanted: rich and famous, and one of France's most prominent authors. Ultimately, his success would kill him.

The year 1956 brought the publication of his fifth novel, the 443-page *Les racines du ciel* (*The Roots of Heaven*), along with France's premier literary award, the Prix Goncourt. (The eleven-member jury included Maurice Blanchot and Jean Paulhan.) In truth, the prize was a mixed blessing. For Gary, winning meant a surge in sales, of the kind that only the imprimatur of Oprah Winfrey's book club can inspire today. Along with that, however, came the need to address the demands of promotion and celebrity, while also managing a confused identity and increased self-doubt. He and other winners over the years found themselves derailed by what they had most coveted. One winner of the prize referred to the "GP" as his "General Paralysis." Another, Jean Carrière (who won in 1972), expressed a similar sentiment. "After having believed that one was writing for a couple hundred or thousand readers, one finds oneself in front of an arena packed with spectators who gasp every time they spot a sign of failure—or the renewal of the artist's exploit," he wrote. "It is enough to paralyze your pen and call into doubt the slightest word traced by your hand." Following his award, Carrière expressed a sense of resigned duty toward the writing that had once been his passion, saying he felt as though his identity had been hijacked and "a puppet was bearing it in my place." His disillusion worsened over time, to the point, he said, that "names strike me as fraudulent." Still, Carrière would survive his plunge into depression and feelings of profound alienation. Romain Gary would not.

Between his celebrated debut and his fifth novel, a strange thing had happened: the adored Romain Gary had been neglected by his public. The novels published after *A European Education* were not well received, and Gary found his career stalled. He sent a despairing letter to his publisher. "I know full well that the public has forgotten me," he complained. "I will have passed like a dream. It's horrible. Sometimes when I look back and see my brilliant beginning and what I am today, a knot forms in my throat."

The Roots of Heaven marked a triumphant comeback. The author whom everyone had once celebrated was again relevant. Gary was no fool; he knew that he had to capitalize on his resurgence. He committed to hundreds of media appearances, and in interviews, he enjoyed inventing amusing and outlandish anecdotes about himself (including a story about his seduction of Clark Gable's girlfriend in a London bar). He treated the "truth" behind his authorial persona like a piece of taffy, something to be stretched and pulled.

One writer noted that "[Gary's] legend as a charmer is not overblown." It worked in his private life, too. In 1959, he met the Iowa-born film actress Jean Seberg. She was twenty-one; he was forty-five. Nine months later, Seberg divorced her husband, François Moreuil. Gary divorced Lesley Blanch in 1961. (She lived to the age of 102, dying shortly before her birthday in 2007.)

In 1962, Gary and Seberg had a son, Alexandre Diego (known as Diego), and they subsequently married, but Gary would lie about the order in which these events occurred, transposing them so that marriage came first, and even falsifying his son's birth certificate.

Following the publication of his memoir, *S. ou l'espérance de vie*, in 2009, Diego recalled his father in an interview. "Even when he was present," he told *Paris Match*, "my father was not there. Obsessed by his work, he greeted me, but he was elsewhere." Today, Diego maintains his father's literary estate and tends to his legacy.

Seberg and Gary were a glamorous couple whose social whirl included dining with the Kennedys and spending time with famous actors. But the marriage collapsed in 1970. Its failure could be attributed in part to an affair Seberg is said to have had with Clint Eastwood, and another with a college student (while she and Gary were separated). That relationship resulted in a daughter. Seberg and Gary were divorced by the end of the year, yet they remained extremely close. They jointly filed a lawsuit against *Newsweek*, which, along with other publications, had alleged that the father of Seberg's daughter was a Black Panther, a cousin of Malcolm X. The stress from this gossip led Seberg to attempt suicide and to give birth prematurely. The baby died two days later.

Throughout the 1960s, Gary published a number of books, but he also acquired new credentials as a director and screenwriter. (Both of the films he directed starred Seberg.) Others adapted Gary's books for the screen as well, and these productions involved some big names. John Huston directed *The Roots of Heaven*, starring Errol Flynn, Trevor Howard, and Orson Welles. The film *The Man Who Understood Women* starred Henry Fonda and Leslie Caron. Peter Ustinov directed Paul Newman, Sophia Loren, and David Niven in *Lady L*. Charlotte Rampling appeared in an adaptation of *The Ski Bum*.

Gary's amazing feat of self-invention now seemed complete. This Russian Jew turned Frenchman was a war hero, a diplomat, a renowned and widely translated author, and a film director, and for eight years he had been the husband of a young and beautiful Hollywood actress. He owned residences in Paris, Majorca, and Switzerland, and on the French Riviera. He was fluent in Russian, Polish, French, and English, and knew some German, Bulgarian, Arabic, and Hebrew. He was a legend of his own making, and against all odds, he had pulled it off. Even though his reputation as a writer had waned somewhat in the 1960s, he still seemed to lead a rather enviable life. His story should end there, it seems, but instead it starts anew. This is where things get really interesting, and deeply sad.

With all the gaps in biographical information—and all the misinformation—concerning Romain Gary, it is difficult to assemble a comprehensive narrative of his entire life, though biographers in recent years have tried. One fact, however, is well established: at a certain point, Roman Kacew no longer wished to be Romain Gary. Feeling as though he'd been typecast, he reached an impasse. So he became someone else.

In January 1974, the French publisher Éditions Gallimard received a manuscript called *La solitude du python à Paris*. It arrived in an envelope that appeared to have been sent from Brazil, by a French businessman on behalf of his friend. Eventually the publisher passed on it, but sent it along to Mercure de France, a division of Gallimard. The novel, later called *Gros-Câlin* (also known as *Cuddles*) was published that year. It told the story of a lonely IBM employee who lived in a Paris apartment with his pet python. The author was Émile Ajar. It was an immediate best seller.

Only a select group knew that Ajar was Gary: his typist, his son, Seberg, his attorneys in Geneva and New York, and a longtime friend. They carefully protected his secret. Once, when he was young, Diego watched a show on television in which a critic mercilessly trashed the work of Romain Gary. She then exclaimed, "Ah! Ajar—now *there's* a talent of a quite different order!" The boy glanced toward his father and slyly winked at him.

It's unclear how Gary arrived at his nom de plume, but some speculate that "Émile" was derived from the bastard child of Gauguin, whom Gary had fictionalized in a novel. "Ajar" is Russian for "glowing embers" and was also the acronym for a Jewish veterans group.

When *Gros-Câlin* was short-listed for the Renaudot Prize, Gary found himself in an ethical quandary. The prize was intended for the first novel by a new, undiscovered talent. Not wanting to deprive a young writer of a significant prize, Ajar withdrew his work from consideration. This honorable act merely fed the flame of public interest, and Gary quickly enlisted a cousin, Paul Pavlowitch, to play the "real-life" role of Ajar. Now people could put a face to the mysterious author (or so they thought). "Ajar" had his photograph taken and even gave interviews. "It was a new birth," Gary admitted later. "I was renewing myself. Everything was being given me one more time."

Before the birth of Ajar, Gary had already begun planning a second act. Initially he'd considered a kind of performance art ruse, in which an old friend named Sacha Kardo-Sessoëf would sign his name to detective fiction that Gary had written. His friend declined, as did another, so the role-playing idea was tossed. Instead, Gary produced a trial run for Ajar, under a different guise. In the spring of 1974, a spy novel called *Les têtes de Stéphanie*, by Shatan Bogat, was published. This unknown author was praised by critics for writing "with the stroke of a master." The press release featured a detailed (and peculiar) biography: "Thirty-nine years old, son of a Turkish immigrant, Shatan Bogat was born in Oregon. He directs a fishing and shipping business in the Indian Ocean and Persian Gulf. The black market arms trade inspired one of his novels. He won the Dakkan Prize in 1970 for his coverage of international gold and weapons traffickers." The prize did not actually exist, nor any earlier novels, but no one had bothered to verify the information.

The critics loved Bogat. One reviewer said that the author's style was "100% American, both explosive and relaxed, but with an appreciation of the Persian Gulf's local color that is not from the eye of a tourist."

Unfortunately, sales were sluggish. The publisher, Robert Gallimard, decided to out the author in a radio interview, hoping the news might provide a much-needed sales boost. He revealed that "Bogat" was actually Romain Gary. In a later edition of the novel, Gary explained his use of a pseudonym in that instance: "I did it because I sometimes feel the need to change identities, to break free of myself, if only for the duration of a book."

If Gallimard had not exposed the hoax, would anyone have discovered the author's identity? Perhaps not. Journalists can be a lazy bunch.

In any case, now Gary was ready to become Ajar.

His alter ego was an Algerian immigrant, born in 1940, and a former medical student who, after performing an illegal abortion, had fled to Brazil, where he now lived. Some critics were suspicious about Ajar's identity, wondering whether an eminent figure such as Raymond Queneau or Jean Paulhan might have taken a pseudonym. Yet as the scholar Ralph Schoolcraft notes in his fascinating 2002 study, *Romain Gary: The Man Who Sold His Shadow* (the first major examination in English of Gary's life and work), the author had left plenty of clues that Ajar was a mask. Anyone who poked around enough would have found evidence linking Ajar's work to Gary's own novels. (Gary later admitted that Ajar's books "often contained the same sentences, the same turns of phrase, the same human beings.") Yet no one picked up on the trail of crumbs. With Ajar, Gary was trying to shed the influence of the literary establishment of which he was now a familiar member. "I was an author who was classified, catalogued, taken for granted," he later complained. Ajar opened the door to experimentation and novelty, and to another new start for his career. Critics would have to approach the work from a fresh perspective because Ajar was an unknown quantity, free of baggage.

Following the success of *Gros-Câlin*, in 1975 Ajar published a second novel, *La vie devant soi* (also known as *Madame Rosa*). A reviewer in *Le Monde* proclaimed it "a *Les Misérables* for the twentieth century." The novel explored the relationship between an orphaned Arab boy named Momo and Madame Rosa, a heavyset sixty-eight-year-old Auschwitz survivor who was once a "lady of the night." (A film adaptation was released in 1968.) With this work, Ajar's reputation was assured. The first printing of fifty thousand copies sold out quickly and the book became a best seller. The author could count Marlene Dietrich among his fans. Today, the novel remains the top-selling French novel of the twentieth century, with more than a million copies sold.

Although some suspected that Ajar was a pseudonym, no one associated it with Gary. In news accounts, Gary's name had been mentioned, but simply as another example of a pseudonymous author. Some were convinced that Ajar was a Lebanese terrorist; others believed that the eccentric author was an American; still others said that the work was the product of a clandestine collective. And once, Gary met a woman who claimed to have had an affair with Ajar. "He was a terrific fucker," she said.

Eventually, this mystery would prove to be the most scandalous event in the French literary world since the publication of Pauline Réage's *Histoire d'O*. One half-joking theory was that the savvy culprit behind Ajar was Réage's illegitimate son.

All was mere fun and games until *La vie devant soi* won the 1975 Goncourt. Because Paul Pavlowitch had done such a fine job selling himself as Ajar, the jury members had all they needed to see that the author was real, that they were not being played for fools. Satisfied that Ajar really did exist, they awarded the deserving young author his prize.

This event was no happy accident. Gary had worked tirelessly behind the scenes, managing his accommodating cousin like a puppet. Pavlowitch eventually gave in-person interviews, but first he had to trick Ajar's own publishing house, Mercure de France, into believing, beyond any doubt, that Ajar was flesh and blood. It was an absolutely brilliant scheme. As Ralph Schoolcraft recounts in his book:

> Gary then prepared a couple meetings, plotting out Pavlowitch's role in minute detail. The impersonation would be something of a high-wire act, for Pavlowitch had to improvise his demeanor and remarks within the boundaries of Gary's prearranged script. Pavlowitch began by sending Mercure de France a blurry photograph of himself for promotional use (the photo, taken years earlier in Guadeloupe, had the advantage of showing him prior to the growth of the bushy, long hair and extravagant moustache that he was sporting in 1975).

Pavlowitch-as-Ajar even signed the publishing contracts and collected a check in person. He went so far as to enlist his wife, Annie, to play the role of Ajar's girlfriend. When the head of his publishing house wanted to spend more time with Ajar, a weekend together in Copenhagen was arranged, which went off without a hitch. During that weekend, Pavlowitch autographed a stack of "his" books as a favor to the publisher. He dutifully personalized his inscriptions, just as she requested, addressing them to members of various prize juries, including the Goncourt.

As Gary himself would explain later, the politics behind the Goncourt were rather heated, and authors had to make nice to become literary darlings. It was a highly rarefied and incestuous world. "I am not the only person to have spoken of the 'literary terror,' of the coteries, of the cliques with their claques, of cronyism, of 'you scratch my back and I'll scratch yours,' of debts repaid and accounts settled," he wrote. "Outside Paris there is no trace of that pathetic little will to power." The back-scratching was exhausting and humiliating, and after a while Gary had come to detest his critics and the phoniness of his milieu: "I developed a profound disgust of publishing anything."

Pleased with the success of the encounters he'd concocted for Ajar, Gary upped the demands on his cousin, who complied with each new directive. Personal information was given to the press, but not too much; and with his unkempt appearance and slouchy demeanor, Pavlowitch had no trouble passing as a bohemian writer in exile. His performance wasn't always flawless (he occasionally got minor details wrong), but the public was so eager to embrace "Ajar" that discrepancies went unnoticed. After a while, he and Gary could simply sit back and enjoy the fruits of their labors. Journalists did all the rest. "As soon as it became public," Pavlowitch later revealed, "it no longer depended on us." When a reporter once suggested to Gary the similarities between his and Ajar's work, Gary replied that he was flattered, and that perhaps Ajar was guilty of plagiarism.

For some factions in the literary world, the selection of Ajar for the Goncourt was highly controversial, and the usual protests took an especially ugly turn that year. There were bomb threats. Gary, growing nervous, attempted to heed the advice of one of his lawyers, who'd urged him to have "Ajar" decline the prize as a magnanimous gesture. Recusing himself, it turned out, was not Gary's choice to make. The Goncourt jury issued a terse, huffy, unambiguous statement, announcing that "the Academy votes for a book, not a candidate. The Goncourt Prize cannot be accepted or refused any more than birth or death. Mr. Ajar remains the laureate." And that was that.

The problem? An author can be awarded the Goncourt only once. Romain Gary had already won. That he could (secretly) win again gave his ego a significant boost and confirmed that, at sixty-one, he was still an important cultural figure—even if under the cloak of someone else. He'd shown that his talent was still intact. To throw people off the scent, Gary provided a friendly but neutral comment in support of Ajar. "I liked *Gross-Câlin,*" he said, "but I haven't read *Madame Rosa* yet. I don't think the author will stay in hiding much longer."

He was right. Events took another bizarre twist, though, when more than one reporter tracked "Ajar" to Pavlowitch's home, and even uncovered Pavlowitch's relation to Gary. But instead of recognizing that Pavlowitch was a proxy for Gary, who was the real man behind Ajar, the press assumed that the bold Pavlowitch had acted alone—and that the has-been Gary must have envied his relative's turn in the spotlight. Rather than attempt to seize control of this narrative, Gary and his cousin embraced it. Pavlowitch took the hit, crafting a story about how he'd adopted the Ajar pseudonym to launch his own career independently, so as not to exploit Gary's celebrity. This story made Pavlowitch a sympathetic figure and drew attention away from Gary. Meanwhile, Gary cheered on his cousin from the sidelines, joking to the media that there was no way he could have found the time to write Pavlowitch's books as well as his own—and encouraging the literary world to accept the talented Pavlowitch into its fold. He responded angrily to a journalist who persisted in suggesting that Gary himself, not Pavlowitch, was Ajar. "Your maneuver consists of cutting the balls off a newcomer by attributing his work to me," he said, "all the while protecting yourself with a 'maybe.' Even by Parisian standards, this is truly low."

Gary was beginning to come undone, increasingly unable to deal with the pressure of keeping up his fabricated self. Determined to put a definitive end to lingering guessing games, he sat down to write. In a state of almost manic fury—just two weeks after the (false) revelation that Pavlowitch was Ajar—in his "Geneva hideout," Gary finished another manuscript.

Entitled *Pseudo* and published in December 1976, the book purported to be a complete, uncensored confession of the entire Ajar affair. It sold modestly. Written as a novel, it was nonetheless meant to be interpreted as autobiography. The narrator was a madman telling his story from a psychiatric ward, but many of the events and motivations he described were true. (They were, however, told in a highly distorted form, and ascribed to the wrong person.) To the world, it seemed that the story of Ajar had at last been unraveled by the man himself. This should be the end of the story, but it isn't. Not quite.

There was one glitch: *Pseudo* was presented as the confession of Paul Pavlowitch, not Romain Gary. This is a confusing twist, but Gary had largely told the truth about his own story, providing many accurate details—he had simply attached the wrong name to it. Some of the issues he "revealed" as belonging to Pavlowitch/Ajar were invented, but others were actually his own. (There's mention of a doctor telling the author that he masturbates too much, a colorful anecdote that may or may not have been true.) In this way, Gary was able to seek redemption and at the same time deny his identity. He'd told a story that was at once fictional and true. He even inserted himself into the novel as a character called Uncle Bogey. The Princeton University scholar David Bellos, who translated *Pseudo* for the 2010 American edition (as *Hocus Bogus*), called the book "one of the most alarmingly effective mystifications in all literature. . . . Almost every sentence of the book is a double take."

In *Pseudo*, Ajar-as-Pavlowitch describes being pressured to adopt a pseudonym:

> Publish! It'll be good for you. Use a nom de plume. And don't worry! Nobody will guess you could do it. If it's any good, they'll say it's got art and technique and that it can't have been done by a beginner. That it's the work of a real pro. They'll leave you alone. They'll say you're just a straw man or a ghost. Or a whore.

Because Gary was unable or unwilling to speak as himself, he hid yet again, like a coward, behind his cousin. (He phoned Pavlowitch to tell him what he'd done only after it was completed.) At his cousin's expense, Gary had cleared his own name for good, and *presto!* Mystery solved. Ajar was Pavlowitch, who was a lunatic.

But this time Pavlowitch was not a willing accomplice. He'd loved his cousin dearly—and felt grateful that Gary had paid for his education at Harvard—but now his devotion reached a breaking point. He felt used and discarded. The neurotic, paranoid, delusional "narrator" of *Pseudo* had been presented under Pavlowitch's *actual* name, and this was unforgivable. He worried that his reputation might be harmed beyond repair, and he had his wife to consider as well. To Pavlowitch, this book seemed an aggressive and repugnant act. The rift between the men did not heal, as Gary showed little remorse toward his cousin, no gratitude for all that Pavlowitch had done on his behalf, and no real grasp of the perilous implications of *Pseudo*.

Nor does the story end there. Gary wrote yet *another* confession, but this one he gave only to friends, with the assumption that it should be released posthumously. (It was.) Titled *Vie et mort d'Émile Ajar* (*The Life and Death of Émile Ajar*), the piece explained his motivations and frustrations. "The truth is that I was profoundly affected by the oldest protean temptation of man: that of multiplicity," he wrote. "A craving for life in all its forms and possibilities, which every flavor tasted merely deepened. . . . As I was simultaneously publishing other novels under the name of Romain Gary, the duality was perfect."

He signed off the piece, dated March 21, 1979: "I've had a lot of fun. Good-bye, and thank you."

Upon the release of this text, the French literary establishment was outraged. They perceived Gary's doubleness as mockery directed at them, an attack on the very institutions that had crowned him, and they retaliated as they saw fit. Indeed, Gary's posthumous reputation would suffer as a result. Most of his books are out of print in the United States, some have never been translated into English, and those that are available are not easy to find. (In France, however, his books have never gone out of print.)

A few months after the author had written the true confession of his Ajar pseudonym, he was shattered by devastating news: Jean Seberg was dead. On August 30, 1979, having gone missing for eleven days, she was found on the backseat of her car. Her death at age forty was an apparent suicide—a verdict some still consider questionable—caused by an overdose of alcohol and barbiturates. Gary was inconsolable.

On December 2, 1980, in the Paris apartment where he lived alone, he shot himself in the head. He left behind a suicide note in ninety-six words.

For the press—

Nothing to do with Jean Seberg. Devotees of the broken heart are requested to look elsewhere. Obviously it could be blamed on a nervous depression. But if so it would be one which I've had since I became a man and which enabled me to succeed in my literary work. But why, then? Perhaps you should look for the answer in the title of my autobiographical book *The Night Will Be Calm* and in the last words of my last novel: "There's no better way to say it, I have expressed myself completely."

She was bipolar and sexually confused

CHAPTER 13

James Tiptree, Jr. & ALICE SHELDON

On May 19, 1987, a seventy-one-year-old woman and her eighty-four-year-old husband were found lying in bed together, hand in hand, dead of gunshot wounds, at their home in McLean, Virginia.

Just before midnight, the woman had phoned a family attorney to warn him that she planned to kill her husband and herself. She calmly asked that he notify the police. When the officers arrived at the house, they found the couple alive, concluded that the situation was under control, and left. Two hours later, the woman phoned the lawyer to tell him that she had killed her husband. Again she asked him to summon the police. Then she called her husband's son and said that she had shot his father. Although she claimed that she and her husband had agreed in advance upon a suicide pact, she had waited until he fell asleep to kill him. At about 3:30 in the morning, she shot herself in the head.

This event marked the tragic and dramatic end to the lives of Huntington Sheldon and his wife, Alice Bradley Sheldon. It was sick and scandalous, like something out of a gothic novel. In fact, Alice had been a wildly imaginative writer, intensely driven, producing science fiction for more than a decade using a male pseudonym. She kept her alter ego a secret even from those closest to her. ("At last I have what every child wants, a real secret life . . . nobody else's damn secret but MINE," she wrote in her diary in 1970.) Assuming this guise gave her the confidence to write and allowed her to become the "son" she believed her father had always wished he'd had. It also freed her to explore another deeply buried self—one that harbored a shameful yet undeniable sexual desire for women.

Aside from becoming famous—and considered among the most important science-fiction authors of the twentieth century, along with writers such as Philip K. Dick—Alice Sheldon led many extraordinary lives. She was an exceptional painter, a brilliant storyteller, and passionately interested in science; she had eloped at age nineteen, become pregnant, and had an abortion in her first year of marriage; divorced, enlisted in the army, and worked for the CIA; she had become a poultry farmer; and she had earned an undergraduate degree at age forty-three, followed by a Ph.D. in experimental psychology. Literary success came later still.

Born in Chicago in 1915, Alice Hastings Bradley (later known as Alli) was the only child of charismatic, wealthy, glamorous, and eccentric parents. Her formidable mother, Mary, was a prolific travel and fiction author and a popular lecturer; her attorney father, Herbert, was also an explorer and hunter who led expeditions into unmapped regions of central Africa. Those trips into the Congo provided Mary with material for two children's books. Yet Mary did not just accompany her husband on African hunting expeditions; she carried her own rifle and killed lions and tigers herself, proudly bringing back the skins as souvenirs. The Bradleys, both Republicans, were often featured in the society and gossip pages of local newspapers. They had a large circle of friends; loved to give parties; and employed nannies, a chauffeur, and a cook. Alice was pampered and spoiled, but she was also lonely and never felt comfortable in her affluent surroundings. "I was unpopular," she once complained, "except with dull adults."

When Alice was four, her mother gave birth to another daughter, Rosemary, who lived for only a day. Mary never recovered from her grief. "She didn't provide a model for me," Alice wrote later of her mother. "She provided an impossibility." The barrier was, among other things, vocational, but above all, Mary's idealization of femininity left Alice anguished, her identity a blur. As Alice struggled throughout her life to achieve a sense of wholeness, to feel at peace with her gender, Mary projected confidence, accomplishment, and uncomplicated, effortless sensuality.

Alice's artistic inclinations were encouraged—but only so far. Mary's needs and her desire for attention (especially from male admirers) always came first. "She had emotion enough for 10," Alli wrote of her mother, "but I got it all, and was always—perhaps wrongly—aware that had the others existed she wouldn't have cared much for me." Later she would recall that having a mother who seemed to do everything well was "bad for a daughter because you identify with her. And without meaning to, you compete. And to be in competition with Mary was devastation, because anything I could do she could do ten times as well." Alice's father was cool and distant, a welcome contrast to her mother's dependent, possessive behavior.

Mary's emotional neediness was too much pressure for a child to bear. Alice felt compelled to be a compliant "good girl," managing her own anxieties, anger, and unhappiness so as not to upset her mother. Although Alice suspected that "everybody wants to wipe the world out a couple of times a day," she kept such notions to herself. Decades later she admitted that she'd lived with "a silent inner terror" of not succeeding enough to warrant her parents' praise. "[A]ll my early life was lanced with that fear; if I wasn't somehow Somebody, it would represent such a failure I'd have to kill myself to keep my parents from knowing how I'd betrayed their hopes."

She also had to suppress her intense dislike of her own name, which carried "joyless connotations of 'Alice, eat your spinach.' 'Alice, go to bed.'" As she discovered early on, there was power, and a thrilling sense of escape, in naming yourself, in reclaiming your identity. She fled the unpleasantness of daily life through books. Alice was an avid reader and especially loved Kipling. Later she insisted that everything she knew about writing stories and plotting "came from Kipling, and will probably end there." Eventually (following the unmasking of her pseudonym), Alice gave an interview in which she pointedly quoted the end of his poem "The Appeal":

> And for the little, little span
> The dead are borne in mind,
> Seek not to question other than
> The books I leave behind.

As a child, Alice also enjoyed reading science fiction, including H. P. Lovecraft and a pulp magazine called *Weird Tales*. It was exactly the kind of literary material that her mother would have found vulgar and unseemly, and this made her love it even more.

Alice was sent to boarding school in Switzerland, where she did her best to fit in, but she was socially awkward, moody, and a poor student. She made her first suicide attempt there, cutting herself with razor blades. Lonely and struggling with what would be a lifelong battle with depression—fifty years later, Alice was diagnosed as bipolar—she was desperate to return home. But her father wrote to her that "it would not be fair to your school, nor to us, nor to you to come home in the middle of the year." Convinced that the challenge of an academic experience abroad would build character, Herbert urged her not to give up. In any case, he gave her no choice. "I'll trust you to be a good sport and see it through like a little lady," he wrote in another letter. Mary, who deplored candid displays of emotion as much as her husband did, wrote to Alice cheerily, "You are taking life the right way, darling, if you keep jolly and keep going—that's all any of us can do." Eventually Alice attended a small boarding school in New York, and even though she felt happier there, the headmistress observed astutely that "[t]he task of adjusting herself to her contemporaries is not an easy one."

As her sexuality developed, Alice felt ambivalent toward other girls. In some ways she preferred the company of boys, who seemed much more straightforward emotionally. Her relations with them were flirty, easy, and fun. In the presence of girls, Alice often felt annoyed by their frivolous, superficial behavior and their hierarchical approach to friendship, yet she felt strongly attracted to them as well. Girls turned her on. They excited her in ways she found deeply unsettling, but she did not pursue her feelings beyond a few fumbling encounters. The passion she felt was unrequited, anyway, and remained so: her desire for women would never be fulfilled (at least, not as far as anyone knows; it has never been confirmed that Alice had any affairs with women). Sexual love provoked frustration and torment, but nothing more. The only coming out Alice experienced was as a debutante, in 1934, when she was nineteen years old.

That was the year she met a wealthy twenty-one-year-old Princeton student, Bill Davey, who was a guest at her debutante party. Alice was still an undergraduate at Sarah Lawrence College. They eloped almost immediately—the wedding was front-page news in the *Chicago Tribune*—and Mary coldly informed Alice that she had broken her father's heart. The marriage lasted just six years. "He was beautiful, he was charming, he was a poet, he had references from the deans at Princeton," Alice would recall years later, "but they forgot to mention that he was an alcoholic and supporting half the whores in Trenton."

Initially, getting married seemed to promise Alice a chance to liberate herself from her parents, and from her sense of inertia and sexual confusion. It would prove that she was a "normal" heterosexual woman fulfilling what was expected of her. But this marriage was hell. Bill was as unstable as his wife, who also drank too much. Both of them slept with other people. Their fights were often physically violent, and their reconciliations were short-lived. The sex was mutually unsatisfying. (Alice described it in her journal as "a mechanical farce.") She was uncomfortable with her own body, and quite miserable having sex with a man. "Oh god pity me I am born damned they say it is ego in me I know it is man all I want is man's life," she wrote in a notebook five years before her death, "my damned oh my damned body how can I escape it. . . . I am going crazy, thank god for liquor." It was not surprising that Alice's gender dysphoria would lead her to inhabit a male self so that she could feel in control as an author. Even after her second marriage, to Huntington Sheldon, her struggles with sex and sexuality continued. "I am (was) notoriously fucked up about sex," she once admitted in a letter to a friend.

Meanwhile, during her tempestuous first marriage Alice was beginning to find her way as an artist, though as a painter, not as a writer. She started to show her work and was included in a group exhibition at the Art Institute of Chicago. For the next five years, she toiled away at her paintings while struggling through her moribund marriage. "Happy is the person who has never loved another," she wrote in her journal in 1941. Alice became convinced that she was constitutionally incapable of intimacy, and realized that she had to end her marriage. That summer, she left Bill. He promptly filed for divorce and remarried within a few months.

The collapse of this relationship ended her ambitions as a painter, too. Although she knew that she was talented, Alice felt certain that her true vocation lay elsewhere. She offered a harsh self-assessment of her potential as a visual artist: "I was a good grade B, no more, only with a quickness at new tricks which made ignorant souls call me an A." She decided to invest her intellect and energy in writing instead. Her parents helped her get a job as an art critic for the recently launched *Chicago Sun*, where she earned sixty dollars a week. She didn't especially like journalism, but she knew she had to start somewhere.

In 1942, when the controversial Women's Army Auxiliary Corps (later the Women's Army Corps) was created by Congress, Alice decided to join. She wanted to serve her country, move toward a different kind of career, and feel useful and accomplished. She also wanted to put more distance between herself and her failed marriage, and to cultivate more structure and discipline in her life. The pretty twenty-seven-year-old arrived at the recruiting office in "three-inch heels and my little chartreuse crepe-de-chine designer thing by Claire somebody, and my pale fox fur jacket." When she showed up for basic training in Des Moines, Iowa, she marveled at the sight of women "seen for the first time at ease, unselfconscious, swaggering or thoughtful, sizing everything up openly, businesslike, all personalities all unbending and unafraid." At the time, it was the most exciting experience of her life to be surrounded by twelve thousand women. "What a range!" she later marveled.

Eventually she went to the Pentagon, where she did intelligence work during World War II, and spent the next few years having affairs with men. She seemed to have resigned herself to the fact that her romantic future, however imperfect, inauthentic, or unsatisfying, would be with a man. And she spent her spare time writing fiction. Her efforts, filled with autobiographical elements, fell flat. ("'Ouch' simply is not a story," she wrote years later, in a letter to a friend.) It would take the authority and secrecy of a male pseudonym, and the genre of science fiction, to transform her pain, anguish, and desire into compelling material.

Stationed in London in 1945, Alice met the man with whom she would spend the rest of her life: Huntington "Ting" Sheldon, a forty-two-year-old army colonel who had been a Wall Street banker. He fell in love with her—hard. Ting came from the "right" social class; like Alice, he'd found a sense of purpose during wartime and had used military service to escape the confines of his past. He was born in Greenwich, Connecticut, to a family that had earned a fortune in banking and lost it in the Great Depression. He attended boarding school at Eton and university at Yale. Though Ting was a calm, steady, dependable presence, he was not without baggage—he'd already been married and divorced twice and had three children.

But now Ting wanted to marry her, and as a thirty-year-old woman, Alice felt she was in no position to refuse. She wanted children; she wanted to feel cared for and secure. For the most part, Ting proved a supportive, easygoing partner who gave her space when she needed it. He also put up with her mood swings. But there were problems. Like her first husband, Ting drank a lot. He was emotionally distant and did not share her love of reading. And their sex life was terrible. A year later, Alice's literary agent, Harold Ober, submitted a short story she'd written to the *New Yorker*, and it appeared in the magazine on November 16, 1946. "The Lucky Ones" was the first and last piece she would publish under her own name. Nor would she ever submit another story to the *New Yorker*. She had been unhappy with the intensive editing process, complaining that "it was astounding how they edited me into *New Yorker*ese," and she found the magazine as a whole too polished and genteel.

Despite her family pedigree, Alice was anything but polished and genteel. Among the multitudes within her were, she said, "a female wolf who howls, and a gross-bodied workman who moves things and sweats, and a thin rat-jawed person who is afraid and snaps . . . [and] a disastrous comedian who every so often comes roaring out of the wings and collapses the show. Now it seems clear that while one might get one or two of these characters to write for a living, most of them won't go along, and the comedian's opinion is unprintable."

Her impressive publishing accomplishment at such a young age notwithstanding, the next several years hardly indicated that Alice was on her way to becoming a famous writer—one who, in the words of Isaac Asimov decades later, "has produced works of the first magnitude and has won the wild adulation of innumerable readers." In fact she seemed about as far away as possible from a literary life. She felt lost. Depressed by her lack of sexual chemistry with Ting and her ambivalence toward their marriage, she tried to leave him at one point. "What shall I do?" she wrote in a letter to her husband, announcing her departure. "Lie and deceive, put on a bold face and knock the bottom out of everything? Drift in this void and try to work? I cannot hold the beast that is me in check much longer." But she didn't leave, and apparently never even gave him the letter. (Eventually, the couple agreed on an open marriage.) Alice abandoned her attempts at journalism, having experienced little success at selling pieces as a freelancer. Ting, too, was adrift in his work, unable to secure a new job on Wall Street.

After seeing an ad in the *New York Times* offering a chicken hatchery for sale in New Jersey—with promises of high income and working only half the year—the Sheldons impulsively decided to buy the business, which they ran for nearly five years. The work was hard and the routine dull, but at first the rigid structure of their days was good for Alice. When she realized, however, that she could not conceive a child, she was devastated and began spending the little free time she had writing both poetry and prose, including the beginning of a mystery novel and some science fiction. In knowing that she would never become a mother, she felt betrayed by her own body. She decided to confront this issue in an essay, asserting that a woman's body was an "unpredictable, volcanic, treacherous, merry, rather overpowering thing to live with." She likened her body to "a large and only partly tamed animal, day and night the damn thing is being itself, with its own semi-inscrutable operations."

The characteristics of her gender—punishing and restrictive, yet wildly untamable—left her feeling repeatedly "derailed" in life, and she described being a woman as an almost debilitating condition, and certainly a steep disadvantage. She argued (rather reductively, even for the era) that if she had been born male, she might have been more aggressive and could have become "a rather prosy young engineer or research scientist," married with children. "Instead of which, I was born a girl," she wrote, "and my life has been quite different. . . . I have had about four different and disparate careers. I have been married twice. I have seriously upset a great many of the people who came close to me. . . . I have been called brilliant, beautiful, neurotic, suicidal, restless, amoral, anarchic, dangerous, diffuse, weak, strong, perverse, and just plain nuts." It seemed to Alice that the impossible fact of living as a woman was enough to make anyone despondent or crazy. She devised no solutions to her profound quandary, but she did extol the virtues of "a great deal more homosexual activity on the part of women." Rather than adhering to binary notions of gender, Alice proposed five: men, women, children, mothers, and "human beings." Unsure of where or how she fit into her own odd schema, she concluded wearily that it was perhaps best "in most of the waking hours of a non-pregnant woman to consider her a kind of man."

In 1952, when Alice was thirty-seven, she and Ting turned to their former military and government contacts, sold the (woefully unprofitable) hatchery business, and moved to Washington, D.C., to work as analysts for the CIA. Ting worked in high-level intelligence positions for the next seventeen years, whereas Alice's career was low-ranking, much to her frustration, and lasted only a few years. As a woman in a male-dominated agency, she stood no chance of having a powerful or well-paying job, but as someone who placed a high value on secrecy and privacy, she felt entirely comfortable in an environment that promoted covertness as policy. "I always had a feeling there were big things going on in her life that she would share with nobody," one friend recalled of Alice. "She could have been living three or four lives at once."

Alice was by nature flirtatious, but at the CIA she remained sartorially gender-neutral, a look she found appealing. "Boyish clothes look younger, or healthier," she noted in an unfinished memoir in 1957, "because they contrast a woman's features with a man's, rather than with a girl's. In a clean white shirt I still look like a perverse young boy, and this is about my best effect, from the standpoint of attraction."

In 1955, Alice was in her third year at the CIA, on the verge of turning forty and deeply unhappy. Her mood swings were even more pronounced. She became addicted to prescription pills and at times felt suicidally depressed. Like many women, she felt conflicted about the gap between society's demands on women and her own desires. Which should she reject, and at what cost? She felt that as a writer, she had nothing important to say—or at least nothing that would be heard. She was expected to be a devoted wife and a faithful, hard-working CIA operative; with whatever energy was left, she could attempt to write. The most obvious effects of such strong pressure were her increased hostility toward Ting and her general sense of inertia. "O, how I want to be loved, me myself—" she confided in a letter that year, "—and how I fear it—and what bliss it might be—brrr!—and how easy to shelve this whole thing." That summer, she quit her job, left Ting, rented an apartment, and "really destroyed all traces of my former personality."

Self-creation and reinvention are deeply and quintessentially American notions (e.g., *The Great Gatsby*), and their appeal was not lost on Alice. A full decade before she would assume her pseudonym and launch her literary career, she felt the lure of inhabiting another identity. Alice was trapped in her nondescript life, and simply wanted to be someone else. For a start, she wanted the freedom of divorce and solitude. "I figure I have enough sub-personalities so I can build one up to where it is quite companionable," she wrote. She was convinced that "[t]here *is no way* I can be peacefully happy in this society and in this skin. I am committed to Uneasy Street."

After a year of aimless soul-searching, she returned to her husband, having resolved nothing. "So ensued a period of more milling (I'm a slow type) including some dabblings in academe," she later recalled.

Because she was unable to commit herself wholly to one enterprise, she accepted Ting as an essential and permanent part of her life and struggled to find fulfillment elsewhere. Her inability to give herself full time to writing was partly due to her profound ambivalence toward the task itself. She questioned its value and believed that writing was "an act of aggression." It was a betrayal, selfish, an act of exploitation. As Joan Didion famously noted, "Writers are always selling somebody out." Janet Malcolm, too, has described even journalism as "morally indefensible," and has characterized the journalist as "a kind of confidence man, preying on people's vanity, ignorance, or loneliness, gaining their trust and betraying them without remorse."

Alice decided to go to back to school to complete her undergraduate degree, which she earned, summa cum laude, at the age of forty-three. A friend and mentor at the time advised her that "the greatest favor you can do to others is being yourself as much as you can," but Alice was still grappling with what that meant. "Being, I imagine, must be very simple," she wrote back. "It is Becoming which is so messy and which I am all for."

In 1959, Ting and Alice moved to McLean, Virginia. Eight years later, Alice earned her doctoral degree in psychology at George Washington University. Her mother's physical health had severely declined—perhaps freeing Alice creatively—and she herself had survived another long period of depression. "Too much motor for the chassis," she noted of her emotional and mental vulnerability. She was burned out in every sense and on the verge of physical collapse. Amphetamines, cigarettes, and coffee were her sustenance. Just as she was completing her dissertation (and perhaps realizing that academia was too confining for her ambitions, and too boring), Alice began writing fiction again. Sci-fi authors such as Samuel R. Delaney, Ursula K. Le Guin, and J. G. Ballard were gaining prominence. Soon she would take her place among them.

Midlife is often said to be a period of reinvention, and Alice, with typical intensity, accomplished this to an extreme degree. At the age of fifty-two, she abandoned her role as a research scientist and scholar and began submitting her stories to science-fiction magazines. These were hardly highbrow literary publications, but she wasn't aiming for her work to appear in the *New Yorker* again. "I have a modest view of my talent. I haven't the ear for rhythm or the feel for style to encourage me to compete in the serious mainstream," she later admitted.

"And I certainly haven't the stomach to write 'mainstream' schlock, like *Jaws* or *Gone with the Wind*. Science fiction suits me just right. SF is the literature of ideas, and I am, I think, an idea writer."

Starting out, Alice wasn't fearless enough to submit her writings under her own name. Anonymity seemed best. "I am a reclusive type, afraid of meeting people, except on paper," she once admitted. A fateful trip to the supermarket with her husband in 1967 provided inspiration. Spotting a jar of Wilkin & Sons marmalade, she was struck by the label: "Tiptree," in a distinctive cursive print. (The name came from the English village near which Wilkin & Sons owned farmland and orchards.) For the impulsive Alice, it held the key to her new identity. "James Tiptree," she said to Ting. "Junior," he replied, without missing a beat. They laughed, but the name stuck and an author was born. Alice had intended to use a different pseudonym for each short story she submitted to magazines, but as it happened, Tiptree had such a rapid rise to success that she kept him.

In a biographical sketch written more than a decade later for *Contemporary Authors*, Alice offered a cursory description of her bold postdoctoral transformation: "At this point a heart problem forced temporary retirement at semester's end. Meanwhile, some SF stories written as a hobby were all selling, to the author's immense surprise. As health returned, the temptation to write more won out. The author rationalized this activity as a claim for a broader concept of 'science' than rocketry and engineering, and the aim of showing SF readers that there are sciences other than physics, that bio-ethology or behavioral psychology, for instance, could be exploited to enrich the SF field."

She continued: "But this writing had to be kept secret; the news that a new PhD with offbeat ideas was writing *science fiction* would have wakened prejudice enough to imperil any grant and destroy my credibility. . . . Luckily, the challenge of writing exerted its spell; retirement from university work became permanent without any great traumas, and the author found herself with a new line of effort ready-made for somewhat erratic health. . . . The first SF stories were naturally not expected to sell, so a pseudonym was selected at random (from a jam pot)."

By the time of that entry, her secret identity had been exposed for three years and "James Tiptree, Jr." was already buried.

She had enjoyed enviable success as Tiptree, however. On some level, the experience must have been bittersweet: only after she inhabited the role of a male author did she achieve fame. As herself, just another woman writer, no one had paid much attention. "I have this childish fascination with brute power," she admitted in an essay, written in her post-Tiptree years. "And since I have none, I am nothing." As only herself, Alice felt oppressed by a sense of powerlessness and believed that her "authentic" self lay elsewhere. " 'I' am not a writer," she wrote in her diary. " 'I' am what is left over from J.T. Jr., a mindless human female who 'lives' from day to day." Interestingly, in the late 1960s, women writers in increasing numbers had taken up science fiction and fantasy, and although this was a male-dominated field by any measure, it was not impossible for a woman to become successful in the genre. Alice did not see herself among them, but there were women she admired who did just that, such as Le Guin, a contented housewife and mother living a "conventional" life in Portland, Oregon; and Joanna Russ, an outspoken feminist best known for her award-winning, stylistically inventive novel *The Female Man*. Russ was also a lesbian, and this was not without its complications for her writing career—yet somehow it gave her permission to work freely, beyond the standard definitions of gender. Neither of those models would prove a comfortable fit for Alice, but Le Guin and Russ became two of Tiptree's favorite correspondents.

"Becoming" a man had seduced Alice partly because she believed it gave her access to power—and the possibilities that accompany power. "Alli Sheldon has no such choice," she lamented, and imagined what life might have been like if she had been born a boy. No matter how accomplished she was as a woman—and she was extraordinarily so, however hard on herself she was—Alice never felt relief from what she viewed as the constraints of her gender. "Always draining us is the reality of our inescapable commitment," she wrote, arguing that it is only women who "feel always the tug toward empathy, toward caring, cherishing, building-up—the dull interminable mission of creating, nourishing, protecting, civilizing—maintaining the very race. At bottom is always the bitter knowledge that all else is boys' play—and that this boys' play rules the world." Of course, for a woman of her generation, the prospect of being a writer hardly carried the same stigmas and constraints as it had for nineteenth-century iconoclasts such as the Brontës, George Sand, and George Eliot. But the "giants" of literature were men. And to become a major *sci-fi* writer, a woman within a cloistered subculture, she might as well have been living in the previous century. To her, this realm truly seemed an impenetrable boys' club. Things aren't nearly so dire now, but it remains a male-dominated field (less so as a result of her pioneering efforts).

Alice was airing her concerns about gender imbalance in an era of so-called second-wave feminism, but rather than accept herself as a passive victim, she never stopped pushing back. She never gave up. "Maybe all one can do is to say the hell with it," she wrote. "But—life is to *use*. Only, how? How? How? How?"

Writing under the cloak of Tiptree, she soon achieved success. She described once how "this letter from Condé Nast (who the hell was Condé Nast?) turns up in a carton. Being a compulsive, I opened it. Check." Her story "Birth of a Salesman" had been sold to the sci-fi magazine *Analog*; the story "Fault" was bought by another editor for twenty-five dollars. Within a few weeks, a third sold. Letters and checks were addressed to "James Tiptree, Jr.," so her alter ego began to seem like a real person, separate from her. He became a card-carrying member of the Science Fiction and Fantasy Writers of America (SFWA). He even had a nickname—he insisted on being called "Tip." And he enjoyed flirting in his correspondence with women. (Tip complimented one editor's assistant by calling her a "superdoll.") Some women developed crushes on him in return. One editor invited Tip to his wedding; of course, Tip had no choice but to decline. He mentored aspiring sci-fi writers—by mail, of course—and wrote fan letters to fellow authors he admired or envied, including Italo Calvino, Anthony Burgess, and Philip K. Dick. He was generous with praise for his fellow writers. "Who do I admire in SF?" he once wrote. "You and you and you as far as eye and memory reach, sir and madam. Some for this, some for that. All different. But more than that—I love the SF world. And I don't love easy."

When editors asked to meet Tiptree in person, they were given lame excuses. (One editor tried to call him, only to find that Tiptree was not listed in the phone book.) In retrospect, it seems incredible that the ruse was so easy to pull off. But it worked, so Alice simply kept going. Even though she regarded her early sci-fi stories as "mechanical and banal," they were selling, and the act of writing proved a pleasant diversion from the episodes of crushing depression that came on without warning. Yet her two selves were at odds: the charming Tiptree longed to connect, to find acceptance and kinship, to establish a sense of community in the sci-fi realm. He was witty, generous, and kind, a great raconteur, and always supportive of the endeavors and ambitions of his peers. But Alice was forced to act as his vigilant sentry, rejecting intimacy, withholding information, keeping outsiders at arm's length to protect her colossal secret. This internal clash between concealment and revelation was confusing and often painful to bear. "I've lived so deep under masks, my interior was built to satisfy me alone," she wrote in a letter five years before her death. "I have lived 60 years almost totally alone, mentally, and quite content to have it so. I'm fond of a hundred people who no more know 'me' than they know the landscape of Antarctica."

Although other science-fiction writers were secretive, they rarely hid from both editors and readers. Tiptree was especially reclusive and protective of his privacy, which only encouraged rumors about his motivation. Once, a group of curious fans, attending a local sci-fi convention, staked out Tiptree's P.O. box in McLean. Luckily Alice was in Canada at the time.

Readers wondered whether Tiptree was very young, Native American, secretly gay, or working undercover for the CIA. One editor wrote, "It has been suggested that Tiptree is female, a theory that I find absurd, for there is to me something ineluctably masculine about Tiptree's writing. I don't think the novels of Jane Austen could have been written by a man nor the stories of Ernest Hemingway by a woman, and in the same way I believe the author of the James Tiptree stories is male."

Anyone who attempted to extract biographical information met with resistance, aside from learning broad, generic facts. To Le Guin, with whom Tiptree's epistolary friendship endured even after his pseudonymous cover was blown, he once described himself as "an old battered Airedale, one-eyed and droop-eared, whose scarred paws have travelled a lifetime of lava plains." That's about as descriptive as he got about his appearance. He did, however, once venture so far as to send a "baby picture" to one of his correspondents—actually a photograph of Alice Sheldon at age one, in which she might easily have been mistaken for a boy.

In her extensive correspondence, Alice carelessly offered many of her own life experiences as Tip's, rather than making them up entirely—a misstep that would lead to the downfall of her alias. For instance, Tip told people that he was born in the "Chicago area," had traveled around colonial India and Africa as a child, joined the army, and had "some dabblings in academe." When Alice's elderly mother was ill, Tip described the burden of caretaking as his own. "At the moment I'm in and around the Chicago area, partly attending to family matters in the shape of an aged and ornery mother," he revealed in correspondence.

Perhaps Alice's inability or unwillingness to create an entirely fictional background—familial or professional—for Tiptree indicated that on some level she hoped someone would discover her secret and that she would be made whole—freed from the burdens of duality. But for a while, no one did. And because Tiptree had no voice or body for others to know, people gave free rein to their fantasies about him. One person imagined him as Ichabod Crane–like. Another believed him to be exceptionally handsome. One fanzine publisher wrote to Tiptree with his take on the author's physicality: "You like wild shirts and ties. You smoke a pipe. You type fast and grin a lot."

Whenever pressed about personal matters, Tiptree either ignored the queries or pushed back. "Does a writer ever stop telling you who he is?" he wrote in an interview conducted by mail with the editor Jeffrey Smith, arguing that an author's work should speak for itself and that it told readers everything they needed to know. "[M]aybe I believe . . . that the story is the realest part of the storyteller. Who cares about the color of Coleridge's socks? (Answer, Mrs. C.) Of course, I enjoy reading a writer's autobiography—or rather, *some* writers! A few. By far the most of them make me nervous, like watching a stoned friend driving a crowded expressway. For Chrissakes, *stop*!" He also insisted that "my mundane life is so uninteresting that it would discredit my stories." (Well, that was not exactly true.) Tiptree did reveal that "part of my secretiveness is nothing more than childish glee."

He suggested that one way to inhabit authorial identity was to use the "self as an experience laboratory, no sacred wall around the sealed black box of Me." In other words, it was merely a play space. Regardless, he believed (or claimed to believe) that an author's "real" self "leaks at every sentence," so that attempts to shield biographical details from the public were futile, anyway. Justifying his motives a dozen different ways, Tiptree remained defiant. "You know as well as I do we all go around in disguise," he wrote, describing each person as a "roomful" of human beings. Beneath our everyday decorum, he argued, were layers of ugly and messy emotions, including terror, rage, obsession, love, and shame. "So who the fuck cares whether the mask is one or two millimeters thick?"

Tip did a good job most of the time at maintaining his own mask—a little macho posturing here, a little raunchy joking there—

but it wasn't always a flawless performance. "Do you know, there's a good deal about you that seems to me more like women I know than like men I know in the way you handle your feelings?" Joanna Russ wrote to him.

He kept people intrigued by his brilliant talent as well as his demand for absolute privacy. Some claimed that his reticence was a put-on, a "publicity trick," as Alice later wrote. Curiosity about him continued to grow along with his reputation, perhaps because he defied categorizing in every sense. As Jeffrey Smith (who would become Tiptree's literary executor) noted, "What I was most interested in was the fact that in 1970, when there was a virtual war declared between the Old Wave and the New Wave in science fiction, Tiptree was being claimed by both camps."

"It's futile to ask as new a writer as me where he's tending or what his style might become," Tiptree wrote in response to a question from Smith. "Does a kid whose voice is changing know what's going to come out of his mouth?"

For whatever reason, Tiptree was rather expansive in his correspondence with Smith, and developed an unusual closeness and trust with him. Smith, who was respectful without being sycophantic, seems to have impressed Tiptree with astute interpretations of his work. "I'm beginning to feel like this was my last will and personal Time Capsule and it contains more on Tiptree than anybody including me will ever likely see or want to again," Tiptree confided to Smith in the final letter of their interview by mail, which went back and forth from December 3, 1970, until the end of January 1971.

The following year, having inhabited Tiptree for half a decade, Alice Sheldon began to feel constrained by writing as a man. She wanted to express her "feminine" voice, yet she wasn't willing to unmask herself entirely. She did the next best thing: Alice introduced Raccoona Sheldon, another alter ego. What a perfect name: raccoons, after all, are mask-wearing bandits, stealthy and clever.

It was actually Tiptree who announced the arrival of Raccoona—an old friend of his from Wisconsin—to Smith, mentioning that she was a gifted writer. Alice took just as much care of her female pseudonym as she had taken of the enigmatic Tiptree, buying Raccoona her own Olivetti typewriter—this one with a black ribbon to distinguish it from Tiptree's blue ribbon. Raccoona was given a distinct handwriting and signature, and a mailbox in her name at the post office.

Yet just as Alice would slip up in covering Tiptree's tracks, here, too, she was somewhat sloppy. For one thing, she'd given Raccoona her own surname. And supposedly Raccoona had also been published in the *New Yorker*. She was a talented illustrator, had dabbled in academia, and she'd had an abortion. She described herself as a former East Coast resident and a retired schoolteacher, but insisted that "really the less said the better" when it came to talking about her personal life. She had in common with Tiptree the requisite elusiveness, existing entirely on the page. (Raccoona's stories didn't pack the same wallop as Tiptree's work, however; he was by far the better writer.) Tiptree emphasized her shroud of mystery to Smith, warning him that his friend "is even more recessive than me and hard to talk to." When another editor accepted one of Raccoona's stories for publication, he was puzzled to receive no reply from the author. Eventually, she wrote apologetically to explain that her mother "had a heart attack down South." Soon afterward, an "embarrassed" Tiptree dashed off a letter about his friend as well: "I can't imagine what happened to Sheldon (Raccoona), unless she's been abducted by aliens . . . [It's possible] some of her multitudinous parasitic family has her tied up."

Raccoona had mixed success in getting her stories published, and better luck only when her pal Tiptree wrote cover letters of recommendation on her behalf. It is amusing to note that Raccoona felt exasperated and jealous that Tiptree—a man, of course—was getting his stories published by the same editors who were rejecting her work—with Alice being the dutiful midwife to them both. By this point, Alice wished, in a sense, that Tiptree were dead, but killing him off wasn't an option. The strain of maintaining relationships solely by mail was getting to her. "They're real," she wrote privately of the friendships she'd cultivated in the science-fiction world, "yet unreal insofar as they're carried on under an assumed name and gender. A lot of genuine relation comes through, but it's tainted to an unknown degree by falsity. Here I seem to have contrived another odd trap for myself." Why she set these traps is impossible to say, but surely the destructive messages lingering from her childhood had a lot to do with submerging herself in other selves.

In 1974, at least one of Tiptree's friends rightly sensed something amiss in his letters, though it was hard to know how to respond. "Is my friend whom I know and do not know troubled beyond all touch or reassurance?" wrote a worried Le Guin. "Is he *in* trouble? Is there nothing his friends whom he knows and does not know can do, or say, or be? Nothing that would help?"

Alice's ambivalence toward her male alter ego had started to affect her ability to play the role. She was tired and lonely. She asked Ting to lock her prescription pills in the medicine cabinet because she feared she would overdose. And at her lowest depths, she fantasized about killing Ting and then herself, but she wasn't yet able to go through with it.

Tiptree strained her nerves more than ever. He seemed point-less, this man named after a jar of jam at the supermarket. The following year, Alice described herself as descending into a "black pit" and admitted, "I personally am dying." As if to force Tiptree to fade away, Raccoona pointedly downplayed her relationship with him in a letter to Smith: "There seems to be some confusion about me and Tip Tiptree," she wrote. "Several people have written me as though I were an authority on him. I did know him when we were in the local 4th and 5th grades together, but I have not seen him in person for a couple of years." She continued: "We correspond in fits and starts. I take care of his mail when he comes through here to see his mother."

In November 1976, Tiptree sent Smith a letter as intimate and confessional as a diary entry: "Mother died last week," he wrote, "leaving me with a new dark strange place in the heart, and flashes of a lively, beautiful, intelligent, adventurous red haired young woman whom I had once known." The subsequent biographical details about Tiptree's mother, unfortunately, were too specific—they included where Tip's parents had lived for sixty-four years ("Father built the building and they took the whole top and made the first roof garden in Chicago")—and too similar to the newspaper obituaries of Alice's mother. It was already well known that Tiptree's mother (like Mary) had been an African explorer, hardly a typical biographical detail. Tip seemed to recognize that he'd spilled too much personal information. He ended by saying, "Well, this is a weird letter." It was. Yet he mailed it anyway.

The author had (inadvertently? deliberately?) laid out all the clues that would link Tiptree to Alice. It's no wonder: she was exhausted, anxious, and in very bad shape, despite Ting's efforts at managing her moods. She was hooked on prescription pills, including Percodan, Dexedrine, Valium, and Demerol. As for Tiptree, he'd become like one of the distorted figures in Francis Bacon's paintings—tortured and grotesque. The charade had run its course.

The outpouring of fact and emotion in Tiptree's letter was not lost on Smith. Nonetheless, he felt highly protective of the dear friend he'd never met or even spoken with on the phone. He didn't want Tip's cover blown, and didn't want to pry, but he couldn't resist investigating whether Tip's revealing missive was indeed a "road map to a newspaper obituary," as he recalled later. His research didn't take long: the first Chicago newspaper he found at the library, a copy of the *Tribune*, led him to the death notice of ninety-four-year-old Mary Hastings Bradley, who was survived by one child, a daughter. The obituary, aside from a minor element or two, matched the details of Tiptree's letter. How to reconcile "Uncle Tip" with the posh Alice Hastings Bradley Sheldon?

In her 1980 biographical sketch for *Contemporary Authors*, in a section she titled "The Pseudonym That Got Away," Alice wrote that when "the author's mother died after a long illness . . . Tiptree—who wrote only the truth in all letters—had imparted so many of the details of Mary Bradley's unusual life that when her obituary was read by certain sharp-eyed young friends, James Tiptree, Jr., was blown for good—leaving an elderly lady in McLean, VA, as his only astral contact."

To ease the aftermath of Alice's broken secret, Smith opened up to Tiptree first. In a gently honest letter, ever respectful of his friend's privacy, he wrote that he was not making "a demand for information," but warned, "I am going to be getting questions, and whatever you choose to disclose or withhold from me, please pass along the Party Line that I'm supposed to tell others."

He received a response—not from Tiptree, but from Alice Sheldon, who introduced herself. She asked that Smith keep her secret for a bit longer. He agreed. "How great," Alice wrote, but she was relieved beyond measure that the consuming role was no more. Her reply was casual: "Yeah. Alice Sheldon. Five ft 8, 61 yrs, remains of a good-looking girl vaguely visible, grins a lot in a depressed way, very active in spurts. Also," she added, "Raccoona."

To the very end, however, Alice insisted that there was no such thing as "male" or "female" writing. Instead, she believed there were only separate and varying styles of *bad* writing, and whether a weak voice belonged to a man or a woman was beside the point. She allowed that men perhaps had the edge when it came to black humor, and women had a knack for "heart-wringing," which was an odd statement of gender stereotyping by someone whose writing career had defied such notions.

It is intriguing that as Tip, she displayed a certain swagger, while Raccoona was more diffident and a less compelling writer. Alice admitted in an essay ("A Woman Writing Science Fiction," written six months before her suicide) that she didn't feel proud of using a male pseudonym to get ahead. She happened to choose a man's name as a lark, and stuck with it only because it worked so seamlessly. Frankly, she kept exploiting it because of the superior treatment she received as a man: her work was taken seriously, she was well regarded by the women with whom she corresponded as their "understanding" and empathetic male friend, and she occupied a place of power and influence among her peers—allowing her to challenge editors to publish more women writers. Alice said that she was ashamed of using a male guise to earn her place, while other women writers had languished or succeeded entirely on their own terms. "I had taken the easy path," she admitted.

As she began to make amends for her ruse, the responses she received were almost entirely supportive. "Dear Jim or Tip or Alice or Allie," one friend addressed her in a letter, reassuring her, "You are still the same person and I am still the same person and here we are." Ursula Le Guin was similarly kind: "And it is absolutely a delight, a joy, for some reason, to be truly absolutely flatfootedly surprised— it's like a Christmas present!" Joanna Russ, upon learning that Tip was a woman, didn't suppress her delight at the news, admitting that she liked "old women," expressing hope that they could meet "in the flesh"—they never would—and telling Alice bluntly that she should consider herself "well and truly propositioned. I was in love with you when you were 'James Tiptree Jr.' and have been able to transfer the infatuation to Allie Sheldon." Eventually, Alice declared that she was a lesbian in a letter to Russ, but she took things no further with Russ or any other woman.

Alice was crushed to find that some of the male writers she'd considered true friends—those who had ostensibly admired her work as Tiptree—turned their backs on her. ("Oh, how well we know and love that pretentiously amiable tone, beneath which hides the furtive nastiness!" she wrote.) She was heartbroken that some men were suddenly patronizing and condescending toward her, or that they abandoned her altogether. "If that is how I would have been received from the start," she wrote, "my hat is off to those brave women writing as women."

In her "Woman Writing Science Fiction" essay, she couldn't resist a dig at her erstwhile "friends." Noting that some of the male writers who'd been "a touch snotty" to her were perfectly nice to other women writers, she went straight to the core of the problem: "People dislike being fooled, and, quite innocently, I did fool them for ten years. Moreover, it seems to be very important, especially to men, to *know the sex* of the person they are dealing with. What's the use of being Number One in a field of two—i.e., *male*—if people can't tell the difference? I had not only fooled them, I had robbed them of relative status." Apparently, they felt emasculated, something they didn't find funny or even forgivable.

After the initial dizzying rush of revealing her true identity, Alice became severely depressed again. (Rightly so: being exposed meant that a part of her was now dead.) It was something like the shattering remorse that sets in after a breakup. Alice had gotten rid of this troublesome character, and now she wanted him back. Like an ex-lover, Alice could remember only the good that Tip had brought into her life; he had made her a celebrated science-fiction author and given her a supportive community, the likes of which she had never known. Without him, she felt crazy and unable to write.

In her journals, Alice detailed her sense of deprivation. The language she used was like that of someone wanting a sex change: "I do not 'match' my exterior." She wrote of feeling as if she inhabited her body like an alien and even yearned explicitly to become a man. Within her, too, remained a fervent desire to someday love a woman erotically *as a woman:* not to resort to sublimation, as she always had done, but to satisfy raw urges. This pull was profoundly disorienting, and the sudden limbo—for both her professional and her personal identity—intensified her self-hatred.

"Some inner gate is shut," she wrote. The revelation was terrifying. She was left with nowhere to go, no way out. As Tiptree, she'd immersed herself in his unbridled imagination; as Alice B. Sheldon, she noted ruefully that she had no discernible prose style other than "Enclosed please find payment." She was convinced that no one wanted to know her simply as Alice, and she called herself a "poor substitute" for Tip. Although she toyed with the idea of another pseudonym, Sylvester Mule, nothing came of it.

In an interview for *Contemporary Authors* (which would accompany her biographical sketch), Alice expressed her attitude toward separating a writer's work and life, and the damage that results when the latter overshadows the former. She felt this problem was especially acute in science fiction—a genre "that carries some sense of wonder"—and said that when "the camera suddenly pans and picks up the writer himself, he's slouched in a haze of smoke over his typewriter, and it's all come out of his little head. . . . Magic gone." She insisted that most writers were obnoxious or dull (never mind that she was neither), and spoke of façades not in her writing persona, but in daily life. The interview offered plenty of fascinating material. Alice revealed that since she suffered from paralyzing shyness, "Tiptree's elusiveness was no pose." She said that even though she was capable of chatting with people at the grocery store, she had to put on a kind of polite veneer to do it, and "what no one sees is the cost of the façade." (They would after she killed herself.) She spoke of having done two interviews with "pleasant strangers" the previous week, for which she "couldn't help impersonating Miss Vitality" (yet another reference to impersonation), but that the moment those interviews had ended, "I collapsed for the rest of the day in a dark room with a cold rag on my head." She wasn't exaggerating. No one but Ting knew the toll that social interaction exacted from her. This was why he often asked friends to keep their visits short or, better yet, not to come at all.

Her contradictory feelings about the loss of Tiptree were unrelenting and painful. In a passage from the original transcript of her *Contemporary Authors* interview (which she decided to omit in the final version), Alice said that in regard to Tiptree, she would do nothing differently if she had to do it over. Yet she was still shaken by his absence:

> I think that Tiptree's death was long overdue. I had considered taking him out and drowning him in the Caribbean, but I knew I couldn't get away with that. It's a little frightening to find oneself almost being possessed by this personality that one isn't or that only one part of one is. It was an extraordinary experience. He had a life of his own. He would do things and he would not do other things, and I didn't have much control over him.

As Alice felt increasingly dejected after having been outed, she talked openly about wanting to die, telling friends that if Ting's health continued to deteriorate she had no intention of outliving him. She also said that if life got too bad, she'd kill them both. She started seeing a psychiatrist and was taking several antidepressants, but nothing seemed to help. She complained that "so far nobody will give me what I deepest crave, a lead-nose .38 bullet in the parietal lobe. I dream about oblivion the way other people dream of good sex." She would also describe herself with an eerie metaphor to an interviewer in 1982: "I'm a loaded gun, an achingly loaded gun wholly unable to get a shot at those who are my enemies." (Years after her death, one of Alice's editors remembered her as having been "notable for her jocular and ironic determination to survive in spite of her admitted desire to die.")

Alice didn't actively attempt suicide, but she took terrible care of herself. She had "accidents" that caused injuries, health issues (including open-heart surgery), and for a while she lived on nothing but vanilla custard with frozen raspberries. Although she continued to correspond with some of Tip's friends and kept up with people by telephone, her interactions were undeniably awkward. She knew that and withdrew even further. After starting to write fiction again under her own name, she never achieved Tiptree's magic or even came close.

She knew that, too. Maybe her enormous talent would have eventually returned, but Alice didn't live long enough to find out.

Toward the end, Ting had a stroke and was partially blind and deaf; Alice's most serious illness was mental. Her suffering had become intolerable. She'd written a suicide pact for them years ago, but at eighty-four years old, despite his frail health, Ting still wanted to live. Alice had been heading toward oblivion for so long that it was impossible to trace the starting point of her fateful decline. She'd anticipated her premature death, hungrily waited for it.

On May 18, 1987, Alice sent a brief note to Ursula Le Guin, along with a magazine article she thought her friend would find amusing. She signed off, as usual, "Tip/Alli." There was no hint of the gruesome scene to come in the middle of the night: Ting fell asleep; Alice shot him in the head. Then she wrapped her own head in a towel, held Ting's hand, and shot herself. Proving this event had been a long time coming, she left behind a suicide note dated September 13, 1979. Their bodies were donated to George Washington University's medical school.

"She had enormous critical success and was very highly thought of by intellectuals," Alice's literary agent, Virginia Kidd, told the *New York Times* after her death. "But she never made the numbers."

His mother didn't love him
but he was in love with himself

CHAPTER 14

Georges Simenon &
CHRISTIAN BRULLS ET AL.

He claimed to have had sex with ten thousand women, so it is surprising to learn that communication posed a problem. Clearly, he was able to fulfill his needs. But the challenges of verbal intercourse obsessed him throughout his life, as he revealed in an interview with the *Paris Review* in 1955. The Belgian author Georges Simenon was asked about the most significant issues he'd dealt with in his fiction, and which themes he expected to contend with in the future. He replied:

> One of them, for example, which will probably haunt me more than any other, is the problem of communication. I mean communication between two people. The fact that we are I don't know how many millions of people, yet communication, complete communication, is completely impossible between two of those people, is to me one of the biggest tragic themes in the world. When I was a young boy I was afraid of it. I would almost scream because of it. It gave me such a sensation of solitude, of loneliness. That is a theme I

have taken I don't know how many times. But I know it will come again. Certainly it will come again.

For someone so acutely aware of the efforts and failures of everyday speech, Simenon seemed to embody a phenomenal will to express himself to the world. How else to explain his voluminous literary output—hundreds of novels, translated into nearly fifty languages? Many of his novels were best sellers; he sold more than 500 million books worldwide. Preposterously prolific, he was capable of producing eighty pages of prose a day, six books a year; somehow he found time to publish more than a thousand articles and short stories as well. He makes Joyce Carol Oates look like Harper Lee.

Simenon, who died in 1989 at the age of eighty-six, was often more famous for his louche ways than for his work. He brought it on himself. Simenon was "larger than life," known for his hubris, self-infatuation, and a capacity for excess that reached astonishing proportions. He never had an agent, choosing instead to oversee all his own publishing contracts, which he did very shrewdly. His kindness and magnanimity, when he cared to display them, were stupendous in equal measure. He began using pseudonyms at age sixteen and published more than two hundred novels using more than two dozen noms des plume. Nearly two hundred other novels were written under his own name, and twenty-one volumes of memoirs. He was itinerant, moving house dozens of times in his life, including a decade-long stretch in the United States, when he lived in Arizona, California, Florida, and Connecticut. He owned a gold watch that a reporter described as "the size and shape of a brioche." He was an international celebrity and the subject of countless flattering magazine and newspaper profiles. "He Writes a Book in 33 Hours," proclaimed one typically hyperbolic headline. "World's Most Prolific Novelist" was another.

Most of the anecdotes he told about his life were false—they were fantasies he spun to amuse himself and impress (or confuse) others.

He was a legend in his own mind. This was a man as intoxicated by himself as others are by fine wine. But he liked wine, too—also, champagne, whiskey, and beer, even while he wrote. On the advice of his doctor, he restricted himself to two bottles of red Bordeaux daily. (He did go through periods of renouncing alcohol for Coca-Cola.) One friend recalled a common sight: Simenon throwing up a bottle's worth of cognac in the garden, "two fingers down his throat, after he finished a chapter."

He told an interviewer that he had become "hungry for all women" at age thirteen. That was apparent in the vast number of his sexual conquests—ten thousand was perhaps a conservative estimate—most of whom were paid. (He was more often a customer than someone's lover.) Allegedly, Simenon liked to make love several times a day, which would put his stamina right up there with that of Warren Beatty, Wilt Chamberlain, and other reputedly record-breaking sex fiends. He once said that he suffered physical pain at the thought of so many women in the world with whom he would never get to have sex. "I would have liked to have known all females," he said. Simenon married and divorced twice—the first time, at age twenty; the second time, a day after the dissolution of his first marriage—and was an incorrigible philanderer. He was never boring.

Georges Joseph Christian Simenon was born in Liège, Belgium, on Friday, February 13, 1903. Even his birth involved an act of deceit: his superstitious mother insisted that the date be recorded, falsely, as February 12. When his grandmother saw him for the first time, she is said to have exclaimed to her daughter-in-law, *"My God, Henriette, what an ugly baby!"*

Although Georges worshipped his father, Désiré, an insurance clerk, he regarded his domineering, high-strung mother with contempt, and in his later writings, he savaged her mercilessly. Their relationship wasn't helped by her obvious and unabashed preference for his younger brother, Christian, and her blatant disdain for Georges. She adored Christian and always referred to him as "my son"; Georges, however, was "*le fils de Désiré*." Henriette exacerbated Georges's resentment of his younger brother and his bitterness toward the mother he perceived as rejecting him. He acted out in a number of ways, which had the effect not of gaining Henriette's sympathy, as he desperately wished, but of provoking her ire; she found him annoying and peculiar. His parents' marriage was unhappy, too. Désiré died at age forty-four of a heart attack in 1921, when Georges was eighteen years old. Just as his mother's withholding behavior would mark him for life—and surely influence his dysfunctional relationships with women, as well as his writing—so would the loss of his father. "The most important day in a man's life is the day of his father's death," he wrote some thirty-five years later. When Henriette remarried in 1929, Georges considered it an act of treachery. Even more galling was that she kept the name Simenon; he was quite famous by that time and resented her exploitation of his celebrity.

As a child, Georges excelled at school to show his mother that he was no failure, that he was worthy of her love. She was oblivious. He supposedly learned to read at age five, and as a student at a local Catholic school, he was industrious, conscientious, and exceptionally gifted. At age eight, he won a student prize for French composition, earning the praise his mother denied him. By the age of thirteen, the precocious boy was signing his homework using the pseudonym "Georges Sim," just for fun.

Yet by 1918, he'd shed his "good boy" persona, and his grades suffered as a result. "I rebelled more or less against the taboos that imprisoned me and also against the mediocrity that surrounded me," he told a reporter for *Paris Match* in 1967.

Thanks to his brilliance, he got away with a lot. He mocked authority figures, skipped school, rejected any thought of entering the priesthood—the vocation his mother had pressured him toward—and, finally, dropped out of school. "I wanted to get laid, and the Church told me I'd be damned for it," he once said. "So I left." Had he stuck with it, he might have been expelled. Georges didn't care.

He felt he could no longer continue being a mindless slave to any institution, least of all school or religion, and for the rest of his life he would devote himself wholly to two compulsions: sex and writing (not necessarily in that order).

Like nearly every other biographical detail about Simenon, there are multiple versions of the story of how, as a teenager, he landed a newspaper job. Any or all of them may be apocryphal. But it seems that he walked into the offices of the *Gazette de Liège* and talked his way into a position as a reporter, earning forty-five francs a month to start. His debut was an article about the city's first horse fair since the Armistice, and he managed to impress his editors. Although he'd had no burning ambition to become a journalist, he was getting plenty of practice writing. He loved it. Even better, the deadline-driven, high-pressure environment turned him into a writer who could crank out copy quickly, a habit that would help him become the famous author of hundreds of novels.

At the *Gazette*, he resurrected the pseudonym he'd used at school, "Georges Sim," whose byline first appeared in print on January 24, 1919. He happily took on the reporting assignments that no one else at the newspaper wanted, and proved himself a quick study, ambitious, full of energy, and enthusiastic about each new assignment. Soon his editor gave him the crime beat, furnishing him with a paid education that would later serve his detective fiction. In addition to the access he gained to police and criminal matters, he learned a great deal about forensic science.

Within a few months Georges was also given his own daily column, "Hors du Poulailler" ("From Outside the Hen Coop"). He signed it with the pseudonym "M. Le Coq" ("Mr. Rooster"). Whereas Sim was a straight news reporter, Le Coq's tone was funny, cavalier, and snarky. Writing about a criminal trial in 1921, Le Coq described the gathering of journalists in the courtroom: "They form a small, closed circle which lives very much at its ease. There they sit, sharpening their pencils, munching chocolate, swapping jokes, until suddenly the trial takes an interesting direction and they start to scribble furiously. . . . They frequently break off between sentences to swig from bottles which they have brought into court, right under the judge's nose." And at the ripe old age of eighteen, Georges defined a journalist as "a man who can stay awake at political meetings" and "a man who writes a column or two on a subject he knows absolutely nothing about."

He found the world of journalism fascinating, every aspect of it, and perhaps some part of him knew even then that his experiences would prove useful for his fiction writing. As his newspaper articles garnered more attention (a fact that thrilled him), his confidence grew. He knew that he was a real writer and that his ambition and talent extended beyond journalism. He proved it by writing his first book, *Au pont des Arches*, subtitled "A short humorous novel of Liègeois mores." The author was Georges Sim. He followed this a few months later with a second novel, which he later admitted had been written while he was quite drunk. Within a year he cowrote a third novel with a friend—a parody of a detective novel.

In December 1922, Georges resigned from his newspaper job. He was engaged to be married to a painter, Régine Renchon; he decided that he disliked her name and rechristened her "Tigy," which stuck. She was no great beauty, but she was strong-willed and intellectual and three years older than he—and the first woman he'd been attracted to who was not a prostitute. They moved to Paris, as Georges knew he must leave Belgium to truly achieve success. Later, Simenon would confess that when he married Tigy he was in love with her sister, but the marriage got off to a promising start anyway. They had a son, whom they named Marc.

The Simenons felt at home in Paris, where Georges began to submit stories to literary journals and magazines. In 1923, he sent his work to the fiction editor of the daily newspaper *Le Matin*, who happened to be Colette, already famous for her novel *Chéri*. She rejected his work again and again, but one day, she encouraged him by saying that he was close to being published, just not quite there. And she offered some unforgettable advice: "You're too literary. No literature! Get rid of all the literature, and you've got it." He finally did; he was published in *Le Matin*, and felt eternally grateful to Colette for transforming his approach to writing. (He went on to become a regular contributor.) His less-is-more style limited the use of adverbs and adjectives and favored short, clear sentences and brief paragraphs:

> There is not a single light on Quai de l'Aiguillon. Everything is closed. Everyone is asleep. Only the three windows of the Admiral Hotel, on the square where it meets the quay, are still lighted.

Over the next several years, Simenon obsessively honed his craft, trying out different themes and developing his voice. He churned out an absurd number of novels and more than a thousand short stories— all pseudonymously, all pulp fiction—with astonishing economy and efficiency. He would watch movies at night, sleep for a few hours, drink wine, and write and write. Any fear of being "too literary" was gone. These short novels were messy, even incoherent, but they were still good stories—lowbrow page-turners intended for popular consumption. (He was thinking in "chick lit" terms long before that genre ever existed, describing his early works as "novels for secretaries.") They were not works of art, but he had no illusions about that.

In an interview Simenon gave to the *New Yorker* in 1945, he described the rigorous routine of his early career: "Every day was like a prizefight," he said. "My schedule was two hours of work, typing at high speed, followed by an hour of rest or physical exercise. Often my wife would give me a rubdown. Then I would return for another two hours of writing. When evening came, I was depleted."

He admitted that by 1924 he was engaged in "the careful manufacture of semi-luxurious literary products. I became successful. I had a yellow Chrysler Imperial sedan and a chauffeur who delivered my manuscripts to the publishers and collected my checks. Also, I had a servant to fill my pipes for me. Every morning she would place forty filled pipes on my desk, enough to last me for two hours. I did not have to stop to fill my pipes myself and lose valuable time. After a while I worked more slowly, spending as much as two weeks on a single book." Another luxury he enjoyed was what he claimed to be the first private bar in Paris, in his own apartment. He later recalled that after one of his frequent raucous parties, with friends passed out on the floor, "dawn would find me stepping over the cadavers and making my way to the typewriter."

Simenon often boasted about the ease with which he produced books. If he was not ashamed of what he'd written, why had he chosen to write them using multiple pseudonyms? The roster included his old friend Georges Sim; Christian Brulls, a combination of his younger brother's name and his mother's maiden surname; Georges-Martin Georges; Gom Gut; Jean du Perry; Georges d'Isly; Bobette; Plick et Plock; Jacques Dersonne; Germain d'Antibes; and Poum et Zette.

He may have been a pulp fiction factory, but he didn't necessarily want everyone to know. (As in *The Wizard of Oz*, the idea was to "pay no attention to the man behind the curtain.") Perhaps using so many names allowed him to skip from crime novels to steamy romance novels to adventure novels, and so on, employing as many clichés and hackneyed plots as he wished, freely and often hilariously, with no fear of criticism to slow him down. He could write eighty pages a day without breaking a sweat. Because he was in disguise, nothing (nor any dismissive critic) could stop him from exploring his imagination in whatever form or direction he wished. And even here, in what would not unreasonably be called dreck, there were seeds of the glorious Simenon novels to come—including the acclaimed Maigret detective series, which made him one of the best-selling writers in the world—and hints of the author whom André Gide called "the greatest French novelist of our times."

If his writing life was orderly and productive, his personal life was a mess. In 1925, he and Tigy vacationed in Normandy, where he met Henriette Liberge, a local fisherman's daughter whom the Simenons hired as their maid. Just as he'd renamed his wife, Georges started calling Henriette "Boule." His wealth grew along with his writing output, and although he remained as disciplined as ever in his work—Boule woke him at four o'clock each morning with a cup of coffee, and he immediately went to work at his typewriter—his libido was about to wreak havoc.

Boule became Simenon's mistress. But that same year, he saw a nineteen-year-old African-American singer and dancer, Josephine Baker, perform in the show *La revue nègre*. He fell in love. Baker was the toast of Paris, and Simenon was but one of her many lovers and admirers. He was so preoccupied with her that in 1927, his typically manic productivity nearly ceased. His wife seems to have had no inkling of his affair with Baker, even though it consumed his attention. (He and Baker remained lifelong friends.) The following year, he was able to break away from his obsession, at least enough to resume almost his usual output—forty-four novels in 1928. A sense of frustration was beginning to set in; he wanted something more than journalism and pulp novels written under pseudonyms. He had plenty of money now, enough to buy a boat, and then an even larger boat that he had custom-built. Still, he was dissatisfied, maybe because his greatest creation, Inspector Jules Maigret, had yet to be born.

Always self-mythologizing, Simenon claimed that Maigret came to him a fully formed character one day as he sat in a café. "I began to picture the powerful, impassive bulk of a gentleman I thought would make a passable inspector," he told an interviewer decades later. "I added various accessories as the day wore on: a pipe, a bowler hat, a thick overcoat with a velvet collar." Maigret made his first appearance in 1929's *Une ombre dans la nuit* (*A Shadow in the Night*), written under the pseudonym Georges-Martin Georges. In this novel, Maigret is a doctor, and he has only a minor role. It is interesting that Simenon gave the early Maigret a medical profession, as the author frequently mentioned that he might have become a doctor if his writing career had failed.

Simenon published other pulp novels (under different names) that year, some of which featured police inspectors who were essentially composites of the author himself.

The Maigret character was fleshed out over the course of four novels. It was almost as if Simenon was getting to know his signature character, experimenting with his creation before committing an entire novel to the hard-drinking, pipe-smoking detective. Simenon was starting to realize that he could produce higher-quality fiction, but the slow emergence of Maigret was caused by stubborn resistance from publishers, who weren't sold on the character. They viewed Simenon as a reliable cash cow—and if it ain't broke, why fix it? They didn't want to tamper with a successful formula and had little regard for the author's wish to take his career in a different direction. Nor did they see any need for him to publish under his own name, which he was keen to do. It wasn't enough to be a lucrative and prolific author. Simenon yearned to be admired—and moreover, to take credit for his work.

Even several editors he worked with didn't know his real name. In fact, some believed that "Georges Simenon" was Georges Sim's pseudonym. Frustrated by the confusion for which he was responsible, Simenon announced dramatically to a journalist that his days of alter egos were about to end: "From now on I'm going back to my real name, and I'll sign my books as Georges Simenon."

He was taking a huge risk by exposing his true name and attempting a more ambitious, nuanced writing style—placing greater emphasis on character development and shedding the hackneyed plots of his pulp novels. His Maigret series would tweak the detective genre so that the answer to "Whodunit?" was not always wholly resolved, and the unorthodox detective could be counted on for his eccentric, highly unscientific investigative methods and empathy toward criminals. There were no obvious heroes or villains.

Ever fond of excess, Simenon decided that he needed a proper party to introduce his new, improved, more literary self. For someone who had worked pseudonymously for so long, he knew how to win publicity when he needed it. "It's not enough to have talent," he told a friend. "You have to make it known." He was hardly shy. In February 1931, he hosted a decadent society ball in his own honor at a Montparnasse nightclub. The savvy Simenon even hired a company to film his guests as they arrived, just like a Hollywood red-carpet premiere. He invited the most glamorous people in Paris—a mix of high-society types, celebrities, journalists, and artists—ensuring that it would be a much-talked-about event. Nearly a thousand people came. The party lasted all night and, like most other things Simenon attempted, it was a smashing success. Although some critics dismissed him as a publicity whore, he now had all the validation he needed to write under his own name. (He did continue publishing other novels under his nom de plume Christian Brulls for the next few years, but then he retired his alter egos.)

Writing as himself did not slow his output; Simenon could easily complete a book a month, or even every few weeks. A *New York Times* piece once noted that Simenon was a man who "can write a good novel in the time it takes a fallible human to turn out a passable book review." And a *Life* magazine article by Henry Grunwald pointed out that "Simenon turns out a book in about the time the average writer needs to draft a single chapter."

"I write fast, because I haven't the brains to write slow," Simenon once said.

For him, writing provided an equilibrium that kept a darker side under control. He couldn't stand being between books. He took long walks, sometimes for hours on end, as ideas percolated in his mind.

His second wife, Denyse, described the difficulty of living with him during the gestation of each new work: "Normally a happy person, full of vitality and strength, [he] would suddenly look and act strange, become short-tempered and even morose," she said. "I used to think that I had done something to hurt him. The answer usually came three or four days later, when he would announce to me, 'I am going to start a new book!'"

Simenon did not seek approval from his fellow writers, which was lucky, since he had offended so many by behaving like a pompous ass in his interviews. After all, he was only twenty-nine years old in 1932, and he displayed an arrogance that people felt he had not earned. He boasted about never creating outlines for his manuscripts but simply sitting down at his typewriter and essentially allowing the entire story and all its characters to unfold before him. His muse, it seemed, never took a vacation day or called in sick. Further, he didn't hesitate to reveal that all his novels were written "in one take," with no revisions and "no touchups or modifications."

One journalist recounted an irritating interview with Simenon. "I wish I could be anonymous again, walk around unrecognized," he told her, rather disingenuously. "It's terrible, you know, not to be able to go into a bar or restaurant without people elbowing each other and whispering, 'Look! It's Georges Simenon!' They read my books all over the world, you know." He also insisted that he had no taste for the great wealth he'd worked so hard to accumulate, even suggesting that he found money tedious. "If I spend half a million francs a year," he said, "it's only because I have to see the world. I have to know how it feels to lose a fortune in Monte Carlo, or to own a yacht and have a chauffeur. But as soon as I've amassed the material I need, it'll be over with, and I'll go back to a quiet, peaceful, life." Never mind that Simenon enjoyed Savile Row suits, custom-made silk shirts, and expensive wines.

His self-regard was insufferable. "Provide me with a typewriter and this very instant I would be able to get started on a new book," he once boasted, displaying an ego the size of a small nation. "I am fortunate in that I can write anywhere and under any conditions. I do not need to wait for inspiration. I am always inspired."

Simenon argued that he had written his pseudonymous pulp novels to make enough money for writing more "serious" books. Yet he didn't want to limit his literary efforts to an elite readership. He said that his goal was "to write a novel capable of capturing the interest of all audiences." Yet he admitted, "This is not as easy as it sounds: not to repulse the learned while remaining comprehensible to simple folk."

By 1933, Simenon had written nineteen Maigret novels. He felt that he had entered what he called his "literary period," but he was not satisfied with his status. "When I am 40 I will publish my first real novel," he announced in 1937, at the age of thirty-four, "and by the time I am 45 I will have won the Nobel Prize."

It is amazing that Simenon found time for writing at all: because Tigy supposedly had little need for sex, he cheated on her several times a week, with Boule and other women. Sometimes he was unfaithful several times a day. Most years, he was able to maintain the frenzied pace of his writing; when his life was consumed with additional distractions, his average output was still four novels a year (more than some writers produce in a lifetime).

Long after Simenon resolved to publish books openly as himself, the intensity of his writing process caused him to inhabit other selves, in a manner of speaking. Although he was no longer using other names, he adopted the mannerisms, facial expressions, and gaits of his characters, and used sense memory (such as smells, colors, and sounds) to create settings. "[While writing my novels] I shall not be myself," he once said. "Of course, I will eat with my family, but I will not be Simenon but someone else."

Entering into a trancelike state, diving into his subconscious— these were necessary triggers for the act of creation. He was not inventing stories from his imagination, or from an intellectual place. Essentially, he still had to become someone else to write—if not by using a pseudonym, then by allowing a character's "self" to take shape fully, without the author's control or intervention. "I'm not an intelligent man and I don't have an analytical mind," he told a reporter in 1971. "My books are therefore written by intuition alone. . . . The intuition just comes—on condition that I am, in a sense, completely empty."

He would achieve a neutral mind-set in which his subconscious took over, temporarily abandoning Georges Simenon to discover characters that were waiting to rise to the surface. "I actually live the part of my characters," he said. "It's no longer I who write, but they." At one point in the process, the author would pose a question to yield more information, as he revealed in a 1955 interview: "Given this man, where he is, his profession, his family, what can happen which will push him to his limit?"

The first procedure he used to "empty" himself before writing was cleaning his desk, a perfunctory but necessary ritual. "It's the character who commands, not me," he said. His method may have been pretentious (or invented for the sake of a good anecdote), but he claimed that it was the only way his books could be written.

"All the day I am one of my characters," he once said. "I feel what he feels. The other characters are always seen by him. So it is in this character's skin I have to be. And it's almost unbearable after five or six days. That is one of the reasons my novels are so short; after eleven days I can't—it's impossible. I have to—it's physical. I am too tired."

By 1945, Simenon was still married to his first wife, but the marriage wouldn't last. (Still, he managed to stay close to Tigy for the rest of his life.) Within weeks of moving his family to the United States, he began an affair with a twenty-five-year-old French-Canadian woman, Denyse Ouimet. His fixation on name changing continued, as he promptly changed the spelling of hers to "Denise." Because her former lover's name was Georges, he wanted to be renamed as well, and asked her to call him Jo.

Four years later, she was pregnant with the first of their three children: Jean, Pierre, and Marie-Jo. He divorced Tigy in 1950 and immediately married Denyse. They lived for a time in California, where he met and became friends with Charlie Chaplin.

In the same random fashion in which he did most things, Simenon moved his family to Lakeville, Connecticut, where he bought an eighteenth-century home on fifty acres. He woke at six each morning and went to work in a soundproofed office, the curtains drawn.

Denyse would prepare everything for him before he sat down at his IBM typewriter. He placed a "Do Not Disturb" sign—stolen from New York's Plaza Hotel—on the doorknob. His favorite pipes were filled and ready to be smoked, and his stacks of paper, maps, and dictionaries were by his side, as well as the telephone directories from all over the world that he used for naming his characters. In moments of solitary contemplation, he toyed with a monogrammed solid gold ball that Denyse had ordered from Cartier. His dozens of pencils were pre-sharpened daily, and he would switch on a hot plate to keep coffee brewing. He always began by drafting, on the back of a manila envelope, a list of his characters, their addresses and phone numbers, their ages, and other basic information—including places to which they might travel, and possible medical ailments. If his writing "spell" was ever broken by some interruption from the outside world, he immediately shut down and discarded whatever he had written until that point. (Interruptions were rare.)

Supposedly he wore the same outfit while writing each novel. For a normal writer, that might seem eccentric, but for Simenon, who could produce a book in a matter of days or a week, wearing the same clothes for the duration wasn't so odd. And he weighed himself before and after completing each new book, so as to measure how much sweat the project had cost him.

Simenon submerged himself completely while writing at his feverish pace, refusing to see anyone or speak on the phone. It was the only way he could work. There is a well-known story (perhaps a joke?) that goes like this:

Alfred Hitchcock once called to speak with the author. Simenon's secretary apologized, explaining that her boss couldn't come to the telephone because he had just started writing a new novel. "That's all right," Hitchcock replied. "I'll wait."

Between books, Simenon was fully engaged with the people around him. "I'm a bit like a sponge," he once said. "When I'm not writing I absorb life like water. When I write I squeeze the sponge a little—and out it comes, not water but ink."

He would produce twenty-six novels during his five years in Lakeville.

It was there, in 1955, that a reporter from the *Paris Review* came to interview Simenon. The subject was described as "cheerful, efficient, hospitable, controlled," which seemed to be Simenon's manner at all times, unless he was in bed with a woman. In the interview, Simenon provided insight into his revision process, which was brutally efficient and, he claimed, never involved changing the plot in any way. Asked what kinds of cuts he made to his work, he replied, "Adjectives, adverbs, and every word which is there just for the sentence. You know, you have a beautiful sentence—cut it."

He was just as unsentimental about word choice in general. "[M]ost of the time I use concrete words," he said. "I try to avoid abstract words, or poetical words, you know, like 'crepuscule,' for example. It is very nice, but it gives nothing."

Simenon never had any interest in participating in the "literary life," or even reading the work of his contemporaries. His own masters were dead. "I should tell any young man who wanted to follow in my footsteps to read the novels of Dickens, Stevenson, Dostoevsky, Balzac, and Daniel Defoe," Simenon once told an English journalist. "Then—forget them. He must stop reading and start living. He mustn't be like Zola, who cross-examined a carpenter in his workshop about the tricks of his trade, then sat down to hammer out a book on the life of a carpenter."

Yet he did admire a few of his contemporaries, including John Steinbeck, Erskine Caldwell, and especially William Faulkner. He once said in an interview that he wished he could have been Faulkner, because "he was able to contain the whole of humanity in a small county in the south of the United States." Faulkner was also greatly admired by Simenon's contemporary Henry Green. They may have had this in common, but Green couldn't stand Simenon's work.

Simenon regarded Ian Fleming's James Bond novels as insipid, but Fleming was a huge fan of Simenon. So was T. S. Eliot. The film directors Federico Fellini and François Truffaut were admirers, too.

He met Dashiell Hammett and James Thurber, and formed friendships with Thornton Wilder and Henry Miller, both of whom he corresponded with. "For us Americans who have just discovered you in translation," Miller wrote to him in 1954, "it is like a new star rising on the horizon." And in his longtime friendship with André Gide, Simenon opened up about aspects of his personal life that he shared with no one else. But when it came to his writing he was like a magician; he knew better than to reveal too much about how his tricks worked. So when Gide, always awestruck by his friend's extraordinary output, once pressed him in a letter about his creative process, Simenon replied, "It's a form of self-deception, nothing more."

Simenon was flattered by Gide's attention, but he admitted later that he found Gide's work unreadable.

One fan of Simenon (whom he never met) was the British author John Cowper Powys, who described Simenon as "my new favorite writer" and considered him superior to Arthur Conan Doyle. "I never thought I'd live to see the day that I'd be reading detective stories," Powys wrote to a friend, "but the detective element of Simenon's books is their weakest aspect, generally rather unconvincing. All the rest—atmosphere, composition, narration, and characters—is wonderful, at least for me. It's been years since I've come upon an author who has so pleased me, with so many books, all equally charming."

The novelist, critic, and Flaubert scholar Francis Steegmuller (who was married to the author Shirley Hazzard) was an occasional user of pseudonyms in his own novels. Steegmuller wrote that when Simenon was at his best, he

is an all-round master craftsman—ironic, disciplined, highly intelligent, with fine descriptive power. His themes are timeless in their preoccupation with the interrelation of evil, guilt and good; contemporary in their fidelity to the modern context and Gallic in precision, logic and a certain emanation of pain or disquiet. His fluency is of course astonishing. His life is itself a work by Simenon.

Simenon might have acted nonchalant about how others perceived him, but he soaked up the glory. To his credit, he harbored a degree of humility that lingered from childhood. "I like plain people," he explained in a 1953 interview with *Look* magazine, "people who are not all the time thinking about the impression they make and taking notes on themselves. The best thing is for the writer to know the garbage collector."

Even after conquering the world with his Maigret novels, he could not succeed in shaking his mother's critical attitude. When Henriette was well into her seventies, her disapproval had not diminished. "Why don't you ever write a book about nice people and good Catholics," she said to her son, "instead of all these criminals?"

In 1961 Simenon's career was still going strong. His work had been (lucratively) adapted for television and film, and he was deep into another affair, with Teresa Sburelin, the family's Italian housekeeper, who was twenty-three years younger than he. Years later, Denyse offered her opinion of her husband's incorrigible ways. "We made love three times a day every day, before breakfast, after an afternoon nap, and before going to sleep," she said. "Sometimes I wondered whether he didn't think of me as a prostitute. . . . He had contempt for women, but I'm the only one he respected while still showing that contempt. You want to know why he felt the need to cheat on me when he was getting what he needed at home? Definitely to reassure himself. He overdid everything: speaking, writing, publishing, and making love. This was a reflection of his temperament."

Supposedly, one afternoon Simenon enjoyed a marathon session of sex with four women in a row while Denyse packed their suitcases in the adjoining room.

He once said that he viewed sex as "the only possible form of communication with women." Because he had no memory of tenderness from his mother—he claimed that she had never even held him in her lap—his attitude is not surprising. He spent a lifetime trying to move beyond that early abandonment.

"I have no sexual vices," he told Fellini, "just a need to communicate."

Although the author's name was worth a fortune—he was a one-man celebrity brand—his personal life fell apart in middle age. For a man who never met a brothel he didn't like, his sexual fervor remained strong as ever, but it started to take its toll. He went through bouts of depression, and even he recognized that his life was in disarray.

His malaise did not go unnoticed by a French journalist who visited him in 1963, surprised by how grouchy and anxious his interview subject seemed. (Simenon had abruptly moved his family to Switzerland, having enjoyed his time in America but unable to resist his nomadic impulse.) Recalling the interview later, the journalist said he had not come away with a favorable impression. He took a jab at Simenon, describing him as "an industrialist of literature. He produced, and he sold what he produced." Even more damning were his observations of the author's paranoia:

> Simenon dreaded a world war or some other catastrophe; hence the enormous laundry and operating room at his home, driven by a generator ready to go at a moment's notice. The house was replete with microphones, supposedly installed so that Simenon would know if one of his children was calling or crying, but I think he also used them to eavesdrop on what others besides his children might be saying about him. And finally, he detested wood, in which any number of undesirable beasts might find shelter. The furniture was of glass, leather, and metal. A curious impression: I listened to Georges Simenon for hours but never really got to know him.

Whether Simenon's decline had to do with his desperately unhappy marriage is unclear, but it is likely. There were violent incidents between him and Denyse. "He's afraid of her," one of his editors said of the couple's relationship. "She's mad."

Perhaps in denial about how bad things were, Simenon made the reckless decision to custom-build a grand home in Epalinges. In the beginning, Simenon claimed that the house was so immense he did not know the exact number of rooms. It was a fortress designed to accommodate his large staff of servants, nannies, and secretaries, and his paintings by Matisse and Picasso. It provided ample space to park his fleet of luxury cars—including a Mercedes, a Jaguar, and a Bentley. Dollar signs were built into the front gates of the grounds. The house had (depending on the source) either eleven or twenty-one telephones; a vast library of his own works, translated into several languages; a service elevator installed specifically to deliver Simenon's meals; and a pool, among other extravagances. Charlie Chaplin and his family were frequent guests.

Unfathomably rich and famous, Simenon became jaded about his career. In 1969, despite being the world's best-selling author, he had grown tired of his beloved detective. "When I first began Maigret I was 26 and he was 45," he told a reporter that year. "I was his son, he was my father. Now I am 66 and he is only 52, and he is my son and I am his father."

A few years later, having written more than eighty Maigret novels, and thousands of pages in multiple genres under various names, he published the final volume and announced that he would never again write fiction in any genre, under any name. His children and friends refused to believe him—they were convinced that he had another surprise in store—but this time he did not. *People* magazine ran a profile of him accompanied by the headline, "After 500 Novels and 10,000 Women, Georges Simenon Has Earned His Retirement."

Unable to let go of storytelling entirely, he spent years dictating twenty-one volumes of his memoirs into a tape recorder. He addressed the public's immense curiosity about his prolific writing career: "People will speak of a gift. Why not a malediction?" He'd once said that whenever he went to his doctor while suffering from a mysterious illness, his doctor would offer the same prescription: "Write a book." He always did, and noticed that he felt better instantly. Writing was his affliction and his cure. "I'm happy when I've finished," he told a reporter five years before his death. "But during the time I'm writing, it's something awful."

At seventy, he'd endured years of trauma and heartbreak: the collapse of his marriage to the manic-depressive, alcoholic Denyse; the death of his mother, which left him with complicated feelings of grief and anger. And in 1978, his daughter, Marie-Jo, committed suicide at age twenty-five in her apartment in Paris. She shot herself in the chest with a pistol, and a heartbroken Simenon could not recover from the loss. Less than two months earlier, Denyse had published a spiteful, extensively detailed account of their marriage, *Un oiseau pour le chat* (*A Bird for the Cat*). Simenon never forgave her for this betrayal, and refused to say her name aloud.

In his professional life, too, strains became apparent. He felt that he still hadn't received the acclaim he deserved, even though he'd flooded the world with hundreds of millions of copies of his books. The self-described "imbecile of genius" could not overcome his spite at being passed over for the Nobel Prize. It had been bad enough when his friend Gide won in 1947, but Simenon felt even more bruised when Albert Camus became the Nobel laureate in 1957. (There had been international rumors that perhaps Simenon would win that year.) The choice of Camus made him furious. "Can you believe that asshole got it and not me?" he had complained to Denyse.

Having abandoned fiction, he also gave up the house at Epalinges. He and Teresa, now his companion, moved first into a high-rise apartment, then into a small, cramped house in Lausanne. (After his death, his ashes would be scattered under an old cedar tree in their garden.) He placed most of his possessions in storage. He changed the "Occupation" line of his passport from "*homme de lettres*" to "*sans profession.*" He took a daily nap after lunch. It was a simple life. He and Teresa were devoted to each other.

The profile in *People* magazine described a blissful couple: "[L]ife with Teresa appears serene. They are inseparable. They take a daily promenade together and eat their meals on a precise schedule."

As his health declined and he was confined to a wheelchair, he was philosophical about dying: "I don't fear death, but I fear causing trouble by my death to those who survive me. I would like to die as discreetly as possible."

Perhaps because Simenon had so effortlessly inhabited his many pseudonyms and had experienced such huge success, even writing as himself, he was never unduly preoccupied with how others regarded him. "I have a very, very strong will about my writing," he once said, "and I will go my way. For instance, all the critics for twenty years have said the same thing: 'It is time for Simenon to give us a big novel, a novel with twenty or thirty characters.' They do not understand. I will never write a big novel. My big novel is the mosaic of all my small novels. You understand?"

He had always drawn attention because of his gargantuan appetites, including his sexual escapades, yet in private he was an ordinary man who followed a rigid routine—as cited in a 1969 *New York Times* profile, just a few years before his final novel was published: "Mr. Simenon lives by order and discipline. Not only does he rise at 6 on the dot, but he also goes to bed at the first stroke of 10, whether he is in the middle of the sentence or watching a drama on one of his seven TV sets. He falls asleep immediately."

He had the luxury of adhering, without interference, to the simple routine he had designed—never having to do a single thing, for work or pleasure, that he did not schedule himself. And on September 4, 1989, he didn't feel like waking again. With nothing left to say, the great Simenon died serenely in his slumber at 3:30 in the morning.

He could not have written a better ending.

She kept snails as pets

CHAPTER 15

Patricia Highsmith & CLAIRE MORGAN

She was one of the most wretched people you could ever meet, with mood shifts that swung as wildly as the stock market. Patricia Highsmith was born eleven years before Sylvia Plath, and the two women had a similar temperament. Like Plath, Highsmith possessed a legendary cruel streak and harbored feelings of murderous rage that were directed at family members, lovers, and innocent bystanders alike. One friend said that although she appreciated Highsmith's startlingly direct manner, unaccompanied by tact, she did not care for "the ranting and raving, the nastiness, the hatred which would overflow." When a biographer of Highsmith was asked why she'd become interested in her subject, she replied, "I have always been interested in women who go too far—and Highsmith went further than anyone."

That point is hard to dispute. Highsmith was a heavy smoker (Gauloises), an alcoholic, and sexually promiscuous. She had affairs with both men and women—almost all of these relationships were intense and unhappy—and she compulsively recorded her sexual encounters. She revised her work by retyping her manuscripts in their entirety "two-and-a-half times" on a manual typewriter. She was living proof that not all women have a maternal instinct. She was secretive, misanthropic, gruff, cheap, rude, and generally mean. She had wanderlust. She collected maps. She had an eating disorder and described food as her "bête noire." She felt disgusted by feminists. She was openly and relentlessly anti-Semitic, and felt that the Holocaust didn't go far enough. She wrote hateful letters, critical of Israel, to politicians and newspapers, using more than forty pseudonyms (including "Phyllis Cutler" and "Edgar S. Sallich") and disguised signatures. She saved, in her edition of the Holy Bible, an old article with the headline "Archaeologist Finds the Tomb of Caiphus, the Jewish High Priest Who Handed Jesus Christ Over to the Jews." She said that she refused to sell Israel the rights to publish any of her books, and when the ham sandwiches she liked were no longer served in first class on airline flights, she blamed "the yids" for it. Yet she had Jewish lovers and friends. She had huge hands. She loved cats and owned many books about cats. She was a racist who believed that if black men didn't have sex many times a month, they became ill. She simultaneously cursed her fame and courted it. She was a compulsive liar. She had a febrile imagination and boasted that she had ideas "as often as rats have orgasms." One of her editors described her as being like a "child of 10 or 11." On her left wrist, she had a tattoo of her initials in Greek letters. She enjoyed watching violent scenes in movies, but shielded her eyes during sex scenes, which repelled her. She always wanted to play the harpsichord. She did play the recorder. She kept snails as pets because she enjoyed watching them copulate, liked their indeterminate gender and self-sufficiency, and said they provided a sense of tranquillity—this from someone almost incapable of relaxation. Her fondness for snails was such that she kept three hundred of them in her garden in Suffolk and insisted on traveling with them. When she moved to France in 1967, she smuggled snails into the country by hiding them under her breasts—and she made several trips back and forth to smuggle them all. Her favorite snails were named Hortense and Edgar. Her favorite flower was the carnation. She liked her Scotch neat. She had bad teeth.

She was lonely and anxious, ambidextrous, and physically clumsy. She was sensitive to noise and despised it. She was obsessed by routine and repetition in all areas of her life. She believed that her phone was being wiretapped by people who wanted to steal her money. She liked to read the dictionary every evening before dinner. She was known to start drinking screwdrivers at seven o'clock in the morning. She made furniture. She felt that her best quality was perseverance. She was a gifted visual artist and admired the work of Francis Bacon because "he sees mankind throwing up into a toilet." She was tall, dark, and handsome. She slept with many women named Virginia. She was paranoid and controlling. She contemplated suicide, but rejected the act as too selfish.

Patricia Highsmith was born in Fort Worth, Texas, in 1921, and grew up in New York City. She never felt at home in the United States and left permanently for Europe in 1963. Expatriate life suited her well. "My most persistent obsession—that America is fatally . . . off the mark of the true reality, that the Europeans have it precisely," she wrote in her notebook at age twenty-seven. Her childhood could hardly be described as happy; she despised her equally vicious mother, Mary. Highsmith said that she "learned to live with a grievous and murderous hatred early on."

After falling out with Mary in 1974, Highsmith did not see her for the last seventeen years of Mary's life. (It rankled her that her mother lived to the age of ninety-five.) Among what she considered countless slights and misdeeds, Highsmith deeply resented Mary's refusal to accept responsibility for her daughter's character, "or to put it bluntly queerness." When she was fourteen years old her mother asked, "Are you a les? You are beginning to make noises like one." This belittling remark served to alienate Highsmith further from everyone around her.

When she was nearly sixty years old, Highsmith was asked by a reporter why she did not love her mother. "First, because she made my childhood a little hell," she said. "Second, because she herself never loved anyone, neither my father, my stepfather, nor me." One of Highsmith's former lovers once commented that Mary was "high-strung, jealous, and possessive," and that mother and daughter "enjoyed a certain *folie à deux*." Although Highsmith dedicated a few books to her mother, she said that she did it only to impress the woman who found fault with everything she did.

In her diary, Highsmith described herself as feeling "like a glacier or like stone" until the age of thirty, but that sense of remove would never leave her. She had a lifelong aversion to being touched, and she bristled when someone shook her hand. (Many acquaintances learned never to do this with her.) Highsmith was perpetually anxious about maintaining boundaries with people. She viewed living with a romantic partner as "catastrophic." Being alone was her preferred state: "My imagination functions better when I don't have to speak to people," she said.

She was well aware that her taut, self-protective carapace had been caused partly by her upbringing and that it was "certainly tied up with the fact I had to conceal the most important emotional drives of myself completely." Those yearnings were directed toward other women, a fact that drew baffled contempt from her mother.

Highsmith's parents divorced a few days before she was born, and five months before the birth, Mary had tried to abort the fetus by ingesting turpentine. "Highsmith" was actually the name of Patricia's stepfather, who the girl believed was her biological father until she was ten years old. (Her initial surname, Plangman, belonged to her father, but she never used it.) When she learned the truth about her stepfather, she wasn't terribly shocked, because she'd suspected for a while that he wasn't her real father. Still, the revelation added another confounding element to her already fragmented sense of identity. The experience of shifting and shedding selves would prove a recurring theme in her work. It was a conundrum she was never able to solve and one that never ceased to fascinate her.

As a child, Highsmith was reticent, hypersensitive, and self-conscious; she had difficulty forming attachments. By age six, she was aware of an inchoate longing for other girls, which she tried to suppress. An itinerant childhood added to her struggle with (and ambivalence toward) making new friends. But she was a sophisticated and voracious reader, which provided solace. She immersed herself in Dostoevsky, Kafka, Poe, Woolf, and Proust, among others.

When she was just eight years old, she discovered *The Human Mind*, the first book by the influential American psychiatrist Karl Menninger. "He writes about pyromaniacs, kleptomaniacs, schizos and so on; their case histories, whether they're cured or not," she later recalled. "I found this very interesting, and it was only much later that I realized that it had had such an effect on my imagination, because I started writing these weirdo stories when I was fifteen or sixteen." The opening sentence of the first story she wrote was, "He prepared to go to sleep, removed his shoes and set them parallel, toe outward, beside his bed." (Even when she was a teenager, her obsessive-compulsive tendencies were set. These were efforts at control—a coping mechanism in response to the tumult of her early years.)

She was a lifelong diarist and a relentless maker of charts, sketches, and lists that included ratings of lovers by character trait and category. At her death, she left behind about eight thousand pages from her diaries and "cahiers," as she called her notebooks. (The diaries were for chronicling personal experiences; the "cahiers" recorded ideas for stories, poems, and other creative endeavors.) These writings were searching, anguished, and intimate. "Every move I make on earth is in some way for women," she wrote. "I adore them! I need them as I need music, as I need drawings."

She struggled with the gap between who she was and who she longed to become: "What and why am I? There is an ever more acute difference . . . between my inner self which I know is the real me, and various faces of the outside world." Her identity seemed in perpetual flux, and it was quite a lot to manage. "Dostoevsky is criticized for ambivalence, for illogic, contradictions—worst of all, ambivalences in his philosophy," she once wrote in her diary. "But there are always two. Perhaps this wonderful, magical, creative, public & private number is the mystic secret of the universe. One can love two people, the sexes are within all of us, emotions directly contrary do exist side by side. This is the way I see the world too."

On December 31, 1947, she wrote a private "New Year's Toast": "[T]o all the devils, lusts, passions, greeds, envys, loves, hates, strange desires, enemies ghostly and real, the army of memories, with which I do battle—may they never give me peace." Her own happiness, whatever that meant, was not relevant. Nor did anyone else's well-being matter to her, and in that sense she was a bit like the sociopathic characters in her stories.

In 1942, Highsmith graduated from Barnard College. Thus began a series of failed job interviews with various magazines. This was (and remains) a common entry-level field for literary college graduates in Manhattan. But no one would have her. *Time, Fortune, Good Housekeeping,* and *Mademoiselle* were among the publications that turned her down. Her interview with *Vogue* was comically disastrous, even though she did have a flair for clothing and usually displayed a distinctive, androgynous style. She was also meticulous about ironing, a domestic task she'd mastered at a young age and found satisfying. Yet for some reason, Highsmith showed up for her much-coveted interview looking like a mess. She appeared at the offices of the world's most glamorous and prestigious fashion magazine "with a stained and wrinkled blouse, bad hair, and, in the formal 1940s, a head unadorned by a hat," as her biographer Joan Schenkar noted. She appeared to have rolled out of bed and gone straight to her interview. In her diary, Highsmith was angry about the rejection (which was clearly her fault). "Well, I did wash my hair just before going in," she wrote. "There'll come a time when I shall be bigger than *Vogue* and I can thank my lucky star I escaped their corruptive influences." Unlikely as it was, she would prove to be right.

After Barnard, she had a secret life: writing comic strips (story lines and dialogue) for at least seven years. Later, as Schenkar discovered,

Highsmith attempted to remove, without explanation, all traces of this extensive work from her archives. Still, she seemed oddly suited to writing comics if you consider that she specialized in superheroes with alter egos—secret lives and clandestine identities that shifted from day to night. One of her few pleasures in life was fiercely guarding secrets about herself, down to the most banal details.

In 1950, she would publish her first novel, *Strangers on a Train*. It promptly launched her career. The story—which follows two men, Guy and Bruno, who meet on a train and form a murder pact, as well as a twisted, homoerotic bond—had been rejected by six publishers. Yet upon publication it was an immediate success, and Alfred Hitchcock adapted it into a well-received film. (Highsmith was unhappy that the director had paid only about $7,000 to secure the rights. She never got over it.) The process of getting the script written proved challenging; writers such as Dashiell Hammett and John Steinbeck turned down the project. Raymond Chandler wrote an early draft but was fired by Hitchcock. That was probably for the best, as Chandler admitted that he had struggled with the material. "It's darn near impossible to write, because consider what you have to put over: a perfectly decent young man (Guy) agrees to murder a man he doesn't know, has never seen, in order to keep a maniac from giving himself away and from tormenting the nice young man," Chandler wrote. "We are flirting with the ludicrous. If it is not written and played exactly right, it will be absurd."

Other film adaptations of Highsmith's work over the years included René Clément's *Purple Noon* and Anthony Minghella's *The Talented Mr. Ripley*. In the 1980s, a smart, talented young film director named Kathryn Bigelow, who would go on to direct the Academy Award–winning film *The Hurt Locker*, wrote a script on spec for a Highsmith novel she loved. The project never went anywhere, but Highsmith liked Bigelow very much.

Truman Capote was responsible for helping the author complete her draft of *Strangers on a Train*. In the summer of 1948, thanks to his endorsement, Highsmith was awarded a residency at Yaddo, the prestigious writers' and artists' colony in upstate New York. Also there that summer were Chester Himes and Flannery O'Connor. Highsmith finally got the space and time she needed to finish the manuscript, despite her two-day hangovers. She was thrilled: "If I cannot give birth in the supreme hospital of Yaddo, where can I ever?" Fifty years later, in a rare magnanimous gesture, Highsmith would show her gratitude to Yaddo by naming it the sole beneficiary of her estate, along with a $3 million bequest.

She recalled being instantly taken with the spritelike Capote, if not his writing, and particularly appreciated his openness about being gay. He was entirely unacquainted with the hang-ups that froze Highsmith and left her struggling with her sexuality. Once he told her that at the age of fourteen, he came out to his parents with a simple, jubilant declaration: "*Everybody is interested in girls, only I, T.C., am interested in boys!*"

Highsmith's second novel, as far as anyone knew at the time, was *The Blunderer*, in 1954; it would be followed a year later by *The Talented Mr. Ripley*, the book that would ensure her reputation and fame. With that accomplishment she established herself as a master of crime fiction—even though she disliked being typecast in a particular genre—and a creator of psychologically complex characters who, beneath their mannered façades, were misfits, deviants, and sometimes psychopaths. The British novelist Graham Greene, a great fan of Highsmith's work, described her as a "writer who has created a world of her own—a world claustrophobic and irrational which we enter each time with a sense of personal danger. Nothing is certain when we have crossed this frontier." It was a world that often reflected her interior state and her own disturbing obsessions. Perhaps most troubling of all, Susannah Clapp wrote in a 1999 piece in the *New Yorker*, was that "her narratives suggest a seamlessness between bumbling normality and horrific acts. You never hear the gears shift when the terrible moment arrives."

In truth, Highsmith had published her second novel two years before *The Blunderer*—yet it was not a work she wished to claim credit for. This one was a secret.

The Price of Salt came out in 1952 under the name of Claire Morgan, who did not exist. Although Highsmith would never again use a pseudonym for any of her novels or stories, this radical narrative demanded a furtive identity. "Oh god," she said, "how this story emerges from my own bones!" Homoeroticism was pervasive in her fiction, but always obliquely and within the context of troubled, amoral characters. In a scene from *The Talented Mr. Ripley*, relations between Tom Ripley and the object of his fixation, Dickie Greenleaf, begin to take an ugly turn when Dickie walks in on Tom dressed in his clothes:

> "Marge and I are fine," Dickie snapped in a way that shut Tom out from them. "Another thing I want to say, but clearly," he said, looking at Tom, "I'm not queer. I don't know if you have the idea that I am or not."
>
> "Queer?" Tom smiled faintly. "I never thought you were queer."
>
> Dickie started to say something else, and didn't. He straightened up, the ribs showing in his dark chest. "Well, Marge thinks you are."
>
> "Why?" Tom felt the blood go out of his face. He kicked off Dickie's second shoe feebly, and set the pair in the closet. "Why should she? What've I ever done?" He felt faint. Nobody had ever said it outright to him, not in this way.
>
> "It's just the way you act," Dickie said in a growling tone, and went out of the door.

The Price of Salt, however, depicted consensual (and satisfying) romantic love between two women. It was Highsmith's most autobiographical novel, and it laid bare the emotional drives she had worked hard to keep hidden for so long. Moreover, it was the first gay or lesbian novel with a happy ending. This was not pulp fiction. No one went insane, committed suicide, or was murdered. No one "converted" to heterosexuality or found God. This was a breakthrough for the era in which it was written, and surprisingly, the novel was well received by critics. The paperback edition, issued by Bantam a year later, sold more than a million copies. Grateful letters trickled in for years afterward, from both men and women, addressed to Claire Morgan in care of her publishing house. "We don't all commit suicide and lots of us are doing fine," wrote one fan.

If it was true, as Highsmith wrote in her diary in 1942, that "[a]ll my life's work will be an undedicated monument to a woman," then *The Price of Salt* was the culmination of that ambition. No wonder it demanded concealment.

The idea for the novel had arisen from a single but transformative moment. In December 1948, in need of cash and feeling depressed, she took a temporary job during the pre-Christmas rush in the toy department of Bloomingdale's in Manhattan. Though she was hired for a month, she lasted only two and half weeks there. She'd gotten the job partly to pay for her psychoanalytic treatment, which she'd begun in a halfhearted effort to "cure" herself of the homosexual urges that alternately tormented her and left her in a manic state of bliss. "When you're in love it's a state of madness," she said.

One morning, a few days after Highsmith started the job, a beautiful blond woman in a mink coat walked into the toy department, purchased a doll for her daughter, then left the store. Highsmith never saw her again. Yet that brief transaction captivated Highsmith, who had a habit of projecting her fantasies and yearnings onto unsuspecting women she barely knew. "She could be called the balladeer of stalking," Susannah Clapp noted of Highsmith in her *New Yorker* piece. "The fixation of one person on another—oscillating between attraction and antagonism—figures prominently in almost every Highsmith tale."

To Highsmith, the woman she'd met "seemed to give off light." And though it had been a routine encounter in which no flirtation had occurred, she was left feeling "odd and swimmy in the head, near to fainting, yet at the same time uplifted, as if I had seen a vision." That night, she went home to the apartment where she lived alone and wrote eight pages in longhand, a broad version of the novel's plot. "It flowed from my pen as if from nowhere—beginning, middle and end," she recalled. "It took me about two hours, perhaps less." Then she fell ill with chicken pox.

Because this bewitching customer had paid by credit card and asked for the purchase to be sent to her home, Highsmith had the woman's name and address: Mrs. E. R. Senn of Ridgewood, New Jersey. In Highsmith's imaginative retelling, Senn was cast as the seductive older woman, Carol, and Highsmith as the naïve nineteen-year-old shopgirl, Therese. The department store was fictionalized as Frankenberg's. When Carol invites Therese out for lunch, the young protagonist, despite having a boyfriend, feels the first stirrings of love. "An indefinite longing, that she had been only vaguely conscious of at times before, became now a recognizable wish," Highsmith wrote. "It was so absurd, so embarrassing a desire, that Therese thrust it from her mind." Some passages in the novel were taken verbatim from the author's own notebooks and diaries. Although the initial writing of the novel came easily to her, the revision stage brought out dark emotions. As the publication date grew closer, Highsmith suddenly crashed, hitting one of the lowest points of her life. She became self-destructive to a terrifying extent, going on drinking binges and feeling more miserable than ever. At the very moment she should have been celebrating a work that she felt proud of, she experienced an agonizing case of writer's remorse. She wanted to withdraw the novel from publication: it was so deeply personal that she feared it would destroy her, both personally and professionally. The use of an invented name was only a mild anodyne for her anxiety. Mostly, she felt sick with worry and shame: "These days are on the brink again. The least thing depresses me to the point of suicide."

In fact, suicide was the fate of Mrs. E. R. Senn—a grim twist worthy of a Highsmith tale. Married to a rich businessman, the beautiful woman who had aroused Highsmith's ardor was an alcoholic who had been in and out of psychiatric hospitals. She had absolutely no idea that she'd inspired a lesbian love story. In the fall of 1951, Kathleen Wiggins Senn killed herself by carbon monoxide poisoning in the garage of her lavish home in Bergen County.

It wasn't until the 1990 British edition of *The Price of Salt* was released that Highsmith explained in an afterword why she'd decided to publish under a pseudonym. Both her publisher and agent seemed determined to have her keep writing the same books over and over, confining her to so-called crime fiction. After the publication of *Strangers on a Train*, she'd been tagged instantly as a certain kind of writer, even though in her mind it was "simply a novel with an interesting story." (The reductive business of branding and marketing is unchanged even today.) She found this rather frustrating, and in objecting to being labeled she had her share of supporters.

"Patricia Highsmith is often called a mystery or crime writer," a newspaper critic noted, "which is a bit like calling Picasso a draftsman." To Gore Vidal, who shared her expatriate anti-American views, she was simply one of the greatest modernist writers. And the playwright David Hare admired her work because "behind it lies the claim that, once you set your mind to it, any one human being can destroy any other."

Highsmith knew that her literary genius transcended any single genre, and she detested any kind of categorization. She considered herself a neglected master. "If I were to write a novel about a lesbian relationship," she wrote in the afterword, "would I then be labeled a lesbian book-writer? That was a possibility, even though I might never be inspired to write another such book in my life. So I decided to offer the book under another name." She also must have wanted to protect her reputation and nascent career, although she never admitted this outright. (Nor did she wish to upset her eighty-four-year-old grandmother, Willie Mae.)

After all, she noted, those were the days when homosexuals were widely viewed as perverts, when "gay bars were a dark door somewhere in Manhattan, where people wanting to go to a certain bar got off the subway a station before or after the convenient one, lest they be suspected of being homosexual."

The pseudonym gave her the safety she craved. Because the story of her two characters ends on a sweet, hopeful note, this novel seemed an exercise in wish fulfillment for the author. In her own life, Highsmith almost always experienced thwarted love, painfully brief relationships, and bitter rejections.

In 1959, she began an on-and-off relationship with the author Marijane Meaker, who would also publish under pseudonyms, including Vin Packer, Ann Aldrich, and most famously M. E. Kerr. They met at L's, a lesbian bar in Greenwich Village, and in her memoir Meaker later recalled Highsmith wearing a trench coat, drinking gin neat, and looking like "a combination of Prince Valiant and Rudolph [sic] Nureyev." She admired Highsmith's resistance to societal attitudes toward homosexuality: "I don't care for acceptance," Highsmith told Meaker, who was in her early thirties at the time and foolishly believed that she had found her life partner. (The relationship would last two years.) They lived together for a time, but Meaker later confessed that if they hadn't had "such good horizontal rapport," the affair would have ended much sooner.

After breaking up, they stayed in touch—which meant that Meaker had to deal with Highsmith's narcissism by mail instead. "Did I tell you that Bloomsbury liked my latest Ripley so much they gave me an advance that in American money comes to about $115,000?" Highsmith wrote in one letter. "I never got that much for a book. You know, in the U.S. no one really recognizes me, but in Europe I'm often recognized and treated like a celebrity." In other letters she railed against Jews, adding in one postscript that "USA could save 11 million per day if they would cut the dough to Israel."

That wasn't all. Immediately after their breakup, Highsmith wrote a novel called *The Cry of the Owl*, in which an "unsuccessful artist" was a thinly disguised version of Meaker. The character was viciously knifed to death for several pages at the end.

By 1983, many people suspected that Highsmith had been the author of *The Price of Salt*; although she refused to address the truth in any way, it had become a poorly kept secret. When contacted by Barnard's alumni magazine for an article about her, and asked directly whether she had written the novel, Highsmith replied that the less said about the subject, the better, and left it at that. In the same year, Naiad Press bought the rights to reissue the book, but Highsmith declined to publish it under her own name. Naiad tried to tempt her by offering a $5,000 advance for publishing with full disclosure, or $2,000 for publishing under a pseudonym. She refused to take the bait.

For the 1990 UK edition, Highsmith finally came around to coming out. She had stubbornly resisted even then, but she did consent to putting her real name to the work. The novel was also released with a new title, *Carol*. Although Highsmith had no wish to analyze her decision for the press or the public, the book spoke for itself. Writing it had been an act of courage, even if the author wanted no part in acknowledging that fact. Today, it remains one of her best works, a novel worth reading and revisiting.

Highsmith spent her last thirteen years alone in a two-hundred-year-old farmhouse in southern Switzerland. She died of cancer in 1995, at the age of seventy-four, and her body was cremated. Of the author's final weeks, a neighbor recalled, "There was a tranquillity about her. She seemed to be quite peaceful, and as lucid as could be."

She liked whips and chains

CHAPTER 16

Pauline Réage & DOMINIQUE AURY

Not many authors can boast of having written a best-selling pornographic novel, much less one regarded as an erotica classic—but Pauline Réage could. Make that Dominique Aury. No: Anne Desclos.

All three were the same woman, but for years the real name behind the incendiary work was among the best-kept secrets in the literary world. Forty years after the publication of the French novel *Histoire d'O*, the full truth was finally made public. Even then, some still considered it the most shocking book ever written. When the book came out, its purported author was "Pauline Réage," widely believed to be a pseudonym. Although shocking for its graphic depictions of sadomasochism, the novel was admired for its reticent, even austere literary style. It went on to achieve worldwide success, selling millions of copies, and has never been out of print. This was no cheap potboiler. There was nothing clumsy, sloppy, or crude about it. *Histoire d'O* was awarded the distinguished Prix des Deux Magots, was adapted for film, and was translated into more than twenty languages.

Desclos (or, rather, Aury, as she became known in her early thirties) was obsessed with her married lover, Jean Paulhan. She wrote the book to entice him, claim him, and keep him—and she wrote it exclusively for him. It was the ultimate love letter.

Whips and chains and masks! Oh, my. When *Histoire d'O* appeared in France in the summer of 1954, it was so scandalous that obscenity charges (later dropped) were brought against its mysterious author. Even in the mid-twentieth century, in a European country decidedly less prudish than the United States, the book struck like a meteor. That the writer had evidently used a pen name provoked endless gossip in Parisian society. Speculation about the author's identity became a favorite sport among the literati: was the author prominent, obscure, male, female, perverted, crazy? The authorial voice was too direct, too cool, to be that of a woman, some argued; others insisted that no man could have offered such a nuanced exploration of a woman's psyche. One thing was certain: the person who wrote this novel had no shame.

Story of O, the title of the English edition, is an account of a French fashion photographer, known only as O, who descends into debasement, torment, humiliation, violence, and bondage, all in the name of devotion to her lover, René. Over the course of the novel she is blindfolded, chained, flogged, pierced, branded, and more. As the story opens, O is a passive figure who does precisely what she's told:

> Her lover one day takes O for a walk in a section of the city where they never go—the Montsouris Park, the Monceau Park. After they have taken a stroll in the park and have sat together side by side on the edge of a lawn, they notice, at one corner of the park, at an intersection where there are never any taxis, a car which, because of its meter, resembles a taxi.
>
> "Get in," he says.
>
> She gets in.

The book is like an erotic version of those childhood tales in which a character steps accidentally into an alternate reality and is induced into a hallucinatory state. (Paulhan once insisted that "fairy tales are erotic novels for children.") Think of Alice falling down the rabbit hole, or the magic wardrobe leading to Narnia. That was *Story of O*, albeit with a much darker vision. By the novel's eleventh page, O has been abandoned by her lover at a château outside Paris. Alone, she is subdued, quietly following instructions without resistance. She undresses and is fitted with a locked collar and bracelets and a long red cape. Blindfolded, she cries out as a stranger's hand "penetrated her in both places at once." Thus begins her odyssey as a sexual slave to the mostly anonymous men and women who have their way with her. "O thought she recognized one of the men from his voice," Réage writes, "one of those who had forced her the previous evening, the one who had asked that her rear be made more easily accessible." Willing to do anything with anyone, she reveals an existential longing for release. Aury once observed that "O is looking for deliverance, to thrust off this mortal coil, as Shakespeare says."

Years after the book was published, Aury offered insight into her protagonist's apparent façade of passive acceptance. "I think that submissiveness can [be] and is a formidable weapon, which women will use as long as it isn't taken from them," she said. "Is O used by René and Sir Stephen, or does she in fact use them, and . . . all those irons and chains and obligatory debauchery, to fulfill her own dream—that is, her own destruction and death? And, in some surreptitious way, isn't she in charge of them? Doesn't she bend them to her will?"

The novel also featured scenes of women seducing women. Those encounters seemed genuine rather than forced, contrary to accusations that the author had written such scenes to satisfy the "male gaze." Aury considered herself bisexual and admitted her preference for the female body. Describing her first real-life exposure to male anatomy, she said, "I found that stiffly saluting member, of which he was so proud, rather frightening, and to tell the truth I found his pride slightly comical. I thought that that must be embarrassing for him, and thought how much more pleasant it was to be a girl. That, by the way, is an opinion I still hold today."

Throughout the story, O readily offers herself. She responds to pain and suffering with acceptance or gratitude. The narrative culminates in an all-night party in which she is led along on a dog leash, naked, wearing an owl mask. After she has had a depilatory, to please her master, a chain is attached to rings inserted into her labia. (Her journey seemed to confirm the French writer Georges Bataille's dictum: "Man goes constantly in fear of himself. His erotic urges terrify him.") O's response to such terror is absolute surrender, allowing her experiences to lead her into a realm of no pathology, analysis, or consequence. As just about every self-help book advises, opening yourself to the unknown can feel very good. It can transform you. Then again, it can also make you insane.

Depending on your erotic wishes and habits, *Story of O* will disturb you, frighten you, make you angry, make you upset, confuse you, disgust you, or turn you on. Maybe everything at once. Decades after its publication, the novel has not lost its shock value. In 2009, a commentary in the *Guardian* following a Radio 4 program, "The Story of O—The Vice Française," explained that the late-night timing of the program was apt, because the material was "strong stuff" and might have made people queasy. One listener had remarked, on the air, that hearing excerpts from the book provoked "a rush of blood to the non-thinking parts."

As the author once revealed, the character O actually began as Odile, the name of a close friend who'd once been deeply in love with Albert Camus. "She knew all about the name and was enchanted," Aury said. "But after a few pages I decided that I couldn't do all those things to poor Odile, so I just kept the first letter." Contrary to speculation over the years by feminists, academics, psychoanalysts, and general readers obsessed with the book, the name O, she said, "has nothing to do with erotic symbolism or the shape of the female sex."

However depraved her novel seemed, Aury had set out to create a profoundly personal work of art, not cheap porn. ("That Pauline Réage is a more dangerous writer than the Marquis de Sade follows from the fact that art is more persuasive than propaganda," declared an essayist in the *New York Review of Books*.) Aury was making something new, working with conventions as no one had attempted in quite the same way. "Debauchery conceived of as a kind of ascetic experience is not new, either for men or for women," she explained, "but until *Story of O* no woman to my knowledge had said it."

Aury seemed an unlikely candidate to produce a book showcasing violent penetration. From childhood she'd been a serious reader, immersing herself in Boccaccio, Shakespeare, Baudelaire, and the Bible. She once boasted of a period in which she'd read and reread the whole of Proust each year for five years. It seemed inconceivable that a woman with such a drab exterior could explore a sexual compulsion that drove her protagonist toward oblivion. Also distinguishing the novel from what one critic called "volumes sold under the counter" were its intricate ideas about human behavior—that "we are all jailers, and all in prison, in that there is always someone within us whom we enchain, whom we imprison, whom we silence," as she later explained. *Story of O* is about power, the pleasure of having it, and finally the pleasure of letting it go. For her part, the author admitted her comfort with the notion of obedience, at least in certain contexts. "I think I have a repressed bent for the military," she said. "I like discipline without question, specific schedules and duties."

Paulhan, the impetus for Aury's cri de coeur, was one of France's leading intellectuals and the publisher of the preeminent literary journal *Nouvelle Revue Française*. His affair with Aury lasted thirty years, until his death in 1968. Throughout their relationship, Paulhan remained married to his second wife, Germaine, who had Parkinson's disease. She was well aware of her husband's philandering, which he expected her to tolerate without protest. And Aury was not his only mistress. After his death, his daughter-in-law remembered him as "quite the ladies' man." (It's interesting that Aury used precisely the same phrase in recalling her own father.)

When she met Paulhan, Aury was in her early thirties and he was in his fifties. (She was born in 1907; he was born in 1884.) She'd been married briefly and had a son, Philippe. Her father, an acquaintance of Paulhan, had introduced them. At the time, she was hoping to publish a collection of sixteenth- and seventeenth-century French religious poetry, and Paulhan was an editor at the distinguished publishing house Gallimard. She did not describe their meeting as love at first sight. "It was slow, but it went very—efficiently," she said, recalling her initial impression of him as handsome, charming, and funny. They bonded through shared intellectual passion; during the Nazi occupation of France, while doing work for the Resistance, they became lovers. "Dominique Aury was fascinated by intelligence," a friend recalled. "The intelligence of Paulhan was obvious. And for her it became a kind of obsession."

Until her fateful meeting with Paulhan, Aury hadn't yet found the love of her life, and her sexual history was hardly remarkable. "By my makeup and temperament I wasn't really prey to physical desires," she once said. "Everything happened in my head." That would explain the electricity between her and Paulhan, which would exert a hold on her for the rest of her life. Although she could talk extensively about sex, her personal life was fairly tame. She did once joke, however, that she'd considered prostitution as a potential vocation: "I told myself that had to be absolutely terrific: to be constantly wanted, and to get paid besides, how could you go wrong?" she said. "And what happens? At the first opportunity, what do I do but turn into a stupid prude!" Yet she had also wondered what it might be like to become a nun—drawn to it, no doubt, by the stern uniform.

Of course, Aury was destined not for prostitution but to live, work, and breathe intellectual society. She toyed with her identity well before *Histoire d'O* was published. At some point during the war, while working as a journalist and translator, she discarded her original name, Anne Desclos, erasing it entirely from her professional and personal life. Almost no one knew that Aury was not actually her own name; she kept that fact a secret. She had chosen "Dominique" for its gender neutrality, and "Aury" was derived from her mother's maiden name, "Auricoste."

Although it's true that *Story of O* was inspired by Paulhan's off-hand remark to Aury that no woman could ever write a "truly" erotic novel, a more compelling motive was her fear, however irrational, that their relationship might end. "I wasn't young, I wasn't pretty, it was necessary to find other weapons," she later revealed. "The physical side wasn't enough. The weapons, alas, were in the head." She plunged into the task: writing through the night, in pencil, in school exercise books, while lying in bed, and she produced—three months later—her intimate masterpiece. The first sixty pages, she said, flowed "automatically" and appeared in the book exactly as they had come to her.

The novel was written as a challenge to Paulhan's dare (or assignment, if you want to call it that). "I wrote it alone, for him, to interest him, to please him, to occupy him," she told the documentary filmmaker Pola Rapaport shortly before her death. Aury never intended the novel to be made public, but Paulhan insisted on it. For her, the manuscript was simply a long letter that had to be written. She hoped this gift would ensure the permanence of their relationship. "You're always looking for ways to make it go on," she said. "The story of Scheherazade, more or less."

The content of the novel was graphic, but the author's prose was highly controlled, disciplined, and spare. Her "voice" was at odds with the erotic material, making it hard to dismiss as pornography. For Paulhan, the book was "the most ardent love letter that any man has ever received." He did not abandon her.

The author said later that *Story of O*, written when she was forty-seven, was based on her own fantasies. She was influenced, too, by her lover's admiration for the Marquis de Sade. Later she described her feverish writing process as "writing the way you speak in the dark to the person you love when you've held back the words of love for too long and they flow at last . . . without hesitation, without stopping, rewriting, discarding . . . the way one breathes, the way one dreams."

Paulhan was awestruck. When he excitedly asked if he could find a publisher for her work, she agreed on the condition that her authorship remain hidden, known only to a select few. She gave herself the pen name "Pauline Réage": "Pauline" after Pauline (Bonaparte) Borghese, elder sister of Napoleon, who was famous for her sensual, decadent pursuits; as well as Pauline Roland, the late-nineteenth-century French women's rights activist. Despite the apparent blur between "Pauline" and "Paulhan," Aury said later that her appellation had nothing to do with him. (Some insisted, wrongly, that she chose the name because it sounded like the French for "Reacting to Paulhan.") As for "Réage," she'd supposedly stumbled upon it in a real estate registry.

People assumed that aspects of *Story of O* were highly autobiographical, yet Aury wasn't so sure. Some twenty years after the book came out, she admitted that her own joys and sorrows had informed it, but she had no idea just how much, and did not care to analyze anything. "*Story of O* is a fairy tale for another world," she said, "a world where some part of me lived for a long time, a world that no longer exists except between the covers of a book."

She characterized "Pauline Réage" in vague terms as well—someone who "is not me entirely and yet in some obscure way is: when I move from one me to the other the fragments scatter, then come back together again in a pattern that I'm sure is ever-changing. I find it harder and harder to tell them apart anymore, or at least not with sufficient clarity." Like many pseudonymous authors, Aury saw identity as unstable and felt perfectly at ease inhabiting a self that refused to remain a fixed star.

She knew that finding a publisher for her novel (whether or not she took a pen name) would not be easy. It was Paulhan who demanded that the book reach the public, and he fought for it. In this instance, however, his prestige within the literary world carried no clout. Gallimard promptly refused the work, not wanting to deal with the inevitable (and expensive) hassle of a court case. "We can't publish books like this," Gaston Gallimard told her. This was especially disappointing because Aury had worked for him. A few years before her death, Aury said that she had never forgiven Gallimard's rejection of her novel, since he'd already published Jean Genet, whose work was "much nastier."

Paulhan persuaded Jean-Jacques Pauvert—an ambitious twenty-seven-year-old publisher who'd issued Sade's complete works, and who was already a veteran of obscenity trials—to accept *Story of O*. "It's marvelous, it'll spark a revolution," Pauvert said to Paulhan after reading it overnight. "So when do we sign the contract?"

In 1954, Pauvert published a gorgeously designed first edition of two thousand copies. It had a laudatory preface by Paulhan, "Happiness in Slavery," in which he argued that women in their truest nature crave domination; that O is empowered by confessing her desire; and that, in truth, slaves love their masters, would suffer in their absence, and have no wish to achieve independence. Indeed, as one reviewer noted, the more O is brutalized, the more "perfectly feminine" she becomes. This is one of the elements that makes the novel more disturbing than arousing.

Paulhan conceded that there was "no dearth of abominations in *Story of O*. But it sometimes seems to me that it is an idea, or a complex of ideas, an opinion rather than a young woman we see being subjected to these tortures."

The book was a sensation, but hardly a blockbuster. Although it was a topic of titillating gossip among the cognoscenti, a year after publication, the initial printing had not sold out. Aury was not hopeful about the book's prospects; she believed it was doomed to be relegated to the "reserved" section of libraries, if it was ordered at all.

Its status as a best seller was achieved slowly, as the mystique around it continued to build and as other international editions were issued. Initially, because many French booksellers assumed that the novel had been banned, they tended to conceal it under the counter—thus ensuring that sales would be poor. "Everyone talked about it in private," the author recalled, "but the press acted as though the book had never been published."

Whatever attention *Histoire d'O* did receive focused on the author's identity, not on the text itself as something worthy of consideration and analysis. Susan Sontag was the first major writer to recognize the novel's merit and to defend it as a significant literary work.

In her 1969 essay "The Pornographic Imagination," Sontag insisted that *Story of O* could be correctly defined as "authentic" literature. She compared the ratio of first-rate pornography to trashy books within the genre to "another somewhat shady sub-genre with a few first-rate books to its credit, science fiction." She also maintained that like science fiction, pornography was aimed at "disorientation, at psychic dislocation."

If so, that aim is far more interesting than what most generic "mainstream" novels set out to do. No one could describe *O* as predictable or sentimental. Its vision was dark and unrelenting; everything about it was extreme. Sontag also compared sexual obsession (as expressed by Réage) with religious obsession: two sides of the same coin. "Religion is probably, after sex, the second oldest resource which human beings have available to them for blowing their minds," she wrote. In her disciplined effort toward transcendence, O is not unlike a zealot giving herself to God. O's devotion to the task at hand takes the form of what might be described as spiritual fervor. She loses herself entirely—and, after all, the loss of self is a goal of prayer.

If O is willing to sustain her devotion all the way through to her own destruction, so be it. She wants to be "possessed, utterly possessed, to the point of death," to the point that her body and mind are no longer her responsibility. "What does a Christian seek but to lose himself in God," Aury, a devout atheist, once said. "To be killed by someone you love strikes me as the epitome of ecstasy."

Sontag's essay was notable for refusing to conflate all porn as bad or to dismiss it all as "dirty books." It was a thoughtful, rational piece on the aesthetic virtues of pornography at its best. In arguing that some so-called pornographic books were legitimate works of art, she acknowledged that staking such a claim was a daunting task: "Pornography is a malady to be diagnosed and an occasion for judgment. It's something to be for or against . . . quite a bit like being for or against legalized abortion or federal aid to parochial schools."

Her case for the literary value of *Story of O* was compelling and highly specific: "Though the novel is clearly obscene by the usual standards," she wrote, "and more effective than many in arousing a reader sexually, sexual arousal doesn't appear to be the sole function of the situations portrayed. The narrative does have a definite beginning, middle, and end. The elegance of the writing hardly gives the impression that its author considered language a bothersome necessity. Further, the characters do possess emotions of a very intense kind, although obsessional and indeed wholly asocial ones; characters do have motives, though they are not psychiatrically or socially 'normal' motives." All Réage did was bring into the open the kinds of impulses many people harbor in their bedrooms, alone, late at night. And, from Sontag's perspective, *Story of O* was not really pornography but "metapornography, a brilliant parody."

Who would suspect that Dominique Aury was Pauline Réage? In midlife, Aury was a respected figure: an influential editor, a writer, and a jury member for various literary prizes. She'd earned the Légion d'Honneur; she had translated into French works by authors such as T. S. Eliot, Evelyn Waugh, F. Scott Fitzgerald, and Virginia Woolf; and she had been the only woman to serve on Gallimard's esteemed reading committee. Her demure appearance gave no hint of owl masks or dog collars. She was polite, refined, elegant, shy. She could not be described as beautiful. A friend remembered Aury as "very self-effacing," and as having worn "soft, muted colors which really matched her personality." She dressed quite plainly and wore almost no makeup. At least on the surface, nothing about her was subversive. (She said that dressing in a kind of basic uniform made life simpler.) If anything, Aury seemed conservative, even severe—and to look at her, you might assume that her sexual fantasies would be as stimulating as staring at a dusty library shelf.

The glaring incongruity between her work and her personal life was not lost on Aury. That was why the pen name was so crucial. She insisted that "it would have been wrong to mix what was for so long a time secret with something that was always banal and devoid of interest." Aury never felt a need to justify the distinction to anyone; it was what she wanted, and it was nobody's business. She was not "living a lie," because Dominique Aury was not "Pauline Réage," who had produced the scandalous work. "For a long time I've lived two parallel lives," Aury explained. "I have meticulously kept those two lives quite separate, so separate in fact that the invisible wall between them seems to me normal and natural."

Upon the publication of *Story of O*, guessing games were rampant about the author's identity. Contenders included Raymond Queneau, André Malraux, and the most unlikely of all, George Plimpton, founding editor of the *Paris Review*. "It wasn't me," Plimpton told a reporter in the early 1990s, "but it's a rumor I prefer not to scotch." Paulhan, too, was a possibility, suspected at the very least of knowing the enigmatic author's identity. As Sontag noted, the theory that Paulhan was the author seemed credible partly because of his introductory essay for the novel. It called to mind the mask of Georges Bataille, who, having written his *Madame Edwarda* under the pseudonym "Pierre Angelique," also contributed its preface under his own name.

For a while, Paulhan was under intense scrutiny, and his longtime, already volatile friendship with the writer François Mauriac was threatened by the novel's publication. Mauriac, a devoted if somewhat conflicted Catholic, acknowledged that he hadn't read *O*, but nonetheless publicly attacked the book. He was convinced that Paulhan had written it, and Paulhan responded by lashing out, accusing Mauriac of being the real author.

Some readers believed that Paulhan had heavily edited the kinky text. He denied doing so, and Aury, too, insisted later that he hadn't altered so much as a comma. She said the extent of his editing consisted of omitting a single adjective: "*sacrificiel.*" Pauvert, who'd known Aury for more than a decade (and knew of her nom de plume), had no doubt that the novel was Aury's alone. "I recognized her style immediately when I first saw the manuscript," he said. "She is a great writer and absolutely uncopyable. Paulhan said that he could not write like that—that his own style was quite different, very dry, ironic, and he could not change it."

A hastily released English translation came within weeks, issued by Maurice Girodas of the Olympia Press. This edition "horrified" Aury; she found it "vulgar" and said that "it cheapens the character of the book." (She did approve, however, of the translation published by Barney Rosset's Grove Press in 1965.) Fan mail and hate mail poured in. Such a fuss was made that Pauvert and Girodas were interrogated by French police after the novel won the Deux Magots prize. Both men refused to reveal the whereabouts of Pauline Réage, and despite an investigation, no legal action came of it.

As a prime suspect in the making of this scandalous text, Paulhan paid a price. When he was nominated for membership in the elite Académie Française—which consists of forty members known as "immortals"—the opponents of his candidacy are said to have placed a copy of *Histoire d'O* on every Academy member's chair in protest. (He was elected anyway.) He was also forced to provide a deposition to the vice squad in 1955 as it held hearings to determine whether legal action should be taken against the book. Of course he lied in his testimony. He declared that "Mme. Pauline Réage (a pseudonym) paid me a visit in my office . . . and submitted to me a thick manuscript." There was some truth in Paulhan's deposition—his feelings about the manuscript and why he had championed it. He revealed that he was struck by the book's literary quality "and, if I may say, in the context of an absolutely scabrous subject, by its restraint and modesty." He said nothing about being in love with the author, but he was completely honest in recalling his first response to it. "I had in my hands a work that was very important in both its content and its style," he said, "a work that derived much more from the mystical than from the erotic and that might well be for our own time what *Letters to a Portuguese Nun* or *Les Liaisons Dangereuses* were for theirs."

He concluded his statement by reiterating that Réage did not wish to reveal her true identity, and that he intended to protect her desire for privacy. "Nonetheless," he added, "since I do see her fairly regularly, I shall inform her of the statement I have just made, and in case she should change her mind I shall ask that she get in touch with you."

Aury had her own dealings with the police: They showed up at her house one day to interrogate her about the book, and she feigned ignorance. Inexplicably, they chose not to pursue the matter—a courtesy for which she was grateful. But she did feel terribly guilty that the vice squad had focused so intently on her lover and her publisher.

Still, she suffered her share of awkward encounters, snubs, insults, scorn, and ignorant and rude remarks. Because of her anonymity, people felt free to express their opinions about the book. If anyone asked her directly whether she was Réage, she'd simply reply, "That is a question to which I never respond." (It was a clever response, neither an admission nor a denial.) She was startled to read a characterization of her book as "violently and willfully immoral"; such commentary served to confirm that the pseudonym had been the best way to go. Aury was not naïve, and understood that the novel was quite racy, but she didn't think it was offensive. To her, one's sense of morality was assaulted daily by reading the newspaper. "Concentration camps offend decency," she said, "as does the atomic bomb, and torture; in fact, life itself offends public morals every minute of the day, in my opinion, and not specifically through the various and sundry methods of making love."

Once, at a dinner party, she was amused to hear a friend confidently announce that people who wrote books such as *Histoire d'O* were very sick. Another time, in the presence of her mother, a family friend abruptly turned to Aury and said he believed that she'd written *Histoire d'O*. She panicked, but said nothing. There was an awkward silence. Then her mother said, "She never mentioned it to us." After their guest left, Aury's mother offered her more tea and never spoke of it again. "My freedom lay in silence, as my mother's lay in hers," Aury later recalled. "Hers was the refusal to know; mine, the refusal to say."

Although her father had an extensive erotica collection and had spoken frankly to her early on about sex, Aury's mother was another matter. "She didn't like men," Aury said. "She didn't like women, either. She hated flesh."

Some of the vitriol directed against Aury's book was quite shocking. People described it as trash. (How many had actually read the book?) The author was accused of being antifeminist and of dishonoring all women. Never mind that no man who had written pornography was ever blamed for debasing his gender. Aury received plenty of nasty letters addressed to her alter ego: one writer called her a "damned bitch" who catered to the lowest common denominator for money. Another cursed the womb that bore her. Perhaps one of the most perplexing letters was from a man who told her that although the fantasy S&M world she wrote about did exist, it was only between men and boys. He claimed that it was much easier to dominate young boys than women.

As for Aury's son, Philippe, who was in his twenties when *O* appeared, he told a journalist after his mother's death that he'd had no clue what she had been up to. "I didn't know she was the author," he said. "She never told me, really. I only found out in 1974, when there was talk of making a film and people came round to discuss it." The film, made in 1975, is universally acknowledged to be dreadful. However, he added, "It is a very good book."

Jean-Jacques Pauvert once told an amusing anecdote about being on holiday with his wife in 1957 or 1958 and overhearing a conversation at a restaurant. A group of people were seated at a table behind them—"well dressed, in their late forties or fifties, probably notables of the town, quite cultivated people, talking about books." Suddenly, Pauvert recalled:

> One of the men said, "You must understand that since Paulette wrote *Histoire d'O* she has had a very difficult time—isn't that right, Paulette?" His wife, a good-looking woman, about forty-five years old, wearing a fine pearl necklace, replied, "Yes, you know, it's been terrible for me. If I had only known what it would turn into, what with my husband's position. . . . It's absolutely terrible." This seemed to be going on all over France. There were literally hundreds of people claiming to be the author of *O*.

Each of the three introductory notes in the novel expresses bafflement as to the author's real identity. The translator Sabine d'Estrée—and more on *that* pseudonym later—pointed out that Pauline Réage was "a name completely unknown in French literary circles, where everyone knows everyone." Aside from corresponding with the author about the translation, d'Estrée admitted, "I have never met Pauline Réage." The shock of the book itself paled in comparison with the public's curiosity about the name of the person who wrote it. "Until her identity was bared," d'Estrée wrote, "people found it difficult to assume a reasonable stance vis-à-vis the work; if Pauline Réage was the pseudonym of some eminent writer, they would feel compelled to react one way; if she were a complete unknown, another; and if indeed she were a literary hack merely seeking notoriety, then still another."

The quality of Réage's prose made it clear that the last alternative was highly unlikely, if not impossible. "To this day," the translator wrote, "no one knows who Pauline Réage is."

For his part, Paulhan offered no clues. "Who is Pauline Réage?"

he wrote in his preface, describing the novel as "one of those books which marks the reader, which leaves him not quite, or not at all, the same as he was before he read it." He proclaimed it a "brilliant feat" from beginning to end, one that read more like someone's private letter than a diary. "But to whom is the letter addressed?" he asked, disingenuously. "Whom is the speech trying to convince? Whom can we ask? I don't even know who you are."

Nothing about the novel was straightforward, as the *New York Review of Books* noted in 1966 about the Grove Press edition: "[O]ne is struck by an atmosphere of prestidigitation, of double and triple meanings that suggest an elaborate literary joke or riddle which extends even to the question of *O*'s authorship. Pauline Réage, except as author of the present book and of the preface to another, seems not otherwise to exist: None of her admirers claims to have met her, she has not been seen in Parisian literary circles, and it has been said that she is actually a committee of literary farceurs, sworn to guard their separate identities, like the pseudonymous authors of a revolutionary manifesto."

The *NYRB* had a mixed response to the novel but conceded that it was too coolly executed not to be taken seriously: "If it is not a joke then it is madness, though not without brilliance and not without pathos." The reviewer seemed convinced that it was the work of Paulhan, noting (wrongly) that Paulhan's preface was in a style "not unlike that of the novel itself." But this reviewer added, more tenably, that "Pauline (Paulhan?) Réage, whoever she, he, or they may be, is surely perverse and may indeed be mad, but she or he is no fool and is as far as can be from vulgarity."

The Columbia University professor Albert Goldman, reviewing *Story of O* for the *New York Times*, was effusive in his praise, calling it "a rare instance of pornography sublimed to purest art" and describing its "evidently pseudonymous author" as "a more dangerous writer than the Marquis de Sade." Rather than issuing propaganda or a "call to arms," Réage, with her simple, direct style, aims, he argued, "to clarify, to make real to the reader those dark and repulsive practices and emotions that his better self rejects as improbable or evil." Yet the critic Eliot Fremont-Smith, also writing in the *Times*, described the book in more ambivalent terms as "revolting, haunting, somewhat erotic, rather more emetic, ludicrous, boring, unbelievable and quite unsettling." He added that it was of "undeniable artistic interest."

In any case, Pauline Réage stayed silent, and Dominique Aury continued her respectable life as a cultural éminence grise. For years there were rumors, hints, and speculation connecting the two, and at some point the connection had become an open secret in literary circles—yet her privacy was respected.

Paulhan's daughter-in-law, Jacqueline, later claimed that she had learned the truth only at Paulhan's funeral in 1968. "There was a very big bouquet of flowers with no name attached," she told a journalist. "I was standing next to Dominique Aury, whom of course I knew well, and I remarked, 'I suppose they must be from Pauline Réage.' Dominique turned to me and said, '*Mais, Jacqueline, Pauline Réage, c'est moi.*'"

Decades later, Aury offered a full and public confession. Her lover had been dead a long time. Her parents were dead. She felt she was reaching the end of her own life. There was nothing to lose, nothing at stake now.

The August 1, 1994, issue of the *New Yorker* printed an excerpt from a forthcoming book by the British writer John de St. Jorre, *The Good Ship Venus* (*Venus Bound* in the United States), about the infamous novels published by the Olympia Press—including Vladimir Nabokov's *Lolita*, William S. Burroughs's *Naked Lunch*, and Pauline Réage's *Story of O*. When the author interviewed Aury for his book, he was treated to "a double surprise": he learned definitively that she was Réage; and he learned that the name Dominique Aury "was itself a disguise." Although she asked that he not publish her actual name, the now elderly lady was otherwise ready to confess at last.

St. Jorre landed a fascinating interview with Aury, whom he described as a "calm, clearheaded woman who answered my questions easily and with dry humor." She dismissed the scandal that had erupted over her novel all those years ago as "much ado about nothing."

In 1975, Aury had given a long, wide-ranging interview to Régine Deforges, an author whom Aury admired. She was interviewed as "Pauline Réage," and she provided honest answers about her life and work, and her philosophical views on art, sex, war, feminism, and so on, without disclosing her true name or getting too specific in her personal anecdotes. She could open up while remaining anonymous. The interview was published in book-length form as *Confessions of O*, first by Pauvert in France, and then, four years later, by Viking Press in the United States. (No photo of Réage appeared in the book.) The jacket copy noted, "In these pages one senses clearly a presence, a person, where once there had been only a pseudonym. The face may still be shrouded in mystery, but now, at last, the voice is clear, authoritative, and of a rare intelligence."

Aury never intended to give another interview after that one, so the *New Yorker*'s profile was a coup for the reporter. It was the first time Aury admitted in public that she had written *Story of O*.

Although she had led a quiet, comfortable life in the years following the publication of *O*, she did not entirely relinquish Pauline Réage. In 1969, she'd published a sequel of sorts, *Retour à Roissy*, which included the first novel's original (unpublished) final chapter, and a third-person account (titled "Une Fille Amoureuse," or "A Girl in Love") about the genesis of *O*, signed by Réage. She'd worked on it as Paulhan lay dying in a hospital room in a Paris suburb. Aury slept in his room each night for four months, until his death at eighty-three in October 1968. Later, she recalled Paulhan's extraordinary passion for life. "Existence filled him with wonder," she said. "Both the admirable and the horrible aspects of existence, equally so. The atrocious fascinated him. The enchanting enchanted him." One friend of Aury said that after Paulhan died, "She pulled back from the world and lost her short-term memory."

It's clear from St. Jorre's profile in the *New Yorker* that this "small, neat, handsome woman with gray hair and gray-blue eyes" never recovered from the loss of Paulhan and led a fairly solitary life afterward. "Their relationship underscored the centrality of love to life," St. Jorre wrote, "the creative and destructive forces that passion can unleash, and the ease with which a human heart can be broken." He concluded the piece by observing that Aury had no regrets "as her days and nights gather speed, taking her toward what she calls 'a great silence.'" She died in 1998, at the age of ninety.

Aside from its major revelation, the article delved into a subplot of the saga: the pseudonymous translator of the English edition of *Story of O*. There was no evidence of deception, aside from the translator's suspiciously florid name, "Sabine d'Estrée." Yet no one seemed to know the mysterious woman. The Grove edition included no biographical note on her, and she mentioned in her "Translator's Note" that she'd never met Réage but had been "in indirect communication (via the French publisher, Jean-Jacques Pauvert) and received the author's comments." Aury, in her interview with St. Jorre, told him that she had no memory of any contact with d'Estrée, nor any idea who she (or he) might be. St. Jorre had a theory, however: the New York editor, translator, and publisher Richard Seaver.

In the early 1950s, Seaver had lived in Paris as a Fulbright scholar studying at the Sorbonne. He cofounded a literary journal that published early pieces by Jean Genet and Eugène Ionesco in English. He was an early champion of the then-unknown Irish playwright Samuel Beckett, and had been instrumental in arranging a book deal for Beckett with Barney Rosset (who hired Seaver). Eventually, Seaver worked his way up to editor in chief at Grove, where he was celebrated for advocating challenging and censored books. He stayed at Grove for twelve years before moving to Viking and then to Holt, Rinehart; along with his French wife, Jeannette, he founded Arcade Publishing in 1988. Jeannette's middle name is Sabine.

St. Jorre's attempt to extract information from Seaver himself went nowhere. Seaver insisted that he'd been sworn to secrecy about d'Estrée's identity but told St. Jorre that he would seek permission from d'Estrée—whom he called a "very shy, secretive person"—and get back to him. He never did.

So the journalist did his own research, carefully going through the Grove Press correspondence archive at Syracuse University Library's Special Collections Department. He found it curious that there were variant spellings of "d'Estrée," and that one letter purporting to be from d'Estrée herself requested that all payments be addressed to an attorney in Manhattan, Seymour Litvinoff. After St. Jorre tracked down the lawyer, Litvinoff said that had represented both Seaver and d'Estrée, but "I cannot say who Sabine is. I don't know who she is."

St. Jorre also discovered that d'Estrée had continued to translate French erotica—at least four other books—in collaboration with Seaver, who kept "hiring" her even after changing publishing jobs. She did translation work for no one else. Seaver was long believed to be d'Estrée, but he kept quiet about it. The mystery was solved in January 2009, when he died of a heart attack at the age of eighty-two. His wife finally confessed. "He wanted people to guess," Jeannette told a reporter. "But yes, he did it."

Seaver's stint as d'Estrée has been largely forgotten, but the novel still resonates around the world, affecting readers in ways that are deeply personal. "Ever since I remember," an anonymous American woman admitted on an online message board, "I have always used some form of power exchange fantasy in masturbation. I had no words for it, no framework, and *O* was the first book to provide that."

Story of O also influenced writers of erotica for decades after its release, though it set a standard that few, if any, could meet. The person who could perhaps claim the closest literary kinship with Réage is the contemporary author and art critic Catherine Millet, whose "autobiography," *Sexual Life of Catherine M.*, was published in 2002. Edmund White went so far as to call it "the most explicit book about sex ever written by a woman." The book detailed the author's early experiences with masturbation and her abiding fondness for orgies (in which she began to dabble at the age of eighteen), sex in public places, and so on. She said that of her countless lovers, mostly men, she would be able to recognize at best only fifty faces or names. The book was cast as a memoir, but J. G. Ballard wondered if it was "the most original novel of the year."

Although Millet's sexual proclivities hardly mirrored those of Réage—Millet did admit to enjoying having her nipples pinched, along with more aggressive forms of sex—their profiles were strikingly alike. Both women published confessional, shockingly graphic books in midlife. Millet is French, and by day she, too, is a bourgeois intellectual who appears respectable enough. Her book, like *O*, was well written and even literary. As Jenny Diski noted in the *London Review of Books*, Millet "anatomises her sexual experiences and responses as a Cubist might the visual field." That Millet's project was both intellectual and sexual (and possibly even spiritual) calls Réage to mind yet again. "[Millet] takes her radical philosophy from Bataille, and admires Pauline Réage's über-underling O for her perpetual readiness for sex, her propensity for being sodomised and her reclusiveness," Diski wrote. Millet, like Réage, feels no guilt about her sexual life, and similarly writes about sex "as plainly as if she were a housewife describing her domestic round."

Had Réage not published *Story of O*, perhaps Millet could not have published *Sexual Life*, at least not under her own name. Aury had endured stigma and shame and had emerged a success. That legacy gave Millet license to tell her story. And it explains why Jane Juska, for example, could celebrate, in *A Round Heeled Woman*, the pleasures of promiscuous geriatric sex via the *NYRB* classified ads. It also freed a young woman, Melissa Panarello (known as "Melissa P."), to publish an erotic autobiographical novel in 2004. Called *One Hundred Strokes of the Brush Before Bed*, it chronicled, in diary form, group sex, S&M, and other experiences. This book was an immediate best seller in the author's native Italy, and was hailed as "a *Story of O* for our times."

O's enduring significance was evident on the fiftieth anniversary of its debut, when the French government proudly announced that

Histoire d'O would be included on a list of "national triumphs" to be celebrated that year.

Two years later, in 2006, Réage's works were part of an auction at Christie's in Paris, featuring the "Bibliothèque Erotique" of Gérard Nordmann, a businessman in Geneva who had assembled a library of almost two thousand erotic manuscripts and rare books. An edition of *O* from its limited first run of six hundred copies was cited as "First edition of the most important erotic novel of the postwar period." Another lot by Réage was described as "[the] complete holograph working manuscript in pencil and ballpoint of what is arguably the finest erotic novel (1954) of the post-war period and its sequel (1969), which describe unconditional love as total sexual submission carried to its ultimate consequence." The manuscripts of *Histoire d'O* and *Retour à Roissy* sold for $127,000.

In assessing the life and work of Dominique Aury, it is striking how brave she was to risk everything for the man she loved. The pseudonym could have been exposed early on, destroying her reputation and wrecking friendships. "If you care enough about something, you have to pay the price," Aury once said. Hers was a life without compromise, highly moral, and one lived without regret.

After Aury's death in a suburb south of Paris, a longtime friend declared it unremarkable that the author had hoarded a nom de plume for so long. "Everyone is double, or triple, or quadruple," she said. "Every character has its hidden sides. One doesn't reveal one's secrets to all."

Acknowledgments

Above all, I cannot thank enough the amazing Tina Bennett of Janklow & Nesbit. Without her, there would be no book, or it would exist only in my head. I'm grateful for her wisdom, kindness, patience, and enthusiasm, and for always laughing at my jokes. I feel very lucky. Big thanks also to Svetlana Katz and Stephanie Koven at Janklow.

HarperCollins has been wonderfully supportive. Thanks especially to Terry Karten, Sarah Odell, Tina Andreadis, and Heather Drucker.

My friend Barbara Jones helped and encouraged me, from beginning to end, in every way possible. I'll be thanking her for years to come.

Thanks also to Amy Grace Loyd, Nicholas Latimer, Amy Citron, Gretchen Koss, Peter Miller, Dawn Raffel, John McMurtrie, Oscar Villalon, Nick Owchar, Perry Haberman, John Williams, Andy Hunter, and Michael Archer. And to the Community Bookstore of Park Slope.

My gratitude to Alice Quinn and Laurie Kerr; dear Michelle Williams; Devon Hodges, Eric Swanson, Tristan Swanson, and Cecily Swanson; Brian Jackson; Thomas Ranese; the Rosabals; my friends at 37 Montgomery Place; and above all, Sarah (and her parents, Rosalind and Colin) and Oscar and Freddy Fitzharding.

Time Line

George Sand born **1804**
Charlotte Brontë born **1816**
Emily Brontë born **1818**
George Eliot born **1819**
Anne Brontë born **1820**
Lewis Carroll born **1832**
Mark Twain born **1835**

1848 Emily Brontë dies
1849 Anne Brontë dies
1855 Charlotte Brontë dies

O. Henry born **1862**

1876 George Sand dies
1880 George Eliot dies

Isak Dinesen born **1885**
Fernando Pessoa born **1888**

1898 Lewis Carroll dies

Georges Simenon born **1903**
George Orwell born **1903**

Henry Green born	**1905**	
Pauline Réage born	**1907**	
	1910	Mark Twain dies
	1916	O. Henry dies
Romain Gary born	**1914**	
Alice Sheldon born	**1915**	
Patricia Highsmith born	**1921**	
Sylvia Plath born	**1932**	
	1935	Fernando Pessoa dies
	1950	George Orwell dies
	1962	Isak Dinesen dies
	1963	Sylvia Plath dies
	1973	Henry Green dies
	1980	Romain Gary dies
	1987	Alice Sheldon dies
	1989	Georges Simenon dies
	1995	Patricia Highsmith dies
	1998	Pauline Réage dies

Bibliography

The sources below were invaluable to me in researching and writing this book. Dates refer to the editions used, rather than the date of first publication. My supplemental research sources—hundreds of archival magazine, journal, and newspaper articles—are far too extensive to be cited in full here. Any source errors or omissions are wholly unintentional and will be corrected in future editions.

Anne, Charlotte, and Emily Brontë & Acton, Currer, and Ellis Bell

Barker, Juliet. *The Brontës: A Life in Letters*. New York: Viking, 1997.

Bentley, Phyllis. *The Brontës*. London: Thames and Hudson, 1997.

Brontë, Charlotte. *Jane Eyre*. New York: Penguin, 2003.

———. *Villette*. New York: Penguin, 2004.

Brontë, Emily Jane. *The Complete Poems*. New York: Penguin, 1992.

Fraser, Rebecca. *Charlotte Brontë: A Writer's Life*. New York: Pegasus, 2008.

Gaskell, Elizabeth. *The Life of Charlotte Brontë*. New York: Penguin, 1997.

Gordon, Lyndall. *Charlotte Brontë: A Passionate Life*. New York: Norton, 1994.

Miller, Lucasta. *The Brontë Myth*. New York: Knopf, 2003.

George Sand & Aurore Dupin

Jack, Belinda. *George Sand: A Woman's Life Writ Large*. New York: Vintage, 2001.

Maurois, André. *Lélia: The Life of George Sand*, trans. Gerard Hopkins. New York: Harper, 1954.

Sand, George. *Lucrezia Floriani*. Chicago: Academy Chicago, 1985.

———. *Marianne*. New York: Carroll and Graf, 1998.

———. *Story of My Life: The Autobiography of George Sand*, ed. Thelma Jurgrau. Albany: State University of New York Press, 1991.

George Eliot & Marian Evans

Booth, Alison. *Greatness Engendered: George Eliot and Virginia Woolf.* Ithaca, NY: Cornell University Press, 1992.

Eliot, George. *Brother Jacob*. London: Virago, 1989.

———. *Daniel Deronda*. New York: Penguin, 1986.

———. *The Lifted Veil*. London: Virago, 1985.

———. *Middlemarch*. New York: Modern Library, 2000.

———. *The Mill on the Floss*. New York: Penguin, 1985.

———. *Scenes of Clerical Life*. New York: Penguin, 1998.

———. *Silas Marner*. New York: Penguin, 1996.

Hanson, Lawrence, and Elisabeth Hanson. *Marian Evans and George Eliot: A Biography*. New York: Oxford University Press, 1952.

Hughes, Kathryn. *George Eliot: The Last Victorian*. New York: Farrar, Straus and Giroux, 1999.

Maddox, Brenda. *George Eliot in Love*. New York: Palgrave Macmillan, 2009.

Lewis Carroll & Charles Dodgson

Bassett, Lisa. *Very Truly Yours, Charles L. Dodgson, Alias Lewis Carroll*. New York: Lothrop, Lee and Shepard, 1987.

Carroll, Lewis. *Alice's Adventures in Wonderland*. New York: Bloomsbury, 2001.

———. *Alice's Adventures in Wonderland and Through the Looking Glass*. New York: Puffin, 1962.

Cohen, Morton N. *Lewis Carroll: A Biography*. New York: Vintage, 1995.

Wilson, Robin. *Lewis Carroll in Numberland: His Fantastical Mathematical Logical Life*. New York: Norton, 2008.

Woolf, Jenny. *The Mystery of Lewis Carroll: Discovering the Whimsical, Thoughtful, and Sometimes Lonely Man Who Created Alice in Wonderland*. New York: St. Martin's, 2010.

Mark Twain & Samuel Clemens

Fishkin, Shelley Fisher, ed. *The Mark Twain Anthology: Great Writers on His Life and Works.* New York: Library of America, 2010.

Grant, Douglas. *Mark Twain.* New York: Grove, 1962.

Kaplan, Justin. *Mr. Clemens and Mark Twain.* New York: Simon and Schuster, 1966.

Neider, Charles, ed. *Life As I Find It: A Treasury of Mark Twain Rarities.* New York: Cooper Square, 2000.

Powers, Ron. *Mark Twain: A Life.* New York: Free Press, 2005.

Quirk, Thomas, ed. *The Portable Mark Twain.* New York: Penguin, 2004.

Trombley, Laura. *Mark Twain's Other Woman: The Hidden Story of His Final Years.* New York: Knopf, 2010.

Twain, Mark. *Adventures of Huckleberry Finn.* Norton Critical Edition, ed. Sculley Bradley et al. New York: Norton, 1977.

———. *The Adventures of Tom Sawyer.* New York, Penguin, 1986.

Ward, Geoffrey C., and Dayton Duncan. *Mark Twain: An Illustrated Biography.* New York: Knopf, 2001.

O. Henry & William Sydney Porter

Henry, O. *The Complete Works.* New York: Doubleday, 1928.

Langford, Gerald. *Alias O. Henry.* New York: Macmillan, 1957.

O'Connor, Richard. *O. Henry: The Legendary Life of William S. Porter.* New York: Doubleday, 1970.

Smith, C. Alphonso. *O. Henry, Biography.* New York: Doubleday, Page, 1916.

Stuart, David. *O. Henry: A Biography of William Sydney Porter.* Chelsea, MI: Scarborough House, 1990.

Fernando Pessoa & His Heteronyms

Borges, Jorge Luis. *On Writing.* New York: Penguin, 2010.

Monteiro, George, ed. *The Man Who Never Was: Essays on Fernando Pessoa.* Providence, RI: Gávea-Brown, 1981.

———, ed. *The Presence of Pessoa: English, American, and Southern African Literary Responses.* Lexington: University Press of Kentucky, 1998.

Pessoa, Fernando. *Always Astonished: Selected Prose,* ed. and trans. Edwin Honig. San Francisco: City Lights, 1988.

————. *The Book of Disquiet: A Selection*, trans. Iain Watson. London: Quartet, 1991.

————. *The Book of Disquiet*, ed. and trans. Richard Zenith. New York: Penguin, 2003.

————. *The Education of the Stoic: The Only Manuscript of the Baron of Teive*, ed. and trans. Richard Zenith. Cambridge: Exact Change, 2005.

————. *Fernando Pessoa: A Centenary Pessoa,* ed. Eugénio Lisboa and L. C. Taylor. Carcanet, 2003.

————. *Fernando Pessoa & Co.: Selected Poems*, ed. and trans. Richard Zenith. New York: Grove, 1998.

————. *A Little Larger Than the Entire Universe: Selected Poems*, ed. and trans. Richard Zenith. New York: Penguin, 2006.

————. *The Selected Prose of Fernando Pessoa*, ed. and trans. Richard Zenith. New York: Grove, 2001.

George Orwell & Eric Blair

Bowker, Gordon. *George Orwell*. London: Abacus, 2003.

Crick, Bernard. *George Orwell: A Life*. New York: Penguin, 1982.

Crick, Bernard, and Audrey Coppard. *Orwell Remembered*. New York: Facts on File, 1984.

Davison, Peter. *George Orwell: A Literary Life*. London: Macmillan, 1998.

Orwell, George. *Animal Farm*. New York: Plume, 2003.

————. *Down and Out in Paris and London*. New York: Harcourt, 1961.

————. *Essays*. New York: Everyman's Library, 2002.

————. *Facing Unpleasant Facts: Narrative Essays*, ed. George Packer. New York: Mariner, 2009.

————. *Why I Write*. New York: Penguin, 2004.

Isak Dinesen & Karen Blixen

Dinesen, Isak. *Anecdotes of Destiny and Ehrengard*. New York: Vintage, 1993.

————. *Last Tales*. New York: Vintage, 1991.

————. *Letters from Africa 1914–1931*, ed. Frans Lasson. Chicago: University of Chicago Press, 1984.

————. *Out of Africa and Shadows on the Grass*. New York: Vintage, 1989.

————. *Seven Gothic Tales*. New York: Modern Library, 1934.

————. *Winter's Tales*. New York: Vintage, 1993.

Henriksen, Aage. *Isak Dinesen/Karen Blixen: The Work and the Life*. New York: St. Martin's, 1988.

Thurman, Judith. *Isak Dinesen: The Life of a Storyteller*. New York: St. Martin's, 1982.

Sylvia Plath & Victoria Lucas

Kendall, Tim. *Sylvia Plath: A Critical Study*. London: Faber and Faber, 2001.

Plath, Sylvia. *The Bell Jar*. New York: Harper and Row, 1971.

————. *The Bell Jar*. New York: HarperPerennial, 1999.

————. *Letters Home by Sylvia Plath: Correspondence 1950–1963*, ed. Aurelia Schober Plath. New York: Harper and Row, 1975.

————. *The Unabridged Journals of Sylvia Plath*, ed. Karen V. Kukil. New York: Anchor, 2000.

Rose, Jacqueline. *The Haunting of Sylvia Plath*. Cambridge, MA: Harvard University Press, 1991.

Stevenson, Anne. *Bitter Fame: A Life of Sylvia Plath*. London: Viking, 1989.

Wagner, Erica. *Ariel's Gift*. New York: Norton, 2001.

Henry Green & Henry Yorke

Green, Henry. *Loving; Living; Party Going*. New York: Penguin, 1993.

————. *Nothing*. New York: Dalkey Archive, 2000.

————. *Nothing; Doting; Blindness*. New York: Penguin, 1993.

————. *Pack My Bag: A Self-Portrait*. New York: New Directions, 2004.

————. *Party Going*. London: Vintage, 2000.

————. *Surviving: The Uncollected Writings of Henry Green*, ed. Matthew Yorke. New York: Viking, 1993.

Russell, John. *Henry Green: Nine Novels and an Unpacked Bag*. New Brunswick, NJ: Rutgers University Press, 1960.

Treglown, Jeremy. *Romancing: The Life and Work of Henry Green*. New York: Random House, 2001.

Romain Gary & Émile Ajar

Bellos, David. *Romain Gary: A Tall Story*. London: Harvill Secker, 2010.

Gary, Romain (Émile Ajar). *Hocus Bogus*, trans. David Bellos. New Haven and London: Yale University Press, 2010.

Gary, Romain. *The Life Before Us* (*Madame Rosa*), trans. Ralph Manheim. New York: New Directions, 1977, 1978.

———. *Promise at Dawn: A Memoir*, trans. John Markham Beach. New York: New Directions, 1961.

———. *White Dog*. Chicago: University of Chicago Press, 1970.

Schoolcraft, Ralph. *Romain Gary: The Man Who Sold His Shadow*. Philadelphia: University of Pennsylvania Press, 2002.

James Tiptree, Jr. & Alice Sheldon

Phillips, Julie. *James Tiptree, Jr.: The Double Life of Alice B. Sheldon*. New York: St. Martin's, 2006.

Tiptree, James, Jr., *Meet Me at Infinity*. New York: Tom Doherty Associates, 2000.

Georges Simenon & Christian Brulls et al.

Assouline, Pierre. *Simenon: A Biography*. New York: Knopf, 1997.

Carter, David. *The Pocket Essential Georges Simenon*. Chicago: Trafalgar Square, 2003.

Marnham, Patrick. *The Man Who Wasn't Maigret: A Portrait of Georges Simenon*. Harvest, 1992.

Simenon, Georges. *Pedigree*. New York: New York Review Books, 2010.

Patricia Highsmith & Claire Morgan

Highsmith, Patricia. *Carol*. London: Bloomsbury, 1990.

———. *The Selected Stories of Patricia Highsmith*. New York: Norton, 2001.

———. *Strangers on a Train*. New York: Norton, 2001.

———. *The Talented Mr. Ripley, Ripley Under Ground, Ripley's Game*. New York: Knopf/Everyman's Library, 1999.

Meaker, Marijane. *Highsmith: A Romance of the 1950s*. San Francisco: Cleis, 2003.

Schenkar, Joan. *The Talented Miss Highsmith: The Secret Life and Serious Art of Patricia Highsmith*. New York: St. Martin's, 2009.

Wilson, Andrew. *Beautiful Shadow: A Life of Patricia Highsmith*. London: Bloomsbury, 2003.

Pauline Réage & Dominique Aury

Deforges, Régine. *Confessions of O: Conversations with Pauline Réage.* New York: Viking, 1979.

Réage, Pauline. *Return to the Château.* New York: Ballantine, 1995.

———. *Story of O.* New York: Ballantine, 1973.

Sontag, Susan. *Styles of Radical Will.* New York: Picador, 2002.

Bond, Jenny, and Chris Sheedy. *Who the Hell Is Pansy O'Hara?: The Fascinating Stories Behind 50 of the World's Best-loved Books.* New York: Penguin, 2008.

Gross, John, ed. *The New Oxford Book of Literary Anecdotes.* New York: Oxford University Press, 2006.

Halpern, Daniel, ed. *Who's Writing This?* New York: Ecco, 1995.

Hamilton, Nigel. *Biography: A Brief History.* Cambridge, MA: Harvard University Press, 2007.

Jones, Emma. *The Literary Companion.* London: Think, 2004.

Marías, Javier. *Written Lives*, trans. Margaret Jull Costa. New York: New Directions, 2007.

Motion, Andrew, ed. *Interrupted Lives.* London: National Portrait Gallery Publications, 2004.

Mullan, John. *Anonymity.* Princeton, NJ: Princeton University Press, 2007.

Prose, Francine. *The Lives of the Muses: Nine Women and the Artists They Inspired.* New York: HarperCollins, 2002.

Rose, Phyllis. *Parallel Lives: Five Victorian Marriages.* New York: Vintage, 1983.

Schnakenberg, Robert. *Secret Lives of Great Authors.* Philadelphia: Quirk, 2008.

Showalter, Elaine. *A Literature of Their Own: British Women Novelists from Brontë to Lessing.* Princeton, NJ: Princeton University Press, 1999.

Woolf, Virginia. *A Room of One's Own.* New York: Harcourt, 1989.

Who is it that can tell me who I am?

—KING LEAR

Insights,
Interviews
& More . . .

About the author

2   Meet Carmela Ciuraru

3   A Conversation with Carmela
Ciuraru, author of *Nom de Plume*

About the book

10 *The Rise and Fall of Pseudonyms*
by Carmela Ciuraru

15 Questions for Discussion

Read on

18 Recommended Reading List

Meet Carmela Ciuraru

Pieter M. van Hattem

CARMELA CIURARU is a graduate of
Columbia University's Journalism
School. She is a member of the National
Book Critics Circle and PEN American
Center, and has edited several poetry
anthologies, including *First Loves: Poets
Introduce the Essential Poems That
Captivated and Inspired Them* and
Solitude Poems. She has written for a
number of publications, including the
*New York Times, Los Angeles Times, San
Francisco Chronicle, Boston Globe, O, The
Oprah Magazine, Salon, Huffington Post*,
and the *Daily Beast*. She was awarded a
2011 fellowship in nonfiction from the
New York Foundation for the Arts
(NYFA). She lives in Brooklyn.

A Conversation with Carmela Ciuraru, author of *Nom de Plume*

How did the idea for your book come about?

This project evolved from a magazine article I had written. After it was published, I wanted to pursue the subject of pen names further and decided to turn it into a book. It took a while to determine the structure and how many writers I wanted to include.

I've always been fascinated by pseudonyms and what motivates writers to adopt them. Of course, I had no idea just how mysterious this tradition was until I submerged myself in the research. Nor did I know that writers could have such intimate, intense relationships with their alter egos—such as the Portuguese writer Fernando Pessoa, who had more than seventy authorial identities.

On a less conscious level, the other thing that probably drew me to this subject is that I grew up in a household where three languages were spoken. Because my parents were immigrants, I never felt as though I fully inhabited one identity or the other. I felt caught between the two, and often felt like an outsider among my peers. I don't know whether that's a common experience among children who grow up with immigrant parents, but it was mine. So the notion of identity as something ▶

A Conversation with Carmela Ciuraru, author of *Nom de Plume* (continued)

fluid or unstable was familiar to me, and something I'd thought about a lot.

What intrigues you about the subject of pseudonymity?

The layers of complexity. For some writers, a pen name is a hoax, a prank, a stunt. But for others there's a tremendous amount at stake; the motivation comes from a painful or traumatic experience in their past. Perhaps they're fighting for respect, hiding something shameful, or struggling just to keep going. The pen name is a release; it's liberating. Sometimes the motive begins as a superficial or playful device, but it becomes much messier over time— as in the case of Romain Gary. This subject also taps into themes of creativity, ambition, self-doubt, and fame—all of which I find fascinating.

There's a quote I've loved for many years from Diane Arbus. It's about the gap between intention and effect in how we present ourselves to the world. She describes a point "between what you want people to know about you and what you can't help people knowing about you."

Pseudonymous writers are acutely aware of that gap, perhaps more than the average writer. They are always trying to manage, control, and distort the gap in information. A pen name gives you the power to toggle between two selves (or even multiple selves). It can be seductive, at least for a while, yet it can also prove exhausting and disorienting. It can become agonizing. A few of the writers in my book found that they could no longer function, and they committed suicide.

The chapters are organized chronologically, starting with the Brontës in the mid-nineteenth century and ending with the French writer Pauline Réage, who died in 1998. Why did you decide to omit contemporary writers who use pen names, such as Stephen King or Anne Rice?

I avoided contemporary authors partly because they're still alive; their stories are unfinished. And pseudonymity reached its peak in the nineteenth century. There was a tradition of reticence that eventually lost its value.

What's more common now, as with Stephen King or Anne Rice, are authors using transparent pseudonyms—openly using other names to avoid saturating the market with their work. Often it's a way of showing off your versatility, like a branding device. That's not interesting to me. I knew from the start that I wanted to explore the dead rather than the living.

I learned that even in the nineteenth century, authorial reticence was not always what it seemed. Some writers used the cloak of pseudonymity ▸

**A Conversation with Carmela Ciuraru,
author of *Nom de Plume* (continued)**

strategically, to stir up public curiosity
and generate excitement about their
books. Or they used a pen name to
test the waters with a new work. If
the experiment failed, they could
disappear with their dignity intact.
And if it succeeded, they could reveal
their true identities to the world, thus
generating even more publicity (and
sales).

***To what extent are pseudonyms
connected with a writer's creative
process?***

It varies. For instance, Charlotte Brontë
surely would have written under any
circumstances, even if she had never
been published (or if she had not
achieved tremendous success) as
Currer Bell. She and her sisters were
highly imaginative and prolific, even
in childhood. Her creative output did
not depend on her pen name. She never
really inhabited a male identity, a male
psyche, in the way that Marian Evans
did as George Eliot.

Then there's Alice Bradley Sheldon,
a former debutante who came from a
wealthy family in Chicago. For a decade,
starting in the late 1960s, she "passed"
as the science fiction author James
Tiptree, Jr., which was a way of
reinventing herself in midlife and
escaping the oppressive influence of
her mother. Sheldon could not function
creatively under her own name. She was

filled with self-loathing, and Tiptree offered a kind of respite. She really did "become" him, and he made her feel confident and talented in a way that she'd never experienced.

Fernando Pessoa, with his many identities, seemed to depend on all those other voices in his head to be creative. They were his muses and his team of writers. Although his output was vast, he claimed that his alter egos did most of the writing, not him.

If you were to adopt a pen name, what would it be?

The most suitable name would be dictated by the genre I'd want to write in, but I've joked that my pseudonym would be "Carmela von Plume" because it sounds vaguely aristocratic.

After writing this book, what conclusions did you make about pseudonymity?

That there are no grand conclusions to be made. It's true that certain patterns and themes emerged among these authors—mainly having to do with how dysfunctional their lives were—but their motives for taking on a nom de plume were too disparate for me to make any sort of unifying, pithy statement. That would have been reductive, and I deliberately steered clear of it. ▶

**A Conversation with Carmela Ciuraru,
author of** *Nom de Plume* (continued)

*Finally, what was the most surprising
thing you learned during your research
process? Did you have a favorite story?*

I made all sorts of wonderful discoveries
while writing the book. Some authors
I ended up admiring even more than
I had previously. Others I had made
certain assumptions about, but those
ideas were eventually overturned.

As I got deeper into my research,
I was surprised by how much I learned
about the Brontës, for instance, whose
stories I thought I'd known pretty well.
I was inspired by their perseverance,
especially Charlotte's. In her brief life,
she had such great courage, confidence,
and ambition.

I was already acquainted with Patricia
Highsmith's work, but I never knew that
she was a raging anti-Semite. I was also
shocked by how cruel she was to people,
especially those closest to her. By all
accounts, she was quite horrible, and
her meanness was almost comical.

Yet I had to admire her for publishing
The Price of Salt, and after I learned
about her awful childhood, I had to
feel sympathetic. In writing this chapter,
one of the disturbing things I discovered
was that when Highsmith's mother,
Mary, was pregnant with her, Mary
had attempted to abort the fetus by
ingesting turpentine. She later told
this to her daughter. So you can see
where Highsmith acquired at least
some of her spite.

Everything about the charismatic French author Romain Gary amazed me. I could not believe what an extraordinary life he'd led, full of wonderful adventures. He was a master of reinvention who pulled off one of the most elaborate authorial hoaxes in history.

Another chapter I especially enjoyed writing was about the scandalous publication of *Histoire d'O*. That story took lots of interesting twists and turns. I loved that Pauline Réage (or, Dominique Aury), the author of this shocking S&M novel, was such a demure and austere woman in her private life. She was contemplative and intellectual. Her writing was elegant and precise. Despite people's assumptions, she was not some hack turning out pornography. And in fact, she had not even intended to make her book public.

This story is a reminder of how infinitely complex all of us are, and how many of our impulses simply cannot be explained. I ended this chapter with an apt quote from a friend of Aury: "Everyone is double, or triple, or quadruple. Every character has its hidden sides. One doesn't reveal one's secrets to all." ᗒ

The Rise and Fall of Pseudonyms by Carmela Ciuraru

This essay appeared originally in the New York Times Book Review *on June 24, 2011.*

WHEN THE VENERABLE TRADITION of the pseudonym is discussed, it is often in reductive terms. The other day, someone said to me, "There are three reasons why authors use pen names, right?" and went on to cite them: Women writing as men. Writers with dirty secrets to hide. Highbrow writers slumming it in trashy genres. It's true that each of those motives is historically common, but there are many others.

Once you scratch the surface, pseudonyms are rarely straightforward. Mark Twain is universally regarded as a genial, avuncular prankster, but his creator, Samuel Clemens, possessed a bifurcated identity whose ugly fissures became more prominent as he got older: Twain buried the vitriol and shame of the tormented Clemens. (In the Oxford English Dictionary, "twain" is defined as "forming a pair, twin.")

Perhaps what's most remarkable about the nom de plume, and rarely talked about, is its power to unlock creativity— and its capacity to withhold it. Even when its initial adoption is utilitarian, a pen name can assume a life of its own. Many writers have been surprised by the intimate and even disorienting relationships they have formed with their alter egos. The consequences can prove grievous and irrevocable.

There is no greater example of the shape-shifting force of a pen name than that of the Portuguese writer Fernando Pessoa, who took the notion of reticence to unparalleled, even pathological levels. In maintaining more than seventy literary identities he called "heteronyms," he did not employ them as a mode of deception. Instead, he insisted that he was amanuensis to the multiple beings that dwelled within. They transcended gender, ideology, and genre. They bickered with one another, mentored one another, clamored for attention like children. He once described his work, aptly, as "a drama divided into people instead of into acts."

Why Pessoa, whom George Steiner once called "one of the evident giants in modern literature," had to engage in self-breeding will never be known. The most obvious explanation might be mental illness. That he remained an obscure, isolated figure in his lifetime (he died in 1935) only adds to the poignancy of his—their?—vast creative output. One scholar speculated that Pessoa's heteronyms were a way to "spare him the trouble of living real life," which makes his bizarre endeavor seem enviable.

In the 1940s, the Lithuanian-born Roman Kacew spun himself into Romain Gary, one of France's most beloved writers. (When he was a teenager, his mother told him: "You must choose a pseudonym. A great French writer who is going to astonish the world can't possibly have a Russian ▶

The Rise and Fall of Pseudonyms by Carmela Ciuraru (continued)

name.") He earned praise from the likes of Raymond Queneau and Albert Camus. At a certain point, however, he felt imprisoned by his fame ("classified, cataloged, taken for granted") and longed to escape his identity. He adopted yet another pen name, Émile Ajar. As he later explained, Ajar provided a glorious sense of stylistic and psychological freedom, writing books that Kacew or Gary could not have produced. "To renew myself, to relive, to be someone else," he confessed, "was always the great temptation of my existence." Not only did Ajar satisfy his desire for reinvention, but the alter ego sustained him "with my mental stability intact." Alas, what began as an elaborate and successful hoax resulted in terrible anguish. Eventually the pressures of this masquerade became intolerable. In 1980, Gary killed himself in his Paris apartment.

The story of the sci-fi writer James Tiptree Jr., who served as the mask of Alice Sheldon, a former Chicago debutante, had a similarly tragic ending. For Sheldon, the value of an alter ego was beyond measure. At first glance, hers seems a familiar narrative of a woman adopting a pen name so she might succeed in a male-dominated genre. But she wasn't just battling gender bias. Without Tiptree, her prose style, as she once put it, was no more imaginative or compelling than "enclosed please find payment." She passed as Tiptree for a decade, thus allowing an emotionally troubled, sexually confused middle-aged woman to experience life as a charismatic, flirtatious man at the height of his creative powers.

Their relationship was complicated. Despite having considered, in darker moments, "taking him out and drowning him in the Caribbean," Sheldon felt that without Tiptree, she was crippled creatively. In the late 1970s, after her identity was unmasked, she was bereft. Although her fans and peers in the sci-fi world were largely supportive of her "coming out," Sheldon's efforts to keep writing under her own name (and even other pen names) were halfhearted and futile. ("Some inner gate is shut," she admitted to a friend.) In 1987, she shot her husband in his sleep and then herself.

Thanks partly to the Internet, pseudonymity is decidedly less dramatic these days. Fake names are more popular than ever, yet the pseudonym as it once existed is just about dead. In the nineteenth century, when the practice reached its height, or even in the early-twentieth century, authorial disguise often carried considerable psychological investment and a genuine need for secrecy. Today, privacy has become less desirable and less possible. An IP address is easy to trace. Many bloggers use an array of noms de plume, but often as a means of generating publicity or branding a "persona." It's self-promotion under the pretense of hiding.

Anyone with an e-mail account can ▶

The Rise and Fall of Pseudonyms by
Carmela Ciuraru *(continued)*

engage in facile trickery to broadcast personal musings or call attention to political issues. In the most recent case of online duplicity, a media sensation erupted over a half-Syrian political blogger, Amina Arraf, a "gay girl in Damascus," who turned out to be a forty-year-old married man from Georgia. He subsequently apologized for the hoax, however perfunctorily. (It was reminiscent of Laura Albert's defensive response when she was exposed as the creator of the truant-novelist JT Leroy.)

Yet a stark contrast exists between mere cleverness (at best) and what such authors as Lewis Carroll (Charles Dodgson), George Orwell (Eric Blair), and Isak Dinesen (Karen Blixen) possessed: literary merit, rigorous effort, a passionate imagination, an obsessive engagement with language, and an intimate acquaintance with artistic suffering. They had what might be called courage. It's the difference between choosing a Halloween costume and being a transvestite. In the former, you dress up because the occasion suits. In the latter, self-presentation is bound up inextricably, profoundly, and even painfully with your identity. It's the difference between striking a pose and learning to walk.

You can misrepresent yourself online? So can I. That does not make either of us George Eliot. ∾

Carmela Ciuraru is the author of *Nom de Plume: A (Secret) History of Pseudonyms.*

Questions for Discussion

1. We are living in an era of made-up memoirs, semi-autobiographical fiction, social media such as Facebook and Twitter, and an ever-increasing number of "reality" TV shows. In a culture in which privacy is constantly being violated, threatened, and exposed, is it still possible to use a pseudonym without being discovered?

2. Think about some of the most common reasons why authors use pen names. What kind of protection do alter egos give them? Why is it that having a secret identity can prove so seductive?

3. Write your own name on a sheet of paper. What kind of history does it conjure for you? Do you feel ambivalence toward your name? Do you think your name reflects who you are?

4. The use of pseudonyms, in the traditional sense, has declined over the past several decades. Why do you think that's true? What, if anything, does it say about our culture?

5. Do you think that inhabiting another identity to write— whether fiction or nonfiction— is fundamentally dishonest? Do different rules apply for different genres? Is there an instance in ▶

which it's unacceptable for a writer to use a pen name?

6. As Isak Dinesen (Karen Blixen) once said, part of the allure of a nom de plume is to avoid answering personal questions, such as: Which part of your novel is drawn from real life? Which character is actually you in disguise? And so on. Do you think that readers have the right to the details of an author's life, even if the author writes fiction? Are authors obliged to "sell" themselves rather than letting work speak for itself?

7. How would you distinguish between the contemporary use of fake names online—pretending to be someone you're not—and the use of a pen name to publish a book? Is there a difference?

8. The author V. S. Naipual has stated that he always knows when he is reading a novel by a female author. Do any of the works by the pseudonymous female authors in this book (such as Alice Sheldon, who published science fiction as James Tiptree, Jr.) overturn that assumption? If so, how?

9. To what extent were the authors in this book exploring different personalities through their names? In the case of Samuel Clemens, how did Mark Twain provide a buffer against the darker side of his personal life?

10. Consider some of the nineteenth-century women writers featured in this book, such as the Brontës, George Sand, and George Eliot. How do you think their novels would have been received if they had not used pen names? What power did they gain by pretending to be men?

11. As a reader, is it important for you to know about the personal lives of your favorite authors? Why? How does having less (or more) information about an author affect your reading experience, if at all?

12. Have you ever wanted to use a pseudonym? If so, why? Would a secret identity allow you to write something that you would not otherwise attempt? ∽

Recommended Reading List

Romain Gary: A Tall Story
   by David Bellos

Saraband by Eliot Bliss

The Lifted Veil by George Eliot

The Days of Abandonment
   by Elena Ferrante

Hocus Bogus by Romain Gary

Pack My Bag: A Self-Portrait
   by Henry Green

The Posthumous Memoirs of Brás Cubas
   by Joaquim Maria Machado de Assis

At Swim-Two-Birds by Flann O'Brien

Olivia by Olivia (Dorothy Strachey)

The Book of Disquiet by Fernando Pessoa

We Always Treat Women Too Well
   by Raymond Queneau

The Complete Saki by Saki

*The Culture of the Copy: Striking
   Likenesses, Unreasonable Facsimiles*
   by Hillel Schwartz

The Train by Georges Simenon

Don't miss the next book by your favorite author. Sign up now for AuthorTracker by visiting www.AuthorTracker.com.